Slowly, deliberately, the great troll took the axe in his right hand. Still squatting, he placed his left wrist on the ground and stretched his five long fingers before him. With a cruel grimace—or perhaps it was a bizarre smile of wicked ecstasy—he brought the blade down sharply, hissing at the pain that lanced through his hand and arm. Green blood spurted from five wounds, while the severed digits twitched mindlessly on the ground.

His face still locked in that twisted grin, Baatlrap awkwardly transferred the axe to his mutilated hand. Already fingers had begun to sprout from the bloody stumps, while the pieces on the ground continued to twitch and writhe. Sharply chopping, Baatlrap repeated the gesture with his right hand, only then dropping the axe and settling back to nurse the pain in his two mangled limbs. For more than an hour he sat thus, while his own pain abated and ten pieces of his flesh danced at his feet.

Finally he rose, hoisting the axe with hands once more whole. His steps, when he started walking, led him back toward the camp, where he planned to return the axe to Garisa and get some sleep himself. Behind him, moving soundlessly through the shadowy wood and following their new master to his destination, came a file of ten young, wiry trolls. . . .

Other Books by Douglas Niles

FORGOTTEN REALMS® Novels

THE MOONSHAE TRILOGY

Darkwalker on Moonshae
Black Wizards
Darkwell

THE MAZTICA TRILOGY

Ironhelm
Viperhand
Feathered Dragon

THE DRUIDHOME TRILOGY

Prophet of Moonshae
The Coral Kingdom
The Druid Queen

DRAGONLANCE® Novels

Flint, the King
The Kinslayer Wars

FANTASY ADVENTURE

The Druid Queen

Douglas Niles

**The Druidhome Trilogy:
Book Three**

THE DRUID QUEEN

All characters in this book are fictitious. Any resemblance to actual persons, living or dead, is purely coincidental.

This book is protected under the copyright laws of the United States of America. Any reproduction or other unauthorized use of the material or artwork contained herein is prohibited without the express written permission of TSR, Inc.

Random House and its affiliate companies have worldwide distribution rights in the book trade for English language products of TSR, Inc.

Distributed to the book and hobby trade in the United Kingdom by TSR Ltd.

Distributed to the toy and hobby trade by regional distributors.

Cover art by Clyde Caldwell.

FORGOTTEN REALMS and DRAGONLANCE are registered trademarks owned by TSR, Inc. The TSR logo is a trademark owned by TSR, Inc.

First Printing: March, 1993
Printed in the United States of America
Library of Congress Catalog Card Number: 92-61080

9 8 7 6 5 4 3 2 1

ISBN: 1-56076-568-2

TSR, Inc.
P.O. Box 756
Lake Geneva, WI 53147
U.S.A.

TSR Ltd.
120 Church End, Cherry Hinton
Cambridge CB1 3LB
United Kingdom

For "Uncle Jim"

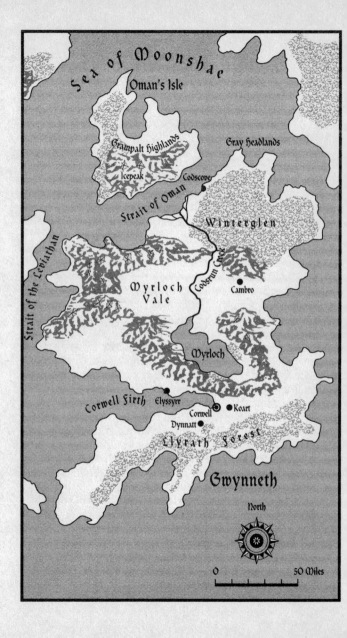

Prologue

She ran as fast as she could, down a corridor walled with black mirrors. The passage stretched to obsidian infinity before and behind her. An intersection broke the smooth perfection, two side corridors leading to more infinities, more impossible distances.

Panic tore at her chest, making her heart pound and her throat dry. Which way? Somehow she understood that it really didn't matter. She darted to the left, the soles of her soft leather boots pounding the smooth floor, the steady cadence the only sound in this eternal maze of nothingness.

That, and the rasping of her breath and the thunderous beating of her straining heart. How could that vital muscle possibly keep her alive, possibly contain the explosive pressure of the blood in her veins? She knew, as instinctively as she understood everything else, that it could not.

Another intersection . . . another frantic turn, between the lines of blackness, the two planes of wall merging into a spot of darkness in the distance. She staggered wearily, her feet shuffling and stumbling until she sprawled headlong onto the marble floor. Astonishingly, her rough fall caused no pain. Indeed, it was more as if she had plummeted into the nest of a warm feather bed, encased by protective down and sheltered against a supernatural chill.

But then she raised her eyes. Still the black walls stretched into the distance, merging into nothing before and behind. Yet, for the first time, she sensed that she wasn't alone within this dim matrix. Someone—some*thing*—lurked here with her.

She knew, with a dull and hopeless sense of terror, that this presence, this being, *awaited* her.

Desperately she scrambled to her feet, slumping against the wall, sliding back along her tracks. She turned and once again broke into a shambling run, the black walls sliding past as she retraced her steps, fleeing the unseen presence, the potent menace she felt in the very pit of her stomach.

She returned to the intersection and stumbled through it, continuing down the passage that was identical to a dozen, a hundred other corridors that had entrapped her during this eternal flight. She wanted only to put that ominous presence behind her.

But as she ran, the threatening aura changed. No longer did it menace her from behind. Instead, once more, she knew beyond any doubt that she approached it.

Stopping on her heels, she spun around again. The intersection! She'd go back there, take a different branch! There *had* to be a way to evade this thing! Stumbling with exhaustion, leaning against the smooth wall for support, once more she retraced her steps, coming to the adjoining passages to the right and left . . . but now there was a difference.

Where there had once been four corridors, she now found six—three pairs, angling off to either side like the limbs of a six-pointed star. She didn't hesitate, fearing all the while the evil drawing inexorably near. She plunged down the closest of the right-hand passages, though the aching strain of her lungs pleaded with her to pause, to rest.

She felt it again, that horror, and now she sensed it behind her—and creeping inevitably, dolorously closer with every passing moment. Opening her mouth, she tried to scream, but no sound issued forth beyond the rattling labors of her lungs. The air seemed impossibly dry, sucking the moisture from her skin and throat, parching her very blood with its persistent, penetrating warmth.

She ran and ran, ignoring the weariness and fatigue, the aches that throbbed in her feet, the stitch of pain that grew steadily longer and deeper in her side. She ran only to get away from this thing she did not know, but that she feared above all else in the world . . . or beyond the world. It loomed nearer now, and this proximity drove extra energy through her veins, propelling her feet into a faster gait.

Another corner beckoned, and she hurtled herself blindly around it, sensing the looming evil as if it reached for her back with rending talons, claws that would rake her ribs aside and rip the heart from her terrified flesh.

Then she stopped in shock, terrified beyond measure. Once again the threat lay *before* her! She *saw* it come out of the darkness, materializing a few steps away, confronting her with an image of monstrous evil, of hopeless despair and infernal betrayal.

This time when she opened her mouth the scream was loud and piercing, a shock wave of sound that echoed down the halls and threatened to shatter the smooth glass of the ceiling. Yet the image of evil confronted her still, coolly inspecting her, red lips twisted into a wry smile . . . an expression of cool contempt, perhaps tinged with a tiny measure of pity.

She screamed again and again, but the image never wavered, never moved away. Finally the woman slumped to the ground in abject surrender, gazing at the shape that loomed above her, abandoning hope . . . giving in to ultimate despair.

For the looming image, the form and visage that embodied the most potent evil known . . . that body and that face were her own.

❧1❧

Gwynneth

"She's sleeping again. That's about all I can say for her." The king reentered the bedroom with a sigh, his shoulders slumping from the weight of his worries. Caer Corwell was still with the silence of the midwatch, night lying thickly about them, though a few embers still glowed red in the large fireplace. A huge dog, blanketed by a coarse coat of rust-colored fur, looked up from the hearthside and thumped his tail once in greeting.

"Better that than the nightmares," Queen Robyn replied, rising from the couch to embrace her husband.

It seemed to the woman that her husband had never looked so old. She noticed that the tint of gray in his hair had grown to an entire fringe. His beard remained full, but even more gray than his once chestnut-colored hair. His dark eyes still blazed with grim determination, but now a hint of despair lurked within them.

It was a despair that Robyn could well understand. Like King Tristan, the queen sagged wearily, and her face was drawn and pallid. Her long hair had lost none of its inky blackness, but now it lay carelessly across her shoulders, uncombed and lacking its usual luster.

The man and woman, High King and High Queen of the Ffolk and the Moonshaes, sat down together on the couch, neither quite ready to return to bed. The great moorhound, Ranthal, rested at their feet, large ears pricked upward to catch any sign of distress or danger, as if the dog, too, sensed that these minutes of nocturnal peace were too rare, too precious to consign them to sleep.

Scarcely a week following their triumphant return to Corwell, fresh from a daring rescue of the imprisoned king, the royal pair had no concerns other than the health of their daughter Deirdre. During the daytime, the young princess lay awake, weak and exhausted from a sleep without rest. Deirdre had little appetite, nor did she ever seem to feel thirst. Indeed, if Robyn did not force her to drink and to eat a few crumbs, she feared that her daughter would take no sustenance at all.

Yet these bleak days were nothing, it seemed, when compared to the nights. Deirdre regarded the approaching sunset with apprehension that steadily built into terror. For hours, she would lie awake, sometimes talking to her sister or one of her parents. On other occasions, she grew shrill and irrational, demanding that her visitor leave, screaming and writhing in apparent agony until her wish was granted.

Finally, then, sleep would claim her. For a precious few moments, her body lay still, relaxed at last. Then, all too quickly, the nightmares began. Or perhaps, the nightmare. Robyn had begun to suspect that each night her daughter suffered the same dream over and over again, so consistent and predictable was the pattern of her distress.

Each night, as the dream began, Deirdre stiffened reflexively in the bed, thrashing with her feet. Her chest rose and fell as if she gasped for breath. Every attempt to awaken her——many had been made—failed to wrest her from the internal trance. Indeed, they seemed only to heighten her terror, so at last there was nothing to do but wait for the nightmare to run its course.

It would not do so until the terror built to the climax that always exploded in a scream of mindless, ultimate terror. Then Deirdre would awaken, and for a short time, her father or mother would hold her as a little girl again, gently rocking her to sleep, not knowing how many hours—or minutes—might pass before the cycle began again.

"She came for me . . . to rescue me!" Tristan groaned softly, acutely conscious of the young woman who finally slept in the next room. "This wouldn't have happened except for that! How can any father bear that guilt?"

The image still burned in his mind: He saw his daughter holding the crystal mirror, the powerful artifact of a dark and evil god, Talos the Stormbringer. The agent of that god had attacked them savagely, but when Deirdre had confronted the beast with the mirror, the glass had shattered and carried the monster to a horrifying demise.

But then, for Tristan, the real horror had begun. The shards of the broken mirror had swirled into a small cyclone, surrounding Deirdre, trapping her in a glittering, whirling column. Then the whirlwind collapsed, and Tristan had stared in horror as the bits of glass had knifed through his daughter's skin, piercing her in a thousand places.

Yet she had lost not a drop of blood—indeed, they could find no physical wound whatsoever upon her. This malaise instead gnawed at her spirit and her soul, they knew.

"She came willingly to your rescue," the queen replied, her voice firm against her husband's despair. "As did Alicia, and many others."

"Aye—and you as well, my queen. So many paid such a grievous cost," sighed the king, wrapping a strong arm around his wife. Unconsciously he raised the end of his arm, not allowing the stump of his wrist to touch his wife's shoulder.

She raised her hand and brought his handless arm fully around her. "We *all* paid our prices—and would do so again!" Robyn declared.

Tristan shook his head, disparaging his own wound. "When Keane gets back with Patriarch Bakar, my hand can be restored, but I suspect no such easy cure awaits Deirdre."

At the mention of the high cleric of Chauntea, Robyn stiffened slightly. She turned to face her husband frankly. "Even the healing of the New Gods doesn't come without its costs. Don't be too quick to assume their success."

Finally Tristan smiled. "Whatever that cost, I'll pay it. And you know Bakar is a good and decent man. After all, he came to Callidyrr and taught you for nearly a decade!"

"It seems like more than a lifetime ago," Robyn said,

clearly uneasy with the subject. "I am a daughter of the goddess again."

"Still, it wasn't long ago that Chauntea offered our hope of growth and guidance . . . when the Earthmother abandoned us to the New Gods."

"She did *not* abandon us!" Robyn replied, her voice tight. "It was weakness—a weakness that I did nothing to soothe! All those years she lay insensate, and I turned to the worship of another rather than labor for her return!"

"We needed the protection of a goddess during those years, and Chauntea gave us her blessing," Tristan countered, shaking his head firmly. "Now her patriarch, I know, will come to answer my need."

"You're right," Robyn said, trying to drive the tension from her body. For once her efforts were not successful. She still felt the lingering pulse of anger in her veins.

"Who knows?" asked the king, drawing his wife beneath his arm again. "Perhaps Bakar can help Deirdre as well." At his feet, the great dog thumped his tail against the floor again, recognizing that some of the tension had drained from his master's voice.

* * * * *

Keane sipped idly at his cup of strong tea, not noticing the fact that it had grown cool while time dragged by. For two days, he had lingered here at the Eagle's Nest Inn, expecting a reply from Bakar Dalsoritan, impatiently awaiting the opportunity to pursue his mission.

True, his expensive suite made for splendid accommodations. High on a hill overlooking the waterfront and wide river at Baldur's Gate, Keane's rooms had a spacious balcony with a splendid view to the west and south. Another, smaller porch provided a sheltered outdoor nook with an excellent view of the rising sun to the east and the road to the shrine, where his messenger had ridden away two days before. It was on this overlook that he spent most of his time, even to the point of sending a petite halfling barmaid up and down the stairs to keep his teacup refilled.

The magic-user lounged against the rail, his narrow face tight with concentration, belying the casual posture of his lanky frame. He was dressed practically, in woolen trousers and soft moccasins and a flowing brown shirt that left his hands free but gave him space to conceal the pouches and vials that contained the components of his trade.

The sun drew near the western horizon before he saw the sleek black horse, flanks covered with foam and nostrils flaring, pounding down the River Highway. He recognized Gapsar, the fellow he had hired to carry his message, lashing the exhausted steed with his riding crop.

"Ho! Lord Ambassador!" cried the rider, spotting Keane on his third-floor perch. "I bring news!"

Urgency in the man's voice—or perhaps the impatience in the magic-user's own mind—propelled Keane through the apartment and down the flights of stairs into the common room. Quickly he passed through the front door and stopped before the dismounting messenger.

"What is it? Will the patriarch grant me an interview?" he demanded.

"Readily, my lord! He was most delighted to hear that an emissary of his former student would be paying a call. Indeed, my lord, he invited you to arrive at the earliest opportunity. He knows that you're a day's ride away, but he wondered if you might have means to, er, expedite the transport."

"That's good news," Keane said quickly, his mind immediately clicking onto the problem. He couldn't teleport directly to the shrine. Since he'd never been there, it would be dangerous and difficult to attempt to transport himself into the midst of buildings and landscape. After all, he wouldn't want to materialize in a place where something else, like a tree or hill, already existed. Such a mistake would be inevitably fatal.

Yet a sense of profound urgency consumed him. The thought of his king, so cruelly mutilated, still outraged him, and *Keane* was the one Tristan had relied upon to get help. Such a mission could brook no delay.

The wizard looked up and saw that the sun was perhaps an hour from the western horizon. Keane noticed the messenger standing awkwardly beside his horse, casting longing eyes toward the inn and the cool barroom beyond. The man had done his work, he reminded himself.

"Here—thanks for your efforts," Keane noted, drawing several gold coins from his pouch and pressing them into the man's suddenly extended hand.

"I hope the news is welcome, my lord," said the fellow, bowing. Leading his horse, he went in search of a liveryman, while Keane returned to the inn. He found the rotund innkeeper, a cheery halfling named Miles, and pressed a few more coins on the not unwilling businessman.

"I'll be gone for a short time, perhaps a couple of days," Keane explained. "I'd like to leave my things in the room upstairs until my return."

"Consider them safe!" Miles proclaimed, with a deep bow. "You will find them undisturbed when you return!"

"Splendid," the wizard replied agreeably. All urgent matters thus attended to, he climbed the stairs to his rooms so he could make the final preparations for the trip.

* * * * *

Bakar Dalsoritan, High Patriarch of Chauntea, enjoyed these hours of early evening better than any part of the day. It seemed so often that the weight of his labors dragged him down during the busy days. Now, with the shrine buildings closed up tight behind him and the apprentices gone to sup, he could let the soothing aspects of his faith revive and revitalize him.

He walked along the low ridge, row upon row of lush grapes stretching to either side of him—sweet to the south, where the sun warmed them fully, and more sour to the shady north. The latter, when harvested, created a highly sought vintage that had put this shrine on the map. Indeed, many merchants sailed to nearby Baldur's Gate, the port that was barely a day's ride away, for the express purpose of seeking out the Shrine of Chauntea and its prized wine. Bakar cheerfully sold each one a barrel or two—no more, in order to preserve the rarity of the vintage—and had employed the profits to create one of the grandest nature shrines on the Sword Coast.

Now the high patriarch approached the crowning glory of that shrine: the orchard. Set in long lines, each trunk perfectly aligned with its neighbors to the four points of the compass, the orchard curled along the ridge, surrounded by swaths of smooth grass and well-manicured hedges. The goddess Chauntea must be well pleased, thought Bakar. All around him was the vitality of fruitful life, the precision of well-managed nature turned to the uses of man.

The orchard was the place where the priest felt most serene, most capable of communion with his goddess. And here each night, during long hours of prayer, he tried to repay the debt he felt to that benign deity, Chauntea. For a lifetime, she had allowed him to serve as her agent, furthering the worship of her name along the length of the Sword Coast—even, for a time, as far as the Moonshae Islands. But in none of those places had he found the sanctuary that he now approached.

Yet memories of past travels now occupied him, and most particularly his thoughts dwelled upon the Moonshaes. Earlier that day he had received a message from one Keane of Callidyrr, requesting the honor of an interview. Keane, it seemed, had arrived via teleportation in Baldur's Gate and awaited the cleric's reply in one of the more comfortable inns of that great port city.

Bakar remembered Keane, though the fellow had been but a gawky adolescent when the priest had finally departed from the Moonshaes. Even then the youth had displayed an uncanny aptitude for magic. Now, in adulthood, he had become a mage of considerable power. Bakar knew him to be a loyal lieutenant to High King Tristan Kendrick, recently returned to his throne from captivity beneath the sea. It was rumored—even a patriarch couldn't depend on absolutely accurate information—that the king had lost a hand during the course of his captivity.

Such a loss could possibly be repaired, but only by means of a powerful spell of the priesthood, the enchantment of regeneration. Bakar was one of but two or three clerics within several hundred miles capable of performing such magic. Besides that, he had tutored the High Queen during the years she had devoted to Chauntea. Bakar had developed a special relationship, of trust and faith and humor, with Robyn and Tristan Kendrick. It seemed only natural that they should turn to him now in this hour of need.

Bakar passed under an arched gate of roses as he entered the orchard for his evening meditations. The sacred fruit trees—apples, pears, even oranges—sheltered and protected him, surrounding the priest with soothing ambience.

But then, in a telltale instant, Bakar realized that something was wrong. The trees, even the carefully mowed grass under his feet, shuddered under the force of a nameless apprehension. Nothing *looked* any different. The rays of the setting sun cast the last of their warmth over the treetops, with their many spots of ripening fruit.

Then, in a flash, he understood. The orchard knew *fear*.

The hair at the back of his neck, where it grew in its encircling fringe beneath his shaved scalp, prickled and stood on end. What menace could cause even the plants to dread?

An immensely powerful man, both physically and in the arcane might of his faith, the patriarch nevertheless stepped nervously backward, casting his eyes about for some sign of danger as he retreated from the orchard. Another step, and after a third, he sensed that he neared the gate.

Suddenly ground ripped open directly beneath his feet, with a sound like the splintering of wet wood. Bakar screamed as he toppled into space. Desperately he reached for the edges, but the wet dirt came away in his fingers, tumbling with him into the crevasse. Slipping down the steep side, aware of the moist, living earth around him, he finally caught himself on a stout root, tangled with dirt and extending from the side of the split.

Earthquake! He sensed the might rending his grove, knowing that this was no act of nature. Power sizzled around him—magical, *clerical* power! Pulling himself upward, the high priest tried to kick a leg over the root, hoping to gain a foothold. Around him, the ground continued to tremble. The deep rumbling seemed to rattle the marrow in his bones, and clumps of dirt showered downward, stinging his eyes and filling his mouth.

Just when he thought he would make it, Bakar looked upward and saw the man standing at the edge of the crevasse, his lips split by an incongruously pleasant smile.

"*You!*" gasped the struggling priest, kicking frantically, knowing he had mere seconds in which to save himself. The other man said nothing but merely raised a hand and pointed at the doomed figure writhing below.

Immediately the walls of earth moved together, rumbling and grinding with unspeakable force. Bakar kicked out frantically at the opposite wall. He braced his feet, trying to scramble upward, but now the root entangled his robe, tying him effectively in place.

In another moment, the walls of earth came together with crushing pressure. Bakar's scream vanished in the thunderous volume of noise as the two surfaces of sod pressed so tightly that no seam was visible in the grass. The other man, the murderer, stood on the ground, hands clasped before his stomach in a posture of reflection, lips still pursed in that slight, enigmatic smile.

* * * * *

The teleport spell carried Keane, in the blink of an instant, from his room at the Eagle's Nest to the vicinity of the shrine some fifty miles inland. However, as a precaution, he employed a unique protection against the threat of striking a solid object on the unknown terrain: He arrived at a place nearly a thousand feet above the sweeping landscape.

At the exact moment the spell concluded, Keane felt himself falling, plunging through cool, evening air in steadily increasing speed. The ground below, a soft carpet of forest broken by the occasional patchwork of fields, villages, and great manors, rushed upward at a dizzying speed.

Then the featherfall spell changed that sensation with the speaking of a single word, and the wizard floated gently toward the ground, which now appeared properly motionless. Drifting easily, he took time to study the lush landscape spreading below. The central feature of the River Highway was a plain track of dusty tan slicing a nearly perfect east-west line into the horizon to either direction.

The sun had already set, but enough light remained for him to identify the marble-walled enclosure, with its long ridge of vineyards to the north. He congratulated himself on his accuracy, for the shrine was less than a mile away.

Something about that ridge caught his eye, and he blinked, certain that the twilight played tricks with his eyes. But when he looked again, he saw beyond doubt that the ground there was *moving!* He saw men there, at least two of them, before the tiny figures vanished amid the tumult.

Trees swayed back and forth, and the hilltop pitched up and down, grass rolling like a rug that a housekeeper shakes above the floor. He saw dark brown tendrils spreading across the ground, and he realized that these were cracks in the turf. In fact, the hilltop was splitting apart right before his eyes!

Alarm jangled in Keane's nerves. The localized nature of the disturbance meant it was almost certainly magical, and the destruction indicated it was not likely done by the one who tended the orchard! By this time, Keane neared the ground, quickly drifting behind the treetops of the grove and losing sight of the turmoil.

Canceling the spell with a snap of his fingers, he dropped

the last ten feet and broke into a run, sprinting between the widely spaced trees of the precise orchard. Reaching the crest of the hill, he felt the strain of his breathing begin to burn in his lungs.

Breaking around a row of trees, he saw a man silhouetted against the glow in the west. The fellow stood as if in great reverence, his hands clasped over an ample belly. There was an aspect both cruel and mocking in his posture. The wizard saw something that must have been illusionary—little sparkles of light gleamed around the man's shape, like fireflies pinned to his tunic.

Then, before Keane could shout or reach him, the fellow raised a bottle to his lips, took a quick swallow, and disappeared.

"Wait!" cried the magic-user, knowing the word was wasted as the blocky form vanished into the pale dusk.

In another moment, the magic-user reached the scene of the earthquake. Fruit littered the ground, though the lush grass showed no sign of its tumult. The cracks that Keane had seen from the air were gone, the sod sewn whole as tightly as any tailor's seam.

What had happened? A warning voice amplified the alarm he had sensed before.

Keane heard voices then, coming up the hill behind him. It occurred to him that if a foul deed had occurred, it might not be good for him to be discovered here. A swiftly murmured incantation rendered him invisible, and he stepped close to the trunk of a tree where he could remain out of the way.

"Patriarch? Patriarch Dalsoritan?" called a reedy voice, emerging tremulously from the shadows below the knoll. Several young men dressed in plain robes came into sight, tentatively approaching the scene. These must be the shrine's apprentices, Keane deduced.

"What happened?" asked one of the young fellows trailing to the rear of the group.

"The patriarch came up here for his evening meditation,

just like always," said the first and apparently boldest of the apprentices, pressing onto the hilltop as his companions hesitated. "Patriarch?" he called again, more loudly this time.

"He's *gone!*" said another in an awestruck whisper.

"But that commotion! Something was *wrong* up here!" suggested an apprentice.

"Very much," said the first one, walking carefully around the hilltop. He came very near to Keane, but the invisible wizard remained completely silent, and the fellow, continuing his inspection, moved past.

"Our master has met with some kind of disaster," the acolyte finally concluded, his voice nearly breaking in despair. "There's no sign of him anywhere!"

"Perhaps we should go back to the shrine," suggested one, to the murmured assent of his fellows. "We can pray for enlightenment, and perhaps the patriarch will return in his own good time."

"No!" insisted the leader. "Spread out and comb the ground. See if you can find something, *any*thing, to tell us what happened here!"

Keane remained silent and observant as the acolytes searched. Finally, fearful and unsuccessful, they started back down the hill, declaring their intention to return when the sun had risen and they could fully inspect the grounds. Keane, in the meantime, had formed his own conclusion: To wit, Bakar Dalsoritan had been murdered.

Turning away in anger, the mage tried to collect his thoughts. What was the reason for the killing? Of course, rival factions exist in any hierarchy, and churches were no exception. Such brutality was an excessive tactic, yet it had happened before and would doubtless happen again: A wary official desires the offices and power of a rival and destroys him to open the path. Or perhaps, he considered, an entrenched ruler might have feared the devout followers and steady advance of a younger rival. Bakar could have fit into either of these categories so far as Keane knew.

But was either role enough to cause him to be killed?

Too agitated to be aware of his fatigue, Keane made his way down to the highway and started walking toward Baldur's Gate. Like any other spell, his teleportation enchantment had been used up when he traveled to the shrine. He wouldn't be able to employ it again until he had studied his spellbook. Still, he uttered no complaints about the mundane travel. If anything, it gave him time to think about the confusing questions whirling through his mind.

He slept in a ditch for a few hours, and then in the morning was fortunate enough to catch a ride from a carter hauling a load of fabric to the markets in Baldur's Gate.

Keane tipped the driver well, for his silence as much as the ride. The mage climbed into the back and rested on the rolls of silk and cotton while he pondered the mystery—who had killed the cleric, and why?

Indeed, the murder of a powerful patriarch was no easy task to accomplish. Whoever would attempt such a thing must have considerable resources at his own disposal, be willing to take great risks in the accomplishment of his evil deed.

Keane's speculations didn't answer why the murder had been committed, but they helped him to accept its truth and its implications to his own mission. By the time the carter reached Baldur's Gate, it was nearing sunset. Thanking the man for the ride, he returned to the Eagle's Nest Inn, finally having decided on a course of action.

For once, the mage didn't feel like hiding out in his room. Instead, he entered the common room and sat down at the bar. Confusion and questions gnawed at him, but he found it pointless—and deeply frustrating—to worry about issues he couldn't address with any accuracy. Instead, he focused on practicality. Namely, what should he do now? The notion of returning to his king with a report of complete failure had absolutely no appeal. Instead, he'd have to think of something else.

The innkeeper, Miles, waddled up to him on the raised platform behind the bar. Miles had installed the walkway so that the bar remained waist-high to humans on the one side, and at a proportional height to the halflings on the other. Most of his barmaids and cooks, Keane knew, came from the ranks of the Small Folk.

"You look like a farmer who just planted his beans in the wrong field," observed Miles wryly. "What'll it be?"

"Make it an ale," Keane said, feeling the truth of the halfling's words. Yet even in his disappointment, his mind had begun to move forward. His original mission remained: to find a cleric who could heal his king. If he couldn't gain the services of his original target, he would have to go about finding somebody else.

"On the house," replied Miles. "Sophtie tells me you're all right, though we wouldn't know that down here, as much as you've kept to yourself."

Sophtie, Keane knew, was the young barmaid who had kept him supplied with tea. He was suddenly glad that he had tipped her well for each trip up and down the flights of stairs.

"Your rooms are just too comfortable," Keane gibed, gratefully accepting a tall, foaming mug. "But tonight perhaps I can share the pleasure of your company."

Miles looked around. The rest of the bar was quiet, the few customers readily handled by two diminutive barmaids. "I'm yours until the dinner rush," noted the halfling, drawing himself a small glass and settling across the bar from Keane.

"Tell me," asked the mage, "what are the major temples in Baldur's Gate?"

Miles sipped at his ale, wiping the foam from his lip while he thought. "Well, there's two big shrines—temples, really— to Oghma and Helm. Right in the center of the Upper City, they are, across the square from each other. Lots of little shrines, too. Seems that just about every god this side of the Trackless Sea has a few followers in Baldur's Gate."

"Oghma and Helm, eh?" Keane knew of both gods—the former, patron of bards, lover of music and knowledge; the latter, hailed as an alert guardian and stern arbiter of justice.

Both of them valued the forces of virtue over evil, and thus a cleric of either faith might fulfill the minimum requirements of Keane's mission.

"Does either have a patriarch—a high priest or priestess?" he inquired.

Here Miles shook his head sympathetically. "None so mighty as Bakar Dalsoritan. Weren't you trying to get in touch with him?"

A tingle of alarm alerted Keane. "How did you know that?" he inquired, trying to keep his voice level.

If Miles thought anything was out of the ordinary, he didn't display it in his manner. "Everyone did," he said with a shrug. "Three nights ago, after you hired that fellow Gapsar to ride out to the shrine, he came in here to spend some of his advance payment. Didn't leave until the morning, you know. From what I understand, he visited half the taverns in the Lower City. Made no secret about your generosity, either. I'd think you'd be flattered."

"No . . . not really." Keane strained to keep his voice neutral as he silently cursed his own stupidity. He'd been obligated to pay the man an advance, but he could have offered it in the morning, before his departure! Instead, he had given it to him as they closed the deal, just after sunset. Apparently Gapsar had wasted no time in spreading the word of his good fortune.

"You tell me there's no high priest at either temple. Do you know of any of the smaller shrines that might have a cleric of note in attendance?"

Miles screwed up his plump face in thought, sipping long and deep from his glass in an apparent attempt to jog his memory. "Nope—but there's one thing, though."

"What?" asked Keane, trying not to snap in his desperation.

"I seem to recall there was an Exalted Inquisitor of Helm touring the temples on the Sword Coast, what with the new trade routes opening up—to Maztica and the like. Some of the clerks were arrested—failure to pay import duties to the church or something. I guess they needed a high-ranking churchman to conduct the trial."

"Yes, yes, of course. When was this 'Exalted Inquisitor' here?"

"Well, he might still be here—that's the thing. It was midsummer when he arrived, a little more than a month ago. I know, because the Four Dukes held a grand reception for him on his arrival. Never did hear about him moving on."

"Exalted Inquisitor of Helm?" Keane didn't know the hierarchy of Helm's worship, but the rank sounded impressive. And not every wayfaring holy man was granted a meeting with the Four Dukes of Baldur's Gate!

"Aye—not a fellow you'd want to be crossing, and that's the truth," continued Miles. "Why, it's said that he had one of his own acolytes whipped—and only for showing a courtesy to a priest of a different faith."

Keane grimaced. He'd forgotten a fact that Miles had just brought home. The clerics of Helm were notoriously stiffnecked and rigid in their approach to worship. One who did not agree with their tenets was, as often as not, branded as an infidel or a faithless swine. In fact, during the initial invasion of Maztica little more than a decade before, the clerics of Helm had been primarily responsible for the ruthless campaign to wipe out the native religions. Helm was indeed a vigilant and jealous god.

Yet he didn't see that he had another choice—at least, not so long as he remained in Baldur's Gate. And he had no idea where else to go. Waterdeep came to mind, of course, but that was a city of commerce and sorcery, little known for clerical accomplishment. In fact, it seemed that his best hope of finding a cure for the king's injury might be found at the local Temple of Helm.

"Do you know where the Exalted Inquisitor stayed when he came to Baldur's Gate?" Keane asked.

"Why, sure I do!" replied Miles enthusiastically. "The temple keeps a great house for luminaries like him. Right across the street from the shrine, it is."

"Tell me how to get there," Keane requested. He had

already decided that he would seek out the inquisitor in the morning.

* * * * *

An infant squalled in one of the rude caves, until the mother cuffed it into silence with a few sharp blows. Elsewhere a wolfdog barked, the gruff sound fading into a low snarl as one of the elders stared the beast down over a well-chewed sliver of elk bone. Fires smoldered, dank wood sending clouds of gray smoke past the dirty cave mouths. Normally a hearty haunch of meat would have sizzled over at least one hearth, casting its alluring scent through the village of Blackleaf, but now there was no meat to be had.

Thurgol, self-appointed chief of the village, decided that he would inspect the other cookfires. His own wench, a stooped but sturdy giant-kin named Karloth, had failed to provide him with a single delicacy in several days. The hulking firbolg chieftain, stooped and misshapen kin to the giant races, had thumped her well tonight. Thurgol let her know that such carelessness would not be allowed to continue, for, in the finest traditions of humanoid logic, he conveniently ignored the fact that his club, snares, and rocks had brought them no game for more than a month, though it was past the peak of high summer!

Scowling from beneath his low-hanging brows, massive hands clamped around the base of a club that was nearly as tall as a full-grown human, the chieftain of Blackleaf stumped around the periphery of his village. Firbolgs and trolls scowled back at him, hungry and afraid. Nowhere did he see food, but Thurgol suspected this was because they all hoarded it for times when their leader was absent.

A flurry of activity caught his attention, and he spun in time to see a huge troll lift something to his tooth-studded gap of a mouth. Baatlrap! Thurgol recognized the hulking form of the ugly beast as Baatlrap hoisted a scrawny rat by its tail. The troll's black eyes glared impassively at the firbolg chieftain, challenging him to object.

A scowl darkened Thurgol's face into an ominous thundercloud as he regarded the insolent troll. He restrained, with difficulty, a brutal urge to attack. Baatlrap was one of the few humanoids in Blackleaf, whether firbolg or trollish of blood, who possessed a true sword. The weapon lay beside him now, the bronze blade nearly as long as Thurgol's club, with a line of sharp serrations down each edge giving it a saw-toothed look. Baatlrap had used the sword, together with his truly impressive size, to bull his way to leadership of the troll community in Blackleaf. Now he tantalized the chieftain with his display of an actual morsel of meat.

But then, in the next instant, the rat disappeared, Smacking his thin, bony lips, Baatlrap grimaced in triumph. Thurgol flushed, knowing that the troll had waited until the chieftain could see him. The firbolg bit back the urge to charge over to the hulking troll, but with the morsel already consumed, there was nothing he could do in any event.

Fools! Rage caused the giant's limbs to tremble, and for a second, his temper threatened an explosion that would certainly have resulted in bloodshed, if not death, but then he whirled on his heel and stalked away, past the dirty caves and through the narrow, rocky niche that gave the village its only easy means of egress. Wolfdogs scuttled from his path, cringing away from the clublike feet that had on previous occasions booted many a canine posterior.

Too long they'd been hungry! Thurgol swung his hefty club, a tapered oak limb studded with round knots, into the base of a pine tree, grunting from the pain that shot down his arm. The tree swayed vigorously, but no sound of splintering treated the firbolg's ears.

That was different, also. As recently as last spring, that pine trunk, or any other of equal girth, would have snapped like a dry twig from such a blow. Now the trees were healthy again, thriving with a vibrancy they hadn't displayed for twenty years. All around him, throughout the great valley of Myrloch, the forests and meadows had surged into life with renewed vitality.

And the failure of the firbolg and troll hunters wasn't because the game had disappeared, either. If anything, the numbers of deer and rabbits, fox and squirrels, had increased during this vibrant season. But at the same time as life invigorated the plants, so had the animals become more alert, quicker, more nimble.

The hunting tactics of Thurgol and his band had always been crude, at best. The thrown rock was the deadliest weapon in the giant-kin arsenal, and the club, however heavy and knotted, was no way to bring down a deer. Of course, during the chieftain's youth, the band had possessed the Silverhaft Axe, and while that was no hunting weapon, at least in design, it seemed that the diamond-studded blade and whichever firbolg wielded it had always been able to provide fresh meat. Indeed, one of Thurgol's earliest memories was of a grand feast—a huge bear, slain by Klatnaught, the former chieftain, with the Silverhaft Axe. Klatnaught's wife, the shaman Garisa, had provided Thurgol with a tender morsel from the beast's ribs.

Yet it had now been two decades since the Silverhaft Axe had been stolen. During these past years, the firbolgs had ranged the width and breadth of the wide valley in the heart of the island of Gwynneth, stumbling across listless animals and bashing their brains out. Now, he knew, those days were gone, along with the mighty axe.

He came to the shore of a pool of still water. Previously he had come here to study his reflection, drawing comfort from the craggy precipice of his brow, the heavy jowls and large, wart-covered nose. Those features, together with his broad-girthed mass of shoulders and chest, his stumplike legs as sturdy as two weathered oak trunks, had combined to make Thurgol lord and master of Blackleaf.

But even that visage was lost to him now, thanks to the cloudy film that colored the previously clear water. Not only did the liquid have a distinct cast of milky white color, but in the full dark of the night, it also actually seemed to *glow!*

Thurgol wasn't terribly certain of the latter fact. On one night several weeks earlier, however, he had certainly gotten the impression that the pool possessed some kind of luminescence. On that occasion, shaken by a dim, supernatural fear, he had hastened back to the village, and he hadn't approached the pond after nightfall since.

Now, in his capacity as ruler, he knew that he had to do something about his people's current malaise. Thurgol liked having his pick of the wenches, and it was a source of great satisfaction for him to lord it over the trolls. In the past, those scaly, hideous humanoids wouldn't have consented to such an arrangement, but now the hard times in the vale had driven them to seek the protection of the firbolgs. Without Thurgol and his giant-kin, the trolls would almost certainly have been exterminated by the dwarves, who were the other significant occupants of northern Myrloch Vale.

For many years, the firbolgs and dwarves had existed in uneasy truce, sharing the large valley to the north of the great lake itself. The dwarves claimed the lands to the east of Codsrun Creek, the firbolgs to the west. Surrounded as they were by rugged highlands to north, east, and west, and isolated by the huge lake to the south, the two tribes had lived in seclusion from the rest of the Moonshae population. Indeed, since the druids had departed, precious few humans had even entered Myrloch Vale, much less tried to live there. The few rash enough to try the latter, of course, the trolls quickly found and devoured.

Suddenly Thurgol scratched his head. The druids, he knew, had begun to return. His eyes gleamed with the fervor of insight. Could there be a connection to the revitalized forest and the men and women who had once tended and preserved it? Grunting in frustration, the firbolg chief shook his head as the cognitive link proved to be too much of a mental challenge.

Still, the unease agitating him remained. He thought of the dwarves, spitting loudly as the image of the small, bearded pests filled his mind. Hateful runts, every one of them! Another thought occurred to him: The game eluded his tribe around Blackleaf, but did the dwarves continue to have plenty? In his heart of hearts, Thurgol became convinced that they did.

Perhaps the dwarves had *stolen* the game that rightly belonged to the tribe of Thurgol! The more he considered this possibility, the more he became convinced it was the truth. The complacency of twenty years of peace had lulled him and his people, and his ancient enemies had taken advantage of that lapse! The question of how the dwarves lured away his game did not trouble the giant-kin's dim intellect. It was enough that he had found a focus for his discontent.

Finally—or perhaps foremost—there was the matter of the Silverhaft Axe. The priceless artifact had been the grand treasure of the firbolg clan during the first decades of Thurgol's life. The hallowed object was attributed a major role in the creation of the firbolg race and had been a wonder to look at.

Then, twenty years earlier, following the giant-kins' defeat in the Darkwalker War, the axe had been claimed by the victors, specifically the dwarves. Those short folk also revered the axe as a legendary artifact, and had regarded its possession by firbolgs as nothing short of heresy. The Myrloch dwarves had been only too glad to seize the axe as the spoils of war. Nevertheless, to Thurgol, it was his own tribe who had been wronged.

And then the gods, or fate, gave him further proof when he turned back toward the village, stepping roughly on a lush lilac. A rabbit scampered away from the foliage, and he swung mightily with his club. The knobbed weapon bounced from the ground scant inches from the terrified creature's puffball of a tail. The hare disappeared as Thurgol grunted in anguish, the rude shock jarring his elbow and wrenching his shoulder. Then his eyes narrowed suspiciously as he understood the import of the event.

For the rabbit had fled eastward, toward the vale of the dwarves.

* * * * *

Day provided no respite for the weary Princess of Callidyrr. Deirdre lay awake, but for the most part unaware. Her eyes remained open, staring vacantly about the room. Occasionally she allowed her mother—but no one else—to feed her broth or water. Other than that, she took no nourishment, responding listlessly or not at all to companionship.

A sense of complete weariness possessed her, an apathy that her mother and attending clerics suspected grew from her troubled nights.

Yet her mind remained alive and active. She knew fear, remembered desire. She felt an unspeakable horror of something that awaited her beyond the curtain of nightfall. Yet there was power there, and a certain allure that she couldn't deny.

Thus, at the same time as her terror grew, she found herself yearning for sunset.

* * * * *

Talos the Stormbringer seethed in his rage. At every turn, it seemed, the revitalized goddess of the Ffolk thwarted and aggrieved him. Yet in his frustration, his immortal will congealed into a last grim purpose: He would strike at these impudent mortals; he would wound and dismay them.

For that task, he had one tool—a tool that was singularly suited to his purpose.

❧ 2 ❧

The Exalted Inquisitor

"Please, Alicia, reconsider! Sail with me to the north!" Brandon's arms held the princess against his brawny chest. Though the pressure of his grip was gentle, she felt suffocated, and gently she broke free.

Alicia looked up while the wind blew her bright golden hair back from her face. Her eyes of green searched the ice-blue gaze of the proud northman prince. Framed by high, proud cheekbones, her face tore at Brandon's heart so intensely that it hurt him to see it. At the same time, he found it absolutely impossible to look away.

Only a trace of this anguish showed on the sailing captain's own stern face. Dressed for sea, the northman had tied his long hair into twin braids, donning leather sandals to protect his feet. The day was warm, and so he wore merely a strap of bearskin across his loins.

"I must stay here in Corwell, at least for now, until Deirdre's better or . . ." She didn't want to voice the alternative.

"The goddess has a way of watching over her own, and your mother is the Earthmother's favored child. Deirdre is in very good hands." The words, soothingly spoken from behind her, told Alicia that Tavish had arrived at the waterfront. The princess felt a measure of relief as Brandon stepped back slightly, reluctant to display his feelings before anyone but his beloved.

The harpist wrapped an arm around Alicia's shoulders and pulled the younger woman close in a hug. Though Tavish neared sixty years of age, she remained as robust as, and a good deal stronger than, most women half her age. The bard's round face was split by her almost constant smile, her ever-present harp slung casually over her shoulder.

"It will be a delight to have music accompany our voyage," Brandon said, warming to the harpist's smile.

"And for my part, I look forward to seeing the lodges of the north again. I've always enjoyed the hospitality of Gnarhelm!"

"My father, I know, will be delighted with your return," the prince said sincerely. "King Kendrick couldn't hope for a more able ambassador!"

"Oh, I'm more of a tourist than an ambassador," the bard said modestly. Though she spoke the truth in bare fact, her presence in the northern kingdom would indeed serve to cement the bonds of peace that had survived for two decades between the disparate human cultures of the Moonshaes.

"Well, you two make your farewells," Tavish said genially. "I'll try to get myself loaded into the boat."

Beyond them, the *Princess of Moonshae* sat in the calm waters of Corwell Harbor. The planks of the graceful longship's hull had been scrubbed until they gleamed, the scrapes from her recent trials fully obliterated. Tavish crossed to the edge of the dock, where a small boat waited to take her and the captain out to the sleek vessel.

"Will her keel hold?" Alicia asked the prince, addressing Brandon's greatest concern during the past week.

"As strong as ever, and six inches wider in the beam!" The northman nodded, his mind reluctantly but inevitably turning to the longship that was his other great love. "But . . . your staff. Are you sure you want to leave your staff as part of the hull? I know it's a treasured artifact. . . ."

"Yes . . . it's only right that the blessing of the goddess ride with the *Princess of Moonshae*," Alicia replied sincerely.

The enchanted shaft of wood, a druid's changestaff given to Alicia by her mother, had become a part of the great vessel when she used it to seal an otherwise fatal breach in the hull. Grown to the size of a small tree trunk, it remained wedged into a wide crack beside the longship's keel. Invisible to outside observation, it provided a smooth outer surface and a perfectly watertight seal beside the central timber of the hull. The ship had suffered grievous damage as Brandon captained the quest to rescue King Kendrick, and she couldn't help but feel that a gift of the staff would begin, in some small way, to restore the balance between her gratitude and guilt.

Yet all of her reflections, even her gift of the staff, Alicia knew, were simply means of avoiding the central issue confronting her now on this dock.

Tell him the truth, a voice whispered inside her head—a voice she forcefully ignored. She couldn't admit even to herself a fact that had slowly been growing in her heart and her mind: that she did not love this generous, handsome man who had risked his life and his ship to aid the rescue of her father.

She wanted to love him—indeed, a part of herself told her that she was *obligated* to love him. But neither of these altered the simple fact that she did not.

"I—I wish I could stay for the rest of the summer," Brandon said sincerely. "But my father must know of our safe return, and I have already been absent from my own kingdom for too long. You return to Callidyrr in the autumn?" concluded the prince.

"Always in the past we've left Corwell before the gales of Harvestide. I assume Father will want to do the same this year, but I'll send word to you about our plans. It's not as if you're sailing to the ends of the world!"

She wanted to speak lightly, but the words came out more harshly than she intended. She saw the hurt on Brandon's face and tried to ease it by taking his hand. "I *will* write," she promised.

He nodded glumly, then kissed her. She returned his embrace, but once again she relished a sense of freedom when he released her. Why can't I tell him? The question nagged at her, but she forced it away. She watched him step into the longboat that several kindly fisherfolk had provided. Tavish already sat near the bow, busily tuning the strings of her harp, though she stopped long enough to wave a cheery good-bye to the princess on the pier.

The Prince of Gnarhelm stood tall in the stern of the little boat as he was rowed to his proud longship. Alicia stood watching, waving finally as he climbed aboard the vessel. Wind quickly billowed the longship's sail, and the *Princess of Moonshae* turned her prow toward the gap in the breakwater. Smoothly she sliced through the waves, shrinking in size as Brandon set a course toward the mouth of Corwell Firth.

By that time, Alicia had already started back to the castle.

* * * * *

Keane saw that the house across from the shrine was indeed a magnificent residence. Set high upon the hill that protected the Upper City, it might have served as a palace to the monarch of some small state. Below swept a vista of the Lower City and its great, encircling arm of the Chionthar River, here widespread and placid, though it had another fifty miles of journey before it reached the sea.

A high wall of whitewashed stone surrounded and screened the grounds, but as he approached the steel-barred gate, Keane saw an expanse of fountains and formal gardens. Several cascading spumes of water splashed merrily, casting streams of spray through the crisp morning air. Detailed mosaics of colorful tile formed a wide walkway leading from the gate toward the columned portico before a grand manor. The house, as white as the walls, gleamed in the morning sunlight.

Though Keane could easily have teleported, levitated, or slipped invisibly into the compound, the nature of his business required him to make a more formal approach. Therefore the tall, lanky wizard wore his finest leather cape, a satin shirt of blue silk, and smooth, high-topped boots of soft doeskin.

A pair of guards in red livery snapped to attention behind the gate as the mage approached. Keane bowed politely before speaking.

"Is the Exalted Inquisitor present? I request the honor of an audience with him."

"The inquisitor is a very busy man," sniffed one of the guards, with a disdainful inspection of the magic-user's finery. "Whom shall we report is calling?"

"I am Keane of Callidyrr, serving as ambassador for His Majesty, High King Tristan Kendrick of the Moonshaes."

The guard's eyes, much to Keane's satisfaction, widened slightly at the information. The man turned and started for the house at a trot while the other guard took pains to effect an absolutely rigid stance. A few minutes later the first guard returned, accompanied by a short, chubby man in a white clerical robe. The symbol of Helm, the All-Seeing Eye encircled by a ring of platinum, bobbed against the latter's ample belly.

"A royal ambassador . . . this is a signal honor! Come in, come in, my good lord!" The cleric beamed at Keane, waddling forward and gesturing imperiously to the guard who still stood rigidly at his station. "Open that gate, man—and be quick about it!"

"Thank you," Keane murmured as the priest bowed and smiled.

"You come from the court of the Kendricks? Your king's name is known far and wide, of course—an honorable man and a wise and beneficent ruler! But, of course, you know that already. Perhaps there is something that I can help you with? I am the bishou of this temple and shrine—Bishou Harmanius." The rank of bishou was not unknown to Keane. Harmanius was an influential man and a powerful cleric—but not powerful enough for the mage's needs.

"Actually, I'm afraid that my business must be conducted with the Exalted Inquisitor. Will he grant me the honor of an appointment?"

"Ahem . . . well, you see . . . he is a *very* busy person these days," the bishou demurred. "Perhaps if I could relay to him the nature of your business . . . ?"

As they spoke, the pair passed between a pair of tall

columns, climbing several large steps to approach the huge, ornately carved doors at the front of the manor. These swung open ponderously at their approach, and Keane saw another pair of scarlet-coated guards, images of immaculate tunics, obsidian-black boots, and buckles of gleaming silver, flanking the entrance.

"It concerns a matter of great importance to my king—a service he desires. Naturally it involves a sizable donation to the coffers of the church." Keane added the incentive on his own responsibility, suspecting from the opulence around him that it would be an effective inducement. He was not disappointed.

"Of course, the business of an esteemed monarch like King Kendrick must supersede lesser concerns," noted the cleric, without a hint of irony so far as Keane could tell. "I shall relay your request immediately. Would you be so kind as to wait in here?" Harmanius indicated a large parlor lined with marble walls, the floor buried beneath an array of lush, silken rugs.

"My pleasure," Keane replied. The cleric bustled into the temple while the magic-user walked slowly about the large chamber, dazzled by the wonders on display.

A large doorway of cut glass led into an enclosed garden, and from it sunlight spilled into the room. Paintings hung along the walls, mostly battle scenes, in which the banner of the All-Seeing Eye floated proudly above the victorious troops. One canvas made a mural along a good-sized wall, depicting the toppling of Maztican gods from their pyramid-shaped temples while the local peoples bestowed gifts of gold and silver on the bishou who had enlightened them. The mage spent several minutes studying the scene, noticing the strong flavor of righteous triumph tinged with bleak and abject conquest.

"Lord Ambassador?"

Keane turned suddenly, surprised that someone had entered the room without being heard. He felt a flash of guilt, as if he had been caught eavesdropping. "Ah, yes—

forgive me. I was just admiring your artwork." He recovered smoothly from his surprise to bow formally to the man he knew must be the Exalted Inquisitor of Helm.

"Splendid, is it not? It commemorates the founding of Helmsport, on the coast of Maztica. Perhaps you know that it has become the major port on that savage shore?"

The cleric, Keane saw, was a very tall man—nearly as tall as the mage himself. He was stout, but not obese. Instead, the inquisitor carried the strong suggestion of a workman's strength in his barrel chest and large hands. A neatly trimmed beard of rust red framed the priest's chin, and his blue eyes sparkled with intensity and, perhaps, curiosity.

"I had heard something of that, yes," noted the mage as the cleric lead him to a pair of comfortable chairs arrayed before a currently unlighted hearth.

"Please, be seated. Allow me to introduce myself—Parell Hyath, Helm's inquisitor along this coast. Harmanius tells me you wish to discuss a matter of import to your king."

"That's correct." Keane had already decided that he wouldn't mention the unfortunate demise of Bakar Dalsoritan. No need to inform the inquisitor that he was the mage's second choice. Instead, he quickly launched into the explanation.

"His Majesty King Kendrick has recently been rescued from a dire imprisonment. His health is good, but his captors, in an act of sheer brutality, cut off one of his hands. He has commissioned me to . . . negotiate for the services of a devout man of the gods, a man such as yourself. I am prepared to offer generous inducements should you be willing to return to the isles with me and perform a spell of regeneration on the king."

Parell Hyath's blue eyes narrowed subtly, but his lips pursed tightly together.

"This is a worthy cause, to be sure—but I'm afraid that the matter of timing creates a bit of difficulty. My business here in Baldur's Gate is sure to occupy me for the rest of the year . . . though perhaps after that?"

Keane shook his head regretfully. He wondered if the cleric spoke the truth or simply raised the issue for negotiation purposes. "I'm sorry, Lord Inquisitor, but His Majesty was most insistent that I return as soon as possible. Isn't there a way that you could make the journey quickly, returning here to resume your business, and not incidentally earn a respectable fee for your good efforts?"

The magic-user knew that clerics did not possess the wizard's ability to teleport instantaneously from one place to another, which had been the means Keane used to reach Baldur's Gate from Corwell. But he also knew that other paths were open to the servants of the gods, such as gates through the astral planes and other-dimensional paths that allowed equally rapid transport.

For a moment, he wondered if the cleric really spoke the truth, for the man's lips remained locked in that firm position, causing his beard to twist into a tight circle around his mouth. But then he relaxed slightly.

"It just might be possible," he allowed, "though I can make no promises. By the way, what sort of, er, 'inducement' did your king have in mind?"

"I'm authorized to offer as much as fifty thousand pieces of gold or the equivalent in jewels, gems, or platinum." Keane knew the amount would put a significant dent in the royal treasury, but it was a fee he felt certain that the king would pay. In addition, he could see, with some satisfaction, that the offer had cut right to the core of the inquisitor's being. Hyath blinked, and this time he forgot to purse his lips. Keane saw his eyes slowly widen as he no doubt considered the charitable works that such a sum would allow him to accomplish.

"As I explained," the priest said after a few moments reflective silence, "my time is difficult to rearrange. But there is a possibility. . . ."

"I truly hope so," Keane prodded. "Do you need a day to decide? I'm afraid I won't be able to linger much longer than that. I'll have to seek help in Waterdeep, or Amn. . . ."

"Bah!" The cleric shook his head derisively. "Neither of them offers a cleric worthy of the title patriarch!"

"You'll forgive me"—Keane's voice was soft, precisely polite—"but I'll have to see that for myself."

The inquisitor smiled then, his expression surprisingly friendly. Nevertheless, the Ffolkman thought he detected a hint of craftiness in the cleric's visage.

"I'll do it," Hyath agreed suddenly. "Give me until tomorrow morning to make my arrangements. Then we can depart. We'll travel together, I hope."

"Certainly," Keane agreed smoothly, not at all sure how the cleric intended to make the journey.

"If you will accept the accommodations of my humble abode for the night, we can be off at first light. Will you be my guest?"

"I'll have to get my bags, but it'll be a pleasure."

"We'll send a man for them. Come, allow Bishou Harmanius to show you the gardens while I attend to my business. The roses are in full bloom, and I've been told that our hedges are the finest along the Sword Coast."

The cleric was already in motion as Keane rose to follow him from the parlor. As if he had known his patriarch's intentions, the bishou awaited them in the central hall, beside a circular marble fountain. The inquisitor instructed him as to his plans, then turned back to Keane.

"Please, treat this home as your own. I'll see you again at dinner—and then, as I told you, we'll depart for Corwell at first light."

* * * * *

The fire burned high, consuming many oak trunks with insatiable tongues and greedy fingers of flame. A keg of firbolg rotgut, horrific of stench and searing of taste, made the rounds of the throng, passed from giant-kin to troll and back again. Thurgol sat near the fire, enjoying the warmth of the gathering and the exalted status that gave him his prime seat. Even the presence of the great troll Baatlrap, squatting across the blaze from him, did nothing to detract from his pleasure.

The eyes of a wolfdog flashed golden in the firelight. The creature raised its shaggy head and blinked at the approach of a stooped firbolg clad in a billowing dress. The giant-kin hag regarded the great canine for a second, and then the beast swiftly rose and slinked away from the fire, yielding its place to the giant female.

Garisa reached the fireside and turned to glare at her comrades. Shaman of the village for many decades, she used the authority of her office to silence the throng merely by the persuasive power of her gaze. Even the trolls ceased their bickering yaps, regarding the female firbolg with expressions of fear, awe, and suspicion.

Thurgol was pleased. If the night was to culminate in success, then it was important that all of them give careful attention to Garisa's words, her story and her prophecy. Though the shaman and the chieftain had discussed in minimal detail what was to occur this night, Thurgol wasn't sure how the old female intended to go about it.

Their task was aided by the fact that Garisa held a unique and honored status in Blackleaf. The old crone of a firbolg was more skilled at healing and medicinal applications than any other resident of that community. In addition, however, she had discovered at an early age that she possessed a modicum of magical ability.

Charming a young warrior into a marriage that had elevated her to most envied female in the tribe, Garisa had worked to develop other talents, such as the healing incantation that worked so well for the broken bones and deep gouges that were the lot of the firbolg warrior's life. Thus her exalted status had remained even after her mate had fallen in the tragic conflict the humans had called the Darkwalker War.

Garisa had also learned to weave simple illusions. She never altered anything very much, but she could create the appearance of a mist in the air, and shape it to match the image she desired. This particular attribute had proven very useful throughout her century-plus of life. And during that entire time, she had kept her slight mastery of illusion a secret from every single one of her fellow villagers.

All the firbolgs of Blackleaf, of course, knew of her skill with herbs. Too, she had a reputation for making accurate predictions based on the reflections created by a few copper coins cast into a bowl of water. Hadn't she correctly guessed the outcome of that wild young Bree filly's mating? She had predicted that within five years the brazen young female would be discovered in the arms of another young buck. Naturally the husband, who had commissioned Garisa's foretelling, spent most of those five years accusing and spying upon his unfortunate bride, until the prophecy had been fulfilled.

Garisa continued to enjoy a unique status among firbolg females, being privy to the decisions of the chieftains and elders. Even young Thurgol, who had come to power when the shaman was already an old giantess, had employed her experience and skills when he had first taken the reins of village leadership, wresting them from old Klatnaught, who had grown just a step too slow to hold on to his post.

Then, of course, the trolls had come. Nearly twenty years ago the gangly humanoids, with their emotionless black holes of eyes—"dead" eyes, Garisa thought—had approached Thurgol with an offer to work for the firbolgs, in exchange for sharing the bounty and shelter of the village. The old shaman had been a lone voice of dissent amid a listless chorus of "ayes," and so the trolls had put up some shacks at the edge of the village and settled in.

In fact, the alliance looked innocuous enough on the surface. After all, there had originally been fewer than two dozen trolls, not nearly enough to threaten two hundred firbolgs. For a year or two, the trolls had labored dutifully, hunting and harvesting for their share of Myrloch Vale's provender.

By this time, there were some fifty of them, though none of the firbolgs ever really noticed the addition of individual members. The green-skinned brutes formed a strong and vocal faction, and Garisa found herself increasingly overruled in the rude and informal councils of the giant-troll clan.

Now Thurgol had come to her with this perilous path of warfare against the dwarves. Garisa blamed the trolls for this, as for most everything else. But unlike Thurgol and virtually every other firbolg and troll in the band, she had at least a dim understanding of the changes occurring in Myrloch Vale.

Garisa remembered the druids, remembered them with fear and envy. For most of her lifetime, they had preserved this valley as a sacred wilderness, forcing the firbolg clans into the highlands around the fertile bottomland. There the giant-kin had dwelled for generations, surviving in more or less pastoral existence, though an occasional conflict brought them to blows with their human, dwarven, and Llewyrr elven neighbors.

Two decades ago, when the druids had vanished, nothing had blocked the firbolgs from moving into the well-watered valley, so the tribe had quickly migrated down from their rocky heights. Now Thurgol wanted to fight for possession of that valley, when to Garisa many a highland hilltop beckoned the giant-kin back to their ancient homes.

Yet she was Thurgol's loyal ally, and together the two of them had concocted the plan that, tonight, would reach its fruition. It was a scheme that, despite its risks, had a strong element of merit. Appropriately, it would begin with a familiar tribal ritual—the Cant of the Peaksmasher.

Slowly, with careful, deliberate rhythm, Garisa shuffled her feet. Raising a knotty fist, in which she clasped a worn rope, she shook the line, causing the clattering of tiny bells to jangle in time with her dance.

Firbolgs and trolls alike followed with their eyes the giantess through her ritual, carefully formalized steps. Then abruptly she spun through a full circle, in a whirl of jangling bells and cackling laughter. Stepping rapidly, she returned to her original place beside the fire, once again fixing her fellow villagers with a gaze of mystery and raw suspense. The fact that they had heard the coming story many times before did nothing to mellow the tension. If anything, it brought the giant-kin to an even higher pitch of readiness.

"In the days before humans," Garisa began, her tone singing, the rhythm of her speech retaining its careful tempo, "there came the greatest giant of them all to an island in the Trackless Sea."

"Grond—Grond Peaksmasher!" The chanted response rumbled from every firbolg throat like imminent thunder from the growing darkness.

"Grond saw that this land was good. In the shelter of its reefs, he beheld the gleaming image of the full moon, and he called his place Moonshae."

"Grond—Grond Peaksmasher!"

"He took his mighty blade—the blade that had carried him through legions of elves, against swarms of dragons and pestilential creatures of hideous evil—he took his blade and he carved for himself a home on Moonshae."

"Grond—Grond Peaksmasher!"

"The axe with the shaft of silver—the axe with the blade of gleaming gemstone! And with his cutting edge, Grond carved the Moonshaes, cut the rock into pieces and left it as many isles. He carved the highland and grotto; he carved the vale and lake," Garisa chanted.

"Grond—Grond Peaksmasher!"

"And from the highest rock, he carved the images of his children. He carved the firbolg, the giant-kin! He made them proud and he made them great. He made them the masters of his world."

"Grond—Grond Peaksmasher!"

"But the rubble from his blade fell under his feet, and the refuse was crushed to gravel. And as the magic of Grond's axe showered around him, some of the brightness fell upon the gravel . . . and these crumbled pieces of stone came to life." Now Garisa's voice fell, the tone becoming low and threatening.

"Grond—Grond Peaksmasher!"

"And the stones of the path came to life, and they scuttled out of the sun, away from the glory of Grond and his fir-bolgs! For these stones were the dwarves, and forever they resented the might of the great one who had made such grandeur of his first children, but left the dwarves mere tiny, misshapen runts."

"Grond—Grond Peaksmasher!"

"And the hearts of the dwarves were black with treach-ery. They tumbled under the great lord's feet and made him to think he stood upon the firmament. But then, as he raised his axe to strike again, the dwarves stole away. They carried the stones from beneath the Peaksmasher's feet, and as he tumbled to the earth, the diamond blade chopped a mighty piece from the mountain."

"Grond—Grond Peaksmasher!"

"And the slide of rock and ice entrapped him, and made of him a piece of the Moonshaes, a sturdy beam of the world itself. And the firbolgs wept and grieved, and the dwarves took up the Silverhaft Axe and carried it away."

"Honored is the name of Grond—Grond Peaksmasher!" chanted the firbolg tribe, moved as a single, solid spirit by the tale of their origin.

"And still the Silverhaft Axe remains in the hands of the dwarves! Still they laugh at our grief. Still they taunt us with their prosperity, torment us with their greed. . . ."

"This cannot pass!" Thurgol stormed, bounding to his feet and raising his fist in the air.

"The axe!" shouted another giant-kin, as if on cue. "Claim it back! Claim it in the name of the Peaksmasher's children!"

"Aye! The axe! Kill the bearded runts!" A chorus of cries rumbled through the camp, growing into a crescendo of fury. Even the wolfdogs sensed the frenzy, adding their yaps and howls to the din rising into the night.

Thurgol sat quietly, watching the growing fervor from beneath his hooded eyelids. The council, he knew at last, had carried him perfectly to his goal.

* * * * *

"Did she sleep at all last night?" Alicia could tell from the haggard look of her mother and father as they joined her at breakfast that Deirdre had had another rough night. Though Alicia's own room was nearby, in the upper chambers of Caer Corwell's keep, she did not share the adjoining apartments where her sister currently stayed with their parents. Thus she was spared the experience of Deirdre's nightmares as they happened, though her parents' attitudes in the morning left little doubt as to the night's ordeal.

Surprisingly, Tristan looked at Robyn instead of answering his eldest daughter's question. The queen's eyes were hooded, dark with concern.

"She did . . . unusually so," Robyn finally said.

"Isn't that good?" asked the princess, sensing the worry in her mother's response.

"I don't know," sighed the queen. "The nightmares came first. She kicked and thrashed in her sleep, tossing her head from side to side and gasping for air as if she couldn't breathe. In the end—when, in the past, she's always awakened screaming—she fell into a deep sleep. It frightened me as much as the nightmares, as if she had given herself up to whatever it was that pursued her. I tried to wake her, but she was beyond reach—or comprehension."

"What can we do? Is it enough to wait for this to pass?"

Again Alicia saw the sharp look between her parents, but then Robyn lowered her eyes in silent defeat. Tristan answered the question.

"When Keane gets here with the patriarch, we'll ask him to examine her," he said slowly while Robyn's eyes remained downcast. He spoke to his wife as much as to his daughter. "We've *got* to try it! Nothing else seems to work, and we *can't* give her up! *I* can't!"

"Nor can I," Robyn replied, surprising Alicia with the softness of her tone.

The princess understood that, with the resurgence of the Earthmother, the druid queen must regard with suspicion the intervention of any other gods into the Moonshaes. The "New Gods," they had once been called, for they were seen to compete with the treasured nature goddess who had so long made these isles an enchanted, magical place.

Yet some problems were beyond the abilities of even the Great Druid to solve, and it seemed that Deirdre's malaise was one of these. Alicia, like her father, hoped that a cleric of one of the New Gods might offer her sister some hope of succor. Yet she could sympathize with her mother as well. Alicia herself had been touched by the magic of the Earthmother, and she understood the special role that the benign goddess played in the life of the Moonshaes. She worried about any threat to that serene balance, the eternal equilibrium of light and dark, good and evil, that provided the fulcrum of her faith.

They spent several silent minutes picking dully at their bread and cheese. Somehow, to Alicia, the former tasted dry and stale, the latter crumbly and sharp—though both were fresh, in varieties she had enjoyed all her life.

"It's not like Keane to waste his time when he's on business for the king. What can be keeping him, anyway?" demanded Tristan, breaking the silence with frustrated words.

"He's *not* wasting time!" Alicia immediately leaped to her former tutor's defense, surprising her father with the vehemence of her statement.

"What makes you so sure?" he pressed, more interested in her reaction than in her answer, for if the truth be told, Tristan felt certain beyond any doubt that the faithful Keane labored diligently in service of his king.

Alicia flushed. The emotions that compelled her beliefs were not feelings she felt ready to discuss with her parents;

indeed, she was just beginning to understand them herself. "He's a loyal subject, that's all. If he's taking overly long, it just means that he's run into unforeseen problems."

"Perhaps the patriarch is busy . . . or absent," surmised the queen, with a sideways look at her daughter. "Keane would certainly try to find some other avenue, some other source of help, rather than return empty-handed."

King Tristan smiled wanly, unconsciously holding his hand over the blunt wrist of his left arm. "You're right, of course. I've had enough demonstrations of loyalty—from all of you—that such complaints are unbecoming. I apologize," he said to Alicia, nodding formally.

The princess blushed even more deeply, for she sensed the teasing in his words. "He'll be back soon!" she finished lamely.

"Brandon departed yesterday?" Tristan mentioned idly. Alicia didn't know if he was changing the subject or pursuing his original tack mercilessly. It was common knowledge that the Prince of Gnarhelm had sought her hand in marriage, and the fact that he had sailed away alone gave a clear enough indication of her reply.

"Yes. He had matters in his father's kingdom to tend. He—he plans to come to Callidyrr over the winter." She wasn't sure how she felt about that. The memory of his determination brought back the sensation of being trapped that she had struggled with earlier.

"A good man, that," the king continued, his appetite growing more hearty as his mind drifted away from his ailing daughter and his own semicrippling wound. "I remember his father, King Olafsson, though I haven't seen him in twenty years. Still, he made a fine impression when we signed the Treaty of Oman."

"The treaty that made it possible for his son to help us," Robyn pointed out. The northmen and Ffolk had been mortal enemies for many centuries until the signing of that historic pact. The peace, arranged by High King Kendrick and the kings of the north, had been reaffirmed during the recent troubles. Also, although Alicia had not been aware of this, the prospect of a unifying marriage had been considered and anticipated by both peoples.

"Indeed," Tristan reminisced. "It was King Olafsson who suggested the place for the ceremony. He thought that the image of the Icepeak above, with the surrounding groves of the Grampalt Highlands, made the proper setting for a peace between two such diverse populations."

"The Icepeak . . . that's the highest mountain in the isles, isn't it?" Alicia asked.

"So high that its summit remains shrouded by ice and snow the full year around," Robyn confirmed.

"I remember often enough sailing through the strait on the voyages from Callidyrr to Corwell," Alicia observed. "A few times the weather was clear enough that we could see the mountain. I remember the first time I saw it. Never did I think that any piece of the world could soar so high into the air!"

"There are summits on the mainland that are higher," the king allowed. "But none within the Moonshaes that even comes close."

The king was silent for a moment, then looked at Alicia with a mischievous twinkle in his eye. "And now the son of Svenyird Olafsson is smitten with my daughter! What a way to seal the peace, eh, my queen?"

"Father!" objected the princess as her mother smiled.

Tristan held up his hand in a gesture of peace. "You didn't imagine it was a secret, did you? Besides, it's time you gave some thought to a husband. He'll marry onto the throne of the High King, remember."

"I believe Alicia knows her own mind—well enough for now, in any event," interjected Robyn, coming to her daughter's rescue. Thankfully the princess made haste with the rest of her breakfast, mumbling some excuse about her horses as she rose from the table and all but raced for the doors.

* * * * *

An acolyte awakened Keane as the first rays of sunlight began to lighten the eastern horizon. He met the Exalted Inquisitor in the plaza, where they shared a quick breakfast of fruit and wine. By the time pale blue stretched across the full arc of the sky, the cleric announced that he was ready to depart.

Bishou Harmanius arrived then with a long, narrow roll of silk. Keane discerned that the fabric was merely a wrapping, protecting a straight object some five feet long. The inquisitor took no note of his underling's arrival.

"What shall I do?" inquired Keane, still mystified as to Hyath's intended mode of transport.

"All questions are answered for the patient man," intoned the inquisitor. "For now, just wait there."

Dressed in splendid white robes etched in trim of gold and silver thread, the inquisitor struck a grand pose, closing his eyes and clasping his hands reverently over his solid stomach.

The words of his prayer mingled into a low chant, in a language that Keane did not recognize. The cleric spoke for more than a minute, his tone modulating from harsh to mild, flowing up and down the scale almost as if he sang.

Abruptly Keane detected a brightening in the air before the cleric. Slowly the illumination grew more distinct, taking on a shape and solidity where before had been only the clear morning air. Soon a spinning wheel of fire resolved itself from the arcane pyrotechnics, crackling and hissing, casting showers of sparks to the paving stones of the courtyard. The shape expanded, and gradually Keane made out two blazing figures—like horses, but made from light and fire. Above the flaming wheel, he saw a platform, well shielded and quite wide enough to carry several riders.

It was the image of a chariot, only both the vehicle and the prancing steeds in harness were etched in colors and lines of fire. The beasts kicked and pranced in their traces, eager to run . . . or to fly. Like ghosts, the apparitions flared before Keane, and the wizard knew he beheld an example of very powerful clerical magic.

"The Chariot of Sustarre," explained the patriarch proudly. "It will carry us in royal fashion."

"Indeed," Keane agreed, more awed than he would have liked to admit.

Now the inquisitor turned to Harmanius, and the bishou passed the silk-wrapped package to his master. Carrying the object in one hand, Hyath stepped into the chariot, turning once to beckon to Keane.

The mage hesitated a bare moment, then climbed in beside the inquisitor. Fire crackled all around him, but he felt no unusual heat, though the chill of the morning air had been fully dispersed.

Then, before he could catch his breath, the cleric shouted another word and the chariot took to the air.

* * * * *

Deirdre finally let herself go, giving up the resistance, the panicked flight and terrified evasions that never allowed her to elude the darkness. With her surrender came a sense of impending destiny, and as she faced her own image, she found that her slumber again restored her, revitalizing and empowering nerve and muscle and mind.

She sensed many things as she looked into her eyes. Certainly the fear, the dark, shrouded terror, still lingered there, but no longer did these emotions boil to the surface. Instead, they lay deep within her, fueling the flames of other things . . . of might and power, greatness and control.

And even more.

* * * * *

Talos the Destructor sensed the growing power of the woman, and he knew well that she was more than she had been now, more than any human was. The soul of his own immortal might had entered her, and now, with each passing evening, that presence sealed its grip upon her will and her soul.

His presence stirred evil and chaos throughout the Moonshae Islands, nourished by the woman's spirit, driven by a growing reality of vengeance. As the power of Talos swelled, others began to take notice—others who included not only mortals but also gods.

❧ 3 ❧

Clash at Cambro

Thurgol saw with pleasure that, during every step of the march from Blackleaf, all evidence indicated that the dwarves remained as set in their peaceful ways as he had hoped they would. The chieftain had led a rude column of more than a hundred firbolgs and half that many trolls through the fertile bottomland of Myrloch Vale, but not once had he encountered sign of a dwarven watch post. Even the wide-ranging wolfdogs, sniffing and snarling in a pack as they accompanied the humanoids on the march, had failed to identify any spoor of dwarven activity. Now, approaching Cambro, Thurgol saw that their foolish complacency continued.

Though he was no moralist, the giant couldn't entirely vanquish a small measure of unease over the attack he now contemplated. After all, twenty years of peace was no mean accomplishment. Yet now, after all those years, things were not as good as they once had been. Perhaps peace was the mistake he had made. In the end, he could see no alternative to attacking the dwarves. Doing nothing meant dying by starvation, and death in battle was an infinitely preferable alternative.

There was also the matter of the Silverhaft Axe. At first Thurgol had felt that the axe made a handy incentive for his less broad-minded fellows, giving them a clear reason to march against the dwarves. But during the march—indeed, beginning with Garisa's powerful recounting of the legend on the night before their departure—the ancient blade had come to mean more to Thurgol.

Now it seemed only right and proper to him that the giant-kin regain the lost artifact of their maker. And the only way to do that, he understood, was to wage war. With the battle looming imminent, the prospects of a victory seemed better than even Thurgol had dared to hope possible. His ragged army had reached the very periphery of the dwarves' village, and the wily chieftain concealed his troops among the underbrush no more than a hundred feet from the nearest wood-and-stone houses.

Many dozens of such sturdy dwellings formed the cluster of homes that made the village of Cambro. A few bearded dwarves, males and females alike, clumped from this building to that, though the activity could hardly be described as bustling. A dwarven hunter carrying a stout crossbow emerged from one of the houses and started toward the forest. The few other dwarves visible all seemed to have business within the village.

Nevertheless, the community possessed an undeniable vitality. Sounds of typical dwarven activity were everywhere—the hammering of smiths, the grinding of millers, and the chiseling of stonecarvers all formed a musical chorus in the background of the town's apparent placidity. It seemed, in a dim and admittedly vague sense, a bit of a shame to charge in there and start killing. Still, Thurgol had made his decision several days earlier. It was much too late to change his mind now.

The decision was taken from him as the crossbow-bearing hunter continued to approach the wood. When the dwarf reached the fringe of shade, a monstrous troll whooped and sprang from cover upon the dwarven hunter. Thurgol immediately recognized Baatlrap. The leaping beast held his huge, saw-toothed sword over his head, bringing it down in a crushing blow toward the astonished hunter's skull. Before the dwarf could utter a sound, the deadly copper edge cleaved him from head to heart.

The firbolgs bellowed, a sound like the rumbling of a nearby rockslide. Branches splintered and trees swayed as the monsters of Thurgol's crude force charged from the underbrush. Thurgol himself raised his great club and led the assault. Beside him, several giant-kin paused to pitch rocks into the dwarven village while the chieftain pounded toward the side of the nearest small house.

Meanwhile the sleek forms of racing wolfdogs passed Thurgol by as a dozen savage canines burst from concealment to charge, snarling, into the village of the enemy. The predators quickly surrounded a struggling dwarven axeman, soon bearing the valiant warrior to the ground, though not before one of the wolfdogs fell dead, its throat slashed by a blow from the sharp blade.

A bearded dwarf darted out the door of the house nearest Thurgol, clutching a puny hammer and crouching before his home. The little fellow had obviously been interrupted at his lunch. A napkin remained tucked into the collar of his stiff leather shirt. The dwarf's eyes blazed with hatred, and he raised the hammer, apparently undeterred by the much larger firbolg lumbering toward him. Through the doorway, Thurgol saw similar small figures scrambling out of his view. Obviously the dwarf's family was within.

The firbolg chief bashed his club downward, ready to squash the insolent dwarf on his very doorstep. At the same time, something about the helpless little ones within the house nagged at him. Thurgol decided that, after killing the warrior, he would let the rest of the family live.

Yet his generosity was shortchanged by the stumpy fighter's quick reactions, for the dwarf rolled away from the crushing blow before the club could land. Thurgol grunted in pain as the knobby weapon sprang from the hard stones of the doorstep. But where was the dwarf?

A searing pain in his buttocks answered that question. With a bellow, Thurgol spun, swinging his club in a furious circle close to the ground. The dwarf would pay for his insolence!

Nevertheless, as low as the giant swept his weapon, the pesky little warrior ducked even lower, dropping flat against the earth as the club whistled past. Then, before Thurgol could recover, the dwarf brought the surprisingly heavy hammer down on the firbolg's foot.

Thurgol's bellow of pain rattled the windows in their frames. He swung back, but again the runt scuttled into the roadway, springing into a crouch perhaps six paces away, facing the firbolg and forcing Thurgol to turn his back to the house. This time the chieftain resolved to attack cautiously, advancing toward the dwarf one step at a time, his club raised, a murderous gleam in his eye.

All thought of guilt and mercy had been banished by this scuttling creature's resistance. Never had Thurgol imagined that a single dwarf could prove so troublesome. Now he took great care, reluctant to commit his club to a swing that would leave him open to a fast counterattack.

A rock sailing through the air solved his dilemma, cracking against the dwarf's bare skull from behind and sending him sprawling face forward into the dirt. Thurgol didn't take the time to grunt an acknowledgement to the stone-throwing giant who had aided him. Instead, the chieftain turned back to the village, bellowing savagely and lumbering forward to renew the charge.

Snapping wolfdogs lunged beside him. Thurgol saw two of the great creatures leap on a slashing dwarf, carrying the unfortunate fellow to the ground beneath their weight. Jaws slashed and came up dripping blood, though one of the beasts suddenly yelped and whirled away, losing its own blood through a gaping wound in its belly. The injured canine, whining piteously, fell to the ground and died beside the gory corpse of its last victim.

Dwarves in various states of disarray, some dressed in business finery, others in homespun—one even shaking bath soap from his beard—popped from the houses and shops, rallying to the defense. They bore a variety of weapons, including axes and hammers as well as an occasional crossbow or spear, and they shouted their hatred and anger at the attackers who had emerged from the brush with such shocking and brutal speed. Dimly the chieftain noticed an odd fact: These dwarves, as a group, seemed unusually old compared to dwarven warriors he had faced in the past. Many of them were stooped of posture and stiff of movement, and a significant portion of the males showed patches of sunburned skin through their thinning hair.

Directly in front of Thurgol, a firbolg screamed and toppled forward, the blunt end of a dwarven crossbow quarrel extending from his eye. Another giant fell nearby, hamstrung by a dwarf who rushed from cover to chop savagely with his axe as the attacker rushed past.

Thurgol loomed behind this valiant dwarf, swinging with all the brutish force of his giant body, and this time his club fell true. The dwarf dropped dead, his skull crushed by the killing blow before he even knew he was being attacked. Stepping over the corpse, the firbolg chieftain felt a savage glee begin to pump through his veins, infusing within him a lust for killing, a desperate desire to strike at these foes wherever they could be found.

A wolfdog yelped and sprang backward, collapsing on a wounded leg to thrash on the ground. A sturdy dwarf, wielding a bloody axe, stood over the fallen creature and glared around, ready for a new foe. More of the great canines leaped forward, and the last the chieftain saw of the fight, the dwarf held the beasts at bay with desperate swings of his axe.

Another dwarf raced forward, his bearded face contorted by his own fury. Thurgol didn't stop to note that the fellow's hair was purest white, with a patch of pink skin showing at the crest of his head. Stooped in posture, his movements showing the stiffness of advanced age, the venerable warrior nevertheless brandished a small axe, challenging the firbolg with jabbered insults and clumsy swings of his pathetic weapon. Behind him, several young dwarves scurried for the safety of the woods.

Swinging his weapon through a sweeping arc, Thurgol crushed the old dwarf's shoulder and sent him flying through the air. Shouting in triumphant glee, the firbolg lunged after the escaping dwarves, ready to crush them all with the bloody end of his club.

In the next instant, stinging pain slashed through Thurgol's calf, and he howled in agony, stumbling forward and dropping to one knee in sudden pain. The white-haired dwarf, gritting his teeth against unspeakable pain, wielded his axe with his one good hand. Somehow he had risen to his feet and hacked through the firbolg's skin as Thurgol lumbered toward his next victims.

Furiously, blindly, the giant swung his club at the insolent pest, but from the awkward stance, he could put little force into the blow, and the crippled dwarf toppled backward, avoiding the weapon by several inches. The firbolg scrambled to his feet, grunting and panting from exertion, and brought the club down once, and then again, against the immobile and helpless target.

Only then did he turn his eyes toward the cowardly dwarves who had fled, protected by the dead warrior's desperate diversion, but by now they were nowhere to be seen. Spitting in disgust, Thurgol looked around to see that the battle had swept through the village, with most of the dwarves either slain or driven into the forest.

Several trolls surrounded a young dwarven axeman. The dwarf's beard had barely come in, yet the little fellow circled like a veteran, striking out with his blade, which was well streaked in green, trollish blood, and nimbly dodging the vicious talons of the slashing monsters. Finally three of the gangly predators leaped at once, bearing the courageous dwarf to earth and rending him with claws and teeth. Even with such an overpowering force, one of the trolls staggered back, clutching the stump of his wrist where the dying dwarf had severed his hand with his last blow.

Howling in fury, the troll sat roughly in the dirt, waiting for the hand to grow back. Disgustedly Thurgol turned away. The unnatural and hideous allies never seemed so obscene to the firbolg as when their innate regenerative ability healed some grotesque wound.

Furiously Thurgol bashed at the stone wall of a small house, satisfied that a few rocks chipped loose from the wall but surprised that the structure didn't come crashing down. Any firbolg-built pile of rocks would surely have crumbled from such a blow! Angrily he pounded against it again and again, ignoring the jolts of pain that shot through his shoulders and arms. He bashed against the wooden door, which splintered satisfactorily, and then smashed the eaves of the roof. The stone walls he left alone, however, out of a real danger that he would shatter his club, or perhaps even his bones, before he chipped away any more of the solid masonry.

Even this rampage of destruction did nothing to improve his mood. Stalking through the ruined village, he looked over the carnage of war. Surprisingly, it hadn't been a massacre. Though the dwarves had been taken by complete surprise, they had fought extremely well. Perhaps two dozen had fallen, and most of these were young adults or very old males. The sacrifices of these dwarves had allowed the rest of the village, primarily females and young, to escape.

In exchange, six firbolgs and a like number of trolls lay on the ground in various stages of serious injury. In addition, a surprising number of the wolfdogs had suffered wounds serious enough to rule out any chance of healing. For the badly wounded canines, Thurgol had no choice but to order them destroyed.

The trolls, of course, would regenerate. Indeed, most of them had already risen to sitting positions, their midnight-black eyes inspecting the gruesome healing process as wounds closed, limbs grew back, and broken bones mended.

The giant-kin were not so lucky. Three of them had been hamstrung, a favorite tactic of the nasty little dwarves, and Thurgol had no choice but to order their throats cut. The others suffered a variety of slices and chops that at least had a possibility of healing. Crudely bandaged, these hapless giants would have to fend as best they could when Thurgol's rude army moved on.

Nevertheless, all in all, it must be counted as a signal victory for the invaders. The dwarven village was abandoned, and trolls and firbolgs rooted through the various dwellings, seeking treasures and delicacies. Several casks of strong rum yielded themselves to an inquisitive giant, and with great whoops of excitement, he bashed in the cork and took a long swig.

A troubling thought occurred to Thurgol as he watched the rest of his ragged band gather around the valuable find, joining in with their own grunts and whoops and shouts. Why had the fighting dwarves been almost exclusively old men or youngsters barely fully bearded? Where were the veteran warriors, the full-bearded adults, male and female, who had been the doughty enemies of giantkind since time immemorial? The more he thought about it, the more troubling became the notion. The *real* dwarven warriors hadn't even been here for the battle!

As this truth began to grow within him, Thurgol became increasingly nervous. He cast his tiny eyes about the thick fringe of underbrush surrounding the village, imagining that a deadly ambush took shape there. He saw the firbolgs and trolls, many of them already drunk, and pictured the slaughter that might result from a sudden and unsuspected attack, harboring no illusions that his thick-skulled troops would respond as quickly or in such orderly fashion as had the dwarves.

Abruptly, decisively, he stalked over to a troll who guzzled from the opened rum cask. With a sharp blow, Thurgol knocked the keg to the ground, where it shattered in a splash of amber pungency. With a growl, the troll lunged at him, but the firbolg chieftain smashed a brawny fist into the monster's long, branchlike nose. Yelping, the green-skinned monster stumbled back, both hands clutching his wounded proboscis. Hateful black eyes, sunken like caves beneath the beast's overhanging brows, regarded Thurgol with undiluted venom.

The troll backed away from the enraged firbolg. Like most of his kin, the beast took great pride in the sweeping expanse of his beaklike nose. Now that it had been shattered, he was obsessed with making sure that it grew back as prominently as ever. Growling and snarling, the troll settled in the doorway of a roofless cottage to tend to his regeneration.

Not all the beasts would be so easily cowed, however. As Thurgol might have guessed, Baatlrap was the one to disagree. The monstrous troll swaggered toward Thurgol, his long arms planting curling fists on his hips.

"Why you stop Lakrunt from drink?" he demanded, his voice an ominous growl.

"More dwarves will come," Thurgol shot back, crossing his arms across his chest and facing the giant troll squarely.

"Dwarves run. We celebrate!"

"What about dwarf warriors? We killed only old ones and young ones! Others might be nearby."

"Pah! We win fight. We drink!" To underscore his point, Baatlrap ripped another keg from the hands of a gaping firbolg and poured a long stream of rum into his mouth.

"We win! We drink!" The cry arose all around him, from firbolgs and trolls alike, and Thurgol knew that he had lost the argument.

"Turn your eyes to this!" The voice screeched through the scene of growing chaos like a sharp scythe through a field of ripe wheat. All eyes turned to Garisa. The hunched giant woman stood in the open after emerging from one of the larger of the dwarven buildings. She raised her hands over her head, and they all saw what she held. They saw, and they trembled in awe and a sense of giddy joy.

"The Silverhaft Axe!" she cried, and the last rays of the setting sun gleamed from the immaculate metal of the weapon's shiny haft.

But it was the blade itself that inevitably compelled everyone's rapt attention, for here the sunlight glittered even more profoundly, shining and reflecting and shimmering off the facets of a great, wedge-shaped surface of purest diamond.

* * * * *

Baatlrap stared at the gleaming axe blade. In it, he saw all the wonders of the world, the most glorious beauties and the grandest achievements . . . and the vision of utmost, terrifying power.

A dim stirring tickled the base of the troll's primitive brain. The coarse, wiry body thrilled to the ecstacy of victory and celebration. The scent of blood still pulsed in his nostrils. His mind lingered on the memories of dying dwarves, squirming desperately in Baatlrap's crushing talons until, very gradually, the wriggling bodies grew still.

But now the sight of the Silverhaft Axe awakened within him an overwhelming craving, and at the same time a reverent sense of of awe. All his dull feeling came together then in a single and compelling urge.

One day that axe would be his.

* * * * *

As a girl, Robyn had spent many hours atop the high tower of Caer Corwell. These had been times of delight and disappointment, of joy and sorrow. Whatever her mood, however, the vista of green moor and gray-blue firth beneath glowering clouds or skies of limitless blue had never failed to soothe her anxieties and focus her mind.

Now, though she was High Queen of the isles, she found that the lofty perch had the same soothing and spiritual effect. Since her return to Corwell, she had spent parts of each day up here, sometimes accompanied by her husband or oldest daughter but more often, as now, alone.

The tower wasn't an eminent structure compared to grand Caer Callidyrr, where the royal family made their permanent home. It loomed high above this small castle, however, and when its height was added to the crowning knob of rock that served as Caer Corwell's foundation, it created a vantage almost impossibly remote from the sweeping grass and water below.

Today the clouds were friendly, clean and white, floating

gently through the field of blue far overhead. Their shadows gave the limitless moor a dappled effect as patches of sunlight brightened the grass to an almost luminescent brilliance between darker shadows.

Some intuition that she couldn't identify drew her attention to the east, where the long line of the King's Road faded into the high distance. There, high above the ground, she detected a gleaming pinpoint of light. At first she thought that a shooting star, bright enough to flare in the daylight, crackled through the sky at the limits of her vision. But the thing didn't seem to *move*—at least not perceptibly. Instead, it remained fixed in place, if anything growing slowly brighter. She observed it for several minutes, far longer than any shooting star could last even if it found a way to stay in one place for the duration of its spectacular life.

Then the High Queen understood: The flare appeared to stand still because it *approached* her! Growing steadily brighter, it passed beneath the clouds, and as it neared Caer Corwell, it slowly began to descend. Now she saw sparks of light falling away from the thing in a stream, like embers dropping from a blacksmith's forge in the wake of his shaping hammer.

A sense of foreboding slowly closed about the queen. Vaguely she heard castle guards shouting an alarm, heard trampling feet as men raced onto the walls and lower towers to gape at the approaching phenomenon.

By this time, she could see that the spot of light was actually an object, and slowly it became more detailed, sweeping into a long curve to approach the courtyard itself. She saw a chariot of crackling flame, pulled through the air by two blazing horses and swooping downward with ever-increasing speed. It looked more like a diving hawk than a galloping horse.

Finally she saw the passengers, two men standing in the box of the chariot, one holding the flaming reins and the other, a tall, slender fellow whose trousers flapped around his long, sticklike legs, standing alertly beside the driver.

"Keane!" she shouted, recognizing the tall man at last.

And then the fact of his arrival struck home. This wasn't Bakar Dalsoritan returning with the magic-user to the Moonshaes.

Immediately her foreboding flared into a full sense of alarm. She wasted no time with the tower stairs. Instead, she pitched herself from the rim of the parapet, immediately altering her features into those of another creature favored by the goddess. As a white hawk, she spiraled through a descent into the courtyard of the humble castle, returning to her human body in the instant before her claws touched the paving stones of the wide enclosure.

The flaming chariot swooped over the castle wall. Keane waving frantically to deter dozens of archers who seemed ready to let fly even without the command of their captain. Fortunately the tall mage was a familiar figure to these men, and they lowered their weapons to stare in astonishment at the enchanted transport.

The chariot finally came to rest in the courtyard just as King Kendrick himself emerged from the great hall. His daughter Alicia trailed close behind.

"Keane!" he shouted in delight, stepping forward to clasp the young mage around the shoulders with his good arm and hand.

"Your Majesty . . . may I present Parell Hyath, Exalted Inquisitor of Helm!"

The patriarch stepped out of the chariot with remarkable agility for a man of his bulk and bowed deeply to the king. If Tristan felt any surprise at the appearance of a priest other than Bakar Dalsoritan, he gave no indication, instead warmly welcoming the huge cleric. The High King graciously apologized for the humble nature of Caer Corwell's surroundings, at the same time announcing that he held a real affection for this, his boyhood home.

By the time they concluded the formalities, the flaming chariot had faded into nothingness. Robyn stood silent, back from the throng that had started to gather. She knew of

Helm's worship, knew that this cleric could not be an evil man and still remain true to his faith, yet she couldn't dispel a nagging sense of unease. After all, life was much more than a simple matter of good and evil struggling for prominence. The central tenet of her own faith remained the Balance, the equilibrium of all things. She couldn't bring herself to trust this man who, she knew, would be dedicated to toppling that equilibrium toward his own desires.

Robyn saw her daughter approach the mage and began to feel more comfortable as the king led the cleric toward the widespread doors of the keep.

"Welcome home," Alicia said to Keane as the priest and king entered the great hall. "That was quite an entrance!"

"It was quite a journey," Keane agreed with a wry grin. "Somehow it's a lot more nerve-racking to fly *over* an ocean than it is to teleport past it. Anyway, I'm glad I've got solid ground under my feet again."

"So am I," the princess said quietly, but with enough meaning to draw her mother's attention. Keane, too, heard the hidden warmth in the words. He looked at the princess sharply, as if he wanted to say something. Instead, he allowed her to take his arm and lead him toward the castle.

"A moment, please," Robyn said as they passed. She had to know something. "Bakar Dalsoritan . . . ?"

The shadow on Keane's face answered her question before he spoke. "He's . . . dead—murdered, as it happened, before I had a chance to speak with him. I'm sorry, my queen. I know he tutored you well and wisely."

Nodding absently, Robyn felt the news flow right through her. She wasn't surprised, had even prepared herself subconsciously to hear this. Instead, her mind focused on questions and answers.

"That's terrible!" Alicia exclaimed, shaking her head sadly. "I haven't seem him since I was a little girl, but he always seemed like a nice man. How did it happen?"

"There'll be time for details later," Robyn interjected, knowing that the story would do little to soothe her apprehensions. "Let's go inside with your father."

They found the king and the inquisitor engaged in a frank discussion beside the sweeping fieldstone hearth of the keep. No fire glowed there now during the heat of summer, but it was still a place where Tristan liked to go for discussion and contemplation. Attendants and servants stood some distance back in the great hall, allowing the two men their privacy.

"Payment will be no problem," the High King was saying as the trio approached. "Of course, my treasury's in Callidyrr. If necessary, we can journey there beforehand. . . ." His tone clearly indicated that he hoped it was not necessary.

"No need," said the patriarch graciously. He stood and turned to face Keane and the two women. "Incidentally, your young ambassador here did a splendid job of recruitment. I set aside my other affairs only by dint of his eloquent persuasion."

"He's a man I'd trust with my life—or my family's," Tristan agreed warmly. "Well done, Keane."

"Thank you, Sire."

"Now then, to this business." The king raised his arm, showing the cleric the wound at his wrist. The cut had healed cleanly, with skin fully grown over the rounded stub at the end of his arm. "Do you have to make a lot of preparations?"

"Very few, actually," said the cleric. He looked around the great hall, with its smoke-stained beams and wooden columns supporting the broad ceiling, the long stone walls, and the broad hearth. "Perhaps we could find a smaller chamber—a bedroom or private apartment would be best. You'll want to rest, I'm certain. As for me, I could use a bite to eat and a glass or two of wine—for my strength—and then we can get started."

"Splendid! We'll use my library upstairs. Alicia, will you have Gretta send up some nourishment for the patriarch? I'll show you the place. It should be perfect." The three men left the hall, ascending the wide stairs to the family's apartments on the second floor while Robyn accompanied Alicia to the kitchen.

"Do you think it'll work, Mother?" inquired the princess nervously after they had requested a tray and bottle for the priest.

"I don't see why not," Robyn said, without conviction. "After all, an Exalted Inquisitor, so I've heard, is a rank achieved by no more than a handful of clerics at any given time. He must be very knowledgeable of his god."

"I *hope* so!" Alicia declared with passion.

The two women joined the priest and the king in the library. Upon Hyath's instructions, they pulled the shutters and shades across the window, darkening the room, while Tristan made himself comfortable on a long, bedlike couch. Meanwhile the patriarch enjoyed some of the salt meats, bread, cheese, and wine of Corwell.

"If you three will wait in the next room, we'll get started," Hyath instructed them after he cleaned his plate and very nearly emptied the bottle.

Robyn rose with noticeable reluctance, following Keane and Alicia into the adjacent anteroom. The inquisitor closed the door firmly behind them, and they settled down impatiently to wait.

For a time, they heard nothing, and then Hyath's voice emerged from the room. The priest performed some kind of chant, his voice following a precise cadence, rising and falling in pitch as he drifted, almost singing, through phrases that none of them could identify. Then his voice dropped again, though the soft murmur of verbal rites still came from beyond the door. Then even that faded into silence.

For several more minutes, they listened but heard nothing, aching with curiosity, not daring to open the door. Robyn rose and began to pace, while Alicia clasped her hands before her and Keane sat in attentive silence, alert for any sound from the darkened library.

The quiet broke suddenly with a sound of gurgling shock growing quickly into a scream of terror. They heard a crash, like a boom of thunder, and Robyn cried out in alarm.

Keane reached the door in less than an instant, twisting the latch and throwing the portal open with a surprisingly powerful push of his shoulder. He stumbled into the room, waving his hands to clear thickening smoke from the air as the queen and princess rushed in behind him.

"What . . . what happened?" gasped Alicia, racing to her father's side.

Tristan lay on the bed, blinking and shaking his head. He groaned softly. At least they could see that he was still alive.

Only then did they notice the patriarch of Helm. The Exalted Inquisitor lay motionless on the floor, sprawled on his back as if he'd been knocked over by some shocking force. His eyebrows were singed, his face blackened, and his huge body displayed no sign of life.

Alicia turned back to the king as Tristan raised his left arm. They both saw that the limb still ended in the blunt stump of his wrist.

* * * * *

The dwarven community proved to have an exceptional number of well-stocked wine cellars—so many, in fact, that the hulking conquerors settled for plundering only a select few. Trolls, sinuous and flexible, searched the small houses while the giants waited outside. Several times trolls reported a solid door in the basement of one of the dwarven homes.

Quickly firbolgs wielding axes and hammers smashed a path to the cellar door, usually by knocking out a wall and then collapsing the floor above the wine cellar's hallway. The roof of the actual chamber, they quickly found, was generally sealed over with a heavy stone arch impervious even to firbolg strength.

Thus they entered the wine cellars by the simple expedient of bashing down their metal-banded, heavy oaken doors.

This was a sport where natural firbolg talent could excel, and thus it became a contest as one of the giants smashed his club, a foot, or perhaps a rock into the portal. If it didn't collapse—and it never did before the fifth blow—another would try, and so forth. The firbolg who actually smashed down the door then crawled inside and earned the honor of sampling the first keg.

Stars stood out in brilliant relief above Cambro as the chill of the night seemed to sap every bit of cloud and vapor from the air. The chieftain stood beyond the circle of buildings, near the impenetrable darkness beneath the forest canopy. He watched the pillage dispassionately, trying to dispel the worry that continued to nag at him. Where were the dwarves?

Thurgol pulled his cloak around him, grumbling about the unseasonal chill. More logs, as well as a few scraps of wooden furniture, added their fuel to the blaze in the center of town, and the bonfire surged higher and higher, challenging the darkness of the sky itself.

The firbolg heard increasingly raucous laughter, a gruff and bawdy song. Still discontent, Thurgol wandered around the village, peering anxiously into the shadows beneath the looming trees.

Harsh words barked above the din. A firbolg insulted the nose of a troll, calling it "short as a corncob." Immediately the chaotic festivities doubled in volume. Thurgol heard bets wagered, with odds going two to one in favor of the giant, and cheerful insults tossed in from the crowd. He returned to the circle of his comrades somewhat heartened by the prospective entertainment of a good brawl. Quickly seizing the keg from a small troll, the chieftain shouldered his way through the tightly packed throng of firbolgs and trolls to get a good look at the fight.

The firbolg participant was Hondor, a great brute of a giant-kin with tiny eyes and a perpetually confused expression on his drooping jowls. Though he couldn't be certain, it seemed to Thurgol that the troll was Essekki, a treacherous, gawking member of his clan who did in fact possess a very undistinguished proboscis. Now the two brutes, almost equal in height, though the firbolg weighed nearly double his opponent, circled each other menacingly. The first clasp had come to a draw, and they gasped for breath as they prepared to close again.

Essekki backed carefully away from the fire, which had temporarily died to a great mountain of glowing embers. Fire was the thing feared above all else by trolls, for the burning of their flesh was one type of wound that even their amazing regenerative powers could not heal. Thus the troll took great care not to leave himself vulnerable to the sizzling danger. Growling wolfdogs circled the fight, their eyes and fangs gleaming in the darkness. They wouldn't attack, Thurgol knew, but the fervor of combat agitated them just the same.

Hondor ducked in again, bashing sideways with a hamlike fist that somehow connected with the troll's head. Essekki flew through the air, crashing to the ground in a heap. In another moment, the firbolg leaped onto his stunned opponent's back, grasping the troll's nose and skull and twisting his head brutally. The snapping of the beast's neck shot through the night, silencing the crowd for the briefest of moments.

Then the din erupted again as winners demanded payment from losers and the latter protested vainly that the troll would regenerate. Thus, they claimed, the fight might not be over yet. It was an argument that had raged after hundreds of such fights since the trolls had come to Blackleaf. As always, the prevailing rule was applied: Once the troll died, the fight was over. If he wished to resume the contest upon regeneration, which rarely happened, the brawl would be considered a new fight.

Once again the band settled down to drinking and arguing. Thurgol took his place among them, allowing the warmth of fire and companionship to dispel the chill of the night. He ignored the whispering voice of concern, which in any event had changed its monotonous tune. Instead, he tried to console himself with the suggestion that the alert wolfdogs would hear anyone approaching through the woods, barking an alarm before any serious harm could be done. Indeed, as the rum flowed and the fire grew, it seemed that the threat of danger drifted farther and farther away.

No longer did his internal voice caution him that the woods were full of dwarves. That was a vague and distant worry. Instead, however, it tried to make him think by asking persistent questions. What should they do next? Where did they go from here?

Then the miracle began.

* * * * *

Amid the sacking of Cambro, as Garisa watched the male trolls and firbolgs cavort and posture around the raging fire, the shaman grew increasingly irritated by the frenzied and mindless chaos, which could only drag the tribe to ruin. Beside her was the mighty Silverhaft Axe, though she still didn't quite believe that the tribe had actually regained it from their despised enemies. But her mind, exceptionally alert and active for a firbolg's, was already looking ahead, trying to imagine ways that this remarkable turn of fortune could be used to propel the tribe in a proper direction.

The stooped and elderly matriarch sat, somewhat removed from the press of raucous males, on a bench made from a dwarf's bed that had been dragged into the street. Here she received some of the most tender meats and the sweetest wines among the entire band's booty, for even if they overruled her opinions, the giant-kin still showed their old shaman a measure of dignity and respect.

Yet these facts were no consolation as she watched her kinsmen dance and whoop in the harsh light of the towering fire. She saw that even Thurgol, who for a brief moment had displayed a modicum of character and leadership, now returned to the fire, betting on the fights and drinking like any mulish adolescent.

Something, Garisa decided, had to be done, and as usual, she had some idea as to what that thing should be. Carefully she pulled an old blanket over the axe, concealing the gleaming haft and the brilliant diamond blade from observation.

Slowly, subtly, the stooped female rose to her feet and shambled forward from her bench. A pair of hulking trolls, eyeing her suspiciously, nonetheless stepped back to let her pass. The crone's sharp walking stick had more than once been employed to open a path between slow-stepping humanoids. The same applied to a great wolfdog, who had somehow snared a place near the roaring blaze. The great canine bounced to its feet and slinked out of the way as the shaman approached.

A young firbolg, his eyes blank and his jaw slack from the effects of many hours of drinking, blinked stupidly as Garisa snatched a massive bowl, foaming over with stout ale, from his hands. She sniffed the beverage, then tasted a gulp or two, smacking her nearly toothless gums in appreciation. The young warrior went off in search of an easier drink, and the old shaman nodded in satisfaction.

Setting the empty bowl on the ground, Garisa reached into the pockets of her apron with her two gnarled, yet surprisingly nimble, hands. Feeling through an assortment of bulbs and roots, pouches of herbs, and bundles of dusty powders, she found the two that she wanted—a touch of ground spice coupled with a moist bit of crushed grub.

Carefully she watched to see that the festivities progressed uninterrupted around her. Several shoving matches drew the attentions of the crowd, and the shaman finally felt certain that no one watched her.

Swiftly she pulled forth her hands, mingling the powder with the mash of crushed grub and casting the entire glob into the fire. A *whoosh* of force sucked the air from the clearing for a moment, bringing every argument to a stop. Stunned into silence, the humanoids of Thurgol's army gaped at the image that slowly floated upward from the fire.

At first they could see nothing more than a shapeless form in the mist, yet even in this vague outline, it had a certain solidity that belied its gaseous nature. Slowly the vapor drew together into a white form that seemed to glow like a full moon in the darkness of the night air.

Not a sound escaped the lips of a single dumbstruck firbolg or troll as they stared at this intangible message from they knew not where. Slowly, gradually, the white shape grew firm and solid, taking on an obvious image . . . the image of a snow-capped mountain summit. A rocky crag jutted sharply upward, surrounded by steep shoulders of sweeping icefields and long, precipitous cliffs.

"The Icepeak!" breathed a firbolg. Garisa didn't see who made the identification, but she had known that one of her tribe would do so. After all, the towering mountain, capstone of Oman's Isle, had long been attributed as the birthplace of the giant clans. There was no other mountain in the firbolg realms that loomed so high, or bore such a distinguishing crown of snow upon its summit.

Then the image began to waver and change. Slowly the picture of the mountain faded, returning to its shapeless circle and then, ever so slowly, forming another likeness, an object that appeared so solid that it might really have floated over the fire before the awestruck watchers.

This time they saw the picture of a monstrous axe, its huge, double-bitted blade nicked and scarred by combat so that the runes inscribed upon its broad surface were all but unintelligible.

"An axe!" gasped the same firbolg who had spoken before, this time quite unnecessarily.

"The Silverhaft Axe!" Garisa broke the silence with a sudden screech of definition. "Such was the blade borne by Grond Peaksmasher at the forging of the clans!"

Murmurs of astonishment, tinged with awe, rippled from the onlookers. They well remembered the tale, chanted by them all, on the night before they had embarked on this adventure. The presence of that very axe, found in this village, could not fail to stir the warlike pride of each and every one of the giant-kin, and even to a lesser measure the trolls.

"What does it mean?" inquired Thurgol after a few moments of stunned silence.

"Does the Ancient One awaken?" asked another giant-kin.

"It's a sign!" croaked Garisa, sensing her cue in the firbolg's question.

"A sign of what?" demanded Baatlrap suspiciously. The hulking troll's black eyes bore into the shaman's skull, but Garisa shrugged away his attention.

"Who knows?" she said, with an exaggerated glance at the heavens. "The will of the gods is displayed, but it remains to us mortals to determine how that will is understood and acted upon. But know this, my villagemates: The gods are well pleased with the Clan of Blackleaf, for we have righted a great wrong in restoring the axe to its proper owners!"

"Aye! The gods are pleased!" A chorus of congratulations rose from the shadows around the great fire.

"They are pleased, but they are not satisfied. This can only mean that our work is not done!" hissed Garisa, fixing them all, one at a time, with the balefully gleaming orb of her wandering eye.

"Tell us!" demanded a troll, nervously following Garisa's glance at the sky. "What is the will of the gods?"

"Tell us!" came the chorus of agreement, a basso rumble of voices, all turning to the ancient shaman for advice and comfort. "What do the gods desire?"

Garisa made a great show of shuffling about the full periphery of the large fire, examining the floating image of the axe from every angle, cocking her head this way and that to confront the different firbolgs and trolls with her challenging gaze. To an individual, they would not meet her eyes.

At last she came back to the place where she had started. The image of the huge axe remained poised in the air; once Garisa had established the simple illusion, she hadn't had to pay attention to it. Instead, the image would remain for some time, unless she chose to adjust it.

Staring back at it, mumbling unintelligibly, she suddenly did just that. The axe disappeared with shocking suddenness. The firbolgs and trolls erupted in gasps of astonishment or murmurs of superstition and fear.

"Bring me my bowl!" declared Garisa, her voice shrill. A pair of firbolgs leaped to obey. "Find me coins—they must be gold! Then I will foretell the will of the gods!"

* * * * *

Deirdre started upward in her bed, aware of the pounding of her heart, the pulsing of blood and life through her veins—all that and *more!* She felt a keen sense of awakening power, of growing mastery.

Her nightly sleep had become a soothing balm for her spirit, such that she could hardly contain her anxiousness during the day. Each darkening eve, it seemed, brought her a new infusion of vitality, energy . . . and sheer, constantly building might. That, more than anything, slowly convinced her to stir; she had to test, to examine this sense of limitless power!

Somewhere in the castle, she sensed the presence of another powerful being, one who had summoned his god to serve him. That god, she sensed, had refused. But why? The pressure of the immortal contact tingled in the air around her, tantalizing her even as it refused to answer her question. Yet within that teasing aura, she sensed she would find more than a simple explanation.

She sat up in her bed, feeling as though she were still in the midst of a dream. Around her was her room, looking as mundane as ever, but now she had a feeling that she could see *through* those walls, beyond the confining borders of her apartments.

And what beckoned there was not Caer Corwell. Instead, she sensed that she rested in the midst of a vast cosmos, a place so immensely huge that the entire Realms amounted to little more than specks of dust. On those specks, the tiny, insignificant islands called the Moonshaes were even less than dust.

Voices called from the spacious void surrounding her, drawing her attention this way and that. She knew them and she was pleased, for these were voices of mighty beings, and they showed her honor and respect. In a flash, she understood, and the knowledge placed her entire existence into perspective.

She had been selected to hear the gods themselves, and it was an honor that dwarfed all the rest of her life.

* * * * *

Ever watchful, Helm took note of the immortal turmoil tearing at the fiber of Gwynneth. He pressed close, his power linked to the life and body of the patriarch, only to find that a strong barrier of power held his full might at bay.

Over the land, the presence of Talos was a rumbling and ominous cloud, not yet ready to unleash its storm. Below, the fertile loam of the Earthmother flourished, as if in challenge or scorn.

The Vigilant One realized immediately that the goddess, not the storming god, formed the barrier to his own power, actively resisting the workings of Helm's might or his agents. The goddess blocked him, while Talos . . . Talos strived to weaken her.

In a flash of immortal understanding, Helm sensed the course of destruction acted upon the world. A horde of monsters ravaged the land. Some of them labored in the name of Talos, though even the beasts themselves did not understand.

And Talos showed his workings freely to Helm. The Vigilant One understood that knowledge of the scourging band could be used to his own advantage—and that such advantage would not be unpleasing to Talos.

Thus, in mistrust and suspicion, but full awareness of mutual desire, the purposes of Helm and Talos became aligned.

❧ 4 ❧

The Earl and the Elfwoman

Two proud steeds crested a grassy hill and paused restlessly, drawn back by their riders. One of the prancing mounts was a huge, shag-hoofed war-horse of chestnut brown; the other was a nimble, long-legged mare of purest white.

The pristine valley of Myrloch Vale swept away below them. Off to the right, the huge lake gleamed in the sunlight, heartbreakingly blue and dazzlingly clear even from a distance of more than ten miles. The placid water filled the southern end of the vast, roughly circular valley. The northern stretch of the vale sprawled beneath a blanket of lush vegetation, forests of pine, oak, aspen, and elm, interspersed by numerous meadows, each dotted with a blazing mosaic of flowers.

The riders were as diverse as the horses: A tall, strappingly powerful man rode the dark gelding. He wore no armor, but a huge sword swung easily at his side, and everything about his appearance suggested an accomplished warrior. He rode with the ease of a man born to horseback, guiding his horse with knee pressure alone as he gazed in wonder across the spectacular vista before him.

The white mare's rider was smaller and female, with straw-colored hair that tumbled about her shoulders and the slender, almost fragile features of an elf. Nevertheless she, too, rode with an easy grace that suggested many years of experience in the saddle. Now, like the human warrior, she paused reflectively to enjoy the sweep of valley below.

"It's spectacular!" said the man, after a few moments of silent admiration. "Every Ffolkman has heard of the Myrloch, of course, but it seems a shame that so few of us have seen it!"

"Perhaps that's why it's still spectacular," suggested the elfwoman dryly. "Do you think that a smelting house beside the stream or a smoking forge in the meadow would help the picture very much?"

The elf was Brigit Cu'Lyrran, Mistress Captain of the Sister Knights of Synnoria, and her prejudices against rapacious and populous humanity ran deep. Still, she smiled at her companion to take the sting from her words. Clearly she regarded him in an altogether different light than she did the vast bulk of his kinsmen.

"You're right," agreed Hanrald Blackstone, the Earl of Fairheight. "So much of its beauty comes from that same isolation."

The two had chosen to enter the vale from one of its eastern passes, taking the long route to Brigit's home in the elven valley of Synnoria. The detour would allow them to see some of the most beautiful terrain in the Moonshaes, according to Brigit. She hadn't said that it would also postpone the homecoming that she anticipated with a feeling akin to dread.

How, after all, could one of the prime protectors of Synnorian fastness go before the rulers of her people and tell them that she had fallen in love with a human? It was a question that Brigit still hadn't been able to answer, and so each day that postponed its necessity was another day of exhilarating freedom.

Hanrald Blackstone had no such weighty concerns. He knew only that he rode beside the woman who had come to mean life itself to him. He would follow where she led, confident in the love that bound them. Of course he knew that sooner or later he would have to return to his holding, in the kingdom of Callidyrr, but for now, that was a distant, unreal eventuality. Even further removed from his conscious thought was the knowledge that he would grow old and die in the space of the next half dozen decades, while his love could look forward to many centuries of vibrant life.

They came through the low pass of Aspenheight after six days of easy riding out of Caer Corwell. Each night they had camped under the stars, the goddess favoring them with clear skies and warm temperatures. Now, as they rode into the valley, they found another pristine meadow, surrounded by a protective ring of rocks arrayed as a perfect windbreak.

"How many more days until we reach Synnoria?" Hanrald inquired after they had built a small fire and settled back to watch the emerging stars.

"I don't want to think about it," Brigit replied honestly. "Let's cross the valley *north* of the lake. I haven't been up here in decades, and besides, I'm still not in any hurry to get home."

"Fine with me," Hanrald agreed, drawing the elfwoman close with a brawny arm. She curled against his side, and they watched—awestruck, as always—as the curtain of daylight drew back from the sky. The stars emerged for their nightly march across the heavens, and the two tiny creatures on the ground sat rapt in wonder, absorbed by the stately dance of the cosmos.

Later, as the night grew just a little cooler, they shared their own warmth and at last fell into a relaxed and restful slumber. In the morning, each awakened with a sense of vitality and alertness that, they deduced, must come from the enchanted nature of the valley itself.

For three days, they meandered easily through the glades and fields of pristine beauty. They crossed a shallow stream at a gravelly ford—Codsrun Creek, Brigit remembered. "Imagine—all the outflow of that great lake compressed into this little stream," she remarked.

They remained beside the splashing rivulet for the better part of an afternoon, diving into a placid pool and letting the sun dry them on the mossy bank. Once again the surroundings seemed so pastoral, so serene, that it seemed quite possible for the two of them to forget the cares and concerns of the outside world.

When they finally mounted again, they planned to ride

only a few more miles before finding a place to camp. The forest was open here, with little underbrush and a wide expanse of grass and fern, so they loped easily along, relishing the rhythm of a good ride after their rest and swim.

Abruptly Hanrald's war-horse reared, almost dumping him from the saddle. Brigit cursed as her own mare sprang backward, whirling to face something that rustled in the bushes.

"Ambush!" cried the earl, spotting a number of small forms rushing toward them. Even as he shouted, he drew his massive sword while the great horse spun through a circle, kicking menacingly at the figures that materialized in the shadowy wood, apparently from nowhere.

The earl kneed his horse, ready to charge through the ring of attackers, when something held his assault. He saw that most of the stocky, bearded figures held metal-barbed crossbows, with perhaps a dozen of the deadly quarrels pointed at his chest and head. Reluctantly he relaxed the pressure of his legs, halting the charge before it began, though he still held both hands firmly around the hilt of his sword.

"Dwarves!" spat Brigit, the term as hateful as any curse.

"Dwarves who caught you in a tidy trap, we did!" proclaimed one of the stocky figures, swaggering forward with brawny hands wrapped around the hilt of a silver-bladed axe. Despite the creature's bristling beard, Hanrald realized, with considerable shock, that the speaker was female.

"You have no claim to this land!" shot back the elfwoman. Hanrald had never seen her so enraged. He worried that, despite the crossbows, she might do something rash.

"I think we're all visitors here," the earl said placatingly. He sheathed his sword as a gesture of goodwill. "There's no need for us to talk behind drawn blades or taut bows!"

"There is if we're going to be ambushed like skulking orcs!" retorted Brigit. She challenged the apparent leader of the dwarves. "By what right do *you* march through these woods?"

The dwarfwoman snorted derisively. "You ought to know. It's because of trouble in Synnoria that we've left the comfort of our village to go on the march!"

"What trouble—when?" demanded the elf, chilling at the thought that some dire fate had befallen her land during her absence.

"Coupla weeks ago," replied the dwarf. Hanrald was relieved to note that the crossbows finally had come down, though the ring of dwarves still held them in its center. "Something *big* came out of the mountain. We wanted to make sure that if it got away from you, we had fair warning up in Cambro."

Brigit shuddered at the memory, even as she felt a measure of relief. The Ityak-Ortheel, the Elf-Eater, had been a nightmarish intrusion into Synnoria, but it had finally been vanquished—with the help of her human companions. "You're too late," she said sharply. "The matter was settled without the necessity of dwarven intervention!"

The dwarf shrugged. "Well, it's been a long time since we marched on the war trail. You could say that we needed the practice—after all, it's been twenty years . . . Brigit."

"Finellen?" The elfwoman's eyes narrowed suspiciously. "I might have known it would be you!"

The dwarf laughed heartily. "You *might* have, but you didn't! Ho—there's a good joke! We march against the Darkwalker together, practically put King Kendrick on his throne, and you don't even remember your old axemate!"

Brigit's attitude remained carefully aloof, but Hanrald sensed that the danger of immediate battle had passed. Indeed Finellen chuckled again, slinging her axe from her belt. "We've got a camp a little ways away from here. That's where we were when we heard you coming, though we thought it might be a troop of giants, judging from the noise you made! Why don't you come and enjoy the hospitality of our fire?"

"That's the best invitation I've heard since the ambush!" Hanrald declared, with sincere relief. The two riders dismounted, and within a few minutes had been welcomed into the rude comfort of the dwarven camp.

* * * * *

The Exalted Inquisitor, as it turned out, hadn't been killed by the reaction to his spell-casting, but he had been very thoroughly stunned. Robyn was the first to realize that he still breathed, though she discovered this only after tending to her husband, who was dazed but apparently unhurt.

Five castle guardsmen were required to carry the hefty cleric to a bed, but finally he was situated comfortably, observed by a watchful maidservant, and covered against the evening's chill. The Kendricks and their companions returned to the library, where the High King lay on the couch, tended by anxious servants.

Tristan slowly recovered his tongue and his memories. "All I remember," he told his wife and daughter, "is a very drowsy feeling. Hyath's chanting seemed like it was going to put me right under. Quite relaxing, too. I was having some very pleasant memories.

"The next thing I remember, it seemed as though I was trapped in the middle of a thunderstorm. I saw lightning and heard the pounding—in fact, the flash was so bright that I was blinded for a moment. The next thing I remember, you were both standing there, and the priest was stretched out on the floor."

"But *how?*" demanded Alicia, frustrated. "What happened?"

"That's what *I* want to know!" the king added, with a look at Robyn. "What do you think?"

"This power, regeneration, is a thing of the New Gods," Robyn said slowly and carefully. Suddenly her voice grew tight, and her eyes shone with unshed tears as she looked her husband full in the face. "I was worried before, but now I'm *terrified!* This is a dangerous thing you try to do! Even the cleric of Helm doesn't have the power to control this magic. Please!" The plea was in her face as well as her words. "Don't venture into these realms. Accept your wound in the name of the Balance!"

"It is not the 'cleric' who lacks power to control this magic!" The stern voice, barked from the doorway, drew their attention in an instant.

The Exalted Inquisitor entered the room, his gold-trimmed robe trailing behind him like a full rank of attendants. He fixed Robyn with a fast, icy glare, an expression she returned in full, before stepping to the side of the king's bed and kneeling.

"Your Majesty, I understand now. During my slumber, Helm blessed me with a vision. I know what must be done!"

"Wait a minute!" blurted Alicia. "After what happened before? You don't mean you're going to try again?"

"Not immediately, no," replied Hyath, smiling benignly at the princess—like a forgiving schoolteacher to a dull student, Alicia thought angrily. "First there is something that must be done."

"What? What is it?" demanded Tristan, flinging aside the covers. "By the goddess, I don't need a sickbed!" he roared, climbing to his feet and crossing to one of the chairs before the hearth. "Sit down and tell me what you want," he said to the patriarch of Helm.

Robyn remained frozen in place, her face gone white with fear. Alicia crossed to her, angry with the priest but not understanding her mother's dire reaction. She sat beside her, taking her mother's hand.

"First there is a matter of honor and gratitude I would address." He raised the silk-wrapped package that Keane had seen him carry into the flying chariot. "It is a gift, if you will allow, from myself and, with your permission, from my god. It would please me greatly if it meets with your approval."

Curious, Tristan took the long shape and rested it across his knees. Awkwardly, limited by his one hand, he pulled the silk away, unrolling it through several layers before he revealed a splendid sword and a smooth leather scabbard.

"By the Great Mother, this is a weapon worthy of a king," Tristan breathed, his tone hushed and awestruck. He seized the gold-embossed hilt, which was narrow and sleek, sized for a single hand. Pulling slowly, he revealed inch after inch of silvery blade until the full expanse of keen steel, fully four feet long, came free of its leather sheath.

"I thank you, Patriarch," Tristan said softly. He stood and flourished the blade, relishing the smooth balance, the slender length and deadly edge, as sharp as any razor. "It is a blade I shall wear with pride."

"And with which, no doubt, you'll strive to do what is right for your people and your land. That will is yours alone. I shall tell you only that the blade is blessed by the gods, and only through its use will their will be known."

"A potent protection indeed," Tristan said, turning back to regard the cleric shrewdly. "Now tell me, priest, what is the nature of your vision?" asked the king, settling himself to listen.

"There is *evil* in your realm!" the cleric intoned firmly. "My god requires—nay, *demands*—that this evil be rooted out and destroyed!"

"Name this evil!" snapped Tristan, not at all happy about anyone demanding anything from him. He slapped the sword back into its scabbard, though he still held the weapon comfortably across his knees.

"It is a force on this very island, marching to war through a valley around a great lake—"

"Myrloch!" Robyn whispered, her pulse quickening.

"Already they ravage the dwarves. Soon they will turn against humans, elves—all who would live in peace!" The cleric spoke intensely, staring into Tristan's eyes. "It is an army that must be destroyed—destroyed by *you!*"

"What nonsense is this?" demanded the king, though his tone showed a trace of doubt. "Who would dare disturb the peace of Myrloch Vale?"

"The vision showed me great, misshapen creatures—

giants, with gnarled tree-trunk legs and low, sloping fore-
heads. They carried clubs and hurled boulders."

"Firbolgs?" Tristan all but gasped. Since their defeat in
the Darkwalker War twenty years ago, the few surviving
giant-kin had withdrawn peacefully to their remote lairs,
offering no disturbance. He stood in agitation, pacing to one
end of the library before turning back to hear the Exalted
Inquisitor continue detailing his vision.

"And other creatures were there, too—greenish of skin,
with great noses and wicked talons. They, too, are monstrous, standing far taller than a man."

"Trolls?" The king shook his head in amazement. "It—it's
preposterous!"

The cleric sat back and regarded the monarch silently.

"Why has there been no word? How long has this destruction been going on?"

Hyath shrugged. "I have no way of knowing. Is this 'Myrloch Vale' a remote place? Perhaps there have been no survivors following the rampages of such villages as can be
found there."

"Not even any villages," the king admitted with a shake of
his head.

"But there are *druids!*" Robyn snapped, rising and crossing the room to confront the two men. She felt confident
now that the discussion had turned to Myrloch Vale. After
all, she had received her training in the druidic arts there,
and no place was more sacred to the worship of the goddess
Earthmother. It was a place that was more than a second
home to her; it was the heart and soul of her goddess's
spirit. "And furthermore, if something threatened the sanc-
tity of the vale, *I* would know it!"

The cleric didn't try to dispute her. Instead, he shrugged,
a maddeningly casual expression, and directed himself to
the king. "I can remain but a short time. However, if you
decide to acknowledge the clear will of Helm, I shall make
every effort to assist you so that we can complete the matter
which has brought me here in the first place."

"There *is* no war—no army of monsters!" Robyn protested. "You'll be wasting your time!"

Tristan looked up at her, and she saw the distress in his eyes, the despair at the notion that he, a proud warrior-king, would remain a cripple for the rest of his life. She also saw the stubborn determination that had brought him to his throne and held him so securely to the wise course the two of them had plotted for the Ffolk.

"Are you *absolutely* sure?" he asked. "That there's no threat, no danger out there?"

She was sure, in her own mind, but again she saw that look of fear on her husband's face. It was a look she had seen very rarely, and now, as always before, it frightened her to think that Tristan was afraid. She couldn't increase that fear with a curt rejection of his hope.

"I don't know how it could be otherwise," she said gently. "But in order to make certain, I'll journey to the vale and see for myself. I hope your schedule will allow you to remain a day or two until my return," she added in an icy tone to the Exalted Inquisitor.

"Of course," he bowed, ignoring her manner. "But isn't this valley some distance away? Can you journey there and back in two days?"

"Patriarchs of Helm," Robyn concluded pointedly, "are not the only persons of faith who can travel with speed."

Her preparations were simple, and ten minutes later the High Queen bid her family farewell. She quickly climbed the steps of the high tower, acknowledging a tiny voice of alarm inside her, a voice that warned that the cleric of Helm might just possibly be right.

No! She *would* know if some evil disturbed the vale! Wouldn't she? Angrily but unsuccessfully, she tried to dispel the nagging doubt.

She reached the platform atop the tower and paused for a moment. Again the sweep of moor and firth spread below, but now the scene did not soothe her. Too many questions disturbed her mood as she stepped to the rim of the parapet.

Spreading her arms out wider, she toppled into the air.

Then a white hawk soared from the high tower, catching a powerful updraft and rising swiftly into the sky. The bird's course remained constantly northward, toward the wide valley of Myrloch.

* * * * *

Almost holding his breath in tense anticipation, Thurgol watched Garisa prepare for her foretelling. She had before her a smooth copper bowl, half filled with clear water. She sprinkled some dark dust into the bowl and stirred it with a grimy finger, smiling with satisfaction as the water dimmed to a murky brown.

She had placed the bowl beside the gleaming form of the Silverhaft Axe, explaining that the nearness of the artifact could only help the accuracy of the foretelling. In this she was right, for she had already decided what the prophecy was to be, and the weight of evidence provided by such a potent artifact, she knew, would make it virtually impossible for the thick-skulled firbolgs to dispute her.

"Now the gold," she declared, holding out a hand behind her. Several young firbolgs hastened to drop shining coins in her hands, coins that had just been liberated from dwarven treasuries.

Beyond the bunch of eager giant-kin, a sullen group of trolls, naturally centered around Baatlrap, looked on in rank skepticism. Thurgol was relieved that his firbolgs outnumbered the gangly beasts. It would be just like trolls, he thought, to ignore the clear will of the gods, the will that Garisa would certainly reveal to them. Wolfdogs skulked restlessly around the periphery of the gathering, nervously sensing the giants' agitation. Growls and snarls accompanied their anxious pacing, the smaller dogs staying well out of the paths of their larger kin.

Before the fire, the shaman spun her fingers around the bowl, bringing the water into a swirling whirlpool that washed up the insides of the bowl without losing a drop over the edge. Eagerly the firbolg chieftain watched the coins plop, one by one, into the water.

"I see . . ." Garisa mumbled after three coins had plunked into the bowl.

"What? *What?*" Thurgol pressed, before his comrades rudely hushed him. To the chieftain, the water had seemed relatively unchanged, still dark in color but quickly swallowing the coins without any display of pyrotechnics or, so far as he could see, any message from a god.

Another coin plopped into the water, then another. "More!" hissed Garisa, and her hand was once again filled with coins. She reached back into the water, stirring it faster and faster, dropping gold piece after gold piece into the swirling liquid until, by Thurgol's best estimate, perhaps twenty pieces of the precious metal lined the bottom of the bowl.

This was a small fortune by any firbolg's estimate, and he became increasingly worried about whatever command of the gods would require so much payment. And still Garisa stirred, while the trolls looked on with obvious scorn and secretly growing curiosity.

Finally all the second batch of coins had been dropped into the water, but this time the shaman did not demand more. Instead, she placed both hands in the water, stirring more diligently than ever, yet still taking great care to spill none of the enchanted liquid.

"I see the Silverhaft Axe—again!" she hissed, her voice taut with wonder. "It glows like a beacon before us! It is the summoning agent of the gods, making their will known in the Realms. And beyond the great weapon, rising to the heavens themselves, I see the pristine summit of the Icepeak!"

Thurgol squinted. He, personally, could see nothing even vaguely resembling a weapon or a landform in the murky water, but he wasn't about to challenge his shaman over the clear will of the gods. Furiously he tried to consider the implications of Garisa's words, but he could fathom no meaning there.

Abruptly, in a sweeping gesture, the old female picked up the bowl and tossed the water over her shoulder, in the direction—no doubt inadvertently—of the skeptical trolls. Baatlrap cursed as he was thoroughly doused, but all other eyes remained fixed on Garisa.

The water was the *only* thing that had flown from the bowl! The gold coins remained in the bottom, lined up in a passable imitation of an arrow. The sign pointed in a clear direction, after Garisa set the bowl down on the ground, and even the dimmest troll or firbolg could understand its import.

For the arrow pointed straight north. There, across the stormy Strait of Oman, they all knew, rose the highland ridge and its crowning glory, the Icepeak.

"Grond Peaksmasher . . ." Garisa said slowly, so that her words rang in the ears of all who were present. "He summons us northward in his hour of need."

"Northward? Where?" mumbled Thurgol, scratching his head as he looked at the golden arrow. It certainly *looked* like an arrow, and no one could doubt the fact that it pointed to the north. But still there was much he didn't understand.

"We must journey to the Icepeak, bearing the Silverhaft Axe before us!" Garisa proclaimed. "There we will find the Forger of Giants, frozen in the ice. Our task can only be to break him free!"

* * * * *

Even in the peaceful forest, Hanrald and Brigit noticed that Finellen's dwarves took careful precautions with their camp. For one thing, it was screened on all sides, concealed in a shallow, bowl-shaped depression and protected by thick stands of pines. Even a large blaze would have been well shielded, yet the dwarves burned small fires, feeding just enough fuel to build up a solid bed of coals for cooking and, later, to produce such warmth as the summer wilderness required.

Dwarves were common enough in the mining cantrev of Blackstone, Hanrald's home, but the young earl found the warriors of Finellen's band to be quite different from those familiar and cantankerous folk. The dwarves of Myrloch moved through the woods like beings who belonged there. They left little sign of their passage, and even their camp was a neatly arranged gathering, organized so as not to destroy several gardenlike clumps of columbine and bluebells.

"Is this just routine, or are you worried about something?" Hanrald asked Finellen, gesturing to the pairs of crossbow-armed lookouts posted around the camp.

"I just like to be careful," replied the gruff commander, whose manner had begun to soften under the influence of a good meal—exceptionally tender venison, Hanrald had been pleased to discover—and the flask of sour rum that the earl and the dwarf had begun to share.

Brigit's initial hostility had relaxed to something like guarded neutrality. Still, she said little during the meal and did not partake of the potent beverage.

"Actually," Finellen continued, "we haven't had any trouble for quite some time now. Old habits die hard, I guess. Why, back when I was young, there were bands of fir-bolgs in these heights that would get together and attack every few years. Life was interesting, then. . . ."

"My father told the same kind of stories about the Fair-height Mountains," Hanrald agreed.

"Now we're lucky if we find an outlaw troll or two during the course of a year. Why, it's getting so a dwarf can't find an honest fight within a hundred miles!"

"I should think that would be cause for celebration," Brigit said acidly, the memories of the Elf-Eater's rampage still fresh in her mind.

"Oh, I suppose it is," Finellen agreed, without any trace of irritation. "Still, a gal who would like to keep her hand in things needs a *little* practice. Unless you think our friend

Tristan's going to live forever."

"You know the High King?" asked Hanrald, astounded. He had never seen a dwarf anywhere near the Kendrick court.

"Knew him, I did," Finellen replied. "Let me see that flask. I don't want you to warm it too much with your big human hands." She took the bottle and swallowed a long, gurgling draft. "There, that's better."

"Finellen commanded the dwarves who served your king during the Darkwalker War," Brigit explained, less hostile than before. "Their services were quite . . . useful in determining the final outcome."

"*Useful?*" Finellen almost sputtered out a mouthful of sour, catching herself just in time to swallow before her outrage exploded. "Why, we cut down more firbolgs than you see trees in this forest!" she proclaimed. "And who stood in the trenches, holding the line, while the fancy-saddled riders pranced about on their horses and waited to steal all the glory?"

"I've heard tales of your valor," Hanrald said soothingly, though Finellen was right about the glory. In the histories of the campaign as the earl had learned them, the Sisters of Synnoria, clad in silver armor and mounted on their white steeds, played a far more dramatic role than had the stolid dwarves.

"I didn't expect anything else, really," Finellen groused good-naturedly. "And I'll swear to this very day, it was worth putting up with our pointy-eared allies in order to put King Tristan on the throne! He's the best thing that's happened to these islands in four generations—that's four generations of *dwarves!*" the bearded warrior concluded pointedly. Hanrald understood that she meant a good four centuries.

"That he's been, for Ffolk and northman too," the earl agreed. "The Treaty of Oman has lasted for twenty years!"

"A brief spark of time," Brigit noted, joining them beside the fire and finally taking a taste from Finellen's flask. "Can his peace last a hundred years, or two hundred, when his life must end in mere decades?"

"Yes!" Hanrald pressed. "Through his family, a dynasty that will carry the weight of his will and his wisdom, as well as that of his queen!"

"But who's to say that the ruler who follows will wield that might well?" countered the elf. It seemed to Hanrald as if she tried to debate contradictions within her own mind as much as with him.

"In Alicia, I believe the first—" Hanrald broke off in mid-sentence as a shadow of movement off to the side distracted him. He turned in astonishment to see a man standing at the very edge of their fireside.

Finellen cursed and sputtered, this time spitting the rum onto the fire so that it flashed brightly.

"Where did—*how* did you get here!" she demanded, bouncing to her feet and reaching for the axe at her side. Other dwarves shouted indignantly and reached for weapons, while the guards at the fringe of the camp began cursing each other for the lapse in diligence.

"Peace," said the man, holding up his hands so that they could see he held no weapon. "I come to speak with you, not to attack."

"How did you get past my guards?" demanded the dwarven captain, still indignant.

"With the help of the goddess," the fellow said quietly. "I am Danrak, druid of Myrloch."

The priest of nature was a nondescript man with long, carelessly tossed hair that was nevertheless full-grown and clean. No more than average size of frame, his shoulders were as broad as a wrestler's, and an unspoken grace and strength lurked in his body, visible even as he walked the few steps to the fire.

"It's all right," Finellen assured her warriors, and the members of the band grudgingly returned to their own fires. She kept her eyes on the druid, however. "Why was this necessary?"

"I had thought, under the circumstances, that your guards might be a little edgy. I preferred to speak with their captain before taking an arrow through any part of me."

"Circumstances?" demanded Finellen. "*What* circumstances?"

The druid's eyes widened in surprise—and something else. Sadness, Hanrald realized with a strong sense of foreboding.

"I—I'm sorry," Danrak said, faltering for the first time.

"What is it, by the goddess?" stormed Finellen, trying unsuccessfully to keep her voice to a low hiss. The dwarven captain shared the earl's dire sensation of threat, Hanrald could tell.

"It's Cambro," the druid said quietly. "It was attacked yesterday by an army of firbolgs and trolls."

Finellen sat in absolute silence for a moment, a silence that was as painful to Hanrald as a consuming explosion of temper. Finally she exhaled, a long, drawn-out breath that seemed to continue for the better part of a minute.

"How bad was it?" she asked, in a voice like the dull rasp of a saw.

"Many dwarves escaped—most, I think," Danrak said. "Though they left the village in the hands of the attackers. When I last observed the brutes, the night before yesterday, they were engaged in a bit of victory celebration."

"I can imagine," growled Finellen. "We'd just poured the last three years' vintage from their aging to their storage casks. I'd guess they would have found plenty of them. Any prisoners?"

"None that I saw," Danrak replied. "And as I told you, many dwarves escaped with their lives—though not much more. I met a number of them in the woods."

"Where are the dwarves now?"

"One of our order, Isolde, has taken them to various shelters in the Winterglen. They are safe there and have plenty of food and drink. Naturally they desire to return to their homes."

"Why did I let myself get drawn away?" groaned Finellen, lowering her head dejectedly into her hands. "I take the best warriors in the village and go off on some wild-goose chase, while the real threat is right in our own back yards!"

"It wasn't a wild-goose chase!" Hanrald interjected. "I saw that Elf-Eater, and if it had gotten out of Synnoria, you'd have desperately needed fair notice!"

"He's right," Brigit agreed, surprisingly sympathetic. "You were wise to examine the threat that menaced Synnoria, just as I have every intention now of finding out about this so-called 'army' of firbolgs and trolls."

"Are the bastards still in Cambro?" inquired the dwarf, only the deadly gleam in her eyes revealing her grim determination.

"I don't know. I was able to eavesdrop on some of their celebration. It seems that they plan to march north," Danrak declared.

"Why, that'll take them right into the Winterglen!" barked Finellen, perceiving the peril to the refugee dwarves.

The druid, however, raised a calming hand. "Your village-mates are well hidden—for the most part, in caves and the like. You don't need to worry about them, even if the beasts march within a dozen feet. More to the point, *why* do they go north?"

"There's nothing in their path except for a few tiny villages of Ffolk and northmen," Brigit pictured, remembering Gwynneth's geography. "Then they'll reach the Strait of Oman."

"Perhaps they want to go for a swim," Hanrald suggested wryly.

"Whatever it is, they've got to be hunted down and destroyed. I've got fifty brave dwarves here who've got just the axes for the job!"

Hanrald looked at Brigit with a raised eyebrow. "As a loyal subject of my king, I'm duty-bound to find out what this is all about," he declared.

"Better get some sleep, then," warned Finellen. "We'll be down the trail before first light."

* * * * *

Deirdre rose from her bed during the darkest hours of the night, relieved to see that heavy clouds obscured the sliver of a moon. She went to her window, casting open the shutters to a scene of absolute black.

Her window faced away from the town, and not so much as a glimmer of lamplight disturbed the invisible blackness of the rolling moor. She stood there for a long time, letting the darkness wash over her.

It was easy to imagine the great void in which she had floated during her dreams. No stars gleamed through the overcast, and the distant expanse before her may as well have been an infinite cosmos. She listened for the voices of the gods. . . .

* * * * *

Talos and Helm circled warily amid the infinite cosmos, each prepared to smite the other with thunderbolt or cyclone, yet each at the moment more concerned with the intransigence of the earth goddess ruling a small and isolated group of islands.

And so to that common foe the two gods turned their schemes, though neither neglected to maintain a suspicious watch upon the other.

Still, against the Earthmother, their powers would be far greater than alone, for each could bring to bear his most powerful tool—and both tools could be made to serve the common end.

In the case of Helm, this asset was his most accomplished servant, the Exalted Inquisitor himself. For Talos, the living weapon was none other than the Princess Deirdre, with her secret and crystal-hard soul.

❦ 5 ❦

Old Campaigners' Council

Garisa snored, each exhalation flapping lips and cheeks like sails teased by a vagrant breeze. The sound itself was lost amid the chorus of similar rumbles and snorts from the giant-kin and trolls who slumbered all around, blissfully unmindful of the mass hangover awaiting the army with the coming dawn. A soft wash of light blossomed beside the giantess as she clutched the Silverhaft Axe even in sleep, while the massive bonfire had once again settled into a small mountain of glowing coals. Otherwise the village lay in darkness.

Only one shape stirred among this gathering of humanoids—a tall form, casting a long, almost sticklike shadow in the fading light of the coals. Baatlrap crept silently, stepping across firbolg and troll alike with uncharacteristic care. His black eyes, as devoid of obvious feeling as any walleyed salmon's, fixed unwaveringly on the gleaming blade.

Finally he crouched beside Garisa and carefully, moving no more than an inch at a time, tugged at the blade. Very slowly the axe moved out of her grip. Once the giantess snorted and stirred restlessly, and the hulking troll froze, talons poised above her neck. Then she settled again, and the gangly troll completed his surreptitious theft.

Clutching the weapon to his wiry chest, Baatlrap darted for the shelter of the surrounding forest, sprinting through the trees until he reached a point far removed from the village. Only then did he squat to the ground and examine his treasure.

A pattern of runes, indecipherable to the troll, danced across the broad blade. The surface was a mosaic of many diamonds, so masterfully cut that from the evidence of sight and touch, it might have been one flawless stone. The handle, of cold metal, was as smooth and shiny as silver, yet it seemed to possess an inner strength greater than any steel.

Yet beyond the physical beauty of the object, Baatlrap sensed a power in his hands that was deep and fundamental. He wondered if this was the power of Grond Peaksmasher, god of the firbolgs. Or could it be something more direct, more useful to the troll? In the dim recesses of his brain, he found images of dark thunderheads, leaden with storm and crackling with jagged bolts of lightning. In the destructive power of those storm clouds, he sensed his duty, his mission.

Slowly, deliberatly, the great troll took the axe in his right hand. Still squatting, he placed his left wrist on the ground and stretched his five long fingers before him. With a cruel grimace—or perhaps it was a bizarre smile of wicked ecstacy—he brought the blade down sharply, hissing at the pain that lanced through his hand and arm. Green blood spurted from five wounds, while the severed digits twitched mindlessly on the ground.

His face still locked in that twisted grin, Baatlrap awkwardly transferred the axe to his mutilated hand. Already fingers had begun to sprout from the bloody stumps, while the pieces on the ground continued to twitch and writhe. Sharply chopping, Baatlrap repeated the gesture with his right hand, only then dropping the axe and settling back to nurse the pain in his two mangled limbs. For more than an hour he sat thus, while his own pain abated and ten pieces of his flesh danced at his feet.

Finally he rose, hoisting the axe with hands once more whole. His steps, when he started walking, led him back toward the camp, where he planned to return the axe to Garisa and get some sleep himself. Behind him, moving soundlessly through the shadowy wood and following their new master to his destination, came a file of ten young, wiry trolls.

* * * * *

Persuading the firbolgs and trolls to leave the virtually bottomless wine cellars of Cambro was no easy task, but Thurgol and Garisa set to it with stubborn determination. Even then they wouldn't have succeeded without the clear compulsion of Garisa's foretelling and the concrete and visible reminder of their cause, as embodied by the Silverhaft Axe.

Surprisingly, Baatlrap and the trolls proved remarkably enthusiastic. No sooner had Garisa hoisted the Silverhaft Axe to her shoulder and started toward the trail than the huge troll barked to his fellows and ordered them to fall in behind.

In fact, Baatlrap loped after the giantess with such a grimace on his gnarled features that Thurgol feared he would try to snatch the weapon out of Garisa's hands. While the chieftain didn't care who carried the artifact, he felt certain that the old hag would take exception, so he stepped into the troll's path to block him. The massive creature seemed even larger than normal to the giant chieftain, somehow looming higher into the air, his posture quivering on the verge of outright menace. Finally Baatlrap's tension relaxed. With a sneer at the diamond blade, the troll relaxed his pace, apparently content to follow a few steps behind Garisa.

They marched northward along the general course of Codsrun Creek, though the humanoid column remained miles to the east of that stream. Before them lay the only access to Myrloch Vale that did not require the traversing of a highland pass. Instead, the land remained generally flat, interspersed with forest and glade.

Thurgol did his best to force some sort of formation over his ragged mob. Ironically, the trolls were the easiest to control here. They had formed themselves into five companies of a dozen each. Baatlrap marched with three of these near the head of the column, his great, jagged-edged sword resting casually across his shoulder, while another dozen trolls brought up the rear. The fifth company scattered through the woods, serving as advance scouts and pickets along the flanks. For this duty, Thurgol admitted, the nimble trolls, with their almost tireless endurance, were far better suited than the lumbering giants.

The firbolgs Thurgol bunched mainly in the middle. A single-file column proved to be too ambitious, so he contented himself with various straggling groups keeping their comrades before and behind them in sight. A small group of firbolgs marched at the head of the column to provide advance warning of any potential trouble. The wolfdogs, several dozen of which accompanied the band on its march, coursed through the woods near this advance guard, frequently scaring up game and, whenever possible, running it down.

Garisa alone bore the Silverhaft Axe, carrying the weapon over her shoulder as if she were a young and swaggering warrior. The firbolg shaman wasn't as spry as the males, but she marched along steadily, without a grumble or complaint. The glittering facets of the great diamond blade drew the giant-kin onward far more effectively than any command or persuasion could have done.

Before they left Cambro, the giantess had applied herself to a dark green piece of burlap, using a bone needle to emblazon her material with white thread. She had gruffly refused to answer Thurgol's questions as to what she was making. Each night, beside a comfortable fire, she vigorously pressed her needle through the cloth.

It was several days after leaving Cambro that the rude army came to the first farmsteads. One of the point guards came lumbering back to Thurgol, panting with excitement.

"Humans! Houses! Cows!" he gasped, his meaty face flushing as he came to a skidding stop before his chieftain.

"Slow down! Where? How many? Did they see you?" demanded Thurgol, fingering his club in agitation.

"Up ahead—we not seen! Hide in bushes to watch. Some men plow in fields. One bangs a hammer against metal."

"How many houses?" pressed the chieftain.

"Dunno. Maybe five or eight."

"Good they didn't see you," he told the young giant,

clapping him on the shoulder. Thurgol considered the options. Obviously they had passed from Myrloch Vale into the fringes of populated country. He knew that there weren't any large towns in this part of Gwynneth, but he didn't know how many villages they'd be likely to encounter. Since they hadn't yet been discovered, it seemed logical to skirt this village and try to put off the initial encounter as long as possible. After all, their goal wasn't to plunder and kill, but to cross the Strait of Oman and return the Silverhaft Axe to the Icepeak. It seemed sensible to delay their initial encounters with humankind for as long as possible. Yes, he decided firmly, this was a wise decision: They could circumvent this settlement by passing around it in the forest.

His self-congratulations were interrupted just then by shrill screams, terrified human voices raised in wails of ultimate horror. In the seconds that followed, the screaming voices ceased one by one, each abruptly silenced.

Bellowing inarticulately in his rage, Thurgol lumbered forward, quickly breaking into a plowed field. Before him, he saw the quaint wooden houses, surrounded by gardens and a few tall trees. Among the trees, large figures moved.

Trolls!

Most of the monsters were hunched over motionless figures on the ground, though a few raised bloodstained muzzles to regard the ranting firbolg charging toward them with impassive eyes.

At first glance, Thurgol counted a dozen of the brutes, and then he understood. The company of trolls that had ranged freely through the woods had come upon these humans and attacked, without waiting to report their discovery to Thurgol, or even Baatlrap.

"Good quick fight, huh?" grunted the latter as he loped up to Thurgol's side. "Good eats." Unlike the firbolgs, trolls commonly devoured the flesh of their human and demihuman victims.

But Thurgol was in no mood to debate differences in dietary etiquette. "Stupid fools! We don't need war with humans—just to carry axe through here!"

Baatlrap stopped in his tracks. The shadowy spots of eyes, beneath the overhanging brows of knobby green skin, seemed to smolder at the firbolg chieftain. "We fight—and kill—when we find enemies!" he snarled.

Furiously Thurgol swung his club at the troll, but Baatlrap blocked the blow with his hands. The force of the attack shoved the monster back several steps, and Thurgol heard bones snap. But Baatlrap still faced the giant-kin boldly. The two creatures stood eye to eye, and for a moment, Thurgol trembled with an almost irresistible desire to savagely attack the arrogant troll.

He noticed that several more of the gangly predators had collected around the pair of them, however. A few firbolgs had followed him from the forest, but they were significantly outnumbered at the moment. Forcing his muscles to obey his will, Thurgol lowered his club.

The plaintive bleating of sheep came to the chieftain's ears. Now the trolls butchered the farm animals! "Save cows and horses!" he shouted as a pair of trolls pursued a lumbering draft horse through the field. At least they could use some of the unfortunate creatures as beasts of burden, instead of killing them all and gaining far more fresh meat than they could possibly carry along.

With grudging satisfaction, he saw the two trolls seize the horse around the neck and drag the kicking creature toward the barn. At least he had *some* authority left.

Trying unsuccessfully to regard that small triumph as a victory, he turned his back on the scene of massacre and returned to his troops.

* * * * *

As soon as she reached the skies over the great lake, Robyn sensed that something was indeed wrong in Myrloch Vale. The High Queen soared almost effortlessly in the body of the great white hawk. Her eyes, keen beyond human conception, studied each leaf, each shady bower and rock-bound grotto in the valley sprawled around her.

The vista below appeared to be as pristine, as vibrantly healthful, as she could have hoped. Crystalline lake waters glistened in the light of the sun, and even the dank fenlands lay beneath a dense blanket of verdure. Tall pines waved their crowns proudly in a fresh breeze, and in places where the forest opened into meadow, dazzling wildflowers gleamed like priceless gems in a carefully crafted setting.

Yet something intangible, invisible to sight and sound and even smell, lingered in the air around her, telling her that violence had indeed invaded this place. As distressing as the discovery itself was the knowledge that she had *not* realized this fact earlier, even though Corwell was but a short distance—as the goddess reckoned distance—from this, the heartland of the Earthmother's realm.

She dove, building up tremendous speed and skimming within a few feet of the water's surface. Huge lake trout dove away from her shadow, but she ignored the prey, intent upon her mission. Nothing unnatural disturbed the waters, and soon she soared upward to crest the woodlands at the lake's northern shore. For hours she swept across the vast wilderness, still tormented by her earlier sense of distress and even more agitated by the fact that she could not more specifically identify it.

The coming of darkness surprised her and finally drew her down to the earth, where she landed in a forest of shadow. Shifting her shape as she touched the ground, she stood once again as a human woman, feet planted firmly beneath her.

But more than merely human, she was a druid—a druid who stood upon the most sacred earth known to her faith. The land welcomed her, and she felt strongly the blessings of the goddess. Yet still the sense of danger lingered, though with no more precise indication than before.

Guiding herself by scent and touch more than sight, since the forest was nearly fully dark around her, she found several ripe apples. She had brought some aged cheese, but preferred to save that for an emergency. The druid made a pleasant supper of the fruit, and finally she curled in a grassy bower to sleep until dawn.

She awakened before then, however, sitting upright with a start. An irresistible feeling came over her, a feeling that she was not alone.

"Who is it?" she hissed into the darkness, sniffing the air and listening for any sound. She heard a faint fluttering sound, as of wings beating quickly in the air.

"*I* get to ask that! Who is it?" The squeaking voice brought a wave of relief washing over Robyn, even as she wanted to reach out and strangle a scrawny neck for the fright she had felt.

"Newt!" she cried with a laugh, giving up her irritation in an instant. "How did you find me?"

"How many white hawks do you think we *have* out here, anyway? And how many humans camping on a pile of Corwellian sharp cheese? Downwind, I could smell it from miles away! Say, that's the aged one, isn't it? I remember the taste . . . a nice bite, just a little aftertaste. . . ."

"Here!" Robyn said, still laughing. She reached into her pouch and pulled out a block of the cheese. "But first I have to see you!"

Immediately a soft light diffused Robyn's bower, coming from no place in particular. In another instant, a small, lizard-like creature popped into sight, hovering in the air before the druid queen.

The first thing Robyn saw about Newt, as always, was that wide, toothy grin that always seemed to extend farther to the sides than the width of his head. The faerie dragon was bright pink in color, reflecting his happiness at meeting his old friend, his hummingbird wings buzzing audibly now as he slowly settled to the ground.

No more than three feet in length, and nearly half of that was tail, Newt's body was nevertheless a reasonable approximation, in miniature, of a dragon's. Tiny scales coated him, except for his gossamer wings, and his face—perhaps in part because of its size—consistently bore a far more cheerful expression than one typically associated with the greater wyrms.

Now, resting on his haunches so that he could hold the cheese with both his forepaws, Newt busily stuffed the food into his mouth. Soon his cheeks bulged outward, and then he paused to chew contentedly. Robyn, relaxing again, let her old friend enjoy his repast. She had many questions for him, but she knew better than to press Newt for information.

Finally he finished, swallowing the better part of a full day's ration in one throat-stretching gulp. "So," he said, curling up in her lap, "what brings you back to the Vale?"

"Curiosity," Robyn replied evasively. The worst way to approach the faerie dragon, she knew, was with direct questioning. "After all, it's been a long time since I've been here."

"Me, too," Newt agreed. "I was over on Alaron for a little while."

A little while! Robyn smiled privately. The dragon had performed a duty there for twenty years! "Alicia told me. She said you were a great help to her and her companions."

"Say, I was, wasn't I?" Newt raised his head and puffed out his chest a measure. "I bet they'd *still* be wandering around the highlands over there if it weren't for me!"

"How long have you been back?" Robyn inquired casually.

"Oh, two or three days now—or is it two or three months? I always get those two mixed up. I got here before the firbolgs went over and smashed Cambro. Does that help? . . . What's the matter?"

Robyn had stiffened reflexively, stunned by the dragon's casual announcement. Cambro was the only dwarven community in Myrloch Vale. The queen had been there several times, albeit many years past. For centuries, the sturdy community had stood, a bulwark against the firbolgs that used to roam so aggressively through the highlands. Now, when the giant-kin had been all but obliterated, what force could propel them into such an attack?

"Anyway," Newt continued, "I came down to the lake here. I was doing some fishing along the shore when I saw you this afternoon. I chased you all the way to the woods, but then I lost you. Good thing you brought that cheese, or I wouldn't have found you. Say, you wouldn't have another little nibble in there, would you?" Newt's twitching nostrils revealed that he already knew the answer to the question.

Carefully Robyn broke a smaller piece off the block, asking as she passed it, "About Cambro—how badly was Cambro smashed? I didn't really hear much about it."

Newt shrugged. "Oh, you know—firbolgs and trolls dancing around a bonfire. They were waving a big silver axe around in the air and making a lot of noise. I couldn't even get to sleep until I flew a couple miles away!" he concluded indignantly.

"Firbolgs . . . *and* trolls. Are you *sure*, Newt?" Robyn asked intently.

"What do you think . . . I don't know a troll when I see one? Sure I'm sure!"

"What about the dwarves? Did you see any of them?" pressed the queen.

Newt shook his head in exasperation. "I *told* you—I saw firbolgs and trolls! You don't think the dwarves would invite them right in, do you?"

Robyn sighed and leaned back on her arms, frustrated and tense. She knew better than to ask Newt how many of the beasts he had seen. Suddenly she itched with the urge to fly north, to see Cambro and this brutal band of monsters. She didn't want to think of it as an army—there *couldn't* be that many of the gigantic humanoids on all Gwynneth . . . or could there?

"I'm going to Cambro today," she announced. "Want to come along?"

"Sure!" Newt beamed. "But why? Didn't I tell you it's full of giants and stuff? Why don't we go to Corwell, or someplace else that's friendly?"

By the time she had convinced the faerie dragon that she

was determined in her choice of destination, a bare minimum of light sifted through the woods, and the stars overhead slowly disappeared into the dawn. Once again Robyn's
body smoothly changed shape, and the figure of the white
hawk soared into the still morning air. Buzzing beside her
came the equally swift faerie dragon.

For a few hours, they flew, guided by Robyn's true sense
of direction. Finally they saw the small clearing in its setting
of low, rock-knobbed hills. As they swooped downward, she
was relieved to see that most of the houses had suffered relatively little damage, though a few had been burned and others smashed into junk. The evidence of battle was all too
indisputable.

Diving lower, she saw that the monsters had gone. Their
tracks formed a plain, muddy rut extending northward from
the village. Other figures, however, stood among the ruins,
and as the hawk soared toward the ground, Robyn identified
many of them. A number of dwarves regarded the great bird
suspiciously, but none of them raised their crossbows—and
in another moment, Robyn settled to the ground, standing
proudly as the dark-haired druid queen. She wasn't surprised when Newt didn't appear, suspecting that he hovered
around somewhere, invisibly observing this large gathering
of strangers.

"Your Majesty!" Hanrald exclaimed, quickly dropping to
one knee as she greeted him and bade him rise. Danrak,
too, formally greeted the mistress of his druidic faith.

"And Brigit . . . and Finellen as well," Robyn said with a
sad smile at the destruction around them. "How unfortunate
that we old companions meet like this."

"It's a regular 'old campaigners' council,'" Finellen
grumbled. "But we're too late."

"You weren't here when this happened? No wonder they
got away with it," Robyn said, clapping the bearded dwarfwoman on the shoulder.

Gruffly, biting back her frustration, Finellen told Robyn
what she had learned from Danrak and the physical evidence

of the scene: the approximate number of the attackers—a remarkably accurate estimate of two hundred—and the fact that the brutes had marched off to the north. Missing from Cambro were considerable stockpiles of strong drink, as well as much treasure and the Silverhaft Axe, the prize artifact of the village.

Danrak added the information about the dwarven refugees. "We also received word just this morning that they've attacked some farmsteads in Winterglen. They're still marching north, toward the coast."

"We're going after them within the day," Finellen noted. "We've sent out a mustering of the clans, and I hope to add a few more warriors before we start out on the trail. But after that, it won't be more than a few days before we track these thugs down and attack!"

Robyn looked around. At best, Finellen had some fifty warriors in her company. Even if that number doubled, which didn't seem likely, they would be vastly outnumbered by the giant-kin.

"I can return to Corwell by tomorrow," she said, calculating distances and effort in her mind. "When King Tristan hears about this, he'll take immediate action—you know that! Why don't you consider holding back until he can join you? He can raise five hundred men-at-arms from Corwell Town alone. They'll be on the march within a few hours of the call. Then, with your forces united, you can make one solid, sure attack!"

Her arguments sounded persuasive and sensible to the humans and the elf, but Robyn could tell that Finellen didn't see them quite that way.

"Was *Corwell* sacked?" demanded the bearded warrior. This was the question that defined the dwarf's approach to the problem. "Since when do you think that we dwarves can't take care of ourselves?"

"That's not the case! What about the lessons we learned together twenty years ago, Finellen? Standing side by side against chaos—dwarves, Llewyrr, and humans—we faced down evil and we prevailed! Have you forgotten?" demanded the queen.

"No . . . I'll never forget," Finellen said sincerely. "But there's a case where the Darkwalker and its minions threatened *all* of us!"

"Didn't you hear Danrak say that human farmsteads have been ravaged by these beasts? Those are King Tristan's subjects. He would come out of duty to them even if Cambro still stood safe and snug! You'll not relinquish any sense of honor by waiting for him. Instead, you'll ensure that you earn the vengeance you so richly deserve!" And take away from the chance you'll lead your warriors into another tragedy, she added silently.

Finellen turned away to ponder for a moment. Finally she made her decision and faced the queen again, her expression skeptical but not unfriendly.

"I'll have to follow the trail . . . keep them in sight," she explained. "But I suppose I could hold off on the attack for a week or so, at least so long as it doesn't look like they're getting away."

How the giant-kin could "get away" on an island the size of Gwynneth eluded Robyn at the moment, but she was grateful for the dwarfwoman's concession.

"Very well," Robyn replied. "I'll start back to Corwell immediately. The king will be on the march shortly after I arrive, I'm certain!"

"A week," Finellen said grudgingly. "After that, I don't think I'll be able to hold back."

* * * * *

"Come in, my child. . . . It's good to see you walking about." It's good to see you period, the Exalted Inquisitor addended silently as Deirdre entered the anteroom of his apartments.

Indeed, the raven-haired princess of Callidyrr was a stunning beauty, with her ice-white skin, high cheekbones, and lush black hair. Her blue eyes, of a hue so dark it sometimes seemed like black, burned with an intensity that dissolved any thoughts of chilly arrogance within her proud, aloof body.

"I'm beginning to feel . . . *alive* again," Deirdre admitted, sinking to a low bench with a sigh. Even a short walk about the keep still exhausted her. Nevertheless, this was a considerable improvement from her nearly comatose state of a week earlier.

She had awakened several days before to find the patriarch of Helm at her side, holding her small hand in both of his large ones. Immediately she had felt a sense of trust toward the man, and as they had conversed—for a few minutes at first; later for hour after stimulating hour—she learned that here was a person who *understood* her!

This made him unique among her currently present family and friends. Deirdre found that the priest was a very devout man, absolutely subject to the will of his god, but the will of his god as Hyath himself interpreted it. The princess had been quick to grasp the fact that this gave him a certain amount of leeway in the pursuit of his doctrine.

And yet Helm did not seem displeased. She sensed an aura of godhood around the man, an indisputable fullness of power that bespoke more than mortal, or even magical, vitality. It was a strength unique from, and seemingly superior to, the druidic faith of her mother.

When Hyath spoke to her, his deep voice rumbled soothingly. He talked, not of *his* god, but of *gods*. Once again Deirdre found him clarifying things that she had never fully grasped before. The full pantheon of gods worshiped by all the peoples of the Realms she saw as a good thing, a strengthening by diversity that for many centuries had been unknown in the Moonshaes.

It was an outlook that differed fundamentally from her mother's interpretation of immortal will, as personified by the goddess Earthmother. Deirdre had heard often enough the central tenet of her mother's faith: According to Robyn, the Moonshaes were uniquely enchanted because of the purity of their goddess. If other deities—the druids called them "New Gods," though Deirdre knew this was a preposterous misstatement—exercised equal power in the isles, then the goddess must inevitably fade.

But for the first time, Deirdre examined this situation in a somewhat dispassionate light. What was such an inherently terrible thing about the acceptance of the New Gods? Hadn't Hyath already shown her how competition for worshipers bred strength, not weakness?

"Did you sleep without dreams last night?" inquired the patriarch.

"I don't know," Deirdre replied with a bemused shake of her head. "I certainly felt well rested in the morning, and Father tells me he didn't hear anything during the night."

"Splendid news," the cleric said benignly. "Tell me, did you have a chance to think about our conversation of last night?"

"Yes, I did. It's true that there's a lot of good land in Myrloch Vale, as you pointed out. Yet for some reason none of the Ffolk have ever farmed there."

"Superstitions perhaps?" supplied the Exalted Inquisitor.

"Yes—ancient fears of the goddess. It's as I told you. Many of the Ffolk don't realize that there are other gods who will watch and protect them."

"The spreading of this message is a great, even an historical, task—one that must be undertaken without any further delay."

For a long time, Deirdre kept silent. The implications of the patriarch's suggestions were not lost upon her. She found them strangely disturbing, but also motivating, in a sense that she couldn't quite identify.

"In any event, dear child, I'm delighted to see that your strength returns with such youthful vigor. If only your father would respond as well. . . ."

"He seems robust enough," Deirdre noted.

"In the flesh, to be sure," the cleric explained. "But it is the wasting of the *spirit* wherein lies his danger. By refusing to accept the requirements of Helm, he denies the aid of a very powerful ally, one who could surely heal his wound and raise him to undreamed of greatness!"

Deirdre shook her head. "My father is a king of the Ffolk, and he holds the goddess in nearly the same reverence as does my mother. It's a thrall that I admit I can't understand. After all, he's shown a willingness to accept many other new concepts during his rule. Yet—for now at least—if Helm requires him to reject the worship of the Earthmother, I don't believe he will do so."

" 'Reject'—such a strong word," the Exalted Inquisitor soothed. "There only need be an implicit acknowledgment of the rights and places of other gods—an equal standing with the Earthmother, no more."

Deirdre sighed. It sounded so simple, so *right* when the patriarch explained things. Yet she knew that in her own life, the situation was a great deal more confused. She sensed an expanse of power and potential that dwarfed anything she had previously known, and she was reluctant, even unwilling, to abandon the spark that had been ignited.

A cry from the castle guards roused her from her meditation. At first she thought that an alarm had been sounded, but as she threw open the windows, she heard the joy and relief in the guardsman's voice.

"The High Queen returns!" he cried as other guards joined in the welcome. Deirdre saw the familiar form of the white hawk circling the castle, settling quickly toward the ground.

* * * * *

"A small army of firbolgs and trolls is on the march. They've sacked Cambro, and now they move to the north, toward the shoreline and the Strait of Oman."

Robyn spoke bluntly, standing before the hearth of the library while Tristan, her daughters, Keane, and the inquisitor listened to her report.

"Have they attacked any humans—any Ffolk?" asked Tristan grimly. The High King paced in agitation, his new sword swinging easily at his side and his gold circlet crown resting atop the fullness of his long, gray-brown hair.

"Yes—isolated villages . . . little more than groups of farmsteads. Codscove lies in their line of march, though they must be a few days away from there still."

"Thus is the prophecy of Helm fulfilled!" crowed the Exalted Inquisitor. He turned to face Tristan. "Your Majesty! This is the evil indicated by my god. Wipe it from the isles, and you will earn the blessings of his power."

"I can do no less, in any event," said Tristan. "Yet I fail to see how this makes any great service for Helm."

"Indeed," Robyn agreed. "The dwarves already march against this force, and I assured them that your help would be forthcoming. Finellen was reluctant to delay her attack, but I convinced her to give you time to get there with a body of men."

"Of course," Tristan agreed, though he sounded vaguely distracted. "That's what I *must* do. However many of the villains there are, I can't imagine that we'll have trouble dispatching them."

The king turned back to the cleric, an expression of puzzlement on his face. "That's why I can't see where this could be the will of your god any more than of my own goddess."

"Perhaps there is a thing about your quest that you have not fully grasped . . . that we have not yet understood."

Tristan, his hand on the hilt of his sword, whirled in agitation. He seemed about to say something, but then angrily shut his mouth, half-drawing the sword from its elegant scabbard. Quickly he resheathed the weapon and resumed his furious pacing.

"We have no *time!*" Robyn interrupted in irritation. "It will take the better part of a day to muster your men, and who knows how long to march them to Winterglen! Why waste that time arguing which god is served by your duty?"

"That's just it!" Tristan said, turning to his wife with real anguish on his face. "I'm confused about that duty. What if I'm missing something . . . going about this the wrong way?" He raised his left arm, with its all-too-abrupt termination.

"Call up the men!" Robyn repeated in tight-lipped urgency. "At least you can gather them to—"

"No!" Tristan barked the word so sharply that the High Queen bit her lip, glowering at the patriarch in barely concealed fury. "That's too *easy!*" the king continued. "There must be more to it . . . something I don't understand!"

"What are you talking about?" demanded the queen.

"My quest, you called it." Tristan seemed to be speaking to himself. "And *time*—that's important, too. Both of you, I think, have given me the guidance I need."

"What do you mean?" asked Robyn, concerned with the stubborn set of her husband's chin.

"There is a way I can face these giants and do honor to the gods, and also a way to reach them in far less time than needed for a column of men."

"No!" Robyn gasped, sensing his intent.

"Yes!" declared Tristan, rising from his chair and standing like the High King that he was in the center of the room. He drew the sword from its scabbard, and the silvery steel gleamed like a beacon in the room. The righteous gleam of the blade challenged even the brilliance of full daylight.

"I ride at once to face these monsters, and I journey in a fashion that places my success or failure in the hands of the gods!"

"You can't mean—" the queen persisted, but her husband cut her off with a chop of his hand.

"Indeed I do—for I shall go alone!"

* * * * *

The image of her father's quest flamed in Deirdre's eyes as she settled into bed on the night following his departure. Tension had crackled through the library following his announcement, with her mother actually reduced to tears at one point by the king's single-minded determination. Alicia, too, had created a scene, declaring that she would ride at her father's side. She had been rudely silenced by the determined king.

Only Deirdre and the inquisitor, it seemed, had watched the scene with dispassion. And then, an hour later, Tristan had ridden through the gates of Caer Corwell on his most powerful war-horse, accompanied only by five of his veteran moorhounds and armed with the gleaming sword.

Now, in the darkness, Deirdre sensed the interest of the gods in the High King's quest. He served the goddess, in his defiance of those creatures who actively wracked the Balance. And he also served Helm, for he placed his faith in the arms of a warlike god and fought against great odds. Perhaps he served all the New Gods, for though his quest was sanctified by the blessing of the Exalted Inquisitor, that patriarch had blessed the endeavor in the names of a full pantheon of deities.

And certainly, Deirdre sensed in the dim recesses of her mind, he served at least one other god besides the goddess Earthmother and the All-Seeing Eye. She sensed this in the core of herself, in the part of her body that was no longer fully human—that part that had been claimed when the mirror shattered and the shards of glass had pierced her without a wound.

She heard the deep voice of an immortal master, and it was not a thing of menace, for it did not try to command her. Instead, this potent deity listened to her needs, paid heed to the desires that had begun to grow in her mind, and slowly, gradually, began to show her the way.

* * * * *

Amid the vast halls of the gods, Talos and Helm observed the consultation in the Moonshaes with particular interest. The two mighty gods, diametrically opposed in almost all facets of value and belief, nevertheless agreed that the reign of the goddess must not be allowed to hold all other faiths aside. Each had his own tool, and each worked toward that aim.

Unknown to them, however, a third immortal power began to stir, to take an interest in the affairs of the Moonshaes. That one was not one of the greatest gods; indeed he was not a true god at all, but a demigod who had once stalked the mortal world of the Realms. Still, he did not lack for worshipers. Once the potent master of a powerful race, he now saw the chance to return to his once mighty glory.

This immortal lord was Grond Peaksmasher, and his children were the giant-kin.

✤ 6 ✤

A Storm from the North

It seemed to Tristan Kendrick that layer after layer of his life—extraneous, civilized levels—fell away as he rode steadily northward. The complexities of gods and humans grew distant and remote as Caer Corwell dwindled to a speck on the horizon and finally disappeared in the haze of distance.

The comfortable weight of his chain mail armor, a long-past gift from his father, settled upon his shoulders. The sword given to him by Parell Hyath swung easily at his side, and the king reflected that the blade's weight felt good. It had been long since he had wielded a sword, and that sword had been a blade for the ages—the Sword of Cymrych Hugh. Yet now, so long after that weapon had vanished in the final triumph over the Darkwalker, it somehow seemed right that he again carry worthy steel.

Five powerful moorhounds, led by the redoubtable Ranthal, coursed proudly through the brush and hillocks. The lanky hound, covered with shaggy rust-colored fur and gifted with a keen nose and virtually limitless endurance, was a descendent of the mighty Canthus himself. Loping tirelessly, the pack leader sniffed and searched through the brush, eager to lead his packmates onto the spoor of any prey.

A high-backed saddle supported the king as the huge stallion, Shallot, easily crested the rises. With his gleaming palomino coat and snowy white mane and fetlocks, Shallot trotted and cantered with head held high, as if he knew that he bore the High King of the Ffolk on his back. As the monarch rode, the moors gradually merged into the highlands, the slopes becoming steeper, the crests more rocky and precipitous.

Even the skies blessed Tristan's endeavor, for the sun shone brightly the whole day long at the beginning of his ride. He rode generally along the line of the northern coast of Corwell Firth, but far enough inland that he avoided the settlements of fisherffolk lining the shore. It was enough that he had the company of his dogs and his horse; indeed, it gave him a sense of freedom and youth such as he hadn't known in many years.

Before sunset, he turned inland, intending to widely skirt the only significant town, Elyssyrr, along this coast. His course would take him northward into a rugged range of mountains, yet he relished the challenge of untraveled valleys and undiscovered passes. He still felt the pressure of time; he had to travel quickly! It was possible, even likely, that his path would take him into a box canyon instead of a pass, and he could lose a day's or more travel time with a long backtrack and detour. Yet, as with the entire concept of his solitary quest, he felt no lack of confidence. He rode in the service of the gods; therefore they would find him a path through the mountains.

Of course, even a moment's reflection told him that he couldn't expect to set his lance and charge into two hundred firbolgs and trolls. Yet here a serene faith took over in his mind, banishing any concern on this score. It was as if the gods around him urged him on, assuring him that they would take care of the rest.

The first night he made a comfortable camp atop a low mountaintop, relishing the brilliant arc of stars overhead. Already he was so remote from humanity that he saw no sign of fire or lamplight throughout the circumference of his horizon. In fact, he elected to eat a cold supper of bread, sausage, cheese, and wine rather than build himself a blaze that would have detracted from the brilliance of the night.

Snugly wrapped in his bedroll, he watched the stars until he drifted off to sleep. For a long time, he dreamed about many things, but most vividly he remembered floating on a dark, rolling sea, supported by a wide raft, yet alone upon a featureless expanse of water. Then he awakened, still hours before dawn, and thought that he beheld a miracle.

The sky to the north was aglow with spiraling lines and twisting columns of fire dancing on the surface of the world. They reached toward the stars, those flames, and flickered through cosmic colors—red and yellow, deep blue and pure, flaring white. For an hour, Tristan watched the lights of the north, and in them, he saw the blessings of the gods. Did they not illuminate the sky over his destination?

As if to confirm the magic of the scene, a chorus of wild voices arose from the forest, a song of joy wailing at the stars. It had been many years since Tristan had heard the call of the wolves, and a smile of contentment crossed his lips as he lay, powerfully moved, and listened to their song.

Considerably heartened, the High King drifted back to sleep. This time he dreamed that his ship was propelled by wide sails, fairly flying across the sea on a true and proper course. When he next awakened, it was dawn.

* * * * *

The village of Codscove huddled against the shore, protected by two outreaching peninsulas that served to wrap the bay and community in sheltering arms. Thurgol and Baatlrap watched the town from the vantage of a high hill only a mile or so inland. Not a large town by any means, Codscove was nonetheless the most populous location in the path of the steadily marching army of trolls and firbolgs.

"Good—no wall around it," observed the huge troll, studying the layout of buildings, streets, and waterfront.

Most of the buildings were small and made primarily of wood, with perhaps one or two walls of stone. In the center of the town, however, were several large stone structures—a small temple, some kind of warehouse or armory, and a sprawling house that must belong to the local lord. These three stood around three sides of a large square of grass, with the fourth side facing the water.

Several companies of men-at-arms, including twoscore armed with longbows, stood at ease in the village commons. Thurgol counted perhaps a dozen horses, with the telltale gleam of plate mail armor reflecting from the knights lounging nearby.

"I don't think they know we're so close," observed the giant-kin. Beside him a great wolfdog, its ears raised suspiciously at the settlement of hated humans, growled ominously.

"They'll find us soon enough," replied the brutal troll.

"There's a lot of people there," Thurgol pointed out, uncomfortable with the dispassionate nature of his companion's planning.

In fact, the firbolg chieftain realized, much of the march through Winterglen had turned into an orgy of destruction, with trolls ransacking and murdering wherever humans had been encountered. They had reached more and more of the farmsteads, increasingly less isolated from each other, as they neared the coast. On the last two days, however, every settlement they found had been abandoned, with all the human refugees apparently gathering in the little fishing hamlet before them. Even the wolfdogs had found slim pickings amid the deserted farms, though in several places, the great canines had run down cows or horses enough to feed the entire horde.

"Lots of people good—make nice booty for us," Baatlrap grunted, smacking his thin, bony lips.

Thurgol shook his head. "We cross water here. Why waste time with big attack?"

The giant troll regarded the firbolg chieftain with his deep, emotionless black eyes. Baatlrap raised a gnarled fist clenched into a ball of knotty green-covered bone. "We have to take boats!" He pointed at the small fleet of fishing craft bobbing in the shelter of Codsbay. "To do that—take town first."

The firbolg warrior was forced to admit that his hulking companion had a point, though it galled him to grant anything to the monster he came increasingly to regard as a dangerous rival.

"Let's go make plan," Baatlrap grunted, turning his back on the town and starting down the hill toward the blanket of forest that flowed halfway up the gradual slope. There waited the ragged army of trolls and firbolgs that had followed these two leaders from Myrloch Vale to the northern shore of Gwynneth.

"Attack tomorrow. I tell trolls," barked Baatlrap.

The two types of creatures maintained separate camps, with the trolls gathered closer to the fringe of the forest. They passed through a muddy clearing where the gaunt, wiry beasts flopped in relaxation after a day of marching. Baatlrap stopped here among his minions, while the giant chieftain continued toward the camp of his firbolgs. As he passed, Thurgol noted with surprise that there seemed to be a lot of trolls—more than he had remembered from the previous day. Then, as he reentered the forest to find the camp of the firbolgs, he met still another band of trolls—a dozen or more—coming to join the group in the meadow.

Finally he saw, hanging listlessly from the branch of a dead tree, the woolen banner created by Garisa. The rectangular flag bore a crude replication of the Silverhaft Axe, a white image sewn on a dark green background. The old shaman had proudly produced it during the course of the march, and now she insisted that the firbolgs fly it as a banner of war wherever the trail of the campaign led. Thurgol took little note of the flag as his brain worked over the implications of the large number of trolls assembled in the adjacent camp.

True, the numbers of the giant-kin had grown somewhat as well. Several bands of firbolgs, totalling nearly a score of new arrivals, had emerged from the wilderness to accompany Thurgol's ragged tribe. He had never suspected that this many giant-kin still dwelled in the fringes of the great valley, but word of this epic march had spread to even these remote reaches. As a rule, these smaller bands had suffered even worse luck on the hunt than had the Blackleaf clan.

Word of the Silverhaft Axe had crystallized within these firbolgs an urgency that had drawn them from fifty miles away, flocking to Garisa's rude banner. Thurgol hadn't done a detailed count of his troops. Since their number clearly exceeded the combined total of his fingers and toes, an accurate numbering was more or less out of the question. Nevertheless, he had begun to suspect that the army now included nearly as many trolls as firbolgs.

Of course, on the good side, this meant that they had a fairly respectable force. They might just succeed at taking Codscove, though Thurgol realized without enthusiasm that it was likely to be a bloody affair. And ever since the first massacre of the small steading in the forest, the firbolg had felt the control of this army, of its march and perhaps even the purpose of the grand quest, slipping away.

While he pondered, a great cheer rumbled upward from the camp through the woods. Obviously Baatlrap had just told his troops of the impending attack.

Sighing heavily—the cheering depressed him—the firbolg chieftain shouted to get the attention of his own troops. The shambling giants gathered into a great circle, and Thurgol began to speak.

He very much did *not* feel like cheering.

* * * * *

Robyn spoke with Alicia and Keane in the library less than an hour after the king's departure. Even through the woman's druidic veneer of tranquility, her daughter could tell that the High Queen was furious. Her face was white, and the muscles in her neck clenched spasmodically, as if she struggled to bite back words of rage.

"How could he do something so *stupid?*" Alicia demanded, bound by no such sense of restraint as her mother. "Does he intend to fight a hundred firbolgs alone?"

Robyn sighed. It seemed that her daughter's fury gave

her the vent she needed to relax, at least slightly. "It's not stupid," she chided Alicia gently. "Never dismiss actions that are motivated by faith as mere lack of intelligence—and remember as well, your father is not a stupid man!"

"I know!" Alicia declared in exasperation. "But at least he could have let *me* go along with him—or Keane, or *somebody!*"

"It may as well have been an army then," Robyn replied with maddening calm. "For reasons understood only by him, he had to do this alone."

"But do we have to *let* him?"

"Yes . . . and perhaps no," Robyn replied. At Alicia's look of frustration, she continued: "I have to respect his wish to travel without an army. Much as I would like to fly above him, watching, perhaps assisting him from a distance, I cannot. It would be too much of a betrayal."

"What *can* we do, then?" demanded Alicia.

"I'm getting to that," Robyn responded, with a calm in her voice that seemed, at least slightly, to settle her daughter's agitation. "First we will raise an army. In fact, I've ordered Earl Randolph to start the criers through Corwell Town and onto the nearby cantrevs. The full companies are to assemble below the castle by tonight."

"Will you lead them?" asked the princess.

"As long as Deirdre remains in need of care, I'll have to remain here. So no, I won't lead them. That duty, my daughter, will have to fall to you . . . and to Keane."

For a moment, Alicia was speechless. Never had she commanded, or even given thought to commanding, troops in the field. Yet as the idea took hold, she felt growing confidence gained from recent experiences, and she found that the notion seemed quite natural. Too, it would be a comfort to have Keane's intelligence to rely on. The fact that he would be there with her gave her a bright flare of confidence.

"Do you want us to follow the king?" asked Keane.

"Not in so many words. That would be impossible, anyway,

given how quickly I expect him to travel. But if you march northward with all speed, it may be that you can reach Winterglen before all is lost."

"Mother . . . the route of our march . . . it will take us through the heart of Myrloch Vale."

Robyn bit back her emotions again. The others could see that this fact troubled her deeply. Yet here she saw no alternative. "Any other route would take at least twice as long," she admitted. "And we don't have enough seaworthy ships in the harbor to transport a large number of men by sea. It breaks my heart to send armed men through the heart of the Earthmother's domain, but if this mission has any hope of success, it lies in a speedy march to the north. I'll try to give you a map of the easiest route—and the one least likely to leave permanent scars on the wilderness."

Robyn paused, thinking, before she continued. "You'll have to carry provisions with you. Take *no* game in Myrloch Vale itself. Do you understand?"

Alicia nodded. The command was no more than what she had already planned.

"Also, we know that you'll face trolls. Be sure to carry a good supply of oil."

Again the princess agreed. She knew that fire was the only way to permanently destroy the regenerating monsters, and the flammable liquid was the best way to incinerate the green-skinned corpses.

The queen continued. "Another thing—Newt's back on Gwynneth, in Myrloch Vale. At least, that's where he was when I flew out there a couple of days ago. Naturally he disappeared when I got to Cambro, and I was in such a hurry to get home that I didn't look for him on the way back."

"That's . . . news," Alicia said guardedly. She couldn't exactly call it *good* news. The faerie dragon's pranks and unpredictable, if well-intentioned, illusions had caused them trouble in the past. "Does he know that we're coming?"

"I don't know how much he heard about our plans. In any event, be warned—if the trees start to talk, or the flowers to dance, you might want to look around for our little friend."

"I will," Alicia sighed. In truth, she wouldn't mind Newt's presence that much. The faerie dragon was ever a bright and cheery soul, and despite his pranks, he had also proven to be a useful ally on more than one occasion.

"Will Hanrald and Brigit remain with the dwarves?" asked Keane.

"As far as I know you'll meet them with Finellen," Robyn replied. "And, depending on how Deirdre fares, I'll try to join you near your destination as well."

"I'm faring quite well, mother—thank you!" The younger daughter's voice came from the door of the library. Deirdre entered just then, followed by the looming bulk of the cleric Hyath. "You needn't post yourself at my bedside!"

Robyn's face flushed, though Alicia wasn't sure if it was because of her daughter's impudent tone or the hovering way the patriarch of Helm accompanied her into this family gathering.

"What are you doing here?" she demanded, curtly confronting the priest.

"I have come to offer my advice . . . and my services. After all, it seems that the High King has embarked on a quest motivated at least in part from his widening grasp of theological reality. Perhaps one, such as myself, who can offer an outside perspective may have useful counsel to offer."

"I agree," said Keane, drawing a surprised look from Robyn. She narrowed her eyes at the magic-user for a moment, and then turned back to the priest.

"Be seated, then," she invited with bare civility. Deirdre had already taken an empty chair when the cleric lowered his bulky form onto a wide couch.

"Now, then—you're discussing the muster of your army, perhaps?" inquired the Exalted Inquisitor. As Robyn's face betrayed her surprise at his timely information, he explained: "Your criers are doing a creditable job of spreading the word. I happened to be in the castle courtyard when the first announcement was made."

"Yes—the king might ride alone, but I intend to send an army as fast as possible on his trail."

"I'm surprised that a spiritual woman such as yourself doesn't put more stock in his chances! After all—Your Majesty—he embarks upon a holy quest!"

" 'Holy' is an altogether subjective term in this matter," Robyn retorted. "I will not disavow the possible connection, but neither am I willing to allow my husband to ride off to his death based on an error in judgment!"

"A sensible attitude," allowed the Exalted Inquisitor. "And one which I wholeheartedly support."

"How?" asked Alicia, frankly skeptical.

"I intend to accompany your army on its march against the giant-kin—that is, given your permission?" he added with a benign smile at the queen.

"I was given to understand that pressing duties called you back to the mainland," the High Queen noted.

"Indeed, Your Majesty—but I cannot absolve myself of this task, now that it has begun. You may recall it was I who first informed him of the menace on your island."

Robyn's jaw tightened. She said nothing.

"I repeat my offer of assistance," said the patriarch.

Robyn wasn't at all sure that her lack of permission would prevent the cleric's involvement in this task. Too, she felt that there was an advantage in having him where Keane and Alicia could keep an eye on his activities. Nevertheless, it galled her to openly allow him to accompany an army of Corwell on business that was rightly a private matter of the kingdom.

"We'll march pretty fast," Alicia objected in the meantime. "The troops answering the muster will be young, and fit—and the terrain won't allow us the luxury of a carriage or wagon."

The priest smiled, amused by Alicia's skeptical glance at his large belly. "I wouldn't worry about that, my princess—these feet have carried me many a mile in the service of my god. No, I won't have any trouble keeping up."

"You have my permission to go," Robyn said suddenly.

"With the clear understanding that the High Princess is the leader of the expedition, and you are subject to her commands in all matters."

"Of course," murmured the priest, with a polite nod toward Alicia.

The queen picked up a small bell on the table and chimed it firmly. In another moment a soft knock sounded at the door, and she called "Enter."

The portal opened to reveal a pair of burly men-at-arms, one mustachioed and bow-legged while the other sported a fully bearded face atop a tall, muscular frame.

"You know, I believe, Sergeants-Major Sands and Parsallas," the queen said as the two men entered and knelt. Alicia and Keane recognized them both as veteran and well-respected members of the garrison.

"Greetings, my queen . . . and princess, too," said Sands, the bow-legged officer, speaking for his companion as well. "The muster has gone out and we stand ready for your commands."

Robyn turned back to the princess. "These two men are loyal in all respects, solid veterans and wise soldiers. I suggest you give their advice some heed during the march." She turned back to the gruff-looking officers. "The Princess Alicia will command the expedition," she concluded.

"Very good, Your Majesty," said Parsallas, winking at Alicia. She remembered him as a good-humored and avuncular warrior, and the presence of the two veterans she found strongly heartening.

"Now," announced the High Queen, rising and speaking with a tone of finality that clearly ended the meeting. "You'd best start making your preparations. I expect you'll want to march with tomorrow's dawn."

* * * * *

The *Princess of Moonshae* encountered the storm on the fourth day out from Corwell, as she sailed steadily northward into the Sea of Moonshae. The hulking mass of Oman's

Isle, gathered around the crowning summit of the Icepeak, had lain off the starboard horizon for more than a day. To port, though invisible in the distance, lay the northman-populated isle of Norland.

Prior to the gale the weather had been, if anything, exceptionally mild, with sporadic and unpredictable winds that kept the longship tacking for long hours with little forward progress. They had come through the Strait of the Leviathan in short order, but now that the sea had opened they couldn't seem to get a helpful wind. If it hadn't been for Tavish, who had amused the captain and crew with a wide assortment of musical tales, Brandon felt they might have all gone mad from boredom.

The Prince of Gnarhelm had begun to chafe at the delay, longing to see the great lodges of his home and to share the fellowship of his father's great hall. Too, the memory of the green-eyed princess he had left behind caused him constant agitation. Every little delay seemed, to Brandon Olafsson, a matter of damning frustration.

Then came the summer storm, boiling upward in the late afternoon, forming looming black thunderheads, dark and ominous even as the slanting rays of the sun outlined them in detailed relief. Within fifteen minutes the air whipped itself into a fury, howling down at them from the north with sudden rage and irresistible force. Winds lashed the formerly placid sea into a frothing maelstrom of angry, whitecapped swells. Spray stung the young captain's eyes, blinding his crewmen too as the veteran sailors crouched in the hull. With the sail trimmed to a small square of canvas, Brandon squinted to the east.

He knew that the rocky shore of Oman's Isle lay somewhere in the murk, but he didn't know how close—so quickly had the waves and wind enclosed and blinded them. Yet he well remembered that this stretch of coast had few sheltered bays, and many long expanses of fang-toothed boulders and precipitous granite cliffs. They would find only disaster if they drew too close to the island.

"We've got to turn and run with the wind!" bellowed Knaff the Elder, Brandon's veteran helmsman. Now he clenched the tiller in his muscular hands as spray lashed his long gray hair back from his head, plastering his beard to his broad chest. He grinned in savage delight at nature's wrath, yet he was too good a sailor to want to risk the ship and crew in such an unequal contest.

Brandon's eyes swung to the north, bitterly reflecting the slow pace of their advance. An hour or two of running before this storm would cost them more than a day's worth of progress. He saw the stocky figure of Tavish, crouched behind the figurehead and staring at the spuming sea. If the bard hadn't been forced to take cover, the gods curse him if Brandon Olafsson would do so!

"Ride her out!" he commanded, squinting into the wind as if to prove that the gale was no match for a northman's determination.

Waves climbed before them, looming like mountains on the horizon, then crashing along the sleek hull. Skillfully Knaff steered between the crests wherever possible, and when the longship had to take a wave full upon her prow he guided her with stoic courage straight into the foaming teeth of the breakers.

The *Princess of Moonshae* wallowed up a steeply sloping wave, barely cresting the summit before a chaotic swirl of spray thundered around them, over the gunwales and washing down the length of the hull. Northman sailors, already bailing frantically, redoubled their efforts. Many cast wary eyes at their prince, wondering whether their captain's grim determination to proceed would prove the death of them all.

But even Brandon eventually had to face the inevitable. The wind drove at them too hard, the waves loomed too high, for the ship to maintain the steady northward course. Cursing silently against the gods that thwarted him, he shook his head in fury.

"All right!" he assented grimly. "Bring her around as soon as you can!"

A series of rolling crests tumbled past them and Knaff held the *Princess* steady through the succession of powerful blows. Then, spotting a momentary lull, he heeled hard on the rudder, bringing the sleek longship through a slashing turn on the inside of a rolling trough of seawater. The vessel lurched sickeningly on her beam, but then a quick adjustment by Knaff righted her atop a breaking crest.

Meanwhile, Tavish had backed away from the prow and settled herself on one of the rowing benches, keeping a secure grasp around a nearby thwart. The seas must have gotten too rough for her, the captain mused, deriving some satisfaction from the fact. He realized, then, that his rash course had been a foolish mistake, brought on by his own desire to confront the feelings that stormed within him. Just as well we turned, Brandon grunted to himself—imagine risking the lives of his crew, the survival of his ship, out of the brooding and longing for a Ffolkwoman!

But now the ship rode with the storm, not against it, and the waves rolled away from beneath the sturdy hull. Sliding forward with dizzying speed, the ship raced southward, propelled by the wind and the storm and careening across the choppy surface.

Full dark settled around them, and the storm's fury lasted for several more hours—hours during which the *Princess of Moonshae* raced with the wind, riding the pitching waves with elegant grace. For a time the strains of Tavish's harp accompanied them through the night, but finally the bard fell into a deep slumber. The ship raced on, surrounded now only by the sounds of the crashing sea.

Yet, as Brandon had feared, the miles swept by with dizzying speed. Though the storm faded into a stiff blow during the middle of the night, there was no longer any question of turning and challenging the wind—in the inky darkness, that would almost certainly prove to be a suicidal course.

Finally a gray light began to diffuse through the mist. A break in the clouds came with the dawn, and Brandon cursed when he saw the Icepeak, now laying far to the stern as it emerged from a low-hanging blanket of clouds. And still the wind blew from the north, blocking any serious attempt to return to their original course.

"The sea stands against us," Knaff noted, with a grunted acknowledgement of the prince's frustration.

"Aye," Brand muttered bitterly. He knew these isles, and knew that the direct route home was not a good path for this trip.

"Mark a course to the east," he said after a few moments consideration. "We'll take her through the Strait of Oman."

That route, known from many voyages to each of the veteran sailors, offered good shelter from a northerly gale, and although it represented an increase in distance, the overall time of the voyage could be reduced.

"Wise choice," Knaff announced in hearty acknowledgment.

Since the *Princess of Moonshae* had already passed the southern terminus of Oman's Isle, the helmsman immediately veered her to an easterly bearing. Within a few minutes, the swells around them grew noticeably smaller, with tops of steely gray or green rather than the angry whitecaps of the storm.

Only then did the crewmen breathe a collective sigh of relief, knowing they had at last entered the sheltered waters of the Strait of Oman.

* * * * *

In the night, Deirdre grew restless, rising and pacing her rooms like a caged animal. She cast a spell of silence around her, for she knew that her mother slept lightly in the next room. That was part of her tension, she knew. She felt trapped by the overweening presence of the druid queen.

Again she thought of her father, riding alone across Gwynneth against the forces of chaos. She felt like one of those forces, a powerful instrument, perhaps even a weapon, poised and ready for use.

And in the spirit of chaos, she had no idea of which way her weapon—herself—would strike.

* * * * *

"Now, my deadly blade . . . now you grow finely honed, almost ready to strike. . . ."

Talos chortled, sound gurgling like the seething of a volcanic caldron. The god of chaos and evil saw that his vengeance was near, yet for once, his attention was not directed at the princess who slowly prepared to serve him.

Instead, his delight was fixed upon a darkened forest clearing. There, repeating a ritual he had begun to master, a hulking troll raised a great axe and deliberately sliced off the fingers of his two hands.

❧7❧

The Battle of Codscove

Thurgol stood atop the same low hill from which he had first observed the human town and its sheltered bay. Though he stood in plain sight of the town, all the firbolgs of his army were gathered close behind, concealed from view and lolling in the morning shade as they awaited their chieftain's command.

Below Thurgol, spreading into six broad columns of about two dozen apiece, Baatlrap's trolls marched steadily toward the village. On his lofty vantage, the giant chieftain was stunned by the multitude of his green-skinned allies. Where had they all come from? They crossed green swaths of crops, leaving great brown trails in the dirt as their clawed feet chewed up the moist dirt and mashed wheat, alfalfa, and corn into mud. The wolfdogs paced eagerly at their heels.

The humans in the village, he saw, reacted predictably to the appearance of the trolls. With no wall to protect them, they gathered into companies and advanced quickly to meet the approaching trolls. The giant-kin saw people scrambling through the streets, racing this way and that. The knights stumbled to their horses and mounted, then stood in a tiny knot on the village green, apparently bickering about what to do next.

Several ranks of archers hastened out of the village, forming a long line between the outlying houses and the approaching trolls.

Good! This was the reaction Thurgol awaited. "Follow me!" he bellowed, immediately dropping below the crest of the hill and gesturing to the waiting band of firbolgs. The giants rose to their feet in a mass, quickly breaking into a lumbering trot as they followed their chieftain down the gradually descending ridgeline, out of sight of the men in the village.

Within a few minutes, they reached an enclosing fringe of forest. This was part of the broad woods of Winterglen, Thurgol had earlier noticed. In fact, the concealment of the trees extended all the way to the shoreline, ending only a few hundred yards from the western fringe of the village. It was the closest an attacker could come without falling under direct observation by the defenders—and, hence, within range of arrow fire from the deadly longbows of the Ffolk.

According to the plan hammered out by Thurgol and Baatlrap, the trolls would take their time reaching the edge of the village, knowing that the barrage of arrows could do the wiry predators little significant damage. During this time, however, they would draw the full attention of the archers, or so it was hoped.

He pictured the scene in the fields, imagining the methodical advance of the trolls. The steel-headed arrows would fly as thick as rain, in volley after volley. Perhaps the humans would raise a ragged cheer when the trolls seemed to falter, the monsters pausing to pluck the missiles from their skin, snap them in two, and cast them to the ground. More and more arrows would fly, to be pulled out and cast aside as the patient trolls allowed their wounds to heal, though doubtlessly growing increasingly irritable and bloodthirsty in annoyance.

That was the plan, anyway. All Thurgol could hope was that the trolls stuck to their part of it. Huffing from the exertion of his pounding gait, the firbolg pushed his way through the woods with growing urgency, knowing that he had no time for delay. Fronds and ferns tickled his legs, but fortunately there was little dense underbrush to obstruct their passage.

Garisa hobbled beside him. The old shaman, with her woolen banner of the Silverhaft Axe fluttering in the wind, moved with surprising speed. She hissed and cackled encouragement to the other firbolgs, waving the pennant with unflagging enthusiasm. Though she hadn't been eager to make this attack, she had embraced the assault wholeheartedly once it had been ordered.

Thurgol heard a soft sound before him, but at first he was uncertain whether it was the wind in the trees or the breaking of waves on the coast coast. Then, in another moment, the trees abruptly gave way to a stark, rocky shoreline. Thurgol slowed cautiously as he saw blue water between the gaps in the trunks, staying back from the sea's edge to avoid exposing himself to discovery.

Though he didn't know his exact location, he knew that he would reach the village if he followed the shoreline to the right. Cautiously now, taking more care with silence and concealment than with speed, the firbolgs crept through the verdant woods. Soon patches of sunlight came into view ahead, and in another moment, they had reached the edge of the forest. Barely three hundred paces away, they saw a collection of ramshackle fishing huts, and beyond, the larger houses of Codscove.

Nevertheless, the defense of this side of the town hadn't been neglected, Thurgol saw. Perhaps a hundred men-at-arms stood or sat in the shade along the town's edge. Some of them stared toward the woods, but most seemed to listen intently to the sounds of the battle raging in the field. Buildings obscured the trolls from Thurgol's view, but he heard bellows and taunts and cries of battle. The snarls and savage barks of the wolfdogs punctuated the chaos, and the firbolg chieftain knew that the great canines pressed savagely forward beside their trollish masters. Judging from the sounds of the fighting, which grew louder with each passing second, Thurgol suspected the gangly monsters had already charged into the town.

Knowing the time for his own attack was ripe, the firbolg chieftain nevertheless paused for a moment's nagging doubt. Once again he couldn't entirely convince himself that this was necessary. He looked longingly at the waters of the strait. The rising bulk of the Icepeak on Oman's Isle was visible in the clear morning air, less than a score of miles away but separated from them by a seemingly uncrossable barrier of water.

More shouts—shrill screams of human agony and blood-curdling cries of trollish triumph—rang from the nearby battlefield, and the men-at-arms before the firbolgs became more agitated. The snarling of the wolfdogs increased in fury, and a hideous shriek of terror signaled another human falling to those implacable jaws. Abruptly, as Thurgol watched in astonishment, most of the humans before him picked up their weapons and ran toward the sound of the fighting. Barely two dozen stood in place now, shouting at their comrades to return to their posts.

"Charge!" Thurgol bellowed, pushing through the last screen of brush to emerge onto the coastal field. All around him, the giant-kin came smashing out of the forest, sounding for all the world like blinded bulls stumbling through a tangled maze of fencework. Their own bellows joined the cries of their chieftain, and the firbolgs lunged across the field toward the gaping humans defending Codscove's shantytown.

A few of these had bows and raised the weapons, casting desultory arrows into the onrushing rank of giants. Thurgol seized one of the boulders from his pouch and hurled it on the run, cursing as it sailed over an archer's head. A dozen other rocks missed the same target, but the one that hit proved sufficient. The bowman dropped like a felled tree, blood flowing from a gaping wound on his skull.

The other archers met similar fates as the firbolgs rushed closer. Thurgol raised his club, the old battle rage once again seizing him in its bloodthirsty grip. He cursed as the few humans before him turned away and vanished into the maze of shacks and sheds. Their cowardice made sense; these were the men, after all, who wouldn't join their comrades in rallying to the sound of fighting, but the disappearance of his quarry enraged Thurgol beyond all his previous fury.

He smashed his club through the roof of a ramshackle building, crudely pleased as the structure splintered into pieces from the force of the blow. Stepping through the shattered remains, he saw a human swordsman darting from the wreckage toward another, more sturdy building. Thurgol caught him in two quick bounds, dropping the man with a crushing blow that almost knocked the wretch's head from his shoulders.

All around him, the firbolgs shouted in triumph, wading into the motley buildings, chasing out and killing the few humans they found there. The giant-kin began to smash the shacks with clubs, fists, and feet, until very little of the shantytown remained.

The sturdy building that had originally attracted Thurgol's victim proved to be an exception. It was some kind of fish warehouse, judging from the smell, but it benefitted from far sturdier construction than the other buildings they had come across. Now a number of men had barricaded themselves inside, jabbing through cracks in the walls with sharp spears at any firbolg who dared approach.

One of the giant-kin near Thurgol grunted in deep, sudden pain. Stumbling to his knees and cursing, the firbolg pulled an arrow from his shoulder.

"Up there!" cackled Garisa, pointing a bony finger at the archer, who tried to duck out of sight on the roof of the fish warehouse. A barrage of rocks followed him into his hiding place, with what effect the firbolgs couldn't tell. No more arrows came down from the roof, however.

"Smash down the door!" shouted Thurgol as battle-crazed giants teemed around him, probing and smashing through the ruined shantytown, shaking fists and clubs, throwing stones, and bellowing savagely at the tightly secured warehouse.

A pair of firbolgs lunged at the door, carrying a heavy timber between them. The foot of the beam crunched into the solid portal, creaking the barrier on its hinges but failing to bash it open. Immediately a long spear snaked from a crack beside the entrance, its barbed head driving deep into the flank of one of the lumbering attackers. The firbolg cried out loudly in pain, stumbling away from the door in panic. His companion, left holding the heavy timber by himself, dropped the beam and hastened after the wounded giant-kin.

"All of you, attack!" shouted Thurgol, his own fury compelling him to focus on this stubbornly defended building. Firbolgs surged against the square structure from all sides, smashing against the walls, crashing makeshift battering rams into the two doors. They smashed the shutters over the place's windows, but these apertures proved too small for firbolg bodies. Instead, they opened the attackers up to murderously accurate short-range bow fire from within the darkened warehouse. The giants, on the other hand, couldn't even see their attackers in the shadows.

Still the doors held firm. Thurgol gathered two dozen firbolgs together, commanding them to hoist a long, stout pole that had once supported the roof of an inn. The giant-kin broke into a lumbering gallop, bearing down on the much-battered front door of the warehouse. Though the leaders flinched out of the way as the inevitable polearms projected from gaps beside the entrance, the bulk of the giants drove the ram home with irresistible power.

The door to the warehouse snapped free from its hinges, tumbling into a pile of barrels that had been used to brace it. The latter scattered like ninepins, rolling through the warehouse amid a tangled mass of firbolgs, battering ram, and the unfortunate defenders, who tried to dodge out of the way.

Thurgol stepped through the door in time to see a human spearman drive his weapon into the unprotected back of a firbolg who had fallen to the floor. The giant bellowed in agony as the man pulled his weapon free, raising it for another, this time fatal, thrust.

But the chieftain of Blackleaf got there first. Thurgol broke the human's body like a twig with a single blow of his club, killing him instantly and sending the corpse flying into the wall like a broken rag doll. The wounded firbolg squirmed on the floor, unable to rise, and Thurgol stepped over him to follow the charge into the warehouse.

Humans with swords tried to make a stand around the breach, while others threw open the back doors of the box-like structure. Here they met the other half of Thurgol's band, however. The chieftain hadn't been foolish enough to commit all his giants against one side of the building. Led by Garisa's shouts of encouragement, these firbolgs charged into the desperately fleeing humans, slaughtering them by the dozen as they poured like lemmings from the door.

Thurgol grunted from the pain of a sword cut beside his knee, bashing out the brains of the insolent human swordsman who had injured him. By this time, the firbolgs roamed throughout the warehouse, more and more of them piling through the two entrances until the entire band had collected around their leader. They raised a lusty cheer, and the chieftain felt a cruel flush of triumph.

Then he reflected: There hadn't been more than a few dozen men in this whole place, and it had taken something like two hundred firbolgs the better part of an hour to root them out. When he put the fight into these terms, it didn't cause his heart to swell with martial pride.

Such concerns were beyond the interest of his troops, however, especially after one of them discovered that the warehouse had stored more than fish. Indeed, this seemed to be the biggest liquor repository a town the size of Codscove could possibly need! Casks were broken open before Thurgol even noticed the discovery, and in moments, the smell of flowing rum began to rival even the stench of gutted fish.

* * * * *

Some four hundred stalwart men-at-arms answered the High Queen's mustering within twenty hours. Mostly they came from Corwell Town, but cantrevs Dynnatt and Koart contributed small companies of footmen as well. Nearly twoscore of the Corwell men were mounted and carried light lances; the others included many with longbows and the rest bearing swords and shields. Each man also carried two flasks of highly flammable oil.

The two sergeants-major organized the recruits in the courtyard of Caer Corwell. Sands barked at the swordsmen and archers, organizing them into four companies of march, while Parsallas shouted and harangued the riders and spearmen, forming a long central formation and assigning the horsemen to assume various scouting duties once the formation took to the march.

Robyn stood upon a balcony in the keep, addressing the men gathered in the courtyard below. Alicia and Keane waited at the head of the great file, with the Exalted Inquisitor of Helm off to the side.

"For the first time in a generation," she exhorted them, "the giant-kin have broken the peace, carving a path of destruction across the face of Myrloch Vale and the Winterglen! Will you men join your king and march against them?"

The resulting cry echoed from the walls of the castle, clearly audible even down in Corwell Town.

"Your king already rides," she continued, turning to look clearly at the cleric of Helm. "In the name of the goddess, go forth and restore the Balance! I name the Princess Alicia as your commander, the noble Sir Keane as her lieutenant."

"For the kings of Corwell!" shouted the men, their deep voices rumbling in unison as they chanted the ancient battle cry of the kingdom: "The kings of Corwell!"

Robyn lowered her gaze to rest upon her daughter's uplifted face. "Go now, Princess. Find the enemies of the goddess and bring them to the right!"

"Aye, my queen!" pledged Alicia, with a bow. In another moment, she sprang into her saddle, waiting as Keane and the cleric mounted somewhat more slowly.

"Forward!" she cried. A thumping song begun by a few veterans, rhythmic in tempo and nonsensical in verse, brought the men into a steady march. Alicia and the other riders circled the courtyard and passed through the gatehouse, followed by each rank of footmen in turn, after they clumped proudly past the queen's balcony.

"For the kings of Corwell!" Once again the battle cry echoed from the walls, ringing firmly as the column of men made its way through the gatehouse and onto the castle road.

Just as Alicia, mounted on her fleet mare Brittany, led the column from the gatehouse down the long, descending curve of the road, another rank of men hove into view, coming across the moor from the south. The princess was delighted to hold up the march until the newcomers, forty keen-eyed crossbowmen from Llyrath Forest, fell in at the end of the line. Despite an all-night march, the hearty woodsmen had no difficulty following the rest of the column.

Robyn stood alone in her window for several minutes after that, watching them start across the moors toward the northern highlands. She had given Alicia a map showing a good pass, hitherto known only to a few druids. It should allow them to reach the western shore of Myrloch by the second day out of Corwell.

"Well, they're gone. *Now* what do we do for excitement?" The voice, from the door of her chamber, whirled the queen around in shock, even as she realized that Deirdre had simply entered without knocking.

"You—you startled me," she said unnecessarily.

"Obviously," Deirdre said, walking into the room but staying away from the sunswept balcony. "There's quite a chill," she added, wrapping her arms around her ribs.

"I hadn't noticed." Robyn quickly stepped into the room and pulled the large double doors shut. "How are you feeling this morning?"

"I feel fine, Mother!" snapped the princess with a suggestion of her earlier vitality. "In fact, this place is starting to drive me crazy. I'd like to get out of here!"

"Go for a walk—perhaps even a ride," her mother suggested. "When the sun gets a little higher, it's sure to be a warm day."

Deirdre shook her head firmly. "No, not like that . . . not out with people. I want to get away . . . from . . ."

She didn't finish the thought. Instead, she rose abruptly and crossed to the door. She stopped, as if she wanted to say something more to the High Queen. But then she spun on her heel and quickly left the room.

* * * * *

The moorhounds coursed after a stag in full voice, wailing across the gentle ridgetop, down through the forested valleys, and into the tangled bottomlands and fens. Tristan spurred Shallot on, and the great war-horse thundered after the racing dogs, carrying the High King down a steep slope and plunging into the dense forest beyond.

Thorns tore at Tristan's leggings, and only his armor allowed him to bull his way through the ensnaring thickets. Hacking with his great sword, the king forced a path for himself and his struggling horse, until finally they broke onto a trail and thundered deeper into the wood, following the baying song of the hounds.

The hunt drew Tristan into its vital embrace, so much so that nothing else mattered. He felt the terror of the stag as a powerful enticement pumping through his veins. His lance trailed behind—there was no other way to carry the ungainly weapon in this tangled terrain—yet he longed for the chance to raise the long shaft, driving the barbed head toward the stag's pounding, fear-stricken heart.

He knew that the hounds would take the beast, and he understood that this was the law of the hunt, right and proper and every bit in keeping with the Balance. Yet at the same time, he felt a tearing sense of jealous rage, a powerful compulsion that told him that he himself deserved to slay the beast, had earned the first bloody taste of fresh meat.

Tristan rode like a wild animal, racing through the hunt,

desperately thrilled at the thought of the kill so close at hand. Above the tangled growth, he caught a glimpse of the antlered head cresting a grass-covered ridge, the baying of the hounds sounding close behind. When the great dogs broke into the clear behind the stag, the mighty animal had already disappeared over the summit.

Baying frantically, their song resounding from the very heavens, the five moorhounds bounded after their terrified quarry. Tristan angrily spurred Shallot into a desperate, thundering gallop, urging the powerful stallion up the steep slope. The High King's surroundings had ceased to matter; he knew only the scent of blood in his nostrils, the imminent fate of his quarry before him.

Cresting the low ridge, he saw the stag splash through a wide, shallow stream below. Still howling, the dogs leaped into the water, bounding through the streambed, their slavering jaws snapping after the bounding form of the great deer.

Shallot plunged down the following slope with admirable courage, the stallion's powerful forelegs bearing the brunt of the rapid descent. The war-horse carried the king around the most tangled thickets, past the more precipitous dropoffs, retaining his balance on treacherous terrain, springing downward as if he sensed his rider's need to complete this hunt with his own arm, his own steel.

The stag plunged into a wide meadow of lush greenery and blazing flowers, but then water gleamed to either side, flying outward in shimmering curtains of spray. The animal's mindless flight carried it farther into a marsh, and as it slowed, the huge hounds sprang into the mire in pursuit.

The stag lunged and kicked, reaching with desperate fore-hooves for solid ground but finding only bottomless muck. Splashing and thrashing, the creature pressed ahead, but now the howling dogs closed in steadily. The stag located a low hummock of mud, perilous fundament amid the morass but the only dry ground within reach. Scrambling out of the water, the cornered beast turned its impressive rack of antlers toward the bounding, wailing hounds.

"Hold!" cried Tristan as Shallot reached the edge of the mire and plunged in without a moment's delay. The dogs, well disciplined to their master's command, froze immediately. They barked and snapped at their quarry, but did not close to bite.

The king spurred his plunging horse, trying to drive Shallot to greater efforts as the huge stallion labored through the clutching mud of the swamp. Here was his chance! Tristan raised his lance, leveling the gleaming steel tip at the trapped stag and kicking the stallion into even greater efforts to charge. Then a strange urge held his hand. He thrust the lance into the mud and instead drew his longsword, feeling a flush of impending victory at the satisfying weight of the blade.

The five dogs snapped and snarled, but obeyed his command not to attack. As Shallot carried Tristan onto the hummock of mud, however, the stallion reared back in fright. Clutching his sword, Tristan stared in shock as gray, skulking figures emerged from the brush beyond. Leaping forward with sleek grace and quick, animal power, a pack of lean wolves gathered in a protective circle around the frightened deer. More and more of the lupine forms, nearly as big as his hounds, pounced forward, forming a ring of bristling fangs and raised hackles surrounding the panting, exhausted stag.

The baying of the hounds rose to a furious pitch as the five dogs confronted the wolf pack. A strange kind of equilibrium seemed to hold them in place, only a few paces apart. Ranthal, leading the hounds, stepped forward, stiff-legged and snarling, but the largest of the wolves moved forward from the pack to meet him.

The wild animal's yellow eyes stared, unblinking, at the huge hound. Unconsciously Tristan held his breath. He felt certain that Ranthal would hurl himself at the wolf unless a command from the king held him back. But so powerfully did the hunting song pulse through Tristan's veins that he gave no thought to restraint, never even considered telling his dog to hold.

Yet, surprisingly, Ranthal did not attack. In fact, after a few moments confronting the wolf's baleful glare, the great moorhound crept backward, rejoining his four packmates with almost palpable relief. The wolves, meanwhile, made no aggressive move, instead holding firm in their protective ring. Any attack against the stag would have necessitated a charge through their bristling fangs.

Astonished, Tristan held his sword before him, angled toward the ground, and considered the merits of a short, deliberate charge. Shallot could carry him through the wolves with little danger, and he knew that the hounds would protect the flanks of the great war-horse. Yet still something held his hand—he didn't know what the cause— as the bloodlust of the hunt slowly drained away. He felt as if he awakened from some kind of dream, not entirely certain how he had come to be where he was. Carefully he lowered his sword, no longer wishing to drive it into the flesh of his quarry.

"Greetings, King of Callidyrr, Monarch of the Ffolk, Uniter of the Moonshaes, and Slayer of Giant-kin!" The voice, heavy with irony, nearly knocked Tristan from his saddle with raw surprise, for the words had come from the great wolf!

"Who—who are you?" he demanded.

"Who am *I?*" The wolf sounded amused. "Rather, ask yourself who are you, High King Tristan Kendrick!"

"You've answered that question yourself!" he retorted, still shaken by the unusual speaker. He knew insolence when he heard it, and it wasn't an attitude he was used to or accepting of.

"Have I? Or is there more to it than that?"

The creature's irritating responses, meeting a question with another question, grated on the king's nerves. Growing angry, he raised the tip of his sword again. "I tire of your word games. Explain your reasons for blocking me from my game!"

If the wolf had heard the king's demand, he gave no indication. Instead, the lanky form sat on its haunches and regarded Tristan with those two impossibly bright eyes.

"Answer me, beast!" snapped the High King, yet even as his anger built, he felt a swirling sense of confusion enclosing him. This wasn't right, he knew—and not just because a wolf spoke to him with a human voice. No, the protection the wolves offered to the stag, *that* was certainly unnatural, and the carefully neutral way they regarded his own dogs both combined to give the man a sense of caution.

"Tell me, human king"—the way the wolf said the word sounded as if humans made a very low grade of king indeed—"what great cause brings you to Myrloch Vale? Why do you ride here, frightening the animals and terrorizing the Earthmother's own deer?"

"What business—" For a moment, outrage wrenched the words from Tristan's mouth, but his brain, although it worked a little more slowly than his jaws, suddenly focused on the wolf's question. Why indeed was he here?

With a quick look at the sun, he saw that his chase of the stag had carried him far to the west of his planned route. He had lost several hours in the exuberant chase, not to mention the time needed to retrace his steps and rest his weary horse.

"I ride against the enemies of the goddess!" he declared, as if to remind himself at the same time as he informed his questioner. He no longer thought of it as a mere beast of the forest. "Firbolgs and trolls have broken the peace of the vale, marching against their neighbors for war and plunder. My mission is nothing less than the restoration of the Balance in Myrloch Vale!"

"An interesting tactic," murmured the wolf, the golden eyes taking on a sly cast. "This stag, for instance—he represents a great threat to the Balance, does he?"

Tristan flushed. "No! I was hunting. I grew tired of trail fare and desired fresh meat."

The wolf cast an amused, skeptical eye at the great deer.

The animal stood nearly as tall as Shallot, with a rack of antlers spreading farther to the sides than a tall man's armspan. Finally the barrel chest had ceased its heaving, and the stag seemed to listen attentively, watching the exchange between the wolf and the rider.

"You must be *very* hungry," noted the great lupine, after completing his comparison.

Shaking his head in annoyance, Tristan was about to retort that he didn't intend to eat the whole stag when a cautious voice urged him to hold his tongue. Suddenly he understood the wolf's point. "My hounds must eat as well," he finished lamely.

"Of course—all things must eat! This is the way of the Balance. But I will tell you something, King of the Ffolk: You were chasing a lord of Myrloch Vale, one who has ruled over his domain for as long as you have held sway in your own. It is a domain that has been free from humans, except for such as honor the vale and its life. Now, is it the purpose of this great animal's life, the purpose of the Balance, that he should feed a human trespasser and his dogs?"

Suddenly Tristan felt an appalling sense of sadness. The wolf was right, of course—the wolf, or whoever this was speaking to him.

Consumed by the force, the magic, of the hunt, he had all but forgotten the threat of the firbolg army, the monsters that even now menaced his subjects to the north. For a moment, he remembered the urgency that had seized him upon the first notion of his grand quest. He had delayed no more than an hour before taking to the trail. Now he had wasted many times more than that on this frivolous chase!

No, he chastised himself, it was *worse* than frivolous. When he looked at the proud stag, which still stood before him even though it had recovered its breath, it occurred to him that slaying the beast might be as great a crime, in its own right, as was the firbolg sacking of Cambro.

"Who are you?" he asked again.

This time, he felt certain that the wolf's long, narrow jaws curled upward into a smile. "A friend," came the reply. Then, in a flash of movement, the wolf whirled and sprang away, followed by the others of his pack. In seconds, they had disappeared into the woods.

The stag remained standing on the hummock before Tristan, facing the five hounds. The dogs sat attentively, eyes fixed upon the stag but hindquarters planted firmly on the ground. Then, as if dismissing the interlopers gathered around him, the great animal lowered its muzzle to the fresh grass and began to graze.

"Come," the High King said firmly, and the dogs fell into file behind Shallot. The war-horse plodded back through the marsh, the hounds bounding along behind as they struggled to keep up. Finally they reached open woods and dry land, and Tristan urged the stallion into a lumbering trot.

He had a good deal of time to make up.

* * * * *

Even the shelter of the narrow strait did not improve Brandon's mood. The blasting of the storm and the lashing of the wind had diminished remarkably, but gray clouds scudded quickly across the sky. For its part, the sea remained angry, too, as a series of long, rolling crests swept against the *Princess of Moonshae*'s hull from the north.

The vessel heeled to starboard, plunging steadily eastward between the islands of Gwynneth and Oman. Despite the smoother waters near the Oman shore, Brandon ordered the ship to follow the southern coast of the strait, for there the wind was stronger and the longship's speed correspondingly improved.

"By Tempus!" muttered Brand, in his usual post beside Knaff at the stern. "Might as well have left it to the whimsy of the gods. I'm sure we could have sailed to the south and met a storm coming from that way as well!"

"As sure as the sunrise," Knaff agreed. "Best to hold steady on a nice, easy course."

Not sharing the young prince's urgency, the old helmsman didn't see any particular problem with their change of course. In fact, he felt that his captain could use a little calming down on that point, and Knaff was the only member of the crew who would dare make even a gentle insinuation along those lines. Even as he reflected, the thickest of the clouds blew past the sun, and bursts of illumination began to break through. Where it struck the water, the sea turned from ominous gray to a dark but powerfully beautiful azure.

"*I* like the change in the weather, myself!" Tavish announced, coming to the stern to join the two men. "Though you did a nice job of riding it out," she added.

"Those are the squalls that give the Sea of Moonshae its character," Knaff joked. The bard was forced to smile. Weeks earlier, before the rescue of King Kendrick, the old helmsman had been appalled at the thought of a female sailing on his ship. Now he welcomed her with easy grace and humor.

"It had quite enough character for me," she replied. "And personally I think that sunlight does a lot to improve the look of the waves."

"Aye—sparkle like diamonds, they do," Knaff said, resting his elbows on the transom with a sigh. Tavish leaned against the stern beside him, and the two of them watched the wake trail across the rolling blue waters of the strait.

"Well, *someone's* got to pilot this ship!" grumbled Brandon, annoyed that the two found it so easy to relax.

The prince cursed softly, then stalked through the hull, irritated that Knaff could be so calming when the prince didn't *want* to be calmed. He didn't want his tension soothed, and he wasn't even certain that his anger was caused by the diversion in their voyage. When he thought about it, he didn't want to be in Gnarhelm now, either.

No. Instead, he wanted to be with Alicia Kendrick.

"Smoke, Captain—off the starboard bow!"

The cry came from a lookout perched near the longship's sweeping figurehead as the *Princess of Moonshae* rushed along the shore of Gwynneth. With one arm wrapped around the proud and beautiful image carved from dark hardwood, the sailor at the bow shielded his eyes against the bright morning sun and then pointed to shore.

They all saw it then: a thin black plume rising a dozen or more miles away. As they watched, the column seemed to thicken, as if more and more tinder was added to the blaze.

"It's coming from the shore, inside a small bay," the lookout amplified.

"Codscove!" Brandon immediately guessed. There were only a few towns along these remote coasts, and though he had never been there, as a good captain he had learned of every possible haven and landfall in the Moonshae Islands.

"Take her into the bay," he commanded without a moment's hesitation. He was propelled mainly by curiosity, but the volume of smoke in the air indicated that they might have come upon a scene of real trouble.

"Hop to those oars, you laggards!" barked Knaff, wheeling on the rudder to send the ship running in toward the shoreline. The sail still bulged from the wind, but the experienced helmsman knew that the crew would likely have to row once they entered the sheltered bay.

Soon the *Princess of Moonshae* swept between the outflung peninsulas that bracketed Codsbay and protected the cozy town along the shore—protected it, at least, from the ravages of impersonal nature.

Now that community was anything but cozy, however, and it was obviously in need of more practical protection. Brandon saw numerous buildings ablaze and struggling figures on the wide commons in the center of the town. Riders dashed back and forth, and hulking attackers loomed beyond. They swiftly drew closer, and more details became apparent. The attackers were large and green-colored, with wiry limbs and beaklike noses, readily identifiable even from half a mile at sea.

"Trolls!" shouted the lookout, for the benefit of his less keen-eyed crewmates.

Once again the men looked to their captain for orders, and again Brandon didn't hesitate. This wasn't their fight. Most of the inhabitants of Codscove were Ffolk, although a few northmen had settled here in centuries past. Nevertheless, the frustration that had nagged at him, plus the knowledge that these were King Kendrick's subjects—*Alicia*'s subjects—gave him no room for consideration or doubt.

"Take up your arms, men!" he bellowed, hefting his own double-bitted axe. "We're going ashore!"

With strong strokes of the oars, his crewmen pushed the *Princess of Moonshae* straight toward the broad docks of Codscove.

* * * * *

Deirdre stalked the halls of the palace, more and more agitated by the enclosing walls, the deferential servants, and her solicitous family. By nightfall, she knew that she had had enough.

She returned to her apartments with the announcement that she intended to go to bed early. Then she barred the door, ostensibly so that no one would disturb her rest. She knew that her mother would no longer hear crying out in the night, nor any of the sounds of distress and agitation that had marked some earlier evenings.

Deirdre shuttered her window, lit several candles, and assumed a posture of meditation in the small parlor beside her bedroom. The princess grew more and more proficient at this ritual of faith. This time she rested in silence for only half an hour before she felt the world falling away from her.

Once again the infinite expanse of the void yawned around her. The Moonshae Islands sank to insignificance, and the words of the New Gods sang in her ears.

This time the songs of these gods called the princess to action. As Deirdre listened, she began to understand. She came to know that she was uniquely positioned to carry this word, this fresh doctrine, across the lands of her people. She was a High Princess of Moonshae, after all, and one of no little knowledge and power. The absorption of the mirror, she knew, was not a crippling thing—instead, it was a birth of power and might undreamed of in what she had come to remember as her mortal existence.

Yet at the same time she knew that she would meet tough, entrenched resistance. Much of that friction would come from the most potent enemy Deirdre had—the only one, in effect, who might be able to block her ambitions and desires.

That one was her mother, Robyn Kendrick—the druid queen of the isles.

* * * * *

"Go now and become the Wrath of Chaos!" The will of Talos passed through the ether, grasping the princess in a smoky but unbreakable embrace. Vigilant as ever, Helm looked on, pleased with the power he saw there.

And in the north, where he slumbered in his glacial vale, the demigod Grond Peaksmasher stirred. There was in existence only one key to his icy prison, but now—after all these centuries—he sensed that this key drew near.

❧ 8 ❧

A Princess in Defeat

"How long do we wait?" muttered Finellen as Brigit and Hanrald joined her around the breakfast fire. The dwarven column had marched the breadth of Winterglen, remaining a day or two behind the giants and trolls. The trail had been easy to follow. Several experienced dwarven woodsmen preceded the main body, probing the forest thoroughly in order to discover any potential ambush.

"It'll take a few days for the king's army to get here," Hanrald cautioned. "We have to hold off until we can unite our forces."

"Bah—*caution!*" exclaimed Finellen, making a curse of the word. "It doesn't become me. It doesn't become any dwarven warrior when there's a plain enemy before us, and a blood foe at that!"

"But think how much more damage you'll do to that enemy once you have the force to properly strike them!"

Finellen huffed, spitting into the coals of the fire. Yet she found it hard to argue with that point. The monsters' trail, a wide swath through Winterglen, bespoke of a large force, and several smaller paths had intersected it along the way. The latter led to speculation that the army of monsters had grown since the sacking of Cambro.

On the other hand, Finellen had merely her fifty veteran warriors. Even if they were motivated to glory by battle against a blood foe, the outcome of such an unequal battle would be a foregone conclusion: a disaster for the outnumbered dwarves. Still, that didn't make it any easier for the dwarven captain to accept her forced inaction.

She looked around the quiet camp. Numerous well-screened cookfires dotted the woods, sending the aroma of bacon wafting through the trees but raising no telltale plumes of smoke. The dwarves took their time about eating, since they all knew that there was no purpose in haste. Still, it agitated Finellen even further to see such a lackadaisical attitude among dwarves on the trail of war.

A human stepped from a clump of trees beside the dwarven captain's group, and Finellen spun on her heel, sputtering with surprise, as Danrak bowed politely and settled to the ground beside the others. The druid's comings and goings were always abrupt, and he had a distressing way of appearing in the center of the dwarven camp without having been observed by any of the pickets.

"Well, what did you find out?" demanded the dwarfwoman bluntly.

"They march on Codscove, as we feared," replied the druid sadly. "I left the army last night as it gathered into two great camps beside the town. I don't doubt that by now they've attacked."

"Damn!" snapped the dwarf. "And we sit here a day's march away! How many towns have to get sacked before we—" Abruptly she clamped her mouth shut, her bristling chin fixed in determination.

"Everybody up!" she bellowed, her voice ringing through the forested camp. "Douse your fires and swallow your bacon! We march in three minutes!" Finellen turned back to her immediate companions. "Maybe we can't take 'em in a fixed battle, but if they're occupied with Codscove, we might be able to hurt them from behind."

"It beats sitting around waiting for help that might come too late," Hanrald agreed.

"It *will* come too late," noted Danrak, "if what I saw last night is any indication."

The dwarves responded with alacrity to their leader's command, and within the allotted minutes, the full column took to the trail. The light-footed scouts scattered to form their wide screen, while the two riders followed at the rear. Finellen had made the indisputable point that the pair of horses were a lot noisier than the sure-footed dwarves leading the formation.

A new sense of urgency propelled the dwarves of Cambro as word of Danrak's information spread through the ranks. They hoisted their weapons, grimly buoyed by the prospects of wetting them in the enemy's blood. As a consequence, the two riders had to urge their horses into a trot just to keep up.

* * * * *

"Thurgol—come here!" hissed Garisa, her piercing voice somehow penetrating the boisterous firbolg celebration. The battle outside remained forgotten as the giant-kin all crowded into the storage house. The noises of combat, with the humans of Codsbay fiercely contesting against Baatlrap's trolls, occasionally came to them through the stout wooden walls. The firbolgs, Thurgol included, had little interest in pursuing the fight.

Over the last few minutes, the chieftain had occasionally thought that perhaps he should hasten his creatures back to the attack, but somehow his heart couldn't support the effort. Hearing the shaman's cry now, the firbolg chieftain looked up from the broken keg he had just seized from a young and undisciplined member of his band, as opposed to the old and undisciplined giant-kin who also celebrated raucously in the huge storage depot.

"What is it?" Thurgol barked at the elderly shaman, irritated by everything going on around him. "Can't it wait? I'm busy!"

"Get over here, you great oaf!" she hissed, in a tone that couldn't help but gain his attention.

For a moment, the chieftain considered responding to the ancient hag with angry words or even a thump from his club, but he well remembered Garisa's command of things of the spirit world. He decided he'd best not tempt such unnatural forces and grudgingly climbed to his feet.

"Look!" she crowed, pointing out the crack beside the warehouse door. It was the same crack the humans had used to thrust out with their deadly spears.

"A ship!" he said, amazed at the appearance of a sleek northman longship gliding toward the wharf.

"Yes—it comes to Codsbay just when we need it!"

Thurgol considered, suddenly intrigued by the shaman's implied suggestion. He peered through the crack again, watching the tall, long-braided captain direct the vessel toward the waterfront. The human's attention remained fixed upon the melee on the great commons square. Obviously he wasn't aware of the large force of firbolgs hidden in the building, even closer to the dock.

The ship drew up to the wharf barely a rock's throw from the battered warehouse, and the strapping northern warrior sprang to the dock, holding a huge battle-axe in one hand and gesturing to his crew.

"For Tempus and Gnarhelm!" he bellowed, and twoscore screaming warriors poured onto the dock at his heels. Howling like madmen, they raced toward the melee on the town commons.

Perhaps a dozen men remained aboard the ship. One of them, a gray-haired veteran, held the rudder as if he were a fixture of the vessel, commanding the other crewmen to push off. The giant watched the northmen raise oars, saw that they would drive them against the dock, pushing the vessel away from shore until their shipmates returned.

In that instant of realization, Thurgol saw an opportunity and acted quickly to seize it before it was perhaps forever removed. Crashing a brawny shoulder into the door, he sent it smashing outward.

"Charge!" he cried, his deep voice rumbling beneath the shrill sounds of battle. Somehow the urgency in his command caught even the attention of the rambunctious giant-kin.

"The ship!" screeched Garisa in support. "Go and take it! Seize our means to the Icepeak!"

A dozen firbolgs followed Thurgol in the first rush out the door. The gray-haired helmsman saw them immediately and cursed loudly for his men to hurry.

But the ship was too close and too heavy to move away instantly. The chieftain crossed the ground to the dock in ten quick strides, and then a leap carried him through the air to land heavily in the bench-lined hull. The craft rocked surprisingly from his weight, not to mention that of his fellows as they, too, sprang into the sturdy vessel. At least, most of them landed in the hull. The momentum of each leaping giant pushed the ship farther from the pier, so that the last few firbolgs splashed into the chill waters of Codsbay.

Aboard the *Princess of Moonshae*, Thurgol recovered his balance quickly, smashing his club against a nimble northman and sending the man flying over the side. Another sprang toward him, his face etched into berserking fury, but two of the chieftain's warriors tackled the fellow, pitching him over the gunwale with ease.

The veteran helmsman, Thurgol saw, raised a heavy axe and stood firm beside his tiller. Several firbolgs advanced against him, and the chieftain was impressed to see that the man exhibited not a flicker of fear.

"Wait—save him for me!" Thurgol shouted, calling off his crewmates.

Hefting his club, stumbling slightly as he tried to keep his balance in the unsteady ship, the chief of the giant-kin stalked down the center of the hull. The helmsman, standing on a raised platform in the stern, met the giant almost eye-to-eye. Neither combatant showed any inclination to flee as they raised their weapons and bent knees into a battle stance.

The longship rocked under Thurgol's feet, and the giant staggered, trying to keep his balance. The northman had no such difficulty. He flicked his axe with uncanny speed, cutting a deep gash in the chieftain's forearm. Cursing from the pain of the wound, Thurgol stepped back and hefted his club protectively.

But the gray-haired helmsman wouldn't be drawn from his post. Thurgol studied his foe as the longship's rocking settled down. He was surprised by how old the fellow was. Despite his wiry limbs and strong, knotted hands, the helmsman's hair was thinning, and his face had been weathered by many decades of sea storms. Still, when the giant-kin advanced again, the deadly axe whirled outward once more, this time carving a niche out of the firbolg's knobby club.

"Take him, Thurgol!" came a taunting cry from one of his young warriors.

"He's only a human!" howled another, enjoying the duel.

From the sounds behind him, the chieftain knew that the other northmen in the ship must already be dead or thrown overboard. It irked him that he faced the last of these determined warriors and that this one guarded an obviously key piece of navigational equipment, though Thurgol was not entirely certain of the rudder's purpose.

"Back, beast!" snapped the man, staging a sudden rush at the looming giant-kin.

Thurgol took a step backward, raising his club as if to parry another blow. The axe whipped out, striking low this time, and the firbolg chieftain lunged toward the charging man. Thurgol ignored the pain as the axe blade bit deep into his thigh. He swung, then cursed as the man ducked beneath the blow. Casting aside the club, he closed his hands about the man's surprisingly frail chest and lifted him up. The man kicked and punched as the giant pitched him over the transom. Thurgol stumbled to the deck, his leg collapsing as the helmsman plunged into Codsbay.

The giant chieftain knelt, watching with surprise the fountain of blood spurting from his wounded leg, yet it was with a grim sense of satisfaction that he looked down the length of the hull at the grinning faces of a dozen firbolgs.

Most of their faces showed delight, though already a few had begun to cast longing glances back to the shore.

* * * * *

Shallot cruised through the open forest at a smooth trot, broad hooves pounding rhythmically against the soft dirt while widely spread tree trunks allowed the king to ride for the most part upright in the saddle. Occasionally he ducked his head beneath a low, knotted limb, and his lance trailed behind in order to avoid entanglements, but he was quite pleased by their rapid progress.

The hounds coursed through the woods before and around him, staying in sight but ranging freely back and forth, frequently scaring rabbits from concealment. The great dogs had become adept at pouncing on the fleeing hares, and Tristan had several skinned carcasses swinging from his saddle. Mindful of his lesson from the mouth of the wolf, he would take only enough meat to feed himself and the dogs at their evening meal. Tomorrow, he knew, the forest would provide him with such additional bounty as he might need.

For three days, he had ridden steadily northward, his mind fixed upon his mission, his concentration rapt on the thought of a monstrous horde that marched through his realm and threatened his subjects.

Yet even as he considered the threat, he never regretted his decision to ride alone. Whether it came from a sense of human arrogance or deity-inspired destiny, his determination remained fixed. It was his quest to challenge the monsters, to teach them to honor the peace and return to their homes, or perish in their defiance.

He passed through realms of forest giants, beauty unsurpassed throughout the Moonshaes. Trees that had lived for a thousand years raised their crowns hundreds of feet over his own, and he rode beneath them with scarcely a glance. Meadows of blossoms more brilliant and varied than gemstones in hue and shade sprawled around him, yet he took no note as Shallot's broad hooves pressed some of the blooms into dirt.

Tristan rode until after sunset, when the darkness began to shroud the forest and make further travel dangerous.

Selecting a sheltered glade, closely surrounded by lush, tall evergreens, he made a small fire and cooked a rabbit for himself, giving a raw carcass to each of his loyal hounds.

As the fire sank to good cooking coals, he stared into the embers, enjoying the sizzling smell of his meat. But his ears remained elsewhere, probing through the forest night, listening for a particular sound.

But he did not hear the wailing song of the wolves.

* * * * *

Brandon sank his axe into the muscle-bound gut of a troll, knocking the hulking beast backward. Kicking with his booted foot, he dropped the creature like a felled tree and hacked again. This time his blow nearly sliced the grotesque head from the thin, knobby shoulders.

"Fire—we need fire!" he shouted, knowing that unless the gnarled body was burned, the monster would climb back to its feet within a few minutes.

Pausing to gasp for breath, he looked around the bloody, mud-stained commons of Codscove. The sudden attack of fifty veteran northmen had, if not turned the tide, at least stabilized the battle for a moment. Indeed, the trolls fell back cautiously before Brandon's howling crewmen, the short, lunging charges of several mounted knights, and the grim determination of the townsmen themselves, many of whom had already paid the ultimate price for their courage, as evidenced by the dozens of bodies strewn through the streets of the town and across the field.

"Captain—the ship!" The panicked cry, from one of his young sailors, sent spears of terror shooting through the Prince of Gnarhelm even before he turned around.

But as he spun, those spears turned to rending knives, for he saw that the unthinkable had happened. The *Princess of Moonshae* rocked in the water as a dozen or more giant bodies—firbolgs!—staggered through the hull. He saw one of the creatures pick up Knaff the Elder and hurl the old helmsman into the bay.

Where had the monsters come from? His heart seemed to wither in his chest as he saw them overrun his beloved ship, and at the same time, he saw more of the creatures pouring from the warehouse at the shore. An ambush! Had the dull creatures waited for just such an opportunity?

Brandon had left a dozen men to guard the ship, commanding them to row it a short distance from shore to prevent such an attack. Groaning in disbelief, he saw oars raised, cracking against each other as the clumsy beasts tried to guide the ship. The hulking beast who had thrown Knaff overboard handled the trailing rudder, using it like an oar, slowly starting the *Princess of Moonshae* through a long, gradual pirouette.

Knaff and several other crewmen, meanwhile, splashed their way to shore, climbing onto the dock some distance from the firbolgs gathering along the shore.

The prince felt as though his heart and soul had been torn away. He loved that ship more than anything else in the world! At the same time, his northman's stubborn courage started him thinking about how to get it back.

An unholy shriek arose from the green behind him, and Brandon whirled in time to see the rank of trolls, reformed and healed, surging onto the commons again. This time a deeper roar emerged from the firbolgs at the wharf. Those who hadn't made it to the longship now turned back to the battle, finally ready to help their trollish allies.

A knight on horseback, apparently the captain of Codscove's militia, thundered past Brandon, his lance lowered, a red pennant trailing from his helm. The lance ripped through the chest of a troll, but the monster fastened long claws into the horse's flanks as it pounded past. More and more of the fearsome attackers leaped onto the valiant horseman, dragging him from the saddle and burying him beneath a slavering pile of horror.

The firbolgs lumbered forward too, more and more of them emerging from the smashed wreckage of the fish warehouse. Beyond them, beyond the dock, Brandon could see his once proud vessel, sail furled, hull rocking uneasily from the weight of her boisterous captors.

But the Prince of Gnarhelm had fought too many battles to dwell for long on the unattainable. He fixed his eyes upon one of the leading firbolgs, planted his feet firmly, and waited for the fellow to approach. The giant saw Brandon, sensed the challenge in his stance, and uttered a bellow of hatred. Raising a knotty club, the brute charged at the smaller human with the thunderous force of an avalanche.

At the last second, Brandon ducked his head and took one step to the side. The ground shook from the impact of the firbolg's club, but the northman's blow was already in motion. The giant-kin grunted, exposed for a moment as he leaned forward, his arms angling down to the ground with his club gripped firmly in his knobby fists. Brandon's axe sliced upward, above the arms, to chop deep into the firbolg's unprotected neck.

The giant fell with a strangled sound of bubbling air, thrashing on his face for only a moment before he perished in a growing circle of blood. By this time, Brandon had deflected the attack of a second firbolg, then stumbled back with the rest of his men, driven by the furious charge of the hulking humanoids.

Trolls shrieked in savage glee as they pressed home their attack, rending screaming humans with tooth and claw. Grunting giants closed from the other direction, pressing the valiant warriors off the now-muddy commons into a neighborhood of shacks and houses. Attacked from three sides, pressed by trolls and firbolgs, the humans of Codscove and their hapless allies from the north had only one choice. As a mass, with a few courageous knights and northmen guarding the rear, they fled toward the forest, abandoning their town to the brutal attackers.

* * * * *

Newt meandered through a clump of fading lilacs, relishing high summer in Myrloch Vale. There really was no better place in all the world, he decided. He wasn't at all hampered in his conclusion by the fact that he knew very little about the rest of the world, at least the parts that lay beyond the Moonshae Islands.

The faerie dragon was one who could find delight in the darkest winter night, in a howling tempest off the sea, or in the whistling scourge of a hot, dry wind. Yet there was something about summertime, and something about this great valley, that made for an unbeatable combination.

The faerie dragon's butterfly wings hummed through the air. Idly, without really paying attention to his appearance, Newt shifted his scales from the brilliant green of the surrounding foliage to the soft blues and purples of a field of columbine. He sniffed at a wild rose and his color became a matching crimson.

A noise in a thicket attracted Newt's attention, and he buzzed over to see what caused the commotion, blinking out of sight as a routine precaution. Pressing the lush branches aside, he saw a huge brown form hunched over a large rotten log.

A bear! The huge ursines were rare in the Moonshaes, and it had been many years since Newt had seen one, but he immediately remembered that the gruff, short-tempered creatures made for splendid entertainment.

Silently and invisibly the faerie dragon hovered above the bear, observing the broad paws, tipped with blunt but exceptionally long claws. The animal tore great chunks away from the log before leaning forward to snatch up plump grubs with a long, pink tongue.

The opportunity was too priceless to waste on a hastily conceived prank, so Newt took his time deciding what sort of illusion would be the most entertaining. Finally he settled upon a plan, staring downward with the concentration necessary to weave his simple spell.

The bear huffed in confusion as it detected something

moving within the log. Rearing backward in surprise, the animal growled ominously, still unable to see the wriggling form.

Then the growl turned to a squawk of dismay as the wedged head of a huge viper slithered from the rotten log and darted toward the bear's shaggy belly.

Yowling in dismay, the huge creature turned a complete backward somersault as more and more of the snake emerged. The green-scaled body gathered into a monstrous coil around the log. A forked tongue flicked toward the bear, and the huge mammal backed farther away from its former meal. Then, with an angry bellow, it turned and blundered away through the brush.

The illusionary snake vanished as Newt chuckled delightedly. A big snake—he'd have to remember that one in the future! Still buzzing aimlessly, he drifted on, poking here and there among the forests and meadows of the vale.

It was some hours later that his nose picked up the scent of another victim. Hurrying forward, Newt came to a wide trail. Pacing easily along the ground below him was the lanky form of a great gray wolf.

Suppressing a delighted giggle, for wolves were among his favorite targets, Newt settled onto a high branch. He knew immediately that he'd use the same prank he had on the bear.

No sooner had he made his decision than the great, coiling serpent squirmed from the underbrush, slithering directly into the wolf's path. Newt forced himself to concentrate, quivering with eagerness as he awaited the canine's reaction.

Surprisingly, the wolf ignored the snake, even though the creature had formed a massive coil right before it! Instead, the wolf sat on its haunches and focused bright yellow eyes directly on the invisible faerie dragon above him.

Newt was so surprised that he almost fell off his limb, grasping with his foreclaws at the last moment. He looked at himself—yes, he was still invisible. Yet he couldn't avoid the sensation that the wolf stared directly at him. Somehow the animal *knew* the faerie dragon was there!

In another moment, the creature rose to his feet and loped quickly down the trail, running right through the snake! Disappointed, Newt looked after the departing carnivore, wondering what had gone wrong.

Then another scent came to him, wafting on the gentle breeze. Newt sprang into the air, the snake, the wolf, and everything else immediately forgotten.

* * * * *

Alicia and Keane followed the clear map Robyn had sketched for them. They found the pass into Myrloch Vale with no difficulty, though the narrow trail required the riders to dismount and the entire column of men-at-arms had to traverse the route in single file. At its crest, the twisting footpath curved around the exposed shoulder of a stony bluff, with a torrential stream carving its way through a gorge four hundred feet below.

Their march remained steady and well paced. Each man carried a knapsack filled with a plentiful supply of rations, and though the weight of the packs slowed them slightly, the fact that they didn't have to take time to hunt more than compensated for their slightly slower marching speed. In fact, each day they didn't seek a place to camp until less than an hour of daylight remained.

True to the queen's prediction, by nightfall, the army had reached the floor of the vale and found a comfortable camping place among the trees.

After giving the order to settle in for the night, the princess found herself reflecting on the responsibilities of her command. She felt humbled by her role, realizing that four hundred men depended on her for direction and leadership, that the benefits or tolls of this expedition would fall upon her shoulders. Yet at the same time, she felt a blazing determination to succeed, to follow her father northward and be ready to strike a blow against the army of giant-kin.

She found the silent presence of Keane reassuring. For once, the mage traveled without complaining, as if he, too, appreciated the splendors of Myrloch Vale.

Even the cleric of Helm blended easily with the rest of the party, despite his large size and the fact that he was one of the few who was mounted. He spoke sometimes to the men, although he camped somewhat off to the side from the rest of the troops. Nevertheless, he rose early and showed no difficulty maintaining the steady pace of the march.

"How far ahead of us do you think Father is?" Alicia asked Keane on the third night of their march.

"I imagine he's picking up a little distance each day. He might be all the way to Winterglen by now."

Alicia's eyes swung unconsciously to the north. For a brief moment, she felt a wave of hopelessness. How would they ever catch up to the king before his foolish quest got him killed?

Keane seemed to sense her unease. He didn't say anything, but instead laid a hand gently on her shoulder. The pressure of his fingers against her skin brought a flicker of hope to the young princess. Then he smiled, and her reciprocal expression came easily. She began to believe that, just perhaps, they would succeed.

* * * * *

Twang!

To Tavish, the sound of her harpstring seemed like a booming crash of thunder, easily the loudest sound that had ever occurred. She froze, pressing herself farther under the rowing bench and listening for the sounds of outraged, suspicious firbolgs.

But instead, the brutes continued to wage their gruff argument in the stern of the *Princess of Moonshae*. Tavish couldn't understand their guttural tongue, but she sensed that the fate of this captured prize was at stake.

The bard had been every bit as surprised as the northmen

by the sudden rush of the giant-kin. She had ducked below one of the rowing benches as the boat had been overrun, and she had been able to squirm into a concealed niche between several water barrels and that lifesaving bench.

Now, however, she wondered what fate awaited her. Hidden in the hull of a ship manned by ungainly giants—none of whom had ever sailed before, she felt certain—Tavish had no idea what had befallen Brandon.

Then she felt a gentle bump against the wooden timbers, and she realized that the ship had been pulled up to the sturdy wooden wharf. Then, before she could digest this information, the boat rocked sickeningly, and the crescendo of giant voices rumbled much louder.

The *Princess of Moonshae*, Tavish realized, had been drawn to shore in the midst of the monstrous army.

* * * * *

The Earthmother remembered the coming of the giants, in the days of her dawning spring. Led by the hulking demigod, Grond Peaksmasher, they stormed across the Moonshaes while humankind still struggled among its own ranks for survival.

The invasion of these massive humanoids might have led to disaster, and it would have, had the giants and their master desired conquest. Yet the great creatures longed for peace, and they went to the secluded places of the Moonshaes, avoiding man, only turning him away from their haunts. They allowed him to live and to multiply, and all the while the numbers of the giants dwindled.

In the end, only the firbolgs—smallest of the giant-kin—had been left. They lived on many of the isles, and if they did not serve the Balance, neither did they work for its destruction. Over the course of centuries, the goddess learned their true nature, and it was not the nature of a threat.

Finally, when she gave them a place to dwell, she chose the realm of her heartland, and she offered them Myrloch.

❦ 9 ❦

Partings

Princess Alicia actually had a very mistaken impression of Tristan's whereabouts. Despite the fact that he had a full day's head start and traveled mounted and alone, the High King hadn't progressed much more rapidly than had the footmen of Corwell. For one thing, he hadn't known about the pass into the vale that Robyn had sketched for Alicia. Also, his untimely stag hunt had carried him far from his proper path, and he meandered a bit as he tried to find his way back.

Now Tristan's eyes opened with the dawn, but it was several minutes later before he could pull his mind from the depths of slumber. He slept out-of-doors, he saw, with a mighty sword held ready in his hand. But where was he?

Myrloch Vale, he realized, the recollection followed by a flood of confusing facts. Shallot was here, and Ranthal and the moorhounds. He wore his chain mail, and he had come here on some sort of mission.

But what?

His eyes wandered to the east, toward the bright flare of the sun as it crept above the tree-lined horizon. His mission, he recalled, was a quest of no little importance, yet now it didn't strike him as strange that he couldn't remember the nature of that purpose.

Instead, it was as if the task would only become relevant when he could put his memory in order. He tried to focus on the direction of his journey, but all he could think about was the sunrise, the gleaming dawn that beckoned in the east. Why was his mind so thick? Was something wrong?

Eastward—that must be it, he told himself. True, he felt a vague lack of conviction about that determination, but he could think of no reasonable alternative.

Thus determined, the High King of the Ffolk saddled his great war-horse and called his hounds to the trail. Obediently they loped toward the rising sun, with the proud warrior on his great steed riding grimly behind. His hand rested on the hilt of his sword, ready . . . but for what?

Tristan's mind sharpened until the king felt a keen pulse of mental power tingling through him. For a moment, he drifted again. Why was he here?

"The Darkwalker is abroad," he announced loudly, the words ringing as an alien sound through the pastoral wood of Myrloch Vale. He saw a momentary image of that looming, reptilian form, but it quickly faded into the mists and disappeared.

Did he campaign against the sahuagin? An image of the spine-backed fish creatures filled his mind, rank upon rank of them emerging from the sea to pillage and slay. Did they lurk in the woods, among the trees? Then, in another burst of lucidity, he knew that he wouldn't be seeking his aquatic enemies in an inland valley. No, it must be the Darkwalker.

Somehow, that thought didn't seem right either. He had a clear picture of a *young* prince pursuing the unnatural horror that stalked the land. Yet for some reason, he felt like a very old king.

What *was* the purpose of his grand quest? The sun rose higher, and after a while he even began to doubt the accuracy of his direction. Eastward didn't seem right, after all.

"Tristan! Hey, King, wait for me!"

The voice took him by surprise but brought a welcoming surge of joy to his heart at the same time.

"Newt!" cried the High King, spinning about as much as possible in the tall saddle. "By the goddess, fellow, it's good to see you!" The blunt, tiny snout widened in Newt's unmistakable smile, while his butterfly wings buzzed easily to keep him in a steady hover.

"Hey, what a great horse! And that dog—why, you'd think Canthus was here!"

Chattering delightedly, the little faerie dragon buzzed through the air, circling Tristan and shifting through colors of red, orange, and violet.

"Canthus?" For a moment, the king was puzzled. "He *is*—" Then he remembered. The great, shaggy moorhound was called Ranthal. Canthus, Ranthal's grandsire, was long dead.

But Newt was here. "Come take a rest, my friend," the king said, raising his gloved hand. Delighted, Newt came to rest on the man's wrist, allowing himself to be lowered to the pommel of the deep saddle.

"Are you out here on a hunt?" asked the faerie dragon, propping himself up on his haunches.

"No, no. I ride because . . ." Awkwardly, Tristan's voice trailed off. Suddenly the appalling state of his mind came driving home with vengeful force. "I don't *know* why I'm here," he concluded miserably.

"I'll bet it's the firbolgs again," Newt said, with a conspiratorial look into the woods on either side. "They sacked Cambro, you kn— Hey, what is it?"

Tristan bolted upright in his saddle and then shouted aloud in combined relief and outrage. The king seized the tiny dragon around his belly and squeezed the air from Newt's lungs.

"Firbolgs! That's it!" he cried as the full wealth of his memory came flooding back.

He squinted into the rising sun. "And not east—I should be riding *north!*"

Abruptly the grim strength of his delusion became clear. Something worked against him, striving to steal his memory, his very mind! The forest around him suddenly seemed a darker, more menacing place. He quickly yanked Shallot's reins to the side, starting the great horse onto a northerly course.

How long had he wandered? He realized, to his further distress, that he had no idea as to the answer.

"*When*, Newt?" he pressed. "When did the firbolgs sack Cambro?"

"Well, *before*." The faerie dragon squinted up at the king as Shallot broke into a loping canter. "I mean, before I saw you. . . . Oh, and I saw Robyn, too!"

"You did?" Tristan had ridden out of Corwell too quickly to hear the full tale of Robyn's experiences on her mission of reconnaissance. He bit back a question about the timing of Newt's encounter with the queen, fearing he had already overloaded the tiny serpent's recollection. "But Cambro—how many days ago was it that the firbolgs came?"

"Oh, lots," Newt said breezily. "But I knew you'd be coming along."

The king realized that the faerie dragon was being as specific as he could. Newt wasn't the one to provide precise details or painstaking answers to questions. Nevertheless, Tristan felt a great lightening of his load from the presence of his old friend.

"So—we're going to thump those firbolgs, I bet!" Newt chirped, raising his neck to look forward past Shallot's streaming mane. Then, in a moment of puzzlement, he squinted and looked to the rear. "Didn't you bring an army with you?" he asked.

Another wave of chagrin washed over Tristan. "No," he admitted. "I came alone."

The faerie dragon's eyes widened in awe. "Wow! This is going to be some battle!"

Tristan shook his head. The fierce determination that had seized him following Robyn's report seemed like a strange dementia now. What had he been thinking? For a moment, he considered spinning the horse about, thundering back to Corwell, and mustering his army, but he immediately discarded that course of action as too time-consuming. He must be near the northern fringes of the vale by now, and he couldn't admit that all this time had been wasted.

Another reason nagged at him as well—pure, royal pride. It shamed him to think of his irrational behavior, and if he returned to Corwell, he would be forced to admit his realization before all the Ffolk of his kingdom. That wasn't something he could bring himself to do.

But why had he made this mistake? That question skirted the realm of his brain but wouldn't come into focus—at least, not now.

He tried to imagine the monster that had led the humanoids on their destructive course. A burning, almost mindless hatred seized the king as he pondered this unknown firbolg. What restless arrogance propelled him onto this destructive path? The lord of the marauding band became a focus of his rage, and Tristan forged an iron determination—one day that brute would die on his sword.

"Where's Cambro—how far away?" he asked, trying a different tack on the scatterbrained faerie dragon.

Again Newt looked at him, squinting like a tutor regarding a particularly thick-skulled pupil. "Cambro's in Myrloch Vale," he said precisely. "And *you're* in Myrloch Vale, too!"

"I know that!" declared the king, unable to entirely squelch his impatience. "But where in Myrloch Vale—how far from right *here?*"

"Oh, I don't know. It's over there somewhere." Newt gestured vaguely, but it was enough for the king. The faerie dragon had pointed to the southeast. Tristan realized that he had indeed traveled almost to the northern fringe of the vale. Perhaps he hadn't lost as much time as he'd feared.

"And the firbolgs?" the king pressed. "Do you know where they went from Cambro?"

"Nope," Newt replied, with a firm shake of his head. "Though I heard the humans talking about Winterglen."

That information, at least, was no less than the High Queen had reported when she returned from Myrloch Vale to the castle. "Which humans?" he asked, to confirm his suspicions.

"The ones *Robyn* talked to—the ones with the dwarves! Don't you pay attention at *all?*"

Tristan grimaced. He'd forgotten what a painstaking process it was to gain information from the scatterbrained faerie dragon, but—for now, at least—it proved well worth it.

"What about wolves—*a* wolf, anyway? Have you seen him?"

"I've seen *lots* of wolves!" Newt boasted. "Remember when the Darkwalker came to Corwell, and so did the wolves? Why, there were at least a thousand of them! The whole pack came running out of—"

"No! I mean wolves here, now!" blurted Tristan.

Newt looked around, his tiny eyes squinting. "Nope!" he announced, full of certainty. The king decided not to press the issue.

"We're riding to Winterglen," he announced casually. "Though I'd like to camp on Codsrun Creek tonight."

"Well, why didn't you *say* so?" huffed Newt. "That's way over there!" he added, pointing to the west. "Say, is that Corwellian cheese I smell?" inquired the little dragon, with a meaningful look at the king's bulging saddlebags.

With his position more or less triangulated, the king chuckled with a small measure of relief. Reaching back, he managed to pull a small morsel out of his saddlebag for Newt. "That'll have to last you until we stop for the night," he warned, knowing that the cheese would disappear within a few moments.

But Newt settled down to munch happily, and the miles rolled away behind them. The spell of delusion had passed, except for the lingering distress caused by the mysterious origin of his confusion. The king kicked Shallot harder than he intended. The great war-horse bucked once in annoyance and then set off for the north at a breakneck gallop.

* * * * *

"Hello, my princess," Keane said softly, folding his long legs below him and settling to the ground beside the small fire. "Do you have a few minutes for your old tutor?"

Alicia laughed and nodded. "Sorry, Keane. I know I've been busy. Just now I was almost falling asleep in my tea."

"You're setting a good pace. It's no wonder that you're as

tired as the rest of us," allowed the lanky magic-user.

Indeed, Keane's own legs were cramped and sore, and the ground made an even less comfortable seat than the saddle, which had come to be a fiendish torture device in the mage's mind. Yet he had carefully avoided complaining, knowing that the weight of her command weighed heavily enough upon Alicia's shoulders. And he at least had the benefit of a mount. The warriors of Corwell who marched with them traveled on foot.

"How are the men doing?" Alicia asked, as if reading his mind. "They all seem cheerful enough when I'm around, but I wonder what they really think."

"I think they'd follow you to the Abyss if you wanted them to," Keane replied truthfully. The mage had mingled with the men-at-arms during much of the march northward. He had observed the genuine affection with which they watched and spoke of the young princess who led them.

They looked up to see the sturdy, bandy-legged form of Sergeant-Major Sands approaching. The grizzled veteran stroked his long mustache until he reached the fire, where he bowed to Alicia and nodded at the magic-user.

"The men're all bedded for the night," he said. "If there's nothing else you'll be wanting, I think I'll turn in myself."

"Thanks, Sands. You've done more for us than anyone could ask," the princess replied sincerely. She watched him swagger off, knowing that his gruff exterior concealed a real affection for his royal commander.

Although she didn't realize it, Alicia unconsciously encouraged this admiration. She remained cheerful even when they faced obstacles, such as the unexpectedly deep stream they had encountered that afternoon. The waterway hadn't been featured on Robyn's map, yet it had raged through a deep gorge and they had lost many hours looking for a suitable ford. Alicia had raced ahead of the column to find a crossing, then galloped back with a whoop and cheer that put great heart in the weary marchers.

And even though she was mounted, the princess put in as

much effort as any footman, riding back and forth along the column of marching men, responding to each loud greeting with a wave or a smile, and then racing ahead to make sure they found and followed the route Robyn had marked for them on the map.

Also, the princess had scorned any privileges of royalty. Like any warrior, she built her own fire and cooked her own meals, though every evening she made the rounds of the camp and was frequently invited to join a small group of men at their own cheery blaze. This she did as much as time allowed, listening to their stories of home and hunt, sharing her own experiences in turn.

Keane had watched admiringly, seeing the way that she earned the men's loyalty, sensing in this young woman all the qualities of leadership that would one day make her a splendid monarch. Yet he could tell that she herself remained for the most part unaware of these feelings, a fact that was part of what Keane found so appealing in the young princess.

"It's so hard to tell about them," Alicia said wearily, leaning forward and allowing a bit of the fire's warmth to soak into her rough, callused hands. "Sometimes I think they're coming along out of loyalty to the king, and they're only following me because I'm going the same way."

Keane shook his head firmly. "That's not it, not at all. Your father is an important symbol to them . . . to all of us. But don't underestimate your own role. You represent the Ffolk's hopes for the future. It's good for them, and for you, that you can get to know each other."

Alicia smiled, albeit wanly. "Thanks, old friend. I don't know if I could do this without you here to help."

"Sure you could," he assured her. But he was privately glad she didn't have to, because he didn't want to be anywhere else.

Keane's silent addenda must have shown on his face, for the princess reached over and clasped one of his hands in hers. "How about the inquisitor?" she asked. "Did you see him settled in?"

The young wizard chuckled ruefully. "As usual, he's pitched that palace of his off to the side. Trampled a good-sized meadow to do it."

Though the patriarch of Helm had accompanied them every step of the way, he remained a distant and mysterious figure. He camped in a manner completely unlike any other member of the expedition. Each night he produced a small square of canvas from his voluminous saddlebags. Casting the object on the ground, he spoke a short incantation, and the thing quickly expanded into the structure the Ffolkmen had immediately dubbed the "palace." In truth, it was merely a tent, but the structure included several rooms and covered more ground than a typical house. Colorful silk adorned its many panels, and from three sharp peaks—one atop each of the main chambers—flagpoles extended upward. Three identical banners, each portraying the All-Seeing Eye in vivid detail, outlined in a gold border with highlights of silver thread, streamed from these shafts, proudly proclaiming the faith of the tent's sole inhabitant.

"I've told him not to do that!" Alicia objected. "Everyone else sleeps on a small patch of ground. Why does he need a full hectare?"

Keane ignored the obvious reply concerning the huge cleric's girth and addressed the more pertinent issue. "To him, the whole concept of Myrloch Vale is superstition, or perhaps even blasphemy, and he's persistent, to say the least, in maintaining his own way of doing things."

"There's something more there," Alicia said quietly. Something in her voice drew Keane's eyes to hers, and he saw that the princess was actually afraid of Parell Hyath. "It's not just that he's of a different faith. It's as if he thinks of the goddess as an *enemy!*"

"If he shows any kind of threat," Keane vowed, "you can be sure that I'll be there to stop him!"

"I know." The pressure of her hand increased, and the wizard's heart swelled with joy. He wanted to wrap her in his arms, to pull her against his chest and shelter her from the world. But this he couldn't do, nor was such protection, he sensed, what she needed or desired.

For a time, they watched the fire in silence, seeing the dry aspen slowly turn to coal, the pieces falling away from their individual limbs to form a soft bed of embers. The gentle glow within, of deep and iridescent orange, made a pleasant companion to the darkness and to each other.

"How much longer until we're out of Myrloch Vale?" Alicia wondered.

"We could cross into Winterglen tomorrow," Keane noted. They followed a course to the west of Codsrun Creek, and five days' march must certainly have carried them out of the wide valley.

"I wish there'd been some sign of Father."

Keane shook his head, trying to hide his own concern. "This is a big place. The chance of us crossing his trail anywhere along the way is pretty remote."

"Then what if he *has* caught up with this army of firbolgs and trolls? Is that any better?" Alicia demanded.

"There's always the dwarves," Keane reminded her. "Finellen's likely to spot him just as she did with Hanrald and Brigit. And she's not about to let him charge off on any suicidal attacks."

"I wish I could believe that. But it seemed so shocking, so sudden. One minute he's standing there talking to us, and the next he's astride Shallot, pounding across the moors! If he hasn't come to his senses, who knows *what* could have happened to him!"

"That bothers me, too," Keane admitted. "It was too sudden. Your father's not a sluggish man, but it's not like him to do something so drastic without a little more reflection."

"Greetings, fellow travelers!" The hearty voice emerged from the darkness, followed quickly by the bulky form of Parell Hyath, Exalted Inquisitor of Helm. The silver and golden thread gleamed against the white silk of his voluminous robe. Somehow he kept the garment immaculate, even after five days on horseback, five nights sleeping in his tent.

Keane cursed silently as the princess sat up straight, removing her hand from his.

"Hello," Alicia replied stiffly. His was an invasive presence, but throughout the march, she had forced herself to treat him with civility. Tonight, however, his arrival might as well have doused ice water over the fire.

"Does our quarry draw near? Are there reports from your scouts?" the patriarch inquired, settling himself on a fallen log a little back from the low fire.

"The men of Llyrath have found the path of the firbolgs," she replied. "But it's a cold trail, nearly a week old."

"Any sign of your father, then?" Hyath's eyebrows, which nearly met in the middle, came together in a questioning, even concerned, frown.

"No, nothing," Alicia said bitterly. She turned back to Keane. "We've got to pick up the pace! Too much time has passed already, and I don't want it to be too late by the time we get there!"

"Now, my child . . . I don't believe—" the cleric began, but Alicia cut him off with a sharp gesture.

"We don't know *what* to believe! That's why it's so important to move quickly." She stopped to think, and both men tactfully remained silent for a few moments.

"Tomorrow we'll break camp an hour before dawn," she declared. "The packs are lighter now, with so much of the food gone, so we'll also add another hour to the evening's march."

Alicia's eyes saddened, and she looked at Keane. "That is, if you think that the men . . ."

"I said they'd follow you to the Abyss, and I meant it!" he replied.

"I hope you're right," she said sadly. For a moment, Keane wondered if he felt any of the warmth in her voice that had been so full just a few moments before. He might have, or it could have been just a figment of his imagination.

* * * * *

"What about the plan? We win the fight—*then* we get a boat!" snarled Baatlrap, confronting Thurgol on the dockside of Codscove. The huge troll's thin lips were drawn back, revealing his jagged fangs, while he held his massive and knobby fists planted firmly on his hips.

The firbolg chieftain and his twelve kinsman had, with great difficulty, pulled the *Princess of Moonshae* to wharfside. Thurgol clambered out of the rocking ship and bumped into the troll, knocking Baatlrap backward a step.

"The boat came to shore!" barked the firbolg. He was too delighted with his prize to pay more than mild attention to the hulking troll. "We took it!"

The pair stood amid the throng of huge, boisterous humanoids on the waterfront of Codscove. Wounded trolls, as they healed, limped across the trampled commons to join them. The remnants of the human defenders, recognizing their cause as lost, had fled the field several minutes before. For the time being, even the trolls were too tired to pursue.

Nearby the ruins of the shantytown still smoldered, while the gruff, profane sounds of firbolg revelry continued to rock the stone-walled warehouse.

"Humans all fled, the cowards!" gloated the troll. "We trolls routed them!"

"Good fight," Thurgol agreed easily. He turned to watch his impromptu crew members grappling with ropes and thwarts, trying to secure the ship to the dock. "Stay there. Hold the ropes!" he commanded finally.

"Leave ship here," Baatlrap said, drawing Thurgol's suspicious attention. "Whole army go after the humans. Kill *all* of them!" The troll's eyes drifted casually over to Garisa, who stood at the waterfront with the Silverhaft Axe at her side. The old hag scowled back, unintimidated.

The firbolg chieftain blinked in surprise, studying the recalcitrant troll. Then he scowled, drawing his heavy brows down over his craggy face in an expression that was very menacing indeed. "We've got the ship. Now we sail to Icepeak!" He pointed across the Strait of Oman, currently too hazy for the far shoreline to be seen. Nevertheless, his firm intent was unmistakable.

"No," declared Baatlrap, stepping closer to the firbolg chieftain. "You follow *me* now."

Thurgol glared at his co-commander in growing fury. "*You* saw the sign of the gods!" he barked. "We have the Silverhaft Axe. Now it's time to take it to Icepeak!"

Baatlrap looked at the ship, skepticism rank on his grotesque face. "Humans flee that way," he said, pointing to the east along the shore. "We should give chase now—catch them and kill them!"

The firbolg chieftain showed no fear of his gangly, powerfully muscled rival. Yet as he remembered the size of the ship, he knew he couldn't squeeze more than his own tribe into the hull. There would be no room for the trolls. And given their utter lack of nautical skill, he suspected that multiple crossings of the surprisingly wide strait would be out of question.

"I take the ship and my warriors," Thurgol said after a moment's thought. "You trolls, and any giant-kin what don't come along, you can chase the humans."

His suggestion seemed, to the powerful giant, to be a model of diplomacy and compromise. He nodded thoughtfully, considering all the ramifications. It was a good idea!

"No!" barked Baatlrap, surprising Thurgol in his self-congratulatory meditation. Then, with not a second's warning, the hulking troll attacked.

* * * * *

How long can a back be twisted before a person became permanently crippled? When an arm or leg remained numb for hours on end, did it wither and die? These questions arose from more than idle curiosity in Tavish. By now, after more than an hour under her bench, she considered them crucial to her chances of survival.

Already she felt as though she had passed the point of ever being able to walk again. A rough thwart jabbed the small of her back, and the low-hanging bench pressed her shoulder into the hull, wearing her skin away with each jolt and roll of the ship. And the firbolgs, she quickly noted, jolted and rolled the ship a good deal more than had Brandon and his crew. The only good news was that the water barrels served to screen her from observation by the giants.

When the humanoids scrambled out of the vessel onto the docks of Codscove, she had risked a little movement, stretching her legs beneath the bench and rolling sideways so that the vicious wooden thwart was removed from contact with her backbone. At the same time, her new position allowed her a small crack of daylight, a space between the bench and a water barrel, through which to observe the longship's captors.

She saw a monstrous troll, easily the largest and ugliest she had ever seen, jabbering angrily with an equally hulking firbolg. The pair stood nose to nose beside the ship, barking guttural sounds at each other. Though she couldn't understand a word of the conversation, Tavish sensed that the troll grew increasingly agitated.

The creature carried a huge, wicked-looking sword, balancing the weapon easily in the palm of one massive hand. The blade was streaked with blood; he hadn't bothered to clean it after the battle on the commons. The giant, on the other hand, leaned casually on a huge, knotted limb. To Tavish, the club looked as large as a small tree trunk, but the monster spun it easily to rest it across one of his broad shoulders.

The firbolg's eyes drifted over the boat, and Tavish flinched, though there was little chance that the creature would see her in the shadowy niche. She was puzzled by something in his eyes. They seemed to stare with longing far into the haze over the strait.

Then, with shocking speed, the troll whipped his sword upward and slashed it toward the unprepared firbolg's neck. Backed by the force of powerful sinew, the blade whistled through the air while the firbolg, still staring out to sea, remained unaware of the treacherous attack.

A deep voice, shrill with warning and—to Tavish, who couldn't see the speaker—unmistakably female, screeched an alarm. With amazing speed, the firbolg flipped his club to the opposite shoulder, spinning back to face his attacker while the great sword bit into the wooden weapon with a loud *chunk*.

Bellowing in fury, the giant-kin twisted his club and almost pulled the blade out of the great troll's hands. As it was, the obscene monster held on to the hilt with both hands, stumbling across the dock before he wrenched the sword from its wooden trap.

An excited hubbub of voices rose from the encircling humanoids, all of whom backed out of Tavish's vision to leave the two combatants a wide, unimpeded arena. The bard felt the strong tension in the air and knew something very important was riding on this duel. The firbolg planted his broad feet firmly, hefting the mighty club and warily holding it before him, guarding against another quick attack.

The troll, however, showed no intention of dashing in for another savage onslaught. The green-skinned humanoid held the sword in the same manner as the giant wielded his club, so that the tips of the two weapons nearly touched, each fighter guarding against a rash attack by his foe.

Tavish heard hisses and catcalls rumble from the unseen onlookers, but the firbolg stood firm, allowing the words to roll off his shoulders. The troll, on the other hand, stepped backward and then angrily barked at the surrounding monsters. His sharp commands only seemed to inflame them more. Even without a knowledge of the language, the bard had no difficulty discerning the derisive tone of the hoots and taunts.

Finally the weight of opinion grew too heavy for the monstrous troll. With a curse and a snarl, he sprang toward the firbolg, bashing at the club with his huge, jagged blade in an attempt to sweep the weapon out of the way.

But he may as well have chopped at a broad tree. The firbolg, muscles knotting in his shoulders and arms, held the club firm. Instead, it was the troll who staggered, though the lanky creature quickly regained its balance and scuttled through a wide circle around the giant-kin.

Now the firbolg uttered a bellow, a blast of sound that nearly deafened Tavish, and sprang forward with a timber-shaking pounce. The club flew through a dizzying arc, and the troll threw himself headlong onto the dock in order to avoid the savage swing, dropping out of Tavish's view. The cacophony of the onlookers' voices rose feverishly while the hulking giant leered in fierce triumph.

The firbolg whirled through a circle, bashing downward with his stout weapon. Tavish heard it crack solidly into the timbers of the dock, not the troll's wriggling body, and she felt oddly disappointed. Though each of the combatants was a mortal enemy, the ghastly appearance and the total and unadulterated evil nature of the troll made that beast the more hateful foe. Nevertheless, she retained no illusions about her fate if the brutish giant-kin should discover her.

The firbolg kicked, and she heard a squawk of outrage from the green-skinned monster. Then the troll bounced back into view, swinging the gory sword in a wide circle toward the giant's midriff. As the firbolg moved to block the attack, the troll pulled the weapon back, avoiding the parry before driving the weapon's sharp point straight toward the firbolg's chest.

Surprised, the giant tried to recover, twisting desperately away, but not before the keen tip ripped through his skin, slicing a wound deep into his flank. Grunting in pain, the huge creature staggered back, weakly flailing with his club to block any immediate pursuit.

But the troll didn't hesitate for long. Utilizing the newly-successful thrusting tactic, he drew the sword back, leveling the blade and angling the point straight toward the giant-kin's heart. The firbolg stumbled awkwardly, almost falling to one knee, and Tavish wondered if the wound in his side was mortal.

So, too, did the troll. Sensing his opponent's weakness, the horrific monster lunged inward, driving the sword with all the power of his taut muscle and tough, resilient bone. Like an arrow, the tip of the blade darted toward the lurching giant's unprotected chest.

Tavish almost shouted a suicidal warning, so certain was the blow and so unprepared seemed its lumbering target. The assembled humanoids grew silent in that instant, the collective breath of the monstrous army held in tense anticipation of the duel's outcome. Ignoring the impulse to close her eyes, Tavish watched in spellbound horror, waiting for the fatal penetration.

But suddenly it was the giant who, with lightning speed, dropped out of sight. In that instant, before even the monsters roared their approval or dismay, she understood. He had *feigned* his weakness.

The troll shrieked in agony and, though she couldn't see the firbolg, this time Tavish heard that mighty club smash into trollish bone. The horrid attacker fell, and the firbolg rose into her line of sight, lifting the club above his head and then driving it downward onto the unseen form below.

Again the troll howled, and for excruciating moments, the hidden bard watched the club rise and fall, hearing the piteous cries grow weaker, until finally they ceased altogether. Even then the club fell brutally three more times before the firbolg finally lowered the weapon to the dock. No sound emerged from the unseen form at his feet. In fact, Tavish couldn't imagine that the troll was anything more than a gory pulp.

At once, the firbolg stumbled, and several of his fellows dashed forward to support him. Tavish saw a stooped old female firbolg, who nevertheless stood at least eight feet tall, step forward to dab something at the giant's wound. Red blood continued to gush from the small slice, and finally the healer insisted that the warrior lie down.

Tavish drew back into her niche, intrigued enough by the

scene she had witnessed to forget momentarily the painful cramps that had once again started to numb her legs. There seemed to be precious little unity in this monstrous army, for unless her guess was way off the mark, she had just observed a battle between the leaders of separate factions.

She wondered what would happen next. The possibility of waiting until dark and then trying to slip onto the dock began to have its appeal. Perhaps she could get ashore and disappear into the night.

Sunset was still many hours away, however, when firbolg after firbolg began to climb into the ship. As the bard drew back from clumping, intrusive feet, she hardly dared to breathe, cringing against the backbreaking thwart and pressing as far as she could under the low overhanging bench. She forced herself to be absolutely silent. At the same time, she wanted to scream her dismay, for she had no doubt as to what was going on.

And in fact, a few minutes later, her suspicions proved correct. The firbolgs pushed the *Princess of Moonshae* away from the dock and floated toward the rolling waters of the Strait of Oman.

* * * * *

Princess Deirdre stalked through Corwell Town in the dark of the night, wearing the guise of her magic as an impenetrable disguise. Those who passed her saw nothing save a ripple in the blackness. Perhaps they felt a shiver of disquiet as they hurried on their way, rationally certain that there was nothing there, yet spiritually unconvinced.

Thus undiscovered, she entered the hutch of a farmyard, finding a proud rooster slumbering peacefully on his roost nearby. With a sharp twist of her hands, she wrung the bird's neck, quickly dropping the feathered body into her large leather sack.

Next she came upon a dog, slumbering before its master's doorstep. The screen of nothingness was so impermeable that the hound didn't sense the young woman's approach, nor did it see the keen dagger that slit the coarse fur of its throat. Withdrawing the dripping blade, the princess lowered a small cup, collecting the blood that flowed from the severed artery.

She repeated the ritual with a great draft horse that stood slumbering in a livery yard, gathering the dying steed's blood in a larger container. Finally, then, she was ready to return to the castle on the knoll, which she did on the wings of her magic, disdaining the winding road that climbed toward the gatehouse and fortress walls.

Settling her feet on the lofty parapet of those walls, she searched for the final element of her brew. Undisguised now, she came upon a pacing guard. The man bowed respectfully, so he didn't see the still-crimson blade dart outward. He fell silently, staring mute and uncomprehending at the young woman who stood over his bleeding corpse.

Her eyes shining in the darkness, Dierdre knelt and gathered the last sample of blood. Then, in a swirl of her dark cloak, she passed through a door and entered the darkened hallways of the keep.

* * * * *

"Splendid . . . the components of might are in your hands, my daughter." The immortal form of Talos twisted and heaved in anticipation. The princess of the Moonshaes was his now! He well knew that, with the striking of her dagger, she had forever turned her back on her people and their dying faith.

In his struggles, Talos had learned an important lesson— that the Earthmother must be struck away from the heart of her power, away from Myrloch Vale. Dierdre had begun that attack, gathering the vital tools of destruction. She would become a powerful agent of the New Gods, bringing the goddess to her knees in final defeat.

For that purpose, she would be linked to another tool. That one still slumbered to the north, but soon he would be awakened,

*emerging for his vengeance from the very shadow of the
Icepeak.*

*The ultimate sword of chaos would be the demigod, Grond
Peaksmasher, finally freed from his goddess-imposed confine-
ment.*

❧ 10 ❧

Perilous Pathways

The muscular steed galloped like a pale ghost along the open floor of the forest, carrying her silver-armored rider beneath overhanging limbs and around large, moss-covered boulders. Brigit gave the fleet war-horse free rein, and the white Synnorian mare flew through misty meadows and dank, overgrown thickets.

Sensing, after several miles, the nearness of her destination, the elfwoman exerted slight pressure with her knees, bringing the mare's headlong race to a gentle, cautious trot. In another moment, a small figure emerged from the brush, and the horse, grown used to dwarves over the past week on the trail, reared back only slightly.

"We're too late," Brigit announced tersely as Finellen and Hanrald came up behind the lead dwarf. "They've taken Codscove even more quickly than we thought possible."

The dwarven column gradually came into view behind the leaders. Hanrald led his great war-horse, while the dwarves, on foot, marched steadily along behind.

"What are they doing now?" asked the dwarven captain.

"It looks like they've started along the shore to the east. There are several small villages and at least one good-sized town in their path."

"Damn!" spat Hanrald. "We can't let them run wild!"

"Just what I've been sayin' for a week now," grumbled Finellen. "Weren't you the one who told me to wait for King Kendrick?"

Hanrald spun away in irritation. His mind whirled through conflicting pictures of his duty. On the one hand, the king was sure to come, with sufficient men-at-arms to confront the horde with a reasonable chance of success. As it was, they had a mere fourscore dwarves or so, coupled with a human earl and an elven sister knight—not a great prospect of victory in any thoughtful analysis.

Yet they had no indication of how long it would take the king's army to arrive on the scene, or how much damage the monstrous horde could inflict in the meantime. Indeed, they had expected Codscove to delay the beasts for several days, and instead, that prosperous hamlet had been ravaged in a few short hours.

"You're right—now, in any event," muttered the proud earl, turning back to the stubborn dwarfwoman. "I don't think we can afford to wait any longer."

"Did you catch sight of the Silverhaft Axe?" Finellen queried.

"No—as much as I could see, they didn't have it with them."

"Damn! What did a bunch of firbolgs want it for? Where did they take it?" the dwarf demanded.

"Speaking of firbolgs, I was surprised to see that there aren't that many giants in this horde—mostly trolls," Brigit noted. "The firbolgs are only a small fraction of the total army."

"I don't care *who* took the axe," Finellen snorted impatiently. "I just want it back!"

"I'll ride toward the town and see if I can confirm their movements," Brigit volunteered quickly. "If they continue along the coast to the east, it might be that you can angle through Winterglen and gain some ground on them."

"That would be too much of a risk—and besides, it's not necessary," Finellen replied with a firm shake of her head. "They've *got* to go east from Codscove. A march in the other direction would take them right into the middle of the biggest swamp on Gwynneth."

"I remember," Brigit agreed. "At the mouth of Codsrun Creek, isn't it?"

"Yup. That little stream just disappears when it gets within fifteen miles of the shore. It turns into a morass of mud flat and fen. Not a road or track through the whole thing, and not good, open forest like this, either," Finellen concluded.

"Then we've got to get ahead of them if we're going to do any good," Hanrald realized.

That prospect was daunting, at the very least. On their sturdy but short legs the dwarves had difficulty maintaining a speedy march. Now they faced the prospect of not only matching the monsters' pace, but also moving quickly enough to get ahead of them and then making a glorious, but quite probably doomed, attempt to block the pestilential advance.

"We're going to pick up the pace," Finellen announced loudly. The doughty warriors uttered not a single word of complaint, Hanrald noticed, impressed. Instead, they followed the cadence of their leader's commands, forming into their file and following steadily behind Finellen, Brigit, and Hanrald, the latter pair leading their trail-weary war-horses.

"We'll cut a line to the northeast," the dwarf explained. "That should put us nearly parallel to their advance, but gradually drawing closer to the coast. I hope they won't know we're here, but we'll have to take precautions."

"I'll ride on the point," Brigit offered. "That should give you fair warning. If I'm spotted, they still won't know there's a company of dwarves in the woods."

"Makes sense," agreed Finellen.

"It's too dangerous," Hanrald objected. "At least let me ride with you!"

Brigit glared at him, her almond eyes flashing. "I don't need you to tell me what's 'too dangerous'! And the chance of us both being spotted is far greater than I alone. After all, my mare has been raised as a woods runner."

Hanrald bit back a blunt reply. He knew that the proud sister knight was right. She'd been waging war, riding on campaign, for years before his birth. Yet a protective part of his nature worried about the thought of allowing her to ride into such danger.

"Besides," Finellen added, her tone surprisingly soft as she addressed Hanrald, "you're the only other rider among us. I was hoping you'd take the outrider position on our left flank. Just to make sure they don't try to get around us . . . you understand?"

"You're right," agreed the Earl of Fairheight. Indeed, he and Brigit had the only two horses in the whole force. What had he been thinking, to waste that speed and mobility by trailing along with Brigit? "But I still don't see how you intend to catch them when they can make such good time."

"Simple," replied Finellen with a casual shrug. "We'll just have to march all night."

* * * * *

A growing sense of urgency propelled the High King of Moonshae. Shallot thundered along at an easy lope, his broad hooves pounding the soft earth in steady cadence. Tristan and Newt had emerged from Myrloch Vale sometime during the previous day, and now they rode through Winterglen at a steady, mile-crunching pace.

"How come we can't stop and look around a little bit?" pouted the faerie dragon, still perched on the high pommel before the king. "I *know* there's waterfalls on the Codsrun, and some of them have great trout pools, too. Don't you like to eat anymore?"

"It's a good thing I don't like it as much as you remember," Tristan retorted cheerfully. "You've put a pretty good dent in my rations!"

"Oh, posh! Though that cheese is every bit as good as I used to think it was. Say, do you think there's another little bit you could do without?"

"Not now! I told you, I'm not opening up these saddlebags until we stop for the night!"

Their course took them very near Codsrun Creek. Since his meeting with the faerie dragon, Tristan's concentration had remained uninterrupted and intense. Yet as the hours and then the days had passed, he grew increasingly perplexed by the confusion which had overtaken him.

Coupled with this mystery were the facts that he still didn't know: How many days had he been riding? How far off his track had he ventured? And what had caused his disturbing lapse in reason?

Always as he rode, he scanned the surrounding brush, studied each neighboring hilltop and tor, searching for sign of a gray body. But the wolves had disappeared, as far as he could tell, from all the world. At night, he listened carefully, but no more did their song rise to the stars.

"Hey! What's that?" wondered the spritely dragon, raising his narrow snout to sniff the air. "I smell a swamp!"

In another moment, Shallot's gait faltered, and Tristan saw that the ground before them grew tangled and thick with vines, enclosing brambles, and dense, thorny underbrush. The war-horse slowed to a walk, then finally halted altogether, unable to proceed through the thicket.

"It *is* a swamp!" declared Newt, rather unnecessarily. The air had become fetid and dank. Flies rose around them, buzzing through the humid air, coming to rest on human and horse alike.

For a moment, Tristan was puzzled. He'd had a mental picture of the Codsrun flowing all the way to the sea, and now the stream itself slowed to a brackish backwater, meandering among reeds and lilies, apparently stopping in its bed. But then he remembered: He'd sailed through the Strait of Oman many times and had never seen the mouth of that splashing stream. He *did* remember a stretch of marsh, however—a dank fen, actually—that covered much of the shoreline near Codscove. The stream, he deduced, must spread out and form the marsh.

But was the fen to the west or the east of that coastal town? This was the crucial fact now, and the king wasn't at all sure of the answer. Still, a sense of motivation propelled him, and he didn't want to allow this terrain to slow him down.

Which way was it? He tried to remember, all but gritting his teeth from the force of his cogitation. Finally the best he could do was to guess, his mind teased by a variety of memories, none of them certain enough to give him any degree of confidence.

"We'll go east," he announced, his voice more firm than his mind. "In another day, we'll get to Codscove."

"What do you want to go *there* for?" Newt whined. "It's a town, isn't it? There's just a bunch of people there. No meadows or trees or fun stuff like that."

"A *fishing* town," Tristan said calmly, knowing that, besides cheese, the bounty of the seas and streams was Newt's favorite repast. "Why, I wouldn't be surprised if there were whole racks of cod and salmon drying in the sun . . . outdoors, where everyone can see them."

"Say, that's right, isn't it?" Newt agreed, perking up. "You don't suppose they'd mind if one or two— No, of course they wouldn't! I don't eat *that* much! How long did you say it would take to get there?"

Tristan chuckled silently, suspecting that the faerie dragon, if he was truly hungry, would pose a serious threat to the season's catch. The inducement worked well, however, as Newt clambered up on the pommel, eagerly looking around Shallot's broad head, tiny nostrils quivering for any advance warning of the destination.

They rode easily, skirting the fringe of the swampland and passing along the same type of open forest that had surrounded them for so much of the ride through the vale and Winterglen. A light breeze wafted through the woods, and the scents of flowers and ferns filled the air, overpowering any lingering stench of the swamp.

In the end, Tristan's estimate proved remarkably accurate, a fact which he found considerably reassuring. They passed several small farmsteads on the very fringe of the marshlands, all of them abandoned—at least, no one responded when the king rode Shallot up to the porch and called out a greeting.

These were rude dwellings, for the most part, the shacks of hunters and trappers or the small cottages of poor homesteaders. None of the places showed any sign of damage, but the absence of the residents was eerie and disturbing.

The king and the faerie dragon finally reached a larger house, several spacious rooms encircled by well-built wooden walls. A neat barn stood nearby, and Tristan heard the sounds of lowing cattle. The beasts sounded hungry, but not desperately so. Several lush grainfields and pastures were visible among the stands of oak and maple.

Here Tristan dismounted and climbed the steps, knocking heavily against the door. He was astounded when the portal swung easily open beneath his fist.

"Hello! Is anyone here?" he shouted. No answer reached his ears.

"Let's get going!" Newt urged, curled up in the saddle now that the king had left it vacant. "I'm hungry for fish."

"Why don't you throw those cows some hay while I go look around?" the king suggested. "It sounds like they're as hungry as you are."

"I'm not hungry for *hay!*" Newt protested. Nevertheless, after he listened to the bellowing for a moment, he popped into the air and flew off toward the barn.

Finally, still hearing nothing from within the house, the High King stepped through the door and looked around a simple but comfortably furnished room. A stone fireplace occupied most of one wall, with a pair of wooden benches facing away from the hearth—a summer rearrangement, no doubt. But what most intrigued him was the table.

He saw dirty plates scattered among half-full goblets and hastily scattered eating knives. One plate had fallen to the floor and shattered, the pieces left where they lay in the family's haste to depart. Crossing to the cookstove, he placed his hand carefully against the burners. Cold.

Feeling a growing sense of urgency, Tristan stalked from the house, taking only the time to latch the door behind him.

"Newt!" he called. "Let's go!" Looking toward the barn, the king saw a number of brown shapes lumbering eagerly into a pasture.

"The hay was too heavy," Newt explained, "so I let them into the grass instead."

"Good idea." Tristan praised him sincerely. "It doesn't look like these folks are going to be back anytime soon." In fact, the hastily abandoned house had sent a real jolt of alarm through him. For the first time, the fact became glaringly apparent—something was terribly amiss in his kingdom. His bemused reaction thus far now struck him as a shameful lapse of rulership.

Climbing back into the saddle, he cursed the awkwardness caused by his missing hand. Quickly the High King urged Shallot into a trot, and the horse paced like an eager colt along a path through the increasingly open woodland. The hounds coursed nearby, no longer ranging through the woods. They, too, sensed their master's tension, responding protectively.

Only Newt remained unaffected. "I don't smell any fish yet," he discoursed petulantly. "How much farther do you think it is, anyway?"

When Tristan continued to ignore his prattle, however, even the flighty serpent began to sense that something had changed. He ceased his noisemaking and raised himself high on the pommel, sniffing the air and peering around like a watchful sentinel.

Then they reached another farmstead, like the previous settlement except that this one was more than abandoned. It was destroyed. Grim fury took hold of Tristan as Shallot cantered past a smoking ruin that had once been a large house. Dead cattle, many cruelly gutted, lay outside what had once been a barn. That structure, like the house, was now a smoking pile of charred timbers.

Yet the heat was not so great that it held Tristan or the dogs at bay, so he deduced that the damage had been done the previous day.

"Go!" the king cried suddenly, kicking Shallot sharply in the ribs. Anything he could do now, he knew, he couldn't do here.

The great war-horse sprang into a gallop, swiftly carrying the king back onto the track that had grown into a narrow forest road. The hounds flew along at the horse's heels, tongues flapping and legs pumping from the effort to keep up. Newt, after bouncing off the pommel several times, took to the air, arrowing along with his wings buzzing frantically a foot or two over Tristan's head. He was too busy flying even to talk.

A scent came to Tristan that he well recognized—the salt air of the sea. Then forest opened away from them, breaking into scattered clumps of trees dotting a broad expanse of pasture and grainfields. Before them, they caught sight of a gleaming surface through the trees, and the High King knew that at last they approached the Strait of Oman.

Then something closer caught his attention as the hounds flew past the horse in a frenzy of barking and snarling. The dogs leaped into a thicket lying directly beside Tristan's path, and the king immediately heard deeper, more unnatural snarls.

In another moment, several large shapes sprang from the underbrush, sending the steady war-horse rearing backward in fright. They were already too close for his lance, so the king discarded the long shaft and grimly his sword, facing the onslaught of no less than a dozen trolls.

* * * * *

The *Princess of Moonshae* finally approached the two enclosing peninsulas, preparing to depart Codsbay—admittedly somewhat less gracefully than she had entered. Nevertheless, Thurgol and his firbolgs had finally begun to, if not master, at least comprehend the art of propelling the sleek vessel through the water.

Also, the giant chieftain had thought of another precaution, one that gave him a somewhat smug sense of satisfaction. Before they sailed from the harbor, he had ordered his crew of giants to paddle to each of the fishing boats floating in the placid bay. They had kicked several planks out of each hull, so by the time they reached the mouth of the bay, every ship of the tiny fleet rested on the bottom.

With the threat of pursuit thus minimized, Thurgol concentrated on getting his villagemates to propel the longship with some modicum of control. By limiting the oarsmen to a pair on each side, the chieftain found that the giant-kin could row with a reasonable chance of striking the same cadence—at least, a good part of the time.

Thurgol himself stood in the stern, holding the long rudder pole. At first, he had tried to help by swinging this pole back and forth, but he soon concluded that the ship progressed better if he just let the rudder trail into the water behind them. It was a lot less work that way, too.

"Row!" he called, his bass voice rumbling across the smooth-watered bay. "Row again!" In this way, he tried to synchronize the pace of the oarsmen. Once these laboring giant-kin had learned to lift the blades out of the water on the return strokes, they actually made pretty good progress.

As the proud longship emerged from the bay, the haze of the strait parted as if by magic. There before them, breathtaking in its majesty, sweeping above the lowlands with snow-covered peak and jagged, rocky slopes, loomed the Icepeak. Though the mist still cloaked the bulk of Oman's Isle, the mountain summit itself stood out in clear relief, outlined by the late afternoon sun into patches of shadow and stupendous, rose-tinted light.

"It seems so close," Garisa said. The old shaman sat upon the stern platform, resting her weary bones, the Silverhaft Axe across her lap. Now that they had seized a ship and embarked onto the water, the withered hag felt a sense of profound wonder.

"Won't get there before dark, though," Thurgol mused, with a rough approximation of their speed thus far. "Row . . . row again!" he shouted as a pair of oarsmen clanked their bladed shafts together.

"But we'll *get* there," the shaman declared, her tone soft

with amazement.

"Didn't you know that?" Thurgol asked, surprised. After all, this had been her idea.

"There was a time when I wasn't so sure," Garisa admitted. Of course, she well remembered her incantation in Cambro, designed to draw the band out of that dwarven stronghold before disaster struck. At the time, she hadn't really considered the goal of the Icepeak an attainable one, practically speaking, but now good fortune, perhaps even the will of the gods, had set her misgivings aside.

"Baatlrap won't be happy," the chieftain remarked with a deep chuckle. Then he shook his head in regret. "Still, I only wish he'd stay dead. When we get back, he'll be trouble."

Garisa looked intently at the sturdy firbolg who was the chieftain of her lifelong village. He still seemed a callow youth in some ways, but she had to admit that his leadership had been steady and forthright in bringing them this far. She honestly liked Thurgol—liked him enough that she couldn't bring herself to tell him that she didn't think they'd ever be going home again.

That feeling had been growing steadily in her mind, solidifying, it seemed, with each night's sleep, each day's progress in their march to the north. It wasn't a feeling that she sought or desired. More to the point, as they had left Myrloch Vale behind, she had been possessed by a sense of melancholy, as if a powerful voice within told her that she looked on the trees and blossoms of that favored place for the last time.

Now, as the coastline of Gwynneth itself fell away, as she took the first waterborne voyage of her life, Garisa couldn't suppress this wistful conclusion. Of course, if she was right, that meant that Baatlrap wouldn't be a problem for them at any time in the foreseeable future, and that was a fact she could welcome with something like genuine enthusiasm.

"Trolls are no good for us anyway. More trouble than they're worth," she observed. "They make the humans too mad. You wait. Soon comes an army to chase them down."

"What army?" growled Thurgol, looking at the shore behind them. He had begun to assume that his force was the greatest army in the Moonshaes, but Garisa's reminder made him remember that was not the case.

"King's army, probably. Maybe dwarves. Who knows?" Garisa said with a shrug.

"Northmen, too," observed Thurgol. For the first time, he wondered about the odd chance that had brought the crew of this vessel to the aid of Codscove. Twenty years earlier, the firbolgs had allied themselves with the long-haired raiders of the sea, both groups waging war against the Ffolk. Yet here were the sons of those same men, sailing up to a battle and joining in on the side of their former enemies against their allies of that same campaign!

"Northmen come after *us*," Garisa suggested. "We got their ship. They won't like it."

"Yup," Thurgol agreed.

He wondered what kinds of men—what nature of enemy—they would find upon Oman's Isle. Looking forward, he saw that the sunset now cloaked the Icepeak in a mantle of rich purple light, while the lands below it and the sea around them had all fallen into shadow.

The moving scene seemed heavy with promise, certainly magical in its potential. The picture lingered before his eyes for almost another hour, until the last rays of sunlight vanished from the world, and the outline of the Icepeak was silhouetted only by the stars.

* * * * *

Once more Robyn stood atop the high tower of Corwell, watching the stars break into the clear night sky. She longed to take wing, to fly across the isle and find her husband. His strange quest had unsettled her more with each passing day, until she could hardly stand to think about it.

Yet she had to content herself with the knowledge that Alicia and Keane rode on the king's trail, and the hope that they would reach him in time for . . . in time for what?

In time to save his life. A flicker of guilt rose within her as she realized that Tristan's life *did* loom as the most important thing. Her husband, her daughters, the people, and the cantrevs—*these* were the true joys of life. All of them, but most strongly her own family, formed for the queen the boundaries of her life, the factors that caused her joy and gave her purpose.

Yet there was still that guilt. Couldn't she serve her goddess and serve a family as well? She tried to tell herself that it was so, but then came the memory of that rampage in Myrloch Vale—an attack she hadn't sensed, that hadn't caused her the faintest inkling of trouble. Did she serve her goddess poorly? Had her life become too focused on people, not attentive enough to the will of her goddess?

That was just one more thing she didn't know. Robyn tried, with minimal success, to tell herself that her ignorance of Tristan and his enemies was the result of distance. She thought of the enigma dwelling in the very castle below her, and realized that it was not her husband who should now be the source of her greatest concern.

In fact, Deirdre's health now seemed as vibrant as ever. Though the princess refused any attempts to discuss her condition, she ate regular meals, apparently slept through the nights—at least, Robyn hadn't heard evidence of the nightmare in more than a week.

Deirdre, however, had taken to sleeping with her door bolted, so the queen had had little chance to observe her slumber. She could have entered the apartment by invoking the power of the goddess, of course—say, in the body of a mouse or a swallow—but Robyn didn't feel justified in such intrusive behavior.

At least, not yet. Still, she found it hard to put her finger on exactly what disturbed her about the dark-haired young woman. Was it Deirdre's total nonchalance, the ease with which she now treated all aspects of life? She had never been a cheerful or outgoing person, but now she seemed infused with a new serenity, a placid acceptance of daily things that took Robyn quite by surprise.

At the same time, the High Queen saw something sinister, a bit frightening, in her daughter's rapid transformation. She recalled as well as her husband the slivers of the enchanted mirror slicing into Deirdre's skin, then vanishing and leaving no wounds. What would be the effect if such a talisman, fusing itself into the young sorceress, actually had become a part of her?

It was a question that Robyn was afraid to answer, and so for the last week, she had simply passed the time in the castle, knowing that her daughter avoided her company but not at all sure what to do about it.

Yet tonight, as the sun had vanished into the west and the multitudinous stars had broken through the mantle of the sky, all her calm emotions, all her serenity, seemed to the queen like a cruel masquerade. She didn't know what to fear, yet she felt that something was powerfully amiss. Though her unease could perhaps have been caused by fear for her husband or for her eldest daughter, she knew this wasn't the case. By the time full darkness had claimed the heavens, she knew that she had to descend from the tower and confront Deirdre.

Never had the spiraling stairway seemed so long as it did to Robyn Kendrick on that unseasonably chill summer night. She pulled her woolen cape more tightly about her, though the stonework of the tower walls effectively blocked any trespassing hint of a breeze. Torches flickered from wall sconces, only a pair of them to light the long descent, so the queen still had to watch her step carefully.

Reaching the door to the keep, she hesitated, restrained by unnamed fear. Finally she entered the upper hallway, striding purposefully into the royal apartments, across the foyer to the door blocking access to Deirdre's chamber.

Here Robyn stopped again, but only for a moment. Drawing a deep breath, she raised her hand and knocked firmly on the solid wooden portal.

The sharp sound rang eerily through the silence of the keep. It seemed that even the normally bustling kitchen was quiet. She could hear nothing else in the wide halls, the empty and open great room below.

She waited for several moments, and when she heard nothing within the room, she knocked again, more firmly. This time it seemed that the echo had an empty, vague quality, a lack of resonance. She knocked again, confirming that the sound was somehow improper.

The next noise in the keep came from outside the walls, but it filled her with unspeakable terror. "Murder!" came the cry. "Murder on the parapet!"

The queen stepped to a window and looked along the top of the castle wall. Several guards gathered around a motionless shape—a body, she sensed, as if she could feel the warmth of blood pooling around the form. A body that lay outside the door closest to the royal chambers . . . closest to Dierdre's room!

A sense of urgency infused Robyn Kendrick, and she returned to her daughter's door. The High Queen placed the palms of her hands flat against the door. She cast a simple enchantment, and the wooden panels flared warm to her touch.

Magic! Something arcane protected the door, or the room within, and this was enough for the High Queen.

"*Arqueous telemite!*" she cried, drawing upon the power of her goddess. Her hands pressed against the wood, seizing the essence of the trees that the Earthmother had grown, taking the firm grain and straight lines and warping those shapes in the name of Robyn's own magic.

The spell twisted the solid planks that formed the door, warping them so powerfully that they popped free from the iron bands confining them. With rending shrieks, the hinges tore from the walls of stone, leaving the doorway to the room blocked only by a tangle of twisted wreckage.

Pulling sharply against the planks, Robyn broke the pieces away with two quick tugs. In another moment, she stepped through the entrance, seeing immediately that Deirdre was not in her bed.

A glimmer of candlelight in the adjoining parlor caught her eye, and Robyn raced through the bedroom, noticing that her footsteps made no noise even as she kicked pieces of the door out of her path. She understood immediately that Deirdre had concealed the room beneath a magical spell of silence, a fact that only increased her sense of alarm.

She pushed through the hanging curtain dividing the parlor from the sleeping chamber, and for a moment, she saw Deirdre before her. The queen's younger daughter sat in a trancelike silence, her eyes closed, her hands clasped on her knees before her. Several pairs of candles flamed about the room, flickering from the wind of Robyn's entry. Four platters sat on the floor before her—shallow bowls of dark, thick liquid. The pungent smell of fresh blood assaulted the High Queen's nostrils.

Still, unnaturally, there was no sound. Robyn opened her mouth, demanding Deirdre's attention, but no words emerged—and the princess remained inert and entranced.

Then the candles flared brightly, the tiny flames surging upward to illuminate the room with a brightness like sunlight. Robyn felt as though she were mired in mud, watching her daughter's face, cold and icily aloof, etched in the detail of the clear white light.

"No!" screamed the queen, the spell of silence swallowing the sound but not the icy fear that gripped her heart.

In the next instant, Deirdre disappeared.

* * * * *

The princess flew, lending herself to the wings of magic and the power of unknown gods. Plunging through the space of ether, she traveled with dizzying speed through a whirl of colors and chaotic noise. She rode the void like the wild wind, feeling the blessings of a multitude of gods, growing steadily in might and power . . . and ambition.

The pulse of godhood thundered in her veins, carried through the artifact of Talos, the shards of mirror that had become part of her body and made of her so much more than she had been.

She felt the hand of a storming god clasping her own, and then those daggers of glass within her flared into light. Deirdre glowed like a sky speckled with stars, her flesh the cold night and the gleaming points of light coming from the immortal artifact that had torn into her flesh.

But not rending her—no, not at all. There had been no wound, no pain, when those fragments had pierced her. Now, for the first time, she understood that it had not been an assault against her.

In fact, it was the mirror of Talos that had made her whole.

❊11❊

Trollcleaver

Tristan's sword flashed in his hand the instant he saw the
springing trolls. Even so, he barely raised the blade as the
first of the beasts reached wicked talons toward his leg.
Chopping frantically, he hacked at the monster's wrists,
sending it scuttling backward with a shriek of pain.

A pair of trolls closed from his left, and he lowered his
shield. The buckler's tight straps, modified to secure it to his
handless arm, held firm as he bashed the shield firmly into
the face of the first troll. The second monster stumbled to
the ground, borne downward by the leaping Ranthal. The
great moorhound locked his jaws around the troll's neck
while the other dogs tore into the creature's legs.

Shallot whirled through a full circle, lashing out with his
rear hooves to crush the chest of a troll leaping at them from
behind. Newt had vanished, either in sudden flight or, more
likely, concealed by his power of invisibility. A bark of pain
from one of the trolls as tooth marks appeared in its shoulder solved that mystery.

"Go!" Tristan barked to Shallot, and the stallion sprang
forward immediately. The sword flashed brightly in the sunlight, and a bleeding head flew from the body of a suddenly
lurching troll. The corpse fell to the ground in a moment,
growing still as dark, greenish black blood pumped from the
gaping wound onto the ground.

The hounds cried out a challenge and followed, abandoning their original victim to pounce upon another pair of the
monstrous humanoids. One of the dogs yelped and fell to
the ground, and in a quick glance, Tristan saw the gaping
wound along her side.

His sword dropped again, cleaving into the shoulder of a

muscular troll. Shallot whirled away as another lunging monster narrowly missed dragging the High King from the saddle. Desperately stabbing, Tristan drove the point of his sword through the creature's face, almost losing the weapon when the troll dropped to the ground. With a powerful heave, he tore the blade from the bony wound as the stallion charged into another troll.

A ball of fire flared in the air, sending trolls scuttling away in panic, though as Tristan rode past the apparition, he could feel no heat. Newt's illusion was realistic enough to momentarily scatter the trolls, however.

Shallot trampled a troll while the hounds dragged another to the earth. Tristan's sword slashed to the right, decapitating one of the creatures as its claws raked across the king's chest and belly. Pivoting in the saddle, the man chopped to his left, scarring the face and long nose of another attacker. The stallion plunged and bucked, driving heavy hooves into the writhing body below it, and then Newt popped into sight, hovering in front of Tristan's eyes and gesturing behind him in agitation.

"Look!" cried Newt, pointing over the king's shoulder. "Look at *that!*"

Twisting in alarm, Tristan propelled Shallot through a quick spin. The king raised his shield to ward off the anticipated attack, but he could see no threat there! Instead, he saw the wreckage of the fight, muddy hoofprints, the dying hound, and several dead trolls, including two he'd beheaded. But no attacker menaced him.

"What is it?" he demanded, spinning back just in time to see the remaining trolls bolt into the brush.

"Look!" blurted Newt again, his face twisting in sublime frustration.

And then it struck him. Stunned, Tristan looked back again, checking carefully—and it was true! The trolls he had killed *were still dead!* The import slowly dawned on him.

Then he saw one of the previously slain monsters move, carefully and stealthily drawing its legs and arms beneath it.

He remembered the beast—the dogs had torn its green skin to ribbons, leaving the creature dead in a pool of fetid blood. Now it was whole again, ready to attack or flee. Tristan readied his sword, intentionally riding closer to the monster.

With an ear-stunning roar, the troll sprang from a prone position into a flying leap toward the human rider. Tristan was shocked by the power of its arms and legs, the springing speed of its leap, but that didn't stop him from bracing in his saddle and raising the shield to meet the beast with a smashing clang. Lurching backward from the impact—the troll weighed at least twice as much as the man—Tristan nevertheless chopped savagely with his sword, cleaving the grotesque face from forehead to neck. The monster fell like a dead tree, slain again.

"*Now* do you see?" Newt persisted, popping into sight beside the king's ear.

"I think I do," he said softly, not entirely certain he could believe what he saw.

Once more Tristan looked around the scene of the skirmish. The two headless trolls lay still. Though the gaping neck wounds had ceased to bleed, they showed no sign of healing. Another troll lay dead nearby, killed by a sword cut through its neck and into the chest. That wound, too, showed no sign of regeneration. On the contrary, it had clearly been the mortal blow. And there was the one he had stabbed in the face, the tiny wound belying the severity of the thrust that must have plunged all the way into the evil brain.

"Hsst! Over here!" said Newt, in an exaggerated whisper. The faerie dragon hovered over a dense patch of underbrush, pointing down with a tiny claw.

A furtive movement beneath a screening bush drew Tristan's eye. He dismounted, more and more curious, wondering what prevented so many of the slain trolls from returning to life. Shield raised protectively, sword held at the ready, he approached the dense thicket. Ranthal, hackles standing on end, snarlingly advanced beside him, while Newt remained in his bouncing hover.

flame that suddenly burst through Deirdre's room. When she next tried to look, her vision was a series of glowing spots, brilliantly dancing before her eyes, blocking out the darkness of the room itself. Yet even with her shadowy vision, the High Queen could see that her daughter was gone.

Cries of alarm came from the hallway, and she heard persistent pounding at the door. She heard the echoes of her own scream ringing from the walls and understood that the spell of silence had vanished with Deirdre.

"My queen? Are you all right? What's happened?" She recognized the voice of a loyal sergeant-major, a man-at-arms who had served the family all his life and now had been entrusted the security of the royal apartments.

"It's all right, Kaston. I'm fine—just a little surprised, that's all."

"Can I get you something, Your Majesty? Shall I send for the healer?"

"No!" Robyn snapped, her own agitation hardening her voice. A cleric of the New Gods was the last person Robyn wanted to see right now! "I said that I'm *fine!*"

"Of course, my queen," Kaston replied, humbled. Nevertheless, she heard no sound of footsteps walking away and presumed the loyal guard had taken up station right outside her door. The feeling gave her a small sense of security as she wandered around Deirdre's room.

Something jutted from beneath the rug, and she knelt to retrieve it. It was a small medallion, platinum circling a golden image of Helm's All-Seeing Eye. She dropped the icon on the floor as if it had burned her. Looking around more carefully then, she noticed other objects—figurines of wax and clay, and tiny images of gems set on plates or discs. She recognized the rounded lute of Oghma, the tiny skull that was the symbol of Myrkul, lord of the beasts.

She saw the bowls of liquid, only reluctantly admitting that the stuff was blood. Dimly she recalled the shout of alarm—"Murder!"—but her mind refused the implication. A shiver passed along her spine, and slowly, carefully the High Queen backed through the warped doorway, collapsing into a chair when she reached the apartment anteroom.

Where had the princess gone? That question, Robyn decided, was secondary to the central issue. At the core of Deirdre's disappearance, the queen now knew beyond doubt, lay her daughter's dangerous devotion to the gods of the other Realms, the deities who so wanted to overwhelm and suffocate the sublime will of the Earthmother.

For a long time, she sat still in the chair, her mind working feverishly while her body rested, storing physical strength and energy for the task she now inevitably faced. Her husband seized by madness, gone alone to war. By the goddess, she loved him! She felt a deep, mindless terror that he would face some unknown harm, some deadly fate, and she would not be there to help him. Deirdre, too, occupied much of her mind. Why had she killed? What had stolen her away? But all of her cogitation, all of her musing, couldn't give her the guidance she needed. They couldn't tell her where she would find her daughter.

Yet gradually, through the curtain of her despair, she began to sense that she was being tested by these onslaughts against her family. Mysteries assailed her, a thousand unknown questions that she could try to answer, but came instead upon still more enigmatic problems. Finally, in her heart, she began to suspect the truth. She might find comfort, but she would never gain the necessary wisdom, if she stayed here in the castle, in her home.

To answer these questions, the druid queen knew, she would have to seek her explanations upon a higher plane, at a different place. By now she knew this with certainty. Her body tingled with energy, and her spirit soared to the calling of the goddess who was mother to the Ffolk. Only the Earthmother could show her the course to follow, could provide her with the means to counter this threat.

And so once again the white hawk winged toward Myrloch Vale.

* * * * *

"*One* human chased you off your post?" Baatlrap snarled in astonished disbelief. He growled and blustered at the half-dozen trolls standing before him, cuffing each several times as he belittled their parentage and their courage. Nevertheless, the monstrous humanoid was considerably distressed by their arrival and their story.

As a lot, the warriors cowered before him, a craven remnant of a dozen savage brutes Baatlrap had left to guard the approaches to Codscove. Three of them had deep sword wounds, wounds that showed no sign of regenerating!

"And a pack of dogs—hounds from the Abyss itself!" one of the trolls jabbered in the trollish tongue.

"He rode a hell horse, too—a steed that bore me to the earth and rended my back with hooves of steel!" another bore witness.

"Wait here!" shouted the giant troll as the rest of his column of trolls and firbolgs meandered out of sight in its march along the northern shore of Gwynneth. The ragged army, still strong and belligerent despite the defection of Thurgol and his stalwart firbolgs, came to a halt, the trolls and the few dozen giant-kin who had ignored Thurgol's leadership flopping in the shade of trees and trying to understand the reports of the panicked rear guards.

"Did this human ride before an army?" demanded Baatlrap.

"Almost assuredly!" pledged one of the survivors.

"It must have been close behind," mused another. "Else why would he stand and fight us when our numbers should have put him to flight?"

"Your numbers should have *slain* him!" Baatlrap bellowed, smacking the speaker on the side of his head. "And you should have buried him beneath the bodies of his horse and his hounds! How is it that you can fail me thus?"

No answer came from the defeated trolls, though the creatures grew increasingly sullen in the face of Baatlrap's abuse. The hulking brute looked back and forth, along the assembled rank of his monstrous company. It was a potent band, he knew—two score giant-kin and five times that many trolls.

Of course, he would have liked to create still more trolls, but that scheme had been prevented when Garisa and the Silverhaft Axe had sailed to the north. Vaguely Baatlrap felt a desire to go after the weapon. Perhaps one day he would. As for now, he had a hard time imagining a human army that could stand against his present force, nor had he yet seen any evidence that the humans had mustered any men-at-arms even to challenge him.

Yet if there were such a force, it could just as easily be behind him as before him. And this human warrior, the one whose sword sliced the wounds that would not heal, could well be a harbinger of such an army. Indeed, the more Baatlrap thought about it, the more he became convinced: There could be no other explanation.

Certainly any lone human knight, well mounted, who found himself attacked by a dozen trolls would try to ride away from the fight, wouldn't he? Common sense would allow no other interpretation! Since this warrior had elected *not* to flee the battle, it could only mean that he was followed by many more of his own kind.

The prospect did not alarm the great troll. Instead, the thought of such a battle gave him a sense of pleasant antici- pation, together with a self-congratulatory nod for his shrewd analysis of the enemy's situation. This way, Baatl- rap's army would be ready to face the pursuing humans in a fair fight, at a place of the troll lord's choosing.

"Stop the march!" he shouted to the humanoid monsters of his command. "We meet the humans here!"

* * * * *

Finellen tried to conceal her worry from the rest of her troops and from her human and elven companions. She wasn't entirely successful in either case.

"It's going to be tough to catch them, isn't it?" Hanrald asked softly, leading his war-horse along the trail beside the dwarven captain.

"Aye," she grunted sourly. "They move so damned fast. Even a whole night's forced march puts us two leagues behind them!"

The column of dwarves had unquestioningly followed their leader's command, tromping grimly through the night. Hanrald had ridden or walked along with them in silent amazement, for the doughty warriors stumped along at an exhausting rate hour after hour, and yet not one of them raised a voice in complaint or showed any sign of faltering. Brigit's scouting report had indicated that the monsters camped at dusk, and this news propelled all of them into a steady, draining pace.

Before sunrise, the dwarves paused for an hour's rest. Some tried to nap for a few minutes, while others simply stretched muscles battered and bruised from long days on the trail. Brigit rode forth on her fleet mare, ready as always to scout the enemy force. Shortly after her departure, however, the druid Danrak entered the camp with news that alarmed them all.

The monsters, he told them, broke camp even before the coming of daylight. Once again they marched away from the dwarves, increasing the distance between the two forces faster than Finellen and her warriors could close it.

"Still, are you sure it's as bad as all that?" questioned the earl as he and Finellen made their way along the trail. "After all, Brigit hasn't gotten back yet. She might have some good news."

Finellen shook her head in frustration and disappointment. "You heard what Danrak said. They were already on the march an hour before dawn!"

The courageous druid, Hanrald knew, had been observing the camp of the trollish army from nearby vantage points in the brush and trees, no doubt concealed in the body of some fleet forest creature, perhaps a rabbit or squirrel, or maybe even a sparrow or jay. Such disguises had enabled him to give them excellent reports on each of the monsters' camps and their subsequent lines of march.

"Same direction as yesterday, I assume?" the Earl of Fairheight queried.

"Yup. They're heading for the Gray Headlands!" Finellen said disgustedly. "It looks like they'd take the axe all the way to the Sword Coast if they could swim!"

The day after the ravage of the town, the raiders had marched northeast, staying near the shore of Gwynneth. Though the beasts had looted a few small fishing villages—isolated huts and cottages, for the most part—there were no sizable villages in their immediate path. Still, the eastern shore of the island was populated far more heavily than was the north, so it wouldn't take long before the giant humanoids would begin to encounter victims aplenty.

Hanrald knew, too, that even the hardy dwarves couldn't handle another night of marching. It seemed that, by acting upon his advice, Finellen might have missed her chance for the fight that she so desperately wanted. The long-legged troops of the enemy were just too fast for the dwarves.

Something moved in the trees before them, and then, as she always did, Brigit and her mare materialized. Hanrald's heart jumped with relief as she shrugged away his helping hand to dismount on her own.

"How far ahead are they?" Finellen inquired grumpily. Then something on the sister's knight's face gave the dwarfwoman pause. "What is it? Do you have news?"

"I do, at that," the Llewyrr woman reported. She shook her head in amazement, as if she didn't believe what she was going to say.

"I saw them on the march. They kept on for several hours, into the midmorning. Then, for some reason that I can't figure out, they just stopped. They're waiting near the coast, barely a league and a half away."

* * * * *

"I don't like blundering along in this bottomland. It's too easy for it to drop into a bog," Alicia announced with concern.

Following behind her, Keane cursed as a thorny branch slashed back across his face. "And getting more tangled with every step!" he added sourly.

The two of them pressed forward, ahead of the main body of troops. They had been forced to leave their horses some distance behind but continued to explore in the hope that the ground would open up.

Abruptly Alicia stumbled, a loud sucking noise following her foot from the ground. She grasped a tree trunk for balance as Keane saw that she stood ankle deep in brown muck. Flies buzzed around them, and the air pressed close and humid.

"Help!" cried the princess, suddenly in real distress as her feet continued to sink.

Keane reached for her hand and pulled, but it took all of his strength to break the princess free of the clutching mire. Finally he jerked backward and Alicia came free, falling into his arms as he collapsed against the rough bark of a tree trunk.

Exhausted, he held her, and she was content to lie in his arms as they gradually caught their breath. Finally, in a regretful moment for Keane, she sat up and brushed the hair back from her face before she looked at her mud-stained boots.

"Thanks," she said, squeezing his hand. "That stuff surprised me." His heart swelled, and he wanted the moment to last forever.

"Let's rest a bit," Keane urged gently. *I want to be here alone with you!* his mind whispered. It was a selfish reason, but the mage told himself that the princess really did look exhausted.

"Yes. It's nice to sit still for a moment," she agreed softly.

She looked at him, and her deep, bright eyes filled his vision and his heart. Again he felt the urge to take her into his arms, to cover her mouth with kisses, but his innate reserve would not weaken enough for him to act.

And then, in the next instant, her thoughts had turned back to the men under her command. "It doesn't seem that we can go any farther this way," she said. "We'll have to chance the course to the east."

Keane nodded, reluctantly turning to practical matters. "I think you're right, though it surprises me to find this much of a swamp here. Are you sure eastward is the course you want to follow?"

"Father must have encountered this morass too," Alicia continued. "If we halt the men here and explore to either side, we'll probably lose a whole day!"

Keane nodded. Even if he used magic—a spell of flying, for example, to carry him birdlike over the tangled fen—he would need the remaining hours of daylight to complete a moderately thorough reconnaissance. Those would be precious hours when the men of Corwell would not be marching. He well understood Alicia's desire to keep moving. The welfare of King Kendrick had become a growing concern to the magic-user as well. Privately he grew increasingly concerned that they hadn't come upon any sign of the king's passage. It was a fact that did not bode well for their chances of eventually finding Tristan, the mage suspected.

"So all I can do is try to guess at his track," Alicia concluded. "Codscove *must* lie to the east of here, and that seems like the most logical place for him to go!"

They followed the tangled trail back to the main body of the troops. There, the Exalted Inquisitor, still clad in his immaculate white robe, greeted them with expressions of concern.

"This place looks dangerous," he said, clucking in reproval. "I was just about to come after you!"

"That wasn't necessary or called for!" Alicia snapped, discouraged enough to dispense with the niceties of diplomatic language.

"Forgive my overindulgent concern," the inquisitor apologized solicitously.

"We've got a problem," Keane interjected. "This swamp blocks our path to the north."

"So we're angling to the east," Alicia concluded. Stalking past the cleric, she went up to Sands and Parsallas, who had been lounging in the shade of a wide oak. The two sergeants quickly got to their feet when they saw her approaching.

"How are the rations?" Alicia asked Sands, who'd served as unofficial quartermaster.

"Enough for a couple days yet, Your Highness," replied the bowlegged veteran.

"Aye, a few more fine meals of beans and dry bread!" added Parsallas with a hearty chuckle. The lanky warrior seemed to remain cheerful about whatever irritating setbacks they encountered.

"We've got to start up in five minutes," she said quickly. "I'll lead the way. We need to find a path around this swamp."

Each of the sergeants saluted smartly and proceeded to gather the troops into column. They started to march exactly a minute earlier than Alicia had ordered.

Mounted upon Brittany, the princess scouted ahead for the best path through the tangle of underbrush. Keane rode behind her, not wanting to slow her up with his own clumsy horsemanship but ensuring that she remained within sight so that he could reach her side in seconds if need be.

Soon Brittany broke through a tangle of vines onto a narrow game trail, and Alicia guided the eager mare along the relatively straight pathway. Keane followed, and then came Sands leading the first company of Corwell. The spirits and step of the men picked up noticeably now that they had a trail to follow.

Keane prodded his old gelding into a trot, and the nag hastened to catch up to Brittany and the princess. Behind him, he heard the approach of other hooves and turned to see the Exalted Inquisitor also riding ahead of the footmen. It seemed that the open trail had infused them all with energy and enthusiasm.

Then Alicia reined in, uttering a crude sailor's curse. Keane galloped to her side, though he recognized frustration, not danger, in her tone. In another moment, he saw why.

The trail suddenly dropped away, dipping into a pool of fetid water and disappearing. All around them here, to the front and to both sides, stretched a seemingly endless expanse of rank swamp.

* * * * *

Sir Koll was a large knight, broad in the shoulders and the waist. Though he was probably twice the Prince of Gnarhelm's age, Brandon found in him a kindred warrior spirit. He was surprised to learn, however, that the knight's parents had been people of the north, originally settling upon Gwynneth after a successful raiding voyage. Only when Koll had been knighted by High King Kendrick had he fully adopted the manners and customs of the Ffolk.

"Lately, of course, there hasn't been much need for my sword," explained the hearty warrior. His horse had been slain in the final moments of battle. Now he walked along at a steady pace, accompanying Brandon and some two dozen men-at-arms, both northmen and Ffolk, as a rear guard for the fleeing townspeople of Codscove. "But I'm glad I had the sense to keep the thing sharpened!"

"I've had plenty of need for my ship," Brandon countered glumly. "You'd think I would have learned to keep a better watch on her."

"*I'm* the fool who lost her for you!" Knaff interrupted dejectedly. The helmsman bore the responsibility for the capture heavily. His shoulders slumped, and his footsteps were more of a shuffle than a march.

"No, old friend. Stop beating yourself with that!" Brandon countered, clapping Knaff on the shoulder. "The responsibility is mine. I came in to shore without scouting, without even considering the possibilities. The blame is mine."

"Pah—bad luck! Could happen to anyone," Koll allowed. "And, besides, we'll get her back!"

The prince wished he could share his companion's enthusiasm, but his current prospects looked less than ideal.

They had spent the afternoon after their defeat in steady flight, attempting to put as much space between themselves and the monstrous invaders as possible. Now, another day later, the women and children had been given time to find shelter in the secluded grottoes and groves of the woodlands. There they would await news.

The warriors, meanwhile, had debated what they should do. Most of the townsmen had no interest in trying to fight the monsters again. After all, they had already lost their property and many of their neighbors or kin, so unless their families' lives were at stake, they didn't see the point of suffering more death and injury.

With a few exceptions, such as Koll, the men of Codscove seemed all too willing to march to the next sizable cantrev, seeing if they could lure the humanoid horde into a long pursuit and then fight on different ground than their own.

The northmen, and Brandon in particular, had no interest in moving too far from the place where the *Princess of Moonshae* had been captured. It was true that they had no assurances that the ship remained in Codsbay. The trolls had chased them several miles from the village after the battle, preventing any attempts to spy on the harbor. Still, even if the monstrous pirates had tried to embark, Brandon suspected that they wouldn't get terribly far. A related fear to that notion, however, was his constant apprehension that they would destroy his ship on some rocky shore or flounder in the surprise storms that were so common in the Moonshaes.

The final resolution had been the dispatching of this small rear-guard party, with Brandon's crewmen and an equal number of volunteers from the town, led by the redoubtable Koll. The men-at-arms advanced in scattered columns, preceded by several scouts. The latter were woodsmen, Ffolk who spent their days hunting in the forest. They knew its paths and prey and were adept at fast, silent movement.

Brandon and Sir Koll led their group back along the route of their flight, seeking to find out if the troll and firbolg army hastened in pursuit.

"One thing—it seems that they didn't come too far after us," Koll observed as they continued to move back toward the town with no sign of pursuing trolls.

"I wouldn't be surprised if they spent a long time drinking up your liquor stocks," Brandon pointed out. "That doesn't mean they won't be coming after us in a day or two."

"You're right about that. And even if a few of 'em took that ship of yours, I think there'd be plenty left on shore."

Brandon shuddered privately at the thought of numerous hulking firbolgs piling into his beloved ship. Any more than a score or so, he felt certain, and the *Princess of Moonshae* would inevitably capsize.

"Still," Koll added after another mile of undisturbed forest had rolled beneath their boots, "as quick as they came after us when we retreated, I think they'd want to hold on to their advantage. You know, keep us on the run."

"It does seem odd," the Prince of Gnarhelm admitted. Yet still another mile passed with no sign of the trolls. "We must be getting close to Codscove," he guessed.

"Not far at all," agreed the knight. Just then one of the scouts stepped into view, emerging from behind an oak trunk where he'd been completely invisible.

"No sign of 'em so far," reported the green-garbed woods-man. "I don't understand it."

"I don't either," groused Koll. "Somehow, though, I don't think they've just up and disappeared."

* * * * *

Deirdre walked the immortal paths of the gods, a sense of might growing, tingling within her. She heard the words of their counsels, learned the challenge of her being.

"You are the *mighty* one!" came the voices, smoothly urging, compelling her toward greatness. "You will bring us through this barrier with which the ancient shell, the withered hag called the Earthmother, would try to block us."

Talos formed the chorus of words, though others of the New Gods propelled him, eager to claim a place in the Moonshaes. But Talos moved carefully. He would not strike the goddess in Myrloch, in her place of strength. No, for this task, another place would serve.

"Yes!" pledged the princess, thrilling to the role and the power. The shards of glass brightened within her, like a flaming wick concealed by a thin curtain of flesh. "But how?"

"For that," replied the voices of Talos, "we shall grant you a tool."

* * * * *

The demigod had languished in an icy prison for the coming and going of many centuries. Most of that time had passed in cold, mindless blackness as, unknown to Grond, the ages had passed him by.

Now, for the first time in many, many years, that darkness began to lift. The demigod felt the warmth of the world at his feet, the chill of the sky against his skull. For all that time he had rested, in the earth . . . and of the earth. Now, as remembrance of another life returned, the Peaksmasher was reluctant to make any acknowledgment.

He had led his giants here in the distant past, and at the time, the will of the Earthmother had stood strong against him. The clash of immortal wills had been powerful and violent, and in the end, the goddess had vanquished the demigod.

Aware of his past defeat, Grond wasn't certain that the result had been such a bad thing.

❦ 12 ❦

The Face of the Enemy

Tristan camped a short distance from the scene of his fight with the trolls. Finding a low, tree-covered knoll where he could see reasonably well to all sides, he picketed Shallot within a screen of evergreens and ordered the hounds to remain silent and vigilant.

Not daring to risk a fire—even Newt agreed that they didn't want to bring the trolls back just yet—the High King and the faerie dragon ate a cold supper. The loquacious serpent shared his companion's somber mood, talking little while they ate.

Then Tristan found himself a comfortable tree. Laboriously climbing a dozen feet from the ground, using his one hand and his feet to pull himself up the rough bark, he found a wide notch between a pair of sweeping limbs. He leaned back against the trunk, secured by a wide limb encircling his left side. Newt buzzed up to him and then found a stout limb a little higher up the trunk. Here he curled up, catlike, and promptly fell asleep.

Laying the blade he had dubbed Trollcleaver across his lap, the High King watched and waited throughout the remaining hours of evening and fading twilight. The hounds had found places to sleep under the tree, but they, too, remained alert and restless. Still there was no sign of any troll returning to the scene of the skirmish, nor did the corpses show any inclination to regenerate.

Finally, after dark, Tristan slept, though he jolted awake at the sound of any scampering creature of the woodland. He longed to hear the cry of the wolves, but his wishes were met with silence, except for the rustling of the small animals. His hounds, under the example of the well-disciplined

Ranthal, didn't even growl at the rabbits and squirrels. They, like their master, waited for bigger game.

Yet during the course of the night and the dawn, that bigger game never materialized. Stiffly climbing down from his perch before the sun had fully cleared the horizon, Tristan began to wonder if he had sent the band into flight. The latter possibility seemed pretty unlikely, given the fact that he was only one man, but why hadn't they returned to the scene of their watch?

It was time, Tristan decided, to find out what the trolls had been guarding. Climbing easily again into the saddle, with Newt curled up in his position on the pommel, the king urged Shallot into an easy trot. With Ranthal leading, the four remaining hounds loped in a protective screen before the horse and riders.

Almost immediately Tristan noticed that the forest opened up into wide grainfields. He skirted a low hill and at last saw water gleaming before him. By the time he had passed the hill, he could make out the towers of the manor house and temple of a good-sized town.

Codscove! Spurring the powerful war-horse into a canter, Tristan approached the community, sensing immediately that this was a scene of trouble. The great tracks through the grain indicated the advance of a large force, and as he drew closer to the town, he saw the blackened ruins of burned buildings.

Yet, for all the signs of life meeting his eyes, it might have been a ghost town. A few piles of charred timbers still smoldered, casting thin wisps of smoke into the morning air, but the damage was at least a day or two old, Tristan knew. As he neared the first buildings, he saw human corpses, bloated and surrounded by flies, and from them he knew for certain that the battle had been two days before.

It was a sight he had witnessed all too often before, though it had been many years since he had seen it in his own realm. A feeling of deep, fundamental violation took hold of him, slowly welling upward into a crescendo of growing rage.

Again he tried to picture the firbolg lord who had brought all this to be. His hand itched to drive a blade into that hateful body, the grotesque image of evil. *Why?* Why do they attack? What do they seek?

Cautiously he reined in, causing Shallot to prance nervously, still a hundred paces from the nearest fringes of the town.

"What're we stopping for?" demanded Newt, raising his head and peering through the horse's white mane. "I'll bet they have *food* in this town!"

"Remember the way those trolls jumped us? I don't want the same thing to happen when we get between those buildings." Tristan could see that the narrow streets of the town created only a few routes he could use, and all of them could easily conceal a deadly ambush.

"Well, if *that's* all, *I'll* go have a look!" huffed the dragon, bouncing into the air and immediately disappearing. Concealed by invisibility, he flew quickly forward, flying over the main street and looking into the buildings and walled yards to either side.

Five minutes later he had returned to the king. "There's nobody there—no humans, no giants, no trolls. Nothing!" he reported. "Now can we go see if we can find some decent food?"

"I'm afraid not, old friend," Tristan replied. He had learned what he wanted to learn. There was no point now in examining the tragic scenarios that would doubtless be evidenced in the houses of the town. "If the raiders aren't here, they must have gone somewhere else, and I intend to find their trail!"

He guided Shallot in a wide arc around the town, riding along the lanes that ran between the once lush fields. Now most of the crops had been trampled in the chaos of battle. At last, as he neared the shore, he found the muddy track left by a marching army. He saw the harbor, now placid and blue, but the masts of many small boats jutted from the surface, each marking the grave of a fisherfolk boat.

On the ground below, huge, booted feet—firbolgs, Tristan recognized with a tingle of alarm that was nonetheless acute for the fact that the memory was twenty years old—had clumped along in the midst of the horde, while the bare, clawed feet of trolls had carved their own distinctive marks in the earth along the army's fringes.

"Maybe they marched into the town while we were riding around and getting hungry," Newt suggested hopefully.

"Look at the toes," Tristan suggested. "They're pointing away from Codscove."

"I guess you're right," Newt concluded glumly. "At least, *some* of them are going that way."

Ranthal bounded along the trail of the army, but now he stopped, a hundred feet ahead of Tristan, to look back at the king with his ears upraised. The other three moorhounds raced after their leader, and Shallot trotted along in the wake of the dogs.

Tristan was about to call the rangy hounds back—he didn't want them too far in the lead—but the steady Ranthal held his pace to a slow walk until the great war-horse drew near. Then the dogs spread into their protective screen, sniffing alertly and poking through the brush and hedges that flanked the path.

The king's shield was a comfortable weight on his left arm. He tugged at Trollcleaver, reassuring himself that the sword was loose in its scabbard. For several minutes, they rode in silence, even Newt peering alertly to the right and left while Tristan kept his eyes to the front.

Abruptly Ranthal sprang away from a thick hedge, barking furiously. The other hounds joined him, hackles bristling, long fangs bared. Growling and snarling, they backed away from the lush greenery. Nothing moved there, but Tristan drew his sword and studied the hedge, knowing beyond any doubt that he approached a watch post of the predatory raiders.

Tangled branches grew from the ground to a height of eight or nine feet, creating an impenetrable screen. Did another dozen trolls lurk there? He didn't know, but neither did he hesitate in his cautious approach.

"Look out!" squeaked Newt suddenly, bouncing into the air and vanishing as he chattered the alarm. A flash of movement drew the king's attention to the left, just in time to see a huge troll leaping from the concealment of a muddy ditch.

Desperately he raised his shield, bashing the creature's face but failing to block the long, muscular arms. Claws raked his back through his chain mail as the beast seized him and pulled, trying to drag the king from his horse.

Shallot reared instinctively, and only the deep, well-braced saddle saved Tristan from disaster. Grunting against the pain of the troll's grip, he smashed the hilt of Trollcleaver into the monster's face, but the beast clung tenaciously. The war-horse bucked and kicked, unable to break the troll's hold. The king felt the heat of the monster's breath, smelled the fetid rot of its guts as cruelly slashing teeth attempted to tear off his shield arm.

Twisting as much as he could, Tristan reversed the blade and plunged the steel tip into the troll's gaping mouth. Trollcleaver emerged from the back of the monster's neck in a shower of green blood and gore. Retching hideously, the monster finally let go of his victim, slumping back to the ground and writhing in its death throes.

Before him, the dogs, in stiff-legged agitation, still backed away from the concealing shrubs, but the king's attention was suddenly drawn to the rear. He saw them emerge from trees a quarter of a mile off the trail: scores of lanky trolls, racing through the fields in a shockingly fast sprint toward the High King of the Ffolk. Whirling back, he confirmed what he'd suspected a moment before as more of the creatures leaped from the rocks along the shore, closing the last part of the deadly ring.

Except for the gauntlet of hedgerows before him. Even as he nudged the powerful stallion forward, huge forms pushed through, splintering the shrubs like twigs and sending the courageous moorhounds bounding back toward the king.

Firbolgs! Each of them as tall as the king on his huge war-horse, the giant-kin brought back to Tristan a flood of memories from two decades before. He saw the crude assortment of weapons: clubs, mostly, with a few bearing big hammers, axes, or chipped and rusty-bladed swords. A few hefted rocks, and he eyed these most warily, knowing that a blow from one of them could knock him from his saddle or even kill him.

With the appearance of the giants, the monstrous ring closed around Tristan. Behind him, the racing trolls had slowed to a walk once they reached the road. Those to the right and left seemed content to wait, blocking any escape attempt he might make. The firbolgs spread into a broad line, ambling toward the king with caution, more worried about keeping the ring closed than they were about rushing in to attack.

Finally they all stopped, except for one truly colossal troll. That one carried a huge sword, the blade itself as long as Tristan was tall, carved with jagged, wicked-looking teeth down each edge. The massive humanoid swaggered forward with an unmistakable air of command. This one came from the right, where he could see all the components of the monstrous horde and the quarry caught so nicely in the middle of the ring.

Ranthal and the other moorhounds formed a protective circle around their king, facing outward with jaws set firmly. Deep growls rumbled from each canine chest. Newt, of course, was nowhere to be seen.

Holding his sword across his lap, Tristan urged Shallot into a slow walk, leaving the muddy track to push through a field of corn, straight toward the hulking troll.

* * * * *

Thurgol aimed the *Princess of Moonshae* toward a sheltered cove he observed on Oman Isle's shore, but a surprisingly strong current carried him several miles to the east of this destination. Still, the Icepeak remained the crowning feature of their horizon, and the chieftain felt no particular apprehension as he regarded the rock-lined shore. Even if the longship was shattered against those boulders, his primary concern was accomplished if the firbolgs and the Silverhaft Axe could make it onto shore intact, and in the same place.

Finally the firbolgs were fortunate enough to find a stretch of graveled beach, and the longship's keel came to rest against the bottom with scarcely more than a timber-straining shudder that inflicted no damage to the sturdy hull.

"Over the sides!" barked the giant chieftain, and his crew responded with alacrity. These were all firbolgs of his village. The giant-kin who had joined their march in progress had elected to remain with Baatlrap. The fact pleased Thurgol, for it gave him a sense that their quest would end as it had begun. These, his bold and loyal comrades, would see him through.

"You wait here," he told Garisa before he himself dropped over the transom into the gentle breakers.

The sea came barely to the giant-kins' knees for the most part, though at the stern, Thurgol stood in surf that washed as high as his chest. "Push!" he bellowed. "Push it up on the shore!"

Here the steady strength of the firbolgs came to the fore as they raised the longship from the water and hauled it out of reach of the waves. It canted slightly to the side on the flat shore, but Thurgol felt certain that it would remain here—perhaps forever, he admitted, not capable of imagining a future path that would necessarily bring him back to this place, to this ship.

Garisa clambered over the low side of the hull, clutching the Silverhaft Axe in her knobby fist. The giant-kin had brought nothing in the way of cargo beyond the possessions of each individual, so they were immediately ready to start the march.

"There's the mountain," Thurgol said, pointing. "Let's go."

"Remember," the shaman cautioned him, "the Peak-smasher is imprisoned on the north slope of the peak, where the sun can never reach him. We have to approach it from the other side. We should go around the mountain first."

Thurgol considered the suggestion but determined that it didn't make much sense. After all, he could see their objective before them, looming so close in the clear morning air that it looked as though he should have been able to reach out and touch it. "If we have to go to the other side," he responded logically, "then the closest way to get there is to march over the top."

With that course firmly set before them, Thurgol of Black-leaf and some sixty of his villagemates set out to free the godfather of giantkind. Above them, the peak pierced the sky, its fringes of snowy shoulders beckoning the questing giant-kin with a cool beauty that was altogether unlike the difficult challenge presented by its steep slopes and icy, unceasing winds.

* * * * *

Shallot spun easily through a circle, allowing Tristan to get a full view of the encircling monsters. He guessed that there must be at least two hundred of the creatures, and the ring that had formed left him no likely gaps through which to escape. Slowly, steadily, they continued in their soundless advance.

He wasted no time cursing fate or his own carelessness for this predicament. Instead, his mind clicked through options—he had precious few—and in an instant, he made up his mind. If he waited for them to rush him, the fight could have but one possible outcome. The only option available was an attempt to surprise the beasts with something they might not expect—something such as the target of the trap turning the tables on his ambushers.

In the instant of decision, he set his heels into Shallot's flanks, and the war-horse sprang forward like an eager filly, baying hounds coursing at his heels. Tristan rode straight toward the largest troll, the one bearing the massive, serrated blade.

The huge troll gaped at him for a moment, stunned by the apparition of this doomed human having the effrontery to charge! But that moment passed quickly, and the creature raised its great sword while several of its fellows raced to its side. In seconds, Tristan bore down full tilt into a knot of six or eight trolls.

He felt claws rake his leg at the same time as his sword split one green, knobby skull. The frantic baying of the hounds shrilled as they snarled into the monsters, one of the dogs wailing piteously as a huge troll picked up the hound and twisted it into a broken corpse. From the corner of his eye, Tristan saw another of the great hounds meet a similar fate. He slashed blindly, feeling his blade chop into the tangled bodies of his enemies. One of the trolls screamed, staggering backward with its clawed hands pressed to its face.

Shallot pitched and bucked, the stallion's powerful hooves crushing trollish limbs before and behind. The king caught a fleeting image of the huge troll, its jagged blade upraised for a killing blow, but then the horse whirled away and he faced a smaller humanoid. That one lunged for Shallot's neck, but Tristan chopped its hands off with a clean blow. As the creature hissed in horror and hatred, the keen edge of Trollcleaver did the same thing to its head.

"Here! This way!" shouted a familiar voice. Abruptly, from the ground before Tristan, short blades of flame spumed upward, crackling among the feet of the crouching trolls.

"Newt!" shouted the king, recognizing the illusionary magic of the faerie dragon. The trolls squawked in dismay, springing out of the region of flame, opening a path for Tristan's flight.

But then the huge troll with the sword stepped right into

the middle of the illusion, barking something in its bestial tongue. The flames around the creature flickered and grew pale, as Newt's illusion lost its force. The disbelief of the leader proved enough to dispel the magic for the lesser trolls.

More claws bit cruelly into the king's hip while the stallion whinnied in pain. Tristan chopped without looking, feeling the blade bite into bony flesh, while at the same time, he bashed the shield on his left arm against a pair of grotesque, black-eyed humanoids bounding toward him from that side. He saw the hulking leader before him again, waiting with a nasty smirk on its teeth-studded jaws. Trolls sprinted toward them from the left and right, and Tristan knew that his first escape attempt had been blocked.

"Back!" he shouted, again guiding Shallot with his knees while, with sword and shield, he battered at the trolls who had closed in behind him. Two of these fell, slain by Trollcleaver, while the others were forced back by the lunging stallion and the heavy shield.

In another second, the war-horse broke free from the melee, galloping once more into the center of the ring of monsters, trailed by Ranthal and one other moorhound. The great circle had grown considerably smaller during the brief skirmish. Tristan reined in after a sprint of thirty paces, since any farther would have taken him close to the trolls approaching from the direction of the shore. To his right, the firbolgs still advanced in a steady wave, while another large band of trolls blocked any escape to his left.

A whirring form buzzed past his ear, and Tristan ducked instinctively before recognizing the sound of Newt's agitated flight.

"Over here—try *this* way!" came the excited voice out of the air. In his agitation, the faerie dragon had forgotten to make himself visible. But as he dove forward, accompanied by the sound of ripping, tearing earth, it was clear that the trolls weren't going to fall for his illusionary diversions. A great chasm seemed to open in the earth before the feet of the advancing monsters, but the brutes simply stepped onto the apparently gaping fissure, finding the dirt there to be every bit as solid as it was elsewhere.

The ring closed faster, and Tristan knew that his next escape attempt—whether it succeeded or failed—would be his last. Once more he guided Shallot into a charge, and the stallion seemed to sense the raw urgency. Lowering his broad head, snorting aggressively, the war-horse thundered toward a gap between two pairs of trolls.

Immediately the creatures sprang together, closing the narrow opening effectively, while others raced for the point of impact. Tristan hunched low in his saddle, bracing the shield against his leg and shoulder, holding his potent sword like a lance, challenging any trolls to face him on his right.

Shallot smashed into the humanoids, carrying two of the hideous beasts to the earth and trampling them brutally with heavy hooves. Ranthal sprang beside the horse, clamping his jaws to the face of another troll, while Tristan speared one through the chest with the keen sword.

But still more of them surged around him. He felt claws raking his legs, heard Shallot cry out in pain. The king's arm, grown into an unfeeling, leaden weight, chopped, hacked, and stabbed with Trollcleaver, but he couldn't hold the savagely pressing beasts at bay.

The stallion reared back, breaking free of the press for a moment. Then a troll lunged at Shallot's flank, knocking the horse sideways. For a sickening, desperately hopeful moment, Tristan thought that the mighty stallion would recover his balance.

Instead, Shallot fell heavily on his side. The king flew from the saddle, feeling the impact with the ground before it happened. Even as the stunning force of the fall drove the breath from his lungs, he tried to scramble to his feet but found his muscles strangely unwilling to move.

And so he could only lie there, helpless in the midst of his enemies, waiting the blow that would certainly bring the end.

* * * * *

"They haven't come any farther along the coast," reported Brigit, galloping up to the column of exhausted dwarves. Hanrald took her hand as she swung down from the saddle. "They're staying in place near the shore, almost as if they're waiting for something behind them."

"Let them wait for *us!*" snapped Finellen, elated at the news. "How far away are they now?"

"Not far," Brigit replied. "If you keep up the pace, you should get there in a few hours."

"Double-step, now—quick march!" Finellen called. "Make time, dwarves! There's battle awaiting! We'll have the Silverhaft Axe back by nightfall!"

The column of doughty warriors picked up its pace with noticeable enthusiasm. The tromp of booted feet thumped against the ground in rapid cadence, and despite their long hours without any real respite, the bearded warriors looked fresh and eager to meet the enemy.

Hanrald swung into the saddle of his war-horse as Brigit remounted beside him. Pacing themselves with a gentle trot, they rode at the head of the dwarven formation, following the course the sister knight marked to the camp of the trolls and firbolgs.

Because of Finellen's hastened march, they covered the ground in even less time than Brigit had estimated. It was less than two hours before the Llewyrr woman held up her hand, bringing the whole column to a halt behind her.

"Near here?" asked Finellen, squeezing her axe and peering anxiously through the wooded ground ahead of them.

"We break into the coastal fields just up ahead," Brigit replied. "Once we go a little farther, you'll lose the advantage of concealment."

"Let's have a look, then," huffed the dwarf. The riders dismounted to accompany her as Finellen pushed her way through a tangle of underbrush, quickly reaching the trunk of a large tree. Peering around the bole, she saw that the elfwoman had spoken the truth. Fields of lush grain sprawled away before her, blowing gently in the breeze.

But there was nothing lush about the scene drawing their eyes on the far side of the grainfield. There they saw dozens of green, hulking figures—trolls! The monsters had gathered in a large ring, though for the moment, the observers couldn't see what they encircled.

Then a flash of movement whirled beyond the trolls, and they saw a huge war-horse break into a gallop. The steed and its rider were trapped in a ring of savage trolls, and the trio could only stare in wonder at the futile courage of the human rider. His armor gleamed, but they couldn't make out the seal on his dented shield, and he wore no banner, pennant, or other symbol of his identity.

"The poor doomed fool!" Hanrald gasped, his voice tinged with admiration and sorrow.

"By the gods, man, he's giving us a great diversion!" Finellen barked. "Let's get *moving!*"

"You want to *attack?*" demanded Brigit, incredulous. "Why, look at the ground before you! You'd have to charge through that field for half a mile! They'd have plenty of time to get ready to meet you."

"Do you have a better suggestion?" barked the dwarf, regarding the Llewyrr knight belligerently.

"Wait here and watch them for a little while. If you see them get ready to move, then you can take a defensive position in their path. You'll have a better chance against them if you choose the ground and give yourself some cover!"

"No good," Finellen retorted. "If they do pick up and move, there's no guarantee we'll be able to catch 'em. Nope, we've got them here in front of us. I say we're going after them right now!"

Hanrald looked back at the fight, where the lone human rider circled to face the surrounding legion of his attackers. The warrior saw something admirable and grand in the knight's valiant stand. He wished they had a chance to help the man, but even if he and Brigit rode to the fight at top speed, they stood no chance of getting there before the lone rider must inevitably be slain.

Meanwhile, Finellen darted back to muster her company, while the human lord and the elfwoman stared in pity at the doomed fight of the surrounded warrior. His great warhorse reared, raising the rider above even the towering bodies of his enemies, but everywhere the man and horse turned, they faced a closing ring of tooth, sinew, and claw.

Along the fringe of trees, dwarves emerged from the woods silently, starting through the field in a long rank, though only their heads showed above the green, waving grain. And even these the bearded warriors held low, trying to take advantage of their concealment for as long as possible.

Quickly the two riders returned to their horses. "Let's give the dwarves a bit of a start," Brigit suggested. "After all, we'll catch them soon enough, and we'll be a lot easier to see than they will."

"Agreed," said Hanrald, privately chafing at the sensible suggestion. Now that the enemy was in sight, he wanted nothing so much as the chance to thunder across the field in a valiant charge. Though they would be too late to help, certainly, there was something in the doomed rider's carriage and appearance that inspired a fierce and combative drive in the Earl of Fairheight. The rider's battered shield had been through savage fighting, he could tell. Indeed, the insignia had been worn to a shapeless blur of brown. Yet somehow, against these phenomenal odds, that shield had kept the horseman alive.

Then, in a flash, it came to him. That battered seal was the bear's head of Kendrick! The rearing, plunging horse could only be Shallot, the king's prized stallion.

"Sire!" he cried, spurring from the woods, horrified to see no sign of the valiant knight—the knight who could only be the High King of the Ffolk. Now the horse scrambled to its feet, riderless, and a horde of trolls swarmed in.

* * * * *

Ranthal stood over his master as Tristan gasped for breath, holding Trollcleaver across his chest and struggling, but failing, to sit up. The loyal moorhound bled from a dozen gory wounds where troll tooth or claw had rent skin and torn away bristling fur. Yet the dog spun this way and that, lunging and biting seemingly in many directions at once. Snarling, teeth bared in fanged savagery, the great moorhound tore the throat from a troll that leaned in too close.

One of the large wolfdogs of the firbolg camp charged Ranthal from the side, but the hound whirled and broke the wolf's neck with a single bite. Another troll dove, knocking the dog to the side, but Ranthal rolled quickly and came up biting, clasping iron jaws around the troll's wrist until the creature shrieked to the snapping of bone.

The shout of a voice from across the grainfield carried dimly through the fray. Immediately the trolls turned away from Tristan, gesticulating and barking in alarm. The king forced himself to a sitting position, astounded to see the Earl of Fairheight and Brigit Cu'Lyrran galloping at full speed toward the army of trolls and firbolgs.

"No!" Tristan cried, his voice coming out as a strangled gasp. He saw something else then—plumes trailing from helmets, just above the level of the corn. *Dwarves*—a rank of them moving toward him.

Sudden, wild hope infused Tristan's body and soul. Where was Shallot? He climbed to his knees and whistled, drawing the horse toward him at a gallop. Seizing the pommel as the stallion raced by, Tristan awkwardly pulled himself off the ground, finally throwing a leg across the wide back and lifting himself fully into the saddle.

The trolls, still jabbering about the sudden arrival of reinforcements, were taken by surprise when the king on his war-horse, the limping moorhound racing alongside, exploded toward the encircling beasts. One of the wolfdogs sprang at Ranthal, but the powerful hound sent the creature yelping back to its masters with a snap on the muzzle. In

❧ 13 ❧

The Creeping Swamp

Alicia was forced to dismount, leaving Brittany on a small hillock of dry ground while she probed forward for some sign of a trail. Instead of finding a path, however, she saw the plants growing thick behind her even as she passed, and water trickled from somewhere to pool around the trunks of trees. Pads of lilies lay flat upon the stagnant liquid where meadows of flowers and brush should be.

Still the princess pressed onward, growing desperate in the few minutes since she had left her company of men. In fact, she suspected that the trail behind her was now inundated, since by the time she had left the troops, some of the men had already hoisted themselves into the lower branches of trees in order to keep their feet dry. The source of the water remained a mystery, but finding a path through the swampland formed a far more significant problem to Alicia.

Codscove wasn't far away, she sensed. Yet now her entire force threatened to bog down in this impenetrable swamp. Why *now*, of all times?

The dark forest dripped around her, pressing close on all sides. She felt as though something watched her. Nervously, sword in hand, the princess spun through a circle. As far as she could tell, she remained alone.

She wondered, with a flash of irritation, why Keane had been reluctant to accompany her. She hadn't ordered him to do so, but when she had asked he had quietly dissuaded her, suggesting that it was best right now if he remained with the rest of the company. It surprised her and, if the truth be told, it annoyed her, too, this feeling that she needed Keane's presence before she could feel comfortable. But, still, he should have come with her!

"What's he going to do, fly the men out of here?" she muttered, brushing strands of sweat-soaked hair back from her face.

The trees around her seemed healthy and firmly rooted, not what she would expect to find in such a swampland. After her previous experience with the quicksand, she had learned to walk carefully, but even the ground felt surprisingly firm.

Yet in every direction, she quickly found herself facing an expanse of placid, murky water. It pooled around the trees, dark and fetid, concealing the ground, deceptively obscuring any pitfall or irregularity in the terrain. Finally, with considerable disgust, she made her way back to the column of Corwellian men-at-arms.

"Nothing—there's no dry path out of here," she said to Keane in disgust. "Not that *you* would have helped find it!" she added bitterly.

Keane smiled thinly, ignoring her tone, which only made her more irritated. "What did you stay back here for, anyway? Checking to see if it's going to rain?"

"No," he said, quietly. "No rain would make any difference in this flood."

"What do you mean? How can the water level be rising when there isn't any rain?"

"That's the big question, isn't it? If you'll notice, there hasn't been any rain for several days, yet the water flowed in behind us as soon as we passed a certain point."

"And now we're surrounded," Alicia added. "But I'm not so concerned with *why* the water got here as I am with finding a way around it!"

"Then you're making a great mistake," Keane replied bluntly, meeting her indignant gaze with a thoughtful look of his own.

Still annoyed, the princess bit her tongue and tried to understand what he meant. "Well? How *did* this water get here?"

"As near as I can tell, it isn't really here at all. It just seems to be."

"And what's *that* supposed to mean?"

"Perhaps he means that the righteous wrath of the gods wishes to direct your faith in more proper directions," said Parell Hyath, who had approached, unnoticed, to join in their conversation.

"Speak plainly!" Alicia snapped, in no mood for theological discourse.

"I mean this tired obeisance you show to an ancient and withered goddess! You tell us not to trample the grass in that 'sacred' place. You forbid the taking of game for food, and treat each wildflower as some kind of miracle! This goddess holds you in thrall, and by doing so, she holds you, holds your people, *back!*" replied the patriarch, his tone equally firm. "It is time for these isles to welcome the pantheon of deities that are known to all the rest of the Realms."

Alicia's eyes blazed, and for a moment, rage swept through her, fomenting a torrent of angry words that nearly exploded from her. Instead, however, she remembered an early lesson of her mother's: Such rage could only be destructive, and thus it should be conserved for those times when destruction was necessary.

Drawing a deep breath, the princess felt the tension flow from her body, replaced by a serene calm that enabled her to meet the cleric's arguments rationally. In the clarity that followed, she recognized the supreme arrogance that propelled him and knew that her own faith could be strong enough to prevail.

"This 'tired' faith you deride is the lifeblood of my people," the princess explained. "It flows in my veins, and in the veins of all the Ffolk, and it won't wither or weaken in the face of your conceits!"

"Conceits?" Now it was the patriarch who sounded amused. "My dear child, you haven't begun to see the glories that the true gods can work."

"I saw glory enough in Myrloch Vale to last the rest of my life," Alicia retorted. Indeed, there she had felt the magical power of her island, of her home, in a fashion that she had never known before.

"A point in this debate—perhaps minor, but I think significant," Keane ventured, after listening carefully to this exchange. "But it seems that we shouldn't mistake the acts of humans, however potent and arcane, for the will of the gods they purport to serve."

"What do you mean?" snapped Parell Hyath, turning on the lanky tutor with a menacing gaze.

"This swamp, for example," Keane continued, unperturbed. "The will of the gods? The acts of vengeful deities, determined to prove us wrong? Or is it instead the work of a treacherous cleric—one who presents himself as friend and ally, but works instead to thwart the true purpose of our mission?"

"What lies do you speak?" demanded the Exalted Inquisitor.

"There is a spell I know of . . . called 'hallucinatory terrain,' I believe." He turned to Alicia, explaining calmly. "It can only be wielded by a powerful cleric, though I'm certain it falls within the range of ability possessed by our erstwhile companion here."

"Did *you* bring this water around us?" the princess demanded, confronting the patriarch.

"He's *mad!*" protested Hyath, fixing Keane with a baleful gaze. "What would a simple ambassador know about magic and gods?"

Alicia laughed once, a quick and bitter sound. Keane, too, seemed mildly amused. "My 'simple ambassador,' " the princess shot back, "has a certain familiarity with the arcane arts."

"*Denterius—valteran!*"

Keane's sharp, magical incantation cut through the air like a thunderclap, and the blood drained from Parell Hyath's face as he recognized the spell.

"The wizardly enchantment of 'dispel magic,' " Keane confirmed.

But his remark proved unnecessary as, with miraculous speed, the water standing in pools around the tree trunks vanished, leaving ground as dry and musty as a highland forest. Indeed, Alicia saw with astonishment, none of the bark, leaves—nothing near the ground, where the water had stood—was even the slightest bit wet!

"This is preposterous!" sputtered the cleric. "This might even be your own illusion, designed to trick the princess into following an obsolete faith!"

"I'd stay here and argue with you all day," the princess responded curtly, "but now that we've got a path before us, I think it's time that we who are loyal servants of King Kendrick moved out!

"Your treachery might have cost us days of march!" she continued, confronting the flush-faced patriarch. "If it had, it would also have cost you your life! As it is, we no longer desire your presence in this expedition. You are not to accompany us when we march! Return to Corwell or to your own land as you see fit!"

"Your father needs me to heal his wound!" the cleric objected forcefully. "Even now he embarks alone on a great quest in the name of the gods. He'll need me when this matter is concluded!"

"For all we know, it might have been your spell that sent him on this wild errand, your deception that brings this matter onto our heads. Leave us, before I change my mind about your punishment!" Alicia declared, uncowed.

Keane stood firmly beside the princess, and when the cleric's eyes met those of the wizard, Hyath apparently thought better of any further objections. Without a backward glance, he spun on his heel and stalked away. When he was out of earshot, he mumbled an arcane command.

The magic-user tensed, ready for treachery, but then he saw a familiar shape, the glowing wheels bracketing the Chariot of Sustarre, taking shape in the air before the Exalted Inquisitor. Slowly the two horses, prancing eagerly, outlined in fire, materialized.

By the time the cleric took to the air, Alicia had already gone to gather the sergeants, while the wizard watched the final departure of Parell Hyath, the trailing cloud of sparks marking the path of the chariot as the horses lunged into the sky.

Within a few minutes, the men of Corwell had hoisted their weapons and standards to their shoulders and once again resumed the northward trail, accompanied by their chant: "For the kings of Corwell!"

The wizard found Alicia at the head of the column, riding at a fast walk through the once more passable forest. He spurred his old nag up to the side of the princess, lighting up when she turned to him with a smile. Still, a sense of foreboding lingered inside him, and he had to tell her of his twinge of misgiving.

"Good riddance to him, I say," Alicia declared.

"I certainly hope so, but perhaps not," Keane cautioned. "Corwell's to the south of here, Baldur's Gate to the east. Yet when he flew away, he was making straight for the north."

* * * * *

Tavish waited for fifteen painful minutes after she heard the last sounds of firbolg conversation. The rough landing when the giant-kin had dragged the longship onto shore had twisted her spine one final time, and she wasn't at all sure that she'd be able to walk when she *did* dare to venture out.

Nevertheless, she finally crawled forth, wriggling from beneath the bench to lie in the bottom of the hull. Dismayed, the harpist found that she was even more stiff and immobile than she had expected. It took her another ten minutes before she could sit up, and even then her feet remained numb and her arms tingled painfully with slowly returning circulation.

Yet finally she could look around and breathe air unfouled by firbolg feet. White clouds scudded across the mostly blue sky overhead, while a fairly dense forest extended to both sides, just back from the flat and gravelly beach. Above the trees, now with its summit shrouded by wisps of clouds, rose the distinctive cone of the Icepeak.

She raised her head and saw the Strait of Oman to the south, though there was no sign of Gwynneth beyond. It made sense. With no massif such as the Icepeak, the lowland of Winterglen lay below the horizon.

"So they sailed to Oman's Isle," she said aloud. Why firbolgs would do something so unalterably purposeful was a real mystery to the bard. Of course, if this island had been their destination all along, she understood why they'd been so determined to seize the *Princess of Moonshae*.

But this yielded no further light on the issue of why the giant-kin had wanted to come here in the first place. On that question, Tavish could only muse with steadily growing interest and curiosity. She recalled the stooped giantess, clutching that glorious axe so possessively, and she wondered if the explanation lay with that venerable female.

At length, sensation and control returned to her limbs. Twisting and stretching for a few more minutes, she finally felt ready to climb out of the leaning hull. Sitting on the lower gunwale, she crossed her legs over the rail and dropped the short distance to the smooth surface below, landing with a lurch and a jarring of harpstrings, but she suffered no injury.

Once she had checked her lute, determining that it needed a careful tuning but had suffered no damage, she started across the stones. Her curiosity had grown far beyond the realm of idle interest. She felt that, whatever drew these giants, there must be a compelling tale at the end of it.

The trail of the lumbering giant-kin wasn't hard to find. The firbolg band had followed a game trail, widening it frequently by breaking off branches or stomping small bushes underfoot. Hoisting her harp, the bard started along that same path, following the broad footsteps of the giants.

* * * * *

"How did you manage to stay alive the last twenty years without me to bail you out?" Finellen demanded gruffly, the tone of her voice not hiding the real affection she felt for the High King of the Ffolk.

"I've not been in many pickles like this over that time," Tristan allowed, leaning from his saddle to clasp Finellen's fists in his good hand. "But sure enough, when it happened, there you were! Many thanks, old friend."

"Enough about the last twenty years," Brigit said, not unkindly. "What about the next twenty minutes?" She pointed across the cornfield to the trolls who plunged toward them, furious at the escape of the king.

"Back to the woods! Quickstep!" barked Finellen, and the dwarves hastily reversed the course of their advance. With the monsters on the attack, the dwarven leader decided that her company should face the enemy with the benefit of some cover around it.

Fortunately the dwarven charge hadn't progressed far before Tristan broke free, so they quickly reached the shelter of overhanging oak limbs and tangled dogwood trunks. The obstructions would hamper the larger humanoids far more than they would the diminutive dwarves.

"Crossbows about! Fire at will!" cried the bearded captain, and those of her troops with the stocky missile weapons quickly loosed a volley of steel-headed bolts.

Immediately the archers began cranking their heavy weapons to reload, while the first rank of monsters faltered, many falling with the lethal bolts jutting from their bodies. Unlike an arrow from a standard bow, the quarrels from the crossbows struck with great punching power, sometimes with enough force to knock even a troll off its feet.

"Fires!" shouted Brigit. "We need fires to burn the trolls!"

From nowhere appeared the druid Danrak. "I've got tinder piled back here. I'll ignite it," he said to Finellen, "if you'll send some of your dwarves to carry the brands to the fight."

"Aye—good thinking." Finellen nodded and quickly dispatched several trustworthy veterans.

A second volley met the onrushing foe as the giant predators reared only a few paces from the edge of the forest. Following the shot, the archers dropped their missile weapons
and all the dwarves, together with their human and Llewyrr
allies, met the humanoids with sword and axe, hammer and
shield.

Tristan stood near the center of the line, singling out a
strong company of trolls for the attentions of his powerful
sword. As the first of these sprang through the hedge at the
border of the field, the High King split him from chin to
pelvis with a slashing downward blow of Trollcleaver. Spew-
ing gore, the monster collapsed beside him as Tristan
already clashed blades with his next opponent.

All around he heard the gruff cursing of dwarves, the
hissing shrieks of bloodthirsty trolls, and the bellowing cries
of the giant-kin. Ranthal snarled and snapped beside him,
while wolfdogs lunged at the mighty moorhound with slavering jaws.

Trollcleaver met a troll's heavy axe, the resounding clang
driving daggers of agony through Tristan's bones, but he
held firm, and as the troll recoiled for another blow, the
king's sword snaked out, piercing the gristle of the monster's
chest and finally puncturing the knotty ball of its heart.

Smoke wafted through the air. In other places, fallen trolls
were charred by snapping flames, dry timbers piled upon
the corpses to ensure that they wouldn't rise to fight again.
Ranthal, ranging from side to side but always battling close
by Tristan's flank, added his fierce snarl to the din, while
cheering dwarves raised their voices in triumph each time
another of the beasts succumbed to the blaze.

But amid the cheering, the king heard darker, more
painful sounds. Dwarves groaned, and all too often he heard
the piteous exhalation that Tristan recognized as the last
sound of a dying warrior. Wounded dwarves tried to stifle
their moans, but were not always successful. Too many of
them, fallen amidst the chaos of the melee, expired simply
because there was no one to help at hand.

Nearby, the king saw another familiar knight. The Earl of Fairheight, wielding his huge, two-handed sword with deadly precision, stood between two large oaks, anchoring a good portion of the line. The sister knight of Synnoria fought at his side, making certain two razors of sharp steel met any firbolg or troll foolish enough to try to press through.

Finellen moved back and forth along the line of battle, at times lunging forward to help out one of her hard-pressed countrymen, or else carrying flaming brands of dry timber to stack on the temporarily slain corpses of the trolls.

"Need some fire here?" grunted the stalwart dwarfwoman as Tristan carved a deep wound into the leg of a troll, crippling the beast. The monster dropped like a felled tree, scuttling crablike away from the fight.

Gasping for breath, the king shook his head. Already half a dozen troll corpses lay motionless around him, and in the lull, Tristan grinned at Finellen's look of astonishment.

"Good sword," was all she said as the High King raised the weapon to face another push, this time three trolls rushing him together.

Fortunately the tangle of trees kept two of them from coming fully to bear, and the third one danced quickly backward to avoid a thrust from Trollcleaver. As one of the others darted in, Tristan's blade chopped into the beast's arm and Finellen's axe carved a deep wound into its thigh. The monster fell, and Tristan stabbed it once in the skull, driving the tip of his blade deep into the fetid brain; the creature wouldn't menace them further. Ranthal, meanwhile, held the third troll safely at bay.

"Nice work," grunted the dwarfwoman as the ebb and flow of battle momentarily gave the pair a berth of space.

But then came a deeper sound, a growing roar of hoarse triumph from firbolg throats. At the same time, dwarven voices hollered in alarm. The scene of the commotion was perhaps twenty or thirty paces to their right, though the humans could see nothing in that direction because of the screening forest.

Finellen, however, didn't need to see in order understand the significance of the alarm.

"That's bad news," she said, starting toward the noise at a jog. "It means that the giants have breached the line!"

* * * * *

The sounds of fighting came to Brandon and Koll through the trees, and their ragged force of northmen and Ffolk broke into a jog, quickly emerging from the forest into a field of trampled grain. Across the broad expanse, they saw the source of the noise—a seething chaos of bloody melee, where the army of the trolls and firbolgs attacked some foe concealed in the woods across the field. The backs of the humanoids faced Brandon and Koll's men, and that was all the incentive that the two veteran warriors required.

"It's them—the trolls, I mean!" barked Knaff the Elder, pacing at his prince's side. "But who are they fighting?"

"Whoever it is, they can use our help!" Koll barked.

"Charge!" the two captains bellowed in unison, and the men who had been driven from the battlefield of Codscove loped steadily into the field. Voices rose in lusty courage, and many an axe and sword blade gleamed in the midday sun as its wielder brandished his weapon overhead.

To an onlooker who purported neutrality, their onslaught seemed like madness. Though they couldn't know what force they aided, their own numbers equaled but a fraction of the foe's. Yet their defeat on the field at Codscove had branded all of these men with a burning desire for vengeance.

As the humans sprinted and shouted and jeered, dozens of trolls broke from the mass of the attackers, drawn by the sounds of the fresh attack. Many firbolgs, too, hoisted their clubs toward the new threat, lumbering at the heels of their green-skinned comrades.

Loping back into the field with their deceptively speedy gait, the trolls met the men of Brandon and Koll's force with savage tooth and rending claw. The human charge stopped immediately as a dozen men were slain in the first shock. In another moment, the courageous warriors found themselves fighting for their lives against an overwhelming press of savage, hulking humanoids.

Brandon chopped hard into the forearm of a troll, sending the creature reeling backward, but another stepped in to take its place even as the wound began to mend. At the same time, a man beside the prince screamed as a pair of trolls ripped his torso in two.

Furiously the Prince of Gnarhelm slashed one troll in the side, but the creature whirled with deceptive speed, knocking Brandon flat onto his back. He lay immobilized, gasping for breath and trying unsuccessfully to move. The monster picked up a longsword, dropped by another slain northman, and thrust it down, straight toward the prince's unprotected chest.

A wiry body blocked out the sun, and Brandon blinked, knowing that he stared death in the face. The troll stabbed, and the muscular shape—a *human* shape—took the piercing blow intended for the Prince of Gnarhelm. Brandon's strength returned in a wave of energy, and he sprang upward, hacking the troll's chest open with his great axe. He chopped again and the monster fell.

Only then did Brandon turn to see the man who'd given his life for him. Knaff the Elder lay upon the ground, blood emerging like a fountain from the puncture wound in the chest.

"No!" gasped the prince, dropping to his knee beside his trusted helmsman and mentor. Desperately, fruitlessly, he tried to stem the flow of blood.

With gentle pressure, Knaff pulled his hand away. "Go and fight, my prince—for Gnarhelm and the Moonshaes!"

And as the warlike gleam in his eyes faded for the last time, Knaff's jaw remained set in a grimace of battle.

Shaking his head in a failed attempt to dispel his numbing grief, Brandon lurched to his feet and chopped savagely at a nearby troll. Sir Koll of Codscove fought nearby, but the prince saw with dismay that most of his loyal fighters had been driven from the field or slain. A sea of the enemy surged around him, and everywhere he saw the fallen bodies of his friends.

He heard a bullish battle cry and saw the armored figure of Koll, bashing several firbolgs back with his great sword. Brandon limped to the knight's side, driving back a troll that lunged at the Ffolkman's back.

Finally Koll and Brandon stood back to back in the center of the field, using sword and axe to hold a seething ring of trolls at bay. Bleeding from a dozen wounds, gasping and staggering from exhaustion, each gave every shred of his mind and muscle to the effort to prolong the fight for just a little longer.

For beyond this battle, both veteran warriors understood, there would be only the eternal peace of death.

* * * * *

The Moonwell looked much the same as Robyn remembered it, thought the last time she saw it seemed more than a lifetime ago. Cool white water glowed with health amid a setting of bright lily pads and brilliant, dew-glistened flowers. Nearby, through a gap in the trees, the crystalline waters of the Myrloch sparkled like diamonds in the sun.

Great, flat-topped arches of stone surrounded her, for this Moonwell had a special significance. Once, for a period of many centuries, it had been the well at the center of the Great Druid's grove. Then, during the Darkwalker War, this well had been corrupted. As the Darkwell, it gave birth to the Darkwalker itself, the young king's mightiest foe.

Now vines of ivy climbed those stone obelisks, some of which had toppled during the intervening years. The druid queen found a stone bench where she remembered it would be, though she had to clear it of fallen leaves before she could use it to rest.

When she had made herself comfortable, she sat there for

a very long time. The sun slipped below the western horizon, and the stars broke into the sky. Then the full disc of the moon came into sight, rising into the night and spilling its creamy rays across the waters of the Moonwell.

For a time, Robyn's mind drifted across the people she loved, those who had given her joy and to whom she had tried to return happiness and affection of her own. Tristan . . . Alicia . . . Deirdre . . . The images and faces began to swim together in the waters, and then they grew indistinct, muddied by the Moonwell into a vague blur. The water . . . the moon . . . the earth beneath her . . . all these images swept across her conscious mind. They did not supplant the memories of the people, but they took on a life of their own, and in that life, they demanded her love every bit as jealously as any member of her family.

Slowly, over a tranquil period of several hours, Robyn felt the waters of the Moonwell grow warm, powerful. At first, the glow within them was something like a pearly luster, a vague illumination originating somewhere deep within the well, viewed as if through a thick, translucent filter. The sensation grew stronger, the warmth turning to a solid heat so definite that the queen half expected the liquid to bubble into steam.

Yet this was not that kind of heat.

Instead, she saw the whirling turmoil of anger, even of killing rage. She sensed that the goddess recoiled, under siege, surrounded by menace and incapable of fending off those threats with her innate power. The druid queen opened her heart and her soul, and the might of her goddess mother slowly began to concentrate, to gain focus.

Robyn's heart slowed to a calm, steady cadence, and she felt the pacing of her life slow to match. And as she watched and meditated through the long night of the full moon, the will of the goddess began to appear.

* * * * *

Thurgol led his band on the course he had chosen for them, and as night fell and moonlight washed their mountaintop vantage, his mind was occupied by one overriding thought: It was unbelievably, unthinkably, *cold* up here!

They had marched up such a barren ridge that they could find no stick of wood for a fire, though it hadn't been until nearly dark that this thought occurred to any of the giant-kin. Naturally, then, it had been Garisa to acidly make the observation.

But there was nothing to do but curl up in their furs and wait for the dawn. Outlined in a clarity of moonlight that astounded him, Thurgol even spent much of the night staring in awe at the vista of the island below him, or the ice-bound, aloof grandeur of the peak that still loomed high above.

When he finally slept, it was fitfully, as if he understood that his life had reached the edge of the future. Tomorrow they would reach the summit and, if the legends were true, the icy bier of Grond Peaksmasher. Garisa still carried the Silverhaft Axe, and the firbolgs remained willing and determined to chop their immortal founder from his icy prison.

Then, Thurgol mused, everything would fall into the hands of the gods.

* * * * *

By nightfall, Tristan knew that the battle was lost, but the knowledge only infused him with a greater will to resist. He fought with a small knot of fighters—Hanrald, Brigit, and Finellen among them—anchored in a crude bulwark formed by four stout oak trunks.

He had seen the brave charge of a few humans into the grainfield, though he hadn't known who they were. It had been a courageous gesture, but the men had been too few to make a difference in the battle's outcome. Now, out there, only a few survivors of that valiant band stood amid the trampled crop, courageously facing the doom that must inevitably claim them. Two warriors in particular stood back to back, outlined in brilliant moonlight, surrounded by a ring of trolls and firbolgs. The pair wielded battle-axe and sword so effectively that they held the horde at bay for long, desperate minutes.

In this spirit of bleak despair, the High King raised his sword and charged out of his rude shelter. Three trolls felt the fatal kiss of Trollcleaver before the monsters even realized that one of the humans had been so rash as to abandon his shelter. They swarmed around him like bees, but when Finellen darted out to cover his back, the king and the dwarf were able to fight their way back to the clump of trees.

Then, when the humanoids closed in once more to attack, the braying of silver trumpets sounded across the field. Looking up with renewed hope, the warriors of Finellen saw fresh banners unfurl over the muddy terrain. Some two dozen riders appeared off to the left, charging into the field and smashing into the flank of the attacking humanoids' formation. As Tristan stared in disbelief, watching the eerie attack unfold in the moonlight, he saw—or did he imagine?—a familiar, golden-haired head above the charging troops.

"Hail the Princess of Moonshae!" shouted four hundred hoarse voices. Banners of Corwell and Llyrath, of Dynnatt and Koart, waved overhead as rank upon rank of armed men marched toward the horde of monsters.

"For the kings of Corwell!" they added, shouting the standard battle cry of that venerable kingdom until their voices could shout no more.

Arrows filled the sky overhead, the missiles appearing like sleek ghosts against the full moon, until they fell among the monsters like the stinging, deadly darts that they were. Tristan heard sergeants-major bark profane commands—was that Sands' voice? And Parsallas, too! He recognized his two veteran leaders, and when the sharp crack of a lightning bolt sizzled into the ranks of the beast horde, he knew that Keane was there as well.

The monsters, this time struck in the flank by a force that was much larger than their own, howled and milled about in confusion, a confusion that proved fatal for many of them as Alicia led the men of Corwell in a vigorous charge. Firbolgs fell before the lances of the horsemen, while trolls, slain in melee combat, were quickly doused with oil and set afire. Within a few minutes of Alicia's arrival, the entire horde was reeling in confusion that verged upon panic.

Tristan's heart swelled with elation. In the instant of their deliverance, he charged once more out of the sheltered clump of oaks.

Then one lanky humanoid moved in front of him, snarling in venomous hatred, looming like a stout but misshapen tree before the tip of the High King's blade. Tristan recognized the brute by the monster's own sword. This was the troll the king had attacked earlier, only to be thwarted when many other monsters had swarmed to this one's aid. Then, as now, Tristan felt quite certain that this was the monster commanding the whole ravaging horde.

Raising its massive, saw-toothed sword, the troll blocked Tristan's path, holding the blade ready to parry any attack the king made. The surge of charging Corwellians rushed closer, and the troll's attention wavered for just a moment as the monster turned its black, emotionless eyes toward the rank of Alicia's charging troops.

Seeing his opening, Tristan lunged in a quick, savage attack, chopping downward with Trollcleaver and aiming for the beast's momentarily unprotected chest. Sensing the attack, the monster whirled back, raising its forearm and that massive, serrated blade to block the charge.

The High King twisted his attack, missing the troll's weapon but also missing the black, corrupt heart. Instead, the keen sword blade bit into the beast's arm at the elbow, slicing through skin and sinew and bone. The monster shrieked—a hideous, bellowing sound of awful pain and agony—and then, still holding its great blade in the other hand, the troll turned and bolted into flight.

* * * * *

Deirdre reached a hand outward, touching the smooth, pale surface of ice. At that moment, the moon crested the towering ridge of the Icepeak, washing the vale in the cool light of the silver orb in all its summer fullness.

The illumination imparted a magical glow to the imprisoned giant, spilling through the valley and washing the princess in a warmth that was the rightness of the gods.

Her past was gone now. A vague part of her mind remembered her murder of the guard at Corwell with a certain sense of curiosity. It was insignificant, that death, except that it clarified for her the stakes, tied her destiny to the battle of the gods.

Reverently, knowing that she served the masters who would grant her ultimate, undreamed of power, Deirdre sat down to wait for that destiny to take shape.

Yet she could not sit for very long. Impatient, she glanced at the sky and rose to stalk across the shallow vale. It was time *now!* She was ready to act, but the pieces of the puzzle were not yet complete. Angrily she cursed, and studied the horizons. They should be here by now, and yet they were not.

Where were the firbolgs—the giants who would bring her the Silverhaft Axe?

* * * * *

The Earthmother beheld her great druid through the window of the Moonwell, and the goddess found the mortal wanting. For too long Robyn had dwelled among men. No longer did her heart beat the deep, fundamental pulse of her faith. The goddess feared that Robyn now lacked the passion, the keen understanding and self-sacrifice that would have blazed a trail of, if not triumph, at least hope.

Instead, the High Queen had enjoyed good food, company, and drink . . . she had languished within the protection of stone walls, used the fire of a rock-walled hearth to negate the winter chill. *Could she muster the strength required for this desperate, final battle?*

Whether she could prevail or not, necessity forced the choice, for the druid queen was the only weapon that the Earthmother possessed.

❧14❧

The Rockbound Ways

"Incendrius!" cried Keane, pointing his finger toward the target of his deadly spell. The lanky mage stood on his feet, his loyal mount having fallen to a firbolg rock early in the attack. A deceptively small pebble of glowing light drifted outward, angling toward the knot of green-skinnned humanoids before him.

In moments, a searing globe of fire erupted amid the rank of fleeing trolls, and when the crackling flames dissipated, it revealed columns of thick, oily smoke smudging upward from nearly a dozen charred corpses. In the moonlight, the smoke resembled solid pillars of dark rock.

Alicia, on Brittany, surged back and forth. Inspired by her leadership, the men of Corwell had attacked with courage and uncharacteristic savagery. The first rush shocked the lumbering humanoids, and the valiant militia never gave them time to recover their balance or their fighting spirit.

Exhausted but elated, the princess rode up to Keane, swinging down from the saddle to seize him in a bear hug of fierce triumph. He hugged her back, flushed with his own sense of victory.

"Look!" called a grinning Parsallas, pointing across the field.

"There's Father! He's got prisoners!" shouted Alicia, elated at the outcome of the sharp, sudden attack. She saw the king and recognized Hanrald and Brigit among a company of bearded dwarves. The group prodded a half-dozen surly firbolgs before them, the entire group limping toward the wizard, the princess, and their company.

The battle had lasted only a few minutes for Alicia and the men of Corwell, but judging from the trampled look of the field and the weary, battered appearance of the human and dwarven survivors, she knew that combat had been joined here long before her own arrival.

"We were none too soon," Keane said quietly as Sergeant-Major Sands led a number of men forward to take charge of the prisoners.

Alicia ran to the High King, overjoyed to see his smile, however wan and exhausted his appearance. He swept her into his arms and embraced her while she hugged and held him with overwhelming relief.

"Father!" she gasped, after she found her voice. "I'm so glad. . . . I was afraid we'd be too late."

"Not too late at all, though five minutes more might have been," he said cheerfully as the rest of his companions joined them. Alicia embraced Hanrald and Brigit in turn, and then Tristan called to her.

"This is an ally from a previous war, but she saved my life here as well. Finellen of Cambro, I present my daughter, High Princess Alicia."

The princess bowed before the bristling beard of the sturdy dwarf, who regarded her with a frank but friendly sparkle in her eye. "The image of your mother, except for the hair. It's a pleasure to meet you, lass."

"The brave Finellen is someone I've heard about in many tales," replied Alicia. "I'm grateful for everything you've done for my father . . . and the Ffolk."

The dwarf shrugged. "Probably exaggerated, though I'm surprised my name came up at all, given the way the Llewyrr usually hog all the glory!"

In the glow of the moment, even Brigit didn't have the urge to dispute the statement. And then another companion joined them, one who caused all of them to stare in shock.

"Brandon!" cried the princess, the first to voice their surprise. Bleeding from a dozen wounds but smiling in obvious joy, the northman joined them, accompanied by an equally battered knight.

"The good Prince of Gnarhelm!" boomed the king, clasping Brandon on the arm. "Good fight, lad—and Sir Koll as well! I might have known. So you were the fellows who came across the field at such a timely juncture!"

"A rash move it was, too, Your Majesty," Brandon explained, his smile fading to a grim sorrow. "Most of our men paid the price."

"Knaff . . . ?" Alicia asked tentatively, and when the prince shook his head, she felt her throat tighten. She had to turn away.

"We are fortunate indeed to have such loyal companions as you," the High King said to all the assembled warriors. "Each, arriving as you did, kept the fight alive for the others, and together we knew triumph!"

"Riding off alone like that was a good way to get yourself killed!" his daughter retorted. "What sort of madness took hold of you?"

Tristan smiled tolerantly, though certainly no one else in the assemblage would have dared speak to the High King in such a tone. He sighed and looked back to the edge of the forest. He thought of the vast woodland that began there, where Winterglen merged with Myrloch Vale . . . and for a week, he might as well have drifted in a different world. Once again he longed to hear the cry of the wolf, wished that the great beast would signal its approval, if not its forgiveness.

"It was perhaps a rash move," he admitted. He drew Troll-cleaver, allowing the gleaming blade to shed gentle light around the gathered humans and dwarves. "Still, this blade gave me a better chance than I'd ever have thought. Perhaps there *was* something to that priest's prophecy."

"Father, that priest was treacherous to the core!" Alicia objected. She quickly recounted the tale of the hallucinatory terrain Parell Hyath had used to try delaying the company from Corwell, while Tristan frowned in displeasure mingled with confusion.

"If it hadn't been for Keane," the princess concluded, "we'd probably still be wandering around in a swamp that doesn't even exist!"

"Then why would he give me such a sword?" asked the king. "This blade is truly as mighty as any weapon I've wielded since the Sword of Cymrych Hugh. I have dubbed it Trollcleaver, and it is aptly named. If he intended for us to fail, what purpose is served by such a gift?"

"The priest is a mysterious figure," Keane suggested. "Some of what he said—about the trolls and firbolgs, for example—proved to be remarkably accurate. Yet our army was surrounded by an illusionary expanse of water, clearly of the cleric's doing. It could only have been placed there to stop us."

"There's more than a hint of madness to this whole affair," Tristan observed somberly, suppressing an ominous shiver as he recalled his aimless wandering. "It's only good fortune, and perhaps the favor of the goddess, that enabled us to prevail."

"And prevail quite remarkably," Hanrald noted. "From the edge of disaster, we earned a victory that destroyed the foe!"

"The foe is not entirely destroyed," Sir Koll amended. His face fell ruefully. "A small knot of trolls escaped into the forest—alas, but the northman captain and I were too sorely pained to give chase."

"Did you note a great one among them, with a bronze-edged sword—jagged teeth on the blade, like a saw?" asked the king quickly. "I believe him to be their leader, and I'm not sure if he was slain by fire."

"I'm sorry, Sire. I couldn't say for certain," replied the knight.

"We'll break into companies and root them out soon enough," Alicia suggested. "The bulk of the horde has been broken."

"Others might have gotten away as well," Brandon said with a cautionary tone. "I assume that you didn't see the *Princess of Moonshae* in Codscove," he said to Tristan.

"No—nothing afloat. Even the fishing boats had been sunk."

"She was taken by firbolgs!" exclaimed the northman

bitterly. "Some of them must have put out to sea!"

"Why would they do that?" Brigit asked, genuinely puzzled.

"Another thing," Finellen interjected. She had just heard the whispered report of dwarven warriors who had been scouring the battlefield. "The Silverhaft Axe isn't here. No one saw it during the battle, and it wasn't found on any of the bodies."

"Perhaps we'd better have a word with one of the prisoners," mused Tristan. He picked a particularly dejected-looking firbolg, a brute who sat on the ground with his head in his hands. "Bring that one over here!" he called to Sands.

The sergeant-major and a few of his men prodded the reluctant creature toward the king and princess. The giant-kin regarded the humans and their allies with suspicion and fear, though there seemed to be little threat in his manner. Low, beetling brows shaded his eyes from the bright moonlight, but the sagging expression of his jowls seemed far more tired than angry.

"Here," said Alicia, handing the brutish fellow a small sausage from a nearby knapsack. The giant sniffed it cautiously, then popped it into his mouth with a quick gesture.

"There was a ship here," Tristan began, speaking in slow, clear common tongue. "Where did it go?"

"Thurgol took ship," the giant said, squinting in concentration.

"Where did he go?" blurted Brandon.

The firbolg turned, looking to the north. Trees screened them from the coastline, and from this distance, the looming summit of the Icepeak was lost in the haze. Yet the giant-kin unerringly pointed across the strait, to the summit rising above Oman's Isle.

"Thurgol took ship there," he said firmly. "To the big mountain with the snow. They go to the place of Grond Peaksmasher."

* * * * *

Baatlrap seethed with such fury and hatred that he felt as though he must certainly explode. His hand was torn away, his army broken. He led a group of no more than twoscore trolls, the only ones who had survived the battle with the human and dwarven armies. Now those of his comrades still alive regarded him with frank skepticism and loathing, as if it were Baatlrap's fault that the fight had eventually swung against them. He stared back at everyone who seemed likely to challenge him and was mildly gratified to see that, even one-handed, he could still cow the trolls of his band.

Yet his mantle of leadership rested insecurely. He knew that no troll could hold the reins of command for long if he proved incapable of leading his followers to victory and plunder, or at least some small measure of prosperity. Thus far Baatlrap *had* given them a great victory, at Codscove. Unfortunately that triumph had been followed by today's less-than-glorious setback.

But more than the memory of defeat tore at the hulking leader. Indeed, he felt nothing whatsoever for the many trolls, many of them lifelong companions, who had fallen in the fight. The firbolgs who had perished mattered even less.

To find the true cause of his bitter rage, he had to look no farther than the end of his left arm. The limb ended in a slashing, gory wound where once his wrist and hand had been. In one moment of chaotic battle, one violent act of combat, his hand had been sliced off by the human's sword.

And it wouldn't grow back!

Other trolls had suffered similar injuries. In fact, as they marched, one of the creatures, sliced across the gut by that same deadly weapon, fell to the earth, writhing. No longer able to hold back the weight of his insides, the creature finally gurgled out his last breath amid a circle of impassive, dead black eyes.

The trolls resumed their trudging march, leaving the last fatality where he had fallen. The hideous creatures moved in silence, each of them grimly aware of the deadly harbinger this sword might signify, for if humans could inflict trolls with wounds that wouldn't heal, the future of the humanoids suddenly seemed to hang by a very tenuous thread indeed.

In Baatlrap's mind, that hatred began to coalesce into an image of an enemy. He thought of the man who bore that mighty sword, the one his entire army had attacked. They had almost slain him then! A deep growl rumbled from the troll's chest as his fury grew. The lone warrior never would have escaped the encircling ring if not for the appearance of his accursed allies!

But to Baatlrap, it was the lone fighter who came to personify all the hatred, all the frustration that the seething predator now endured. If he could blot out that life, he thought, some of that rage must certainly be mellowed.

And another thought occurred to him. If, in the process of besting the human lord—he knew that such a warrior must be a leader of men—Baatlrap could gain control of that deadly sword, than there would be no troll who dared to stand in the path of his rulership over the clan.

With this thought on the great troll's mind, his pace of retreat slowed to a shuffle and finally stopped altogether. Then, with only a barked command for his tribesmen to follow, he turned and started back toward the gathering of their enemies.

* * * * *

"All the boats were sunk?" demanded Brandon, trying to discover a means to pursue his beloved longship. "Not a curragh or rowboat left?"

"I didn't inspect closely," Tristan said, "but there was nothing afloat in the bay."

"*I* looked," offered a newcomer. Newt popped into view above them, hovering lower until he came to rest upon Tristan's shoulder. His cheeks bulged, and the little faerie dragon quickly swallowed a mouthful of raw fish.

"I got *hungry*," he explained in response to Tristan's look of amazement. "And besides, it looked like you guys had the battle pretty well taken care of. Nice work, too. Hi, Alicia!" he added.

"Hello, Newt," she said wryly, amused by her father's reaction.

"Did you see any *boats?*" Brandon persisted.

"Yup. All sunk, though."

Disgusted, the northman turned to stalk angrily across the trampled field. "There must be *some* way to go after them!" he fumed. Spinning back to the dwarves, he confronted Finellen. "They've got your axe, too. You can bet on it!"

"Thurgol took Axe of Silver Shaft," the captive firbolg explained helpfully.

"There *is* a way, if we can be sure that Oman's Isle is where they've gone," Finellen said cautiously.

"The paths of the Underdark?" Tristan guessed quietly, and the dwarf nodded. To the others, the High King explained. "Many of the Moonshaes are connected below the surface of the sea by the rockbound trails of the dwarves. Once those same trails enabled Finellen to come to my rescue on Alaron when I thought all the while that she was still quartered on Gwynneth."

"Aye—and there is reputedly a trail that connects to Oman's Isle as well," the dwarf agreed reluctantly.

"Can you take us there?" Brandon pressed. "Show me how to get across the strait?"

"These are the secret ways of the dwarves," Finellen protested. "They are the pride of our nation, and one of the keys to our survival!"

"And if we use them to recover the Silverhaft Axe?" countered the king. "Doesn't that serve the nation of dwarves as well?"

"Don't play word games with me!" snapped Finellen, but the king could see that the argument had taken hold.

"How far is the nearest entrance?" he pressed.

"The entrances to the ways are known to only a few of the highest-ranking elders among us," the dwarven captain replied. "But we could get there in a day's long march. Still, it would take most of two days to make the march under the strait, and they've already got a day's head start on us."

"Let's go after them!" roared Brandon. "What else are we supposed to do? We know where they went, and *you* know how to get there! What are we waiting for?"

"An important concession from our allies," King Kendrick said sternly. "Finellen's right. The tunnels beneath the isles are the sacred province of her people, their last line of defense and their secure trade routes. She takes some risk by revealing their location to outsiders."

"That's correct!" she barked, mollified that Tristan understood her viewpoint so well. She pondered the matter a little more before she spoke.

"We've done well together as allies so far—and more to the point, I don't see that I've got much choice. I'll lead you along the tunnel," she said finally. "We'll go to Oman's Isle together and finish the job."

* * * * *

Thurgol's hands were numb, his feet frozen into blocks of ice, by the time morning came to the high slopes of the Icepeak. The other members of his band were similarly uncomfortable, but none of the hardy creatures seemed any the worse for their night of exposure. By the time they had followed the chieftain for the first mile, circulation and warmth had returned to them all.

This part of the climb took them across treacherous side slopes, where loose scree and fields of snow skirted the very pinnacle of the mountain's summit. Several times firbolgs fell, often sliding hundreds of feet before they scrambled to a stop, well scraped and thoroughly bruised. Fortunately none of the tumbling giant-kin was seriously hurt, though each exhausted himself during the long climb back up to his fellows.

Thurgol helped the old shaman across these parts, and by dint of careful footsteps, he prevented either Garisa or himself from suffering a fall. The old woman seemed pre-occupied, carrying the Silverhaft Axe in both hands and constantly staring up at the snowcapped peak, her jaw slack with wonder.

"The eternal home of Grond Peaksmasher," Garisa said with an amazed shake of her head. "It's a miracle to finally be here."

During the arduous climb, she had tactfully avoided any mention of her previous day's suggestion. Thurgol realized now that the lower route, though longer, would have been more practical. Still, he appreciated her tact in avoiding the subject.

The sheer summit soaring above them humbled the giant chieftain. Very carefully he skirted the highest region, leading the file of his tribesmen in a long, creeping traverse. Broad hands and wide feet grasped each bare hold on the steep surface as the chieftain slowly crept along. He led the way around a sheer shoulder, gaining a vista of Oman's Isle sweeping away to the north and of the plunging face of the Icepeak's summit directly ahead.

Thurgol stopped abruptly, vertigo seizing his brain with a whirling, overpowering wind. He felt as though it would tear him from the mountainside and he would plummet down the thousand-foot drop yawning immediately before him.

"The trail stops here," he grunted in disgust, returning to the slightly larger ledge where Garisa and the other giant-kin waited.

"Can we go around?" asked the shaman.

Thurgol looked below, ruefully studying a long, sheer ridge that neatly divided their route in half. They would have to go around that barrier, and the only way to do that was to backtrack nearly to the foot of the mountain.

"We'll have to go back," he replied bitterly. "You were right. We should have gone around Icepeak, not over."

Garisa shrugged. "Grond Peaksmasher has been asleep for centuries," she said. "A few more days aren't going to matter."

With more relief than disappointment, the rest of the firbolgs accepted the news of the necessity to backtrack. With
their numbed hands and frostbitten ears, the thought of a
march back to a land of firewood and windbreaks cheered
them nearly as much as the thought of their destination
itself.

* * * * *

The companions stole a few precious hours of rest following the battle, but when they awakened to resume their
march, it was still the full moon, not the sunrise, illuminating
their preparations. Finellen had agreed only to take the bare
minimum of non-dwarves through the tunnel, so Tristan had
declared that Alicia, Keane, Brandon, Hanrald, and Brigit
would accompany them. Sir Koll, with the aid of the Corwellian men-at-arms and their capable sergeants-major,
would be responsible for chasing down any remnants of the
monsters that might still be roaming the area.

"With this start, we should get to the entrance by noon,"
Finellen explained quickly. "I'll tell you right now, though,
the horses will never fit. You'll have to leave them here or at
the mouth of the tunnel.

"Fair enough," Tristan agreed. "Might as well leave them
in good hands." Sergeant-Major Parsallas took charge of
Shallot and Brittany, as well as Hanrald's and Brigit's steeds,
and with that decided, the companions and the column of
dwarves started along the misty coast.

* * * * *

Crazed by rage, Baatlrap loped through the forest, the
heat of his fury compelling action against the humans. Yet
even his flaming anger did not entirely blind his cunning.
When the scent of humans came to him on the breeze, he
slowed to a creeping skulk, ordering his companion trolls to
remain concealed in the woods.

Crawling forward flat on the ground, concealed beneath the green foliage of a thorny bush, Baatlrap observed the humans beneath the cool light of the moon. The great bulk of the army broke into companies and prepared to make camp. These did not interest the great troll.

Instead, his black, unfeeling eyes remained fixed upon the human lord with the great stallion. That man remained with the dwarves, and presently, to the great troll's bitter satisfaction, this small force marched away from the main body of the army.

Swiftly Baatlrap gathered his remaining warriors, staying well away from the human encampment as they started out. They circled the battlefield, then quickly found the trail of the dwarves and the human king.

Carefully, cautiously, staying well back from his quarry, Baatlrap led his trolls along the moonlit coastal trail.

* * * * *

The dwarven captain led the way along the coast for the better part of six hours as the dawn grew into a cloudless, bright morning. The heat began to increase, untempered by any breeze off the strait.

"I *still* can't figure out why they wanted to steal the axe," Finellen groused. "What use is it to them? Why, the dolts didn't even use it in battle!"

"And why did they break a peace of twenty years?" Tristan added, puzzled himself.

"I think the answer to both questions lies with these firbolgs, and the sooner we catch them and beat the truth out of them, the happier I'll be!"

Tristan shared his old companion's eagerness to conclude their pursuit, but he was surprised to find that his own sense of grim determination had begun to flag somewhat. He wanted to answer these questions as much as ever, but the lust for vengeance no longer burned quite so hotly in his heart. It had been replaced by a kind of wondering curiosity.

By midday, true to Finellen's prediction, the bearded dwarfwoman announced that they must turn inland. Tristan noticed a large split rock, jutting from a promontory on the shoreline, and assumed that this was some kind of landmark.

Indeed, after no more than a quarter-mile of hiking, they reached an apparently impenetrable clump of thornbushes. The branches were interwoven so thoroughly that any attempt to push through, or even to hack a passage, would have been painful if not impossible.

Nevertheless, the dwarf ducked low, lifting heavy branches lined with jagged, prickly thorns out of the way. Tristan followed, using his shield to part the thorny branches, but still he and the other humans had to crawl on their knees to make their way through.

Then abruptly the thicket gave way to a small, grassy clearing, completely surrounded by the thorny hedge. Finellen stepped to a broad stump, the only feature of the meadow, and twisted it once. Tristan wasn't surprised when it fell away, revealing a spiraling stone staircase descending into the earth.

Following the High King, Keane produced a small pebble and, with a snap of his fingers, caused it to burst into bright illumination. "Here you go, Sire," he said, passing it to Tristan.

The king lifted the stone as he followed the dwarf into the dank, tightly circling stairwell. Cool white light splashed along the walls and steps before him, clearly showing him the passage. In the confining space, with the ceiling low overhead and the walls constantly pressing against one shoulder or another, the king was profoundly grateful for the illumination.

The others followed, aided by several additional enchanted pebbles. The dwarves, with their natural night vision, had no need of such aid. After twenty or thirty steps, the stairway became a tight-walled, steeply descending corridor. In places, Tristan had to turn sideways just to make the passage, and he began to wonder if it would be possible to follow such a passage for any number of miles.

"It opens up before too long," Finellen said, as if reading his mind. "As soon as we join up with the main passage."

"Good news!" broke in a familiar voice.

Tristan whirled in surprise as Newt popped into sight behind him, hovering in the corridor that was so narrow his gossamer wings nearly brushed the sides. "Let's get going," said the faerie dragon, settling on the king's shoulder.

"I'm glad you're here, old friend," Tristan said, warmly touched by the little creature's courage.

True to the dwarf's prediction, a few hundred paces, all of it steeply descending, brought them to an intersection with a much wider tunnel. Finellen wasted no time in starting down this passageway, where Tristan was relieved to see that he could walk upright with no difficulty. Still perched on the royal shoulder, Newt nonetheless stretched out his wings, enjoying the extra space.

Keane and Alicia followed behind them, with Brandon, Hanrald, and Brigit next. The remainder of Finellen's dwarves marched silently in the rear. The tunnel drew them deeper into the underground world, the darkness seeming to thicken around them with each step.

As they continued on, the descent was much less noticeable, though it was still there. Onward they trudged, through the darkness of the underearth, while the humans became more and more conscious of the weight of seawater overhead.

For long, dark hours, they made their way along these dank passages. Pillars of stone draped from the ceiling overhead or jutted upward from the floor. In places, they did both, looking to Alicia uncannily like great jaws ready to snap shut on unsuspecting prey.

They talked little, listening instead to the sounds of their footsteps scuffing along the smooth stone floor, or else listening to the vast, unfathomable silence of the Underdark. When they paused to listen carefully, they heard only the echoes of their own passage slowly drifting into the infinite distance and darkness.

* * * * *

The lone dwarf stood guard at the thicket of thorns, assigned to wait there by Finellen as a simple precaution. The dwarfwoman had no reason to suspect that the route might be discovered, yet her natural diligence had required the posting of the sentry.

Now the warrior ambled around the periphery of the hedge, noting nothing unusual in the surrounding woods. He turned back to the thicket, where his captain and her companions had disappeared no more than thirty minutes before. He would have liked to have accompanied the war party, yet he pragmatically accepted the necessity of his current post.

In his musings, he failed to hear the faint crackling of undergrowth behind him—at least, not until it was too late. When the guard finally sensed a presence, he whirled, raising his axe. But here again his reactions were a fraction of a second too slow.

The great, jagged-edged blade of bronze dropped into the dwarf's shoulder, nearly severing his head. Instantly slain, the poor fellow tumbled to the ground while his attacker crept past his crumpled body.

The killer was a huge troll, and he had to bend nearly double to force his way into the thicket. He was further handicapped by the fact that he lacked one hand, the left, which had been chopped off above the wrist. A file of ragged trolls followed him through the tangled path.

Nevertheless, the hulking creatures soon reached the central clearing. They tore at the earth and shrubs, seeking something, and it was only a matter of moments before the great, one-handed troll pried open the tree trunk to reveal the passage leading into the ground.

* * * * *

A flaming chariot came to rest beside Deirdre Kendrick, and she welcomed the arrival of her ally. The Exalted Inquisitor joined the princess at the base of the Icepeak, knowing that the schemes of the gods approached fruition.

In preparation for their ultimate triumph, it was necessary for the princess to master a new aspect of clerical might, the enchantment that would enable them to clear the path for the entry of the New Gods. The magical mastery was beyond even the patriarch's skill, yet with his knowledge and experience, coupled with the clear favor of the gods, the man taught the woman what she needed to know.

Deirdre learned a spell reserved for gods and those of near godly power, for it affected the very fundament of the worlds. Through the immortal core of her body—the core formed by the shards of the shattered mirror—the ability came to her from the vastness of the cosmos. The princess was more than an agent to the gods; she was a part of them, an extension of their might in the world.

Thus they gave her the key to control—the thing that would allow her to master those who would, who *must* inevitably serve her. The spell they gave her offered control of the cadence of life, of the grand progression of events and existence that wove itself into the tapestry of life and history.

For Deirdre had been given the power to bring time itself to a stop.

* * * * *

Stirrings on Oman's Isle brought a chill to the body of the Earthmother. For ages of mortal time, the Peaksmasher had lain dormant, safely cocooned beneath the greatest mountain in the domain of the goddess. His threat had been countered once, when she was young and strong, and since that time her body had served as his bier.

Now she felt the assault of Talos and Helm, the powerful

pressure of the New Gods. Her great druid would labor in her name, she knew, but she would not be enough. In order to prevail, the Earthmother would need more.

She would need nothing less than the aid of an immortal ally.

❧ 15 ❧

Grond Peaksmasher

It took three days for the firbolgs to descend from the steep summit of Icepeak and skirt the base of the mountain. After the first steep descent, the trail mellowed into rolling woodland country. The giants traversed a series of gentle ridges that fanned out from the Icepeak like spokes from a hub. Finally they approached the massif from the north. Here only one narrow valley trailed downward, and so the reputed prison of the Peaksmasher was easy to find.

During the course of their long backtrack, Thurgol came to see the wisdom of Garisa's observation. Indeed, what difference *could* three days more or less make to an imprisonment that had already spanned a dozen centuries or more? Also—and somewhat soothing to Thurgol's ego—the shaman hadn't once tried to point out the fact that she had been correct in her initial suggestion of their path. The mountain heights had proven too much of a challenge even for the determined firbolgs. Her restraint was very unfirbolg-like behavior, and even as he appreciated the respite from her sharp tongue, Thurgol found himself wondering about her reasons.

The giantess, marching stolidly with the great axe across her shoulder, gave him some clue when she spoke to him on the trail.

"Grond Peaksmasher . . ." she mused wonderingly. "What will he do? We bring him the axe, chop him free of the ice—and then what will he do?"

"He will be grateful," Thurgol asserted. "We are his children, are we not?"

Garisa didn't answer the question directly. "It was a long time ago when he came to the Moonshaes. Since his imprisonment, we firbolgs have lived a good life. Gwynneth has been a good home."

"Not all so good—remember the dwarves," the chieftain countered.

"Are they evil? Dwarves let us live by ourselves. Maybe we should have left them alone."

"Why say this now? It's too late!"

"You are right, young chieftain. Here we are—our home is very distant."

"True . . . we have gone far," Thurgol agreed. "We're almost to the end now."

"But what end is it? Do we take a new master who will drive the humans from the isles? What purpose does he have—and, through him, do *we* have?"

"We have to wait for that," the chieftain declared pragmatically.

"Wait . . . yet not wait," Garisa muttered, half to herself. "It all comes too soon."

By the middle of the third day, they had ascended far up the narrow northern valley, picking their way in single file along many sheer precipices. Below them splashed a river of ice-cold water, flanked by groves of lush, dark pines. The trail followed the sloping mountainside some distance above the streambed, and the giant-kin beheld a similar, rock-faced ridge across the valley. The chieftain led the way, eagerly looking forward every time they came around a bend or past a thick clump of trees.

And then finally there it was.

Or was it?

They came around a rocky shoulder to see a sweeping wall of ice. The glacier filled the circular terminus of the deep, narrow valley. Thurgol was astounded by the clear reality before him. How could such an expanse of frost survive the hot months of summer? Indeed, though it was still massive, the surface before him was pocked with melting, pitted by dirt and stone and debris. In fact, the ice was more gray on the surface than white or clear.

"It's *true*," the chieftain breathed, awestruck, as Garisa hobbled up behind him. She gasped as she saw what he meant.

Barely visible, solidly encased within the vast sheet of frozen water, the image of a colossal figure was barely discernible, towering as high as a small mountain in its own right. The cloudy ice obscured much detail, but they could see icy ledges that might have been eyebrows, a trailing slope of slate gray rock that flowed like a beard from other granite crags that looked remarkably like cheeks and jowls.

Neither of them saw the human woman concealed in the rocks at the base of the great glacier. Now, her dark eyes flashing, that observer watched the firbolgs from a shadowy, cavelike niche. She had waited days, with growing impatience, but now at last the giants were here!

Gradually the whole file of firbolgs came up the steepwalled valley. Very slowly Thurgol led them in the final stages of the ascent. He thought that the base of the ice sheet was the logical place to go, and Garisa did not demur. Climbing a steep slope of shattered rock, the giantess ignored her chieftain's offers of help. She had carried the axe this far, she declared, and she would see it to its final destination herself!

A few minutes later, the band had gathered at the foot of the massive figure, staring in awe and deference at the form they distinguished amid the ice. The semitranslucent coating obscured all but the crudest details, yet they saw clearly that the colossal object was unspeakably huge, undeniably lifelike in form.

Slowly, reverently, Thurgol took the Silverhaft Axe from the stooped shaman. The shaft felt right and proper in his hands, the blade perfectly balanced in its crystalline beauty. The chieftain felt as if he had been born to the weapon's use, though in fact he had never wielded an axe for other than woodcutting.

He approached the base of the steep glacier, passing between huge, squarish blocks of blue ice, scrambling up several large rocks until he stood before the uninterrupted surface. Gleaming and pure, uncracked, the glacier swept upward, curling through the end of the narrow valley.

In her niche, the black-haired woman remained silent and intent, staring with raw tension at the giant-kin and his mighty axe. She held her breath as he climbed toward the glacier's base, watched him heft the weapon, check its balance in his hands.

Thurgol raised the axe over his head, gathering all the strength of his giant muscles for the most important blow of his life. The ice seemed so smooth, so perfect, that it seemed a shame to scar it, but he felt no regrets. For the first time since embarking from Blackleaf, he had the feeling that he did something purely, unalterably right and proper.

He swung the axe, and the crystal blade bit through the surface of the glacier. A great, twisting crack snarled its way up the smooth face, and chunks of ice, some the size of a human's house, tumbled free, rolling and smashing down the steep slope. But Thurgol stood firm, ignoring the shattering ice on either side, awaiting the results of his action, the will of the gods.

Then the woman in the rock niche raised her hands and whispered the words to a spell, too softly for any of the giant-kin to hear over the din of the crumbling glacier. And as she spoke, the power of her own magic took hold of the valley before her.

And time stood still.

* * * * *

Tavish had traveled a great deal in her life, had endured many months of exposure to weather, many meals of sub-standard food, long days of wearying travel and exhausting nights of frequently interrupted sleep. Yet never in her six decades of life, she knew, had she been so tired, so hungry, and so cold.

She had followed the firbolg party onto the slopes of the

Icepeak, in fact almost blundering into the giant-kin as they backtracked down their trail. Scrambling into a dense stand of pines, Tavish had held her breath as the column marched past within an easy stone's throw of her hiding place.

Then, of course, she, too, had reversed her course, following the plain trail of the giants as they returned to the lowlands and made the long, circuitous passage around the base of the mountain. Her steady pursuit had left the bard little time for food gathering, and she hadn't dared light a fire that might reveal her position, so she had grown progressively weaker, colder, and more miserable during the course of the trek.

Then had come the final, terrifying climb up the steep approaches of this cliff-walled vale, until she once again reached a vantage over the giant-kin. Now she crouched among the rocks on the mountainside, half a mile from the glacier but high enough for a clear view of the ice sheet and the firbolg party gathered at its base. And yet, as fatigued and uncomfortable as she was here, she wouldn't have been anywhere else in the world, given the fascinating nature of the events going on before her.

First came the astounding effect of the axe's blow against the glacier as the gaping crack shivered its way upward across the face of the ice. In the immediate following moment, some kind of magic seemed to halt the firbolgs in their tracks.

Tavish stared in astonishment as the giant-kin froze like statues, immobile and apparently unaware. They remained fixed in the actions they had been engaged in, some who had been walking growing rigid to the point of having one leg raised, ready to take the next step, though not yet coming into contact with the ground. Even more strange, several blocks of tumbling ice hung suspended in the air, their plummeting descent halted by the unseen force.

But Tavish's surprise grew to astonishment as she saw the black-haired young woman emerge from concealment and walk boldly among the unaware humanoids. Squinting—

her eyes were not the keen tools of observation they had been twenty years earlier—she studied the flowing hair with its suggestion of familiarity, and she thought that she recognized the woman's confident gait.

Tavish saw the great chieftain, the one who had bested the troll on the dock and who had guided his ship across the Strait of Oman, now bearing the great, diamond-bladed axe in his hands. He stood as though in thoughtful repose, observing the jagged, narrow crack that shot up the face of ice following the impact of his blow, the axe held loosely at his waist.

As the tiny female figure clambered up the boulders, Tavish saw that her target was the giant wielding the great axe. With some difficulty, the woman scrambled up the last high boulder and tugged the Silverhaft Axe from the frozen hands of the rigid firbolg. The weapon was huge, and appeared to be quite heavy, yet the princess drew it free without apparent effort.

She turned, her black hair swirling around her head as her face exploded into an expression of fierce triumph, and the bard recognized her for certain: This was Princess Deirdre Kendrick! Why the woman, youngest daughter of her friends, should be here remained a mystery to the harpist, yet Tavish sensed something very wrong, dangerously evil, in the scene she currently witnessed.

Carefully Tavish crept through the broken talus, working her way from rock to rock while she kept her eyes on the tableau below. She saw Deirdre climb down, clutching the axe. Then the princess passed through the band of firbolgs and stood still, her back to Tavish, as if she waited for something.

In another moment, the bard saw what that was: the end of the spell that had frozen the giant-kin in time. Tavish heard a popping sound in the air, and abruptly the firbolgs resumed the activities that had been interrupted. Those in the midst of taking a step concluded the gesture smoothly, as if there had been no spell, no delay of any kind.

The suspended blocks of ice tumbled around them, shattering and cracking down the slope. The sound echoed through the valley, but the dodging firbolgs avoided most of the shards. Indeed, they had already dodged the iceblocks several minutes before, moving out of the way and now watching the debris as if it had continued its plunge quite uninterrupted.

Only the chieftain, standing upon the rock and staring up at the glacier, noticed a change. He bellowed in alarm, spinning on the rock and shouting to his tribesmen, shaking his empty fists. Tavish sensed what had happened: No instant of time had passed for the giant-kin within the sphere of Deirdre's powerful spell. To the great firbolg warrior, it must have seemed as if the axe had vanished instantaneously from his hands.

Then the great giant-kin's eyes fell upon the human figure standing beyond his comrades below . . . the young woman who bore the Silverhaft Axe in her hands. His jaw fell in astonishment, but a moment later, fury contorted his face, and he sprang down from the mountainside in great, leaping bounds. The other firbolgs, sensing the focus of their chieftain's rage, turned in astonishment to regard the impudent human.

"Stop!" ordered the Princess of Callidyrr, her voice ringing in countless echoes from the surrounding cliffs. The tone of command was unmistakable, but Tavish was nevertheless astounded when the hulking giant, twice as tall and five times as massive as the woman, slowed his charge to a walk and finally came to a standstill, staring angrily at Deirdre.

"Who are you?" he demanded, his voice rumbling deep in the familiar words of the common tongue.

"I am your mistress—the one who holds the Silverhaft Axe and whose commands you will obey."

"I owe no fealty to the bearer of the axe," shot back the firbolg chief. He took another step toward the princess.

"Would you see it destroyed?" she demanded, raising the shaft and holding the crystalline edge over a chunk of solid granite.

"It would take one mightier than you to break that blade," the firbolg replied, confident again. He took another step toward Deirdre.

A sound rumbled through the valley like a thunderclap, and they all looked to the sky, expecting to see black clouds rolling in, perhaps bolts of lightning exploding toward the ground. Yet the heavens remained blue and pastoral, with a few puffy clouds the only harbingers of moisture. Surely none of these vaporous wisps had issued that mighty clap of thunder!

The sound was repeated, and like Deirdre's voice, the noise echoed over and over, rolling down the narrow valley like a volley of distant explosions. This time, Tavish could see the source, and it was a revelation that drained the blood from her face and set her stomach roiling.

The crack on the giant glacier *grew!* Now spiderweb fissures ran through the ice to the right and left, extending outward from the gash created by the chieftain's original blow. Once again the crashing sound rumbled through the vale, and this time pieces of ice broke from the surface to plummet dizzyingly toward the base of the glacier and the watching firbolgs and human gathered there.

The giant-kin hastily scrambled away from the tumbling debris as more and more sheets of compressed ice broke away and plunged downward. The first of these shattered against the rocks at the glacier's base, exploding upward in shimmering curtains of white frost. Others cracked into larger pieces, sending blocks the size of boulders tumbling through the air, falling and smashing among the fleeing firbolgs.

Only the princess stood firm, facing the breaking glacier and bearing the axe easily in her hands, as if it were a talisman that could protect her from all harm. In fact, Tavish wondered if that might be the truth. Certainly the plunging debris and deadly flying rocks gave the young princess a wide berth, while the panic-stricken firbolgs had been driven well back from the glacier.

Again the crack sounded through the valley, and this time the gap in the glacier widened visibly, revealing in clarity the granite-featured form imprisoned there. More rubble spewed outward, crashing around the figures below. Now the Peaksmasher appeared, and for the first time, Tavish could see that only the giant's torso was visible. The body from the waist downward was sunk into the ground, as if part of the bedrock itself. Though the giant flexed its chest and shoulders, sending more debris tumbling and crashing, it seemed to be firmly rooted in place. Even only half-visible, however, Grond Peaksmasher loomed like a small mountain overhead!

Then finally the echoes faded away, and the dust of crushed rock and ice began to settle. None of the firbolgs made a move, and even the princess stared upward, her posture locked in rigid awe.

A cliff like a huge face was clearly visible in the glacier's gap now. Low brows of granite sheltered shadowy niches that resembled closed eyelids, above cheekbones of mountain ledges beside an overhanging crag of a nose. The beard, of frosty gray, flowed in a thick cascade, a great slope of broken rock that in itself was the size of a high hill.

Then those ledges flexed, rising like brows as the massive eyes opened, freezing all the watchers with a gaze of ice-pure blue. The massive lips moved, rustling the beard and releasing another shower of icy shards. Awestruck, Tavish held her breath, well aware that she witnessed the awakening of a god, or the potent avatar of an elder deity.

The mighty shoulders shrugged, and more sheets of ice fell away, some of them as big as the icecap on a small pond. These, too, shattered, and now the brawny arms came free, knotted with muscle and capped with massive hands. All the surface of the great being was rock, but it was rock that seemed supple, like rough, pliable skin. The fingers, broad-knuckled and blunt, were themselves larger than the firbolgs gaping up at him from below. Finally the entire torso was revealed, though the giant from the waist down remained imprisoned in the bedrock of the earth.

Twisting, Grond Peaksmasher released another deluge of rock and ice, showering down toward those assembled below. The great pieces seemed to fall in slow motion, yet Tavish knew that any one of them could kill an unfortunate victim trapped in the path of the fall. Once again the firbolgs clawed their way back away from the crushing avalanche.

Deirdre still stood firm, unshaken by the thundering wave of destruction, nor did any of the debris fall anywhere near her. Was it the will of the god that she remained unharmed? Or perhaps some barrier of protection raised by the Silverhaft Axe? The bard couldn't know, so she could only stare in wonder at the steady courage of the young princess.

Then Tavish gasped audibly, anticipating the giant's next act even as he began slowly to move. She watched in an awe that began to grow into terror as she understood the import of the Peaksmasher's gesture.

The firbolgs, too, staggered back in dismay and consternation as the face of the giant moved closer and closer to the ground.

For the colossus that was Grond Peaksmasher leaned toward Princess Deirdre, bending so far forward that the great, craggy forehead finally met the earth.

It was a bow of absolute obeisance. Tavish understood beyond question that Grond Peaksmasher was acknowledging his new mistress.

* * * * *

The march beneath the Strait of Oman took the column the better part of two days, though to Tristan, it felt as though it might have been a week. The tiny pebble glowing in his hand became a kind of talisman for him as Finellen led them along dank corridors, across sweeping bridges that spanned apparently bottomless subterranean chasms, along narrow ledges that swept dizzyingly above black, empty space.

They climbed stairways of stone, and waded through knee-deep, chill water that, the dwarven captain claimed, was 'not likely' to get too much deeper. Even Newt remained quiet and subdued during the underground passage, remaining alertly vigilant on the High King's shoulder. Ranthal, meanwhile, paced along at his master's heels, the great moorhound's nose constantly sniffing the dank, stuffy air for some sign of an approaching threat.

The companions stopped to rest once for a period of several hours, but even the dwarves, who were quite at home in the underground environment, seemed to be ready to move on quickly. Tristan and the other humans slept only fitfully, the king with his hand wrapped around the gleaming pebble that he increasingly believed was the only thing preserving his sanity.

At one point, however, just before he drifted off to sleep, Tristan noticed the Prince of Gnarhelm crossing their darkened campsite, settling himself beside Alicia and speaking softly. Tristan didn't see what happened next, but as he turned away, seeking a comfortable position on the rocky floor, the light from his pebble swept across the group. He saw Keane, oblivious to everything else, staring at Brandon and the princess with an expression of raw, unrelieved tension.

Finally they resumed the march, and within a few hours Tristan noted the subterranean corridor beginning to slope upward, first gradually, as it followed a long, winding cavern that slowly ascended toward the surface. Weary and out of breath from the long uphill grade, the party slowed its pace. Finellen and Tristan kept them going until, staggering with weariness, they reached a wide stone stairway, obviously the work of dwarven craftsmen.

They climbed the steps for an apparently eternal interval—at least, it seemed that way to Tristan. He held the pebble before him, and it illuminated dozens of steps disappearing into the darkness above. When he lowered it behind him, he saw the tired faces of his companions and the trailing column of dwarves, extending into the darkness below.

"Here we are," Finellen announced eventually,

At first, Tristan noticed nothing different, but gradually he realized that the passage around them grew lighter, suffused with a dim illumination. Water trickled along the floor, and as they progressed, he heard a steady splashing, like a small waterfall. The light continued to increase until Tristan enclosed the glowing pebble in his hand and found out that he could see sufficiently to prevent a fall.

The sound of the waterfall increased, and the air itself became moist, full of partially condensed droplets. Finally they came around a bend and beheld a shimmering curtain blocking the way, beyond which blossomed pale daylight. Finellen led them along a narrow, slippery ledge, concealed from outside view by the waterfall. They had to duck through a corner of the watery barrier, but then they came out upon the bank of a small pool. Overhead, well-screened by tree branches, they could see a blue, nearly cloudless sky!

Tristan quickly raised a hand to his eyes, shielding against the shockingly bright illumination that spilled through the trees around them. The king was astonished to see that they weren't even looking at the sun or the sky. It was simply the reflection of daylight off an opposite cliff wall, though in the first blast of brightness, it seemed fully sufficient to blind him.

"It always takes a few minutes to get used to the light again," Finellen said helpfully. "You'll be able to see like normal in just a bit."

True to her prediction, the humans and dwarves quickly adapted to the light, and they wasted no time in moving into a rockbound valley. Nearby, the clear bulk of the Icepeak rose into the morning sky.

"Good navigating," Tristan said, with a grin of congratulations and relief.

"Aye," Finellen replied, pleased herself. "The glacier's on

the north slope, and we're just a little to the east of the main ridge."

The party took a short time to acclimatize to the light and fresh air, also taking a few moments to rest from the long uphill climb. Their goal was too near for them to brook any long delay, however, so the column quickly resumed its march over the surface of the ground. Finellen and Tristan led the way, followed by their human companions and Brigit, and finally trailed by the resolute column of sturdy dwarves.

They passed through sun-speckled woods of pine and cedar, with the scent of evergreen needles permeating the cool morning air. On any other day, Tristan would have taken the time to enjoy the forest. It was just the kind of woods where he loved to spend long, quiet hours. He found the smell reminiscent of pastoral outings as a lad, in the company of Old Arlen, his father's loyal weaponmaster.

Now, however, the driving need to confront the firbolgs propelled him, with no thought for the wonders around him. The High King's desire—for retribution, or vengeance— burned strong. Soon he would confront the firbolg chieftain and ultimately destroy him.

Then finally they came around the last ridge, starting a long, winding trail that led into the narrow valley. The enclosing walls prevented them from seeing very far ahead of them, but the northward orientation of the place was obvious.

The trail twisted across a steep climb, leading them past a great boulder in a path so narrow they were reduced to a single file. Moving carefully, with a hundred-foot drop falling away to their right, they crept steadily upward. They worked their way around the shoulder one at a time. Here the view opened up the valley, and after a few more steps, Finellen stopped abruptly, a gasp of astonishment escaping her lips.

Tristan looked up, following her gaze, and at first he thought that some huge pillar of stone blocked their view of the glacier. That impression lasted only a second, however, before the truth came home to him with a shocking wave of force: The pillar he saw was stone, but not normal rock; not a shapeless monolith, but a humanlike being that was *alive!*

The colossal figure was visible only from the belly up, as if the giant stood in a great canyon in the ground. Tristan refused even to consider how huge it would be if it were to stand with feet at ground level.

"By all the gods!" gasped Keane as he and Alicia came up behind the king.

"What is it?" the princess wondered, awestruck. The chiseled, craggy face peered into the unseen distance as the gigantic being stared vacantly over their heads. Yet in the steady rise and fall of his breath and in the massive sweep of his arms, with his fists planted firmly on the ground, she saw evidence of life, of humanlike dexterity.

"Grond Peaksmasher," Finellen answered for them. The dwarf moved forward, allowing the rest of the file to pass around the rock and stare upward at the gigantic figure. They gazed with slack, stunned faces, in the silence of awe, wonderment . . . and fear.

* * * * *

Tavish had remained hidden as Grond Peaksmasher rose before the princess—or, more significantly in the bard's deduction, before the Silverhaft Axe. In the hours that followed, the bard had been alternately thunderstruck and appalled.

Following the example of the gigantic avatar, the firbolgs themselves had bowed in craven obeisance to the young Princess of Callidyrr. Deirdre had coolly accepted the worship as no more than her due. Speaking in the gruff tongue of the giant-kin, she had dispatched several of them to guard various approaches to this valley. Then the princess had put the rest of the band to work.

Deirdre had ordered the firbolgs to excavate a great pit, with steep walls and a depth sufficient that a firbolg within the hole was perfectly invisible to an observer on the ground. The space enclosed was quite large and an almost perfect square, Tavish saw, estimating perhaps thirty human paces on a side. She wondered about the purpose of the pit and was impressed by the sharp, regular outlines of the corners and sides.

Grond Peaksmasher had stood aloof from this project, looming over the valley bottom, his eyes gazing away to the north, as if he could see something a thousand miles away that triggered his deep, primeval memory. Yet while he took no part in the activities around his feet, Tavish had the feeling that he simply awaited Deirdre's command.

No sooner had the giant-kin completed their great, precisely oriented square hole in the ground than one of the lookout firbolgs hastened back from the mouth of the valley. Watching his gestures, Tavish understood that the fellow warned the princess about the approach of intruders—dwarves or humans, the bard guessed from the crude gestures.

She wondered idly who the newcomers were, but from her position of cover, there seemed to be little that the bard could do to influence events. So, instead, she waited.

* * * * *

For the moment at least, the colossus hadn't seemed to notice Tristan and his companions. The group gathered underneath the screen of several tall pines. The king, the dwarven captain, and the princess advanced cautiously to peer through the densely needled branches.

"Legend said that he was frozen in the ice years before the coming of humans to the isles," Finellen explained in a hoarse whisper.

"It's moving!" Alicia hissed.

The giant turned slowly, sweeping its gaze downward, past the silent observers and into the bowl of the valley before its flat, slablike stomach. A low hillock of ground blocked their view into this bowl.

Then a figure came into view, a small *human*-sized shape

that stood on the grassy knoll and looked directly at the three watchers in the woods.

"Father—and you, too, my sister—come here," commanded an imperious voice, a voice that the king and princess recognized at once, even as the wind gusted out Deirdre's long black hair. "And bring the dwarf as well!"

Instinctively Alicia and Finellen pulled back farther into the shadow of their cover, astonished that their presence had been discovered. The High King, however, pressed the branches back to either side and stepped into the daylight. He was stunned by his daughter's appearance here, his first reaction a genuine explosion of relief because she looked so strong, so robust.

But very quickly that relief was tempered by puzzlement and a growing suspicion. The looming form of Grond Peaksmasher rose to the sky behind his daughter, yet now it stood like some placid manservant awaiting its master's whim.

"What do you mean, giving me orders?" Tristan demanded, approaching the young princess.

Deirdre regarded her father with an expression of aloof, icy disdain. For the first time, he noticed her hands. She carried a huge axe, the blade balanced on the ground while she leaned a hand easily against the base of the shaft. "Not just you—I order all of your companions forward as well."

When no one emerged from the tiny grove, Deirdre snapped her fingers once and pointed at the trees. Immediately a shadow fell across Tristan as the gigantic figure leaned forward.

"No!" he cried. "You *can't!* That's your sister in—"

But he was too late—or rather, Deirdre took no notice of his objection. Instead, she watched impassively while massive fingers closed around the treetops. Wood splintered, and the incongruously pleasant scent of pine filled the air through the entire valley as the Peaksmasher lifted the trees from the earth as a gardener might pluck some annoying weed.

Tumbling figures were clearly visible amid the gaping holes of dirt left behind. Alicia and Keane crawled from the debris, then a sputtering Finellen followed. Slowly, one by one, the others appeared, uninjured for the most part, though one of the dwarves had suffered a broken arm in the upheaval of the grove.

In the meantime, Tristan looked back to his daughter, amazed at the cool air she exuded—the air of the conqueror, he decided. Then he saw other figures moving behind her, and his astonishment grew to a numbing kind of disbelief as this rank of new arrivals moved forward to take up station on both sides of the princess.

Firbolgs! Serving his daughter, as loyally obedient as any guard of honor, they arrayed themselves along the grassy hillock as the remainder of Tristan's party dusted themselves off and came forward to join the king. Alicia, he was relieved to see, had suffered no injury except to her pride. Her eyes flashed rage at her sister, but surprisingly she held her tongue.

Keane, Brigit, and Hanrald followed the princess, and they, too, regarded Deirdre with suspicion and silent hostility, since the overwhelming presence of Grond Peaksmasher was more than enough to stifle any obvious resistance.

* * * * *

Tavish risked emerging from her cover as the princess and the firbolgs hurried down the valley to the grassy hillock where Deirdre confronted Tristan and his companions. At last the bard understood what she had long suspected: Deirdre was working against the wishes of her father and family, and hence to Tavish, against the good of the Moonshaes. Furthermore, she had the High King and his companions at a severe disadvantage.

Grimly the bard crept from her rocky niche, working her way from boulder to shrub for concealment as she surreptitiously advanced toward the princess and her gigantic allies.

Slowly, gradually, she narrowed the distance between them. The harpist cursed the infirmities of age; at nearly sixty, she was no woodland scout! Yet her limbs responded with alacrity to the needs of the moment, and the attention of her targets remained firmly fixed upon the party before Deirdre—the group that included her own father and sister.

Tavish heard the arrogance in Deirdre's tone as she spoke to her prisoners, saw the firm set of the young woman's shoulders as she braced herself against the Silverhaft Axe. The princess seemed every bit the cool conqueror, though the harpist couldn't hear enough of the words to understand the purpose of her conquest. Surely it wasn't vengeance or hatred that motivated her! But what then? Ambition? That, too, didn't seemed likely. Tavish would never have suspected the bookish Deirdre of attempting to usurp her father's throne.

She forced the thoughts, the questions, aside. This was not a time to wonder about *why*. Far more important to Tavish, and to the Moonshaes, was *what*. Specifically, what should she do now?

The axe, Tavish sensed, was the real key to Deirdre's power, the tool that enabled her to compel the obedience of Grond Peaksmasher and the firbolgs. The bard's eyes focused on the potent talisman as she squirmed into the scant cover beneath a dense cedar. She had reached a point only twenty paces behind Deirdre, but there was no further cover between herself and the princess.

Yet she had also reached the point of no return. Gathering her legs beneath her, calling on them for one more burst of speed, she concentrated on the Silverhaft Axe. She would try to wrest the weapon from Deirdre. Whatever happened after that would be up to the king, his companions, and the firbolgs. Tavish's own chances of survival, she believed, were slim. If one of the great firbolgs reached her before Tristan or Keane could come to her aid, the bard had no illusions about the outcome.

But she had no choice, as far as she could see. Tense and

alert, she watched Deirdre, waiting until the princess began to speak.

Then, knowing no time would be better, Tavish broke from her cover in a mad dash toward the black-haired Princess of Callidyrr.

* * * * *

"It is your *arrogance!*" Deirdre sneered, speaking to her father. "Your *blindness* to the need for change! That desire, to hold your people back with a primitive religion and a hide-bound fear of progress, *that* is the evil against which I strive!"

"The evil has been wrought by your own 'friends,' " the king replied, with a meaningful glance at the firbolgs flanking his black-haired daughter.

"Bah—they are mere tools, fit only to bear the axe to the place of its use. If their actions draw you here as well, so much the better."

"But think of your people, your kingdom!"

"They are not *my* people—not yet," Deirdre retorted. "Though they will be soon enough!"

"You're crazy!" cried Alicia. "What matter if you kill us? Do you really think—?"

"You will not necessarily die. All of you who serve the will of the New Gods will be spared," Deirdre explained, like a tutor trying to get a plain point across to a classful of thick-skulled students. "This is the way of the future, the destiny of the Moonshae Islands."

"You would betray the faith of your people, the goddess your mother has served all her life?" Tristan challenged. He struggled to understand, knowing that this was his daughter before him but not finding any part of her that he knew.

"My mother serves the enemy. My mother *is* the enemy!" Deirdre snapped. "That's why the rest of you will remain here as prisoners, significant only as bait to draw the true menace into my presence!"

The High King studied the crystal-bladed axe, with its gleaming haft of pure silver. The weapon must weigh a tremendous amount, yet Deirdre had twirled it around as if it were a toy. That artifact! Surely it must in some way be responsible for his daughter's unnatural behavoir.

Then the king stiffened reflexively as he saw something moving behind Deirdre. Tavish! His heart pounded as he saw the bard break from the cover of her tree. The stout harpist's legs pumped steadily as she dashed toward the princess. At the same time, Deirdre's attention, and that of the firbolgs as well, remained fixed upon their captives.

He heard Alicia's intake of breath, knowing that she had seen the bard's desperate venture as well. Desperately he prayed that none of them would betray that knowledge before Tavish could wrest the axe from the princess.

"Bantarius—Helmsmite!"

The voice sent a tingle of alarm through Tristan's mind. Where did it come from? Who had spoken? The words, the tone, were both maddeningly familiar.

A glowing form instantly materialized in the air behind Deirdre. Solidifying quickly, it became a blunt hammer with a head of slate-gray steel and a haft of sturdy oak, suspended behind and above the princess.

But as Tavish passed beneath it, the hammer smashed downward, dropping that solid head straight onto the bard's scalp, bashing her with brutal force. The harpist dropped like a felled tree, collapsing, motionless, amid the rocks and grass.

Deirdre never even turned around. "Welcome, Exalted Inquisitor, to the dawn of a new era!" she said, holding forth a hand. To Tristan's bitter rage, Parell Hyath stepped forward from the concealment of a nearby clump of rocks, advancing to take his place beside Deirdre. Now Tristan recognized the voice of the spell-caster, too late to do any good.

"We suspected some trickery from you," the cleric explained condescendingly. "Therefore we decided it would be best if I remained concealed until your hand was revealed.

Though I must admit," the inquisitor added, turning to Keane and clucking in mock disappointment, "I had expected the principal troublemaker to be you."

"This affront to the goddess will not pass!" Alicia shouted suddenly.

The priest and princess stood together on the knoll, regarding Alicia with amused tolerance. "We do not hope for it to pass . . . not just yet," explained the inquisitor. "For only when the goddess makes her will known shall that will be bent to ours."

* * * * *

Talos and Helm pressed close as the powerful demigod stirred from his age-long imprisonment.

Grond sensed the surrounding presence of his ancient enemy, the Earthmother. Beyond the cloak of the world, he felt other immortal beings—lords who promised mastery, power . . . and freedom. This promise to the Peaksmasher the New Gods sealed with the presence of the Silverhaft Axe, and against that ancient talisman, he could offer no resistance.

The pulse of the goddess was strong in the bedrock below him, but all of the demigod's might was focused on the surface of the world now, against the pitiful and helpless creatures within range of his crushing fists.

❧16❧

Clash of the Avatars

Robyn flew steadily northward, driven by consuming urgency. Her wings stroked the air in rhythmic cadence, and though cool wind streamed past her feathered skin, her entire body burned with a conflagration of fear.

Would she be too late? That question propelled her and terrified her, for she knew that the task before her was the most important of her life. For too long, worldly concerns had kept her content, even complacent. Now she knew the truth—the terrible vulnerability of the goddess, and the threats from within and without her realm. Gods such as Talos and Helm loomed, ambitious and mighty, while the demigod Grond Peaksmasher could tear her apart from within.

This knowledge filled the High Queen with a sense of inadequacy and failure. At the same time, she knew a kind of desperate abandonment, a willingness to do anything in order to thwart these onslaughts.

Of course, opportunity for redemption might already have passed her by. How could she have wasted so much time? Over and over she chastised herself, as if the criticism would infuse her wings with greater strength, her lungs with increased stamina.

Somehow the druid queen's meditations at the Moonwell had occupied her far longer than Robyn had been even vaguely aware. The warmth of spirit had surrounded her, and she had sat entranced throughout the night of the full moon, allowing the spirit of the goddess to take possession of her, to infuse the human body with the immortal power of the Earthmother. It had been an expansive experience, unlike anything she had ever known, and it had carried

Robyn far from her body, far from her world and her mortality. She soared on the wings of the Earthmother, journeying wherever she would, wherever the desires of the goddess took her.

Yet unlike her daughter, who had also walked the paths of the gods, Robyn did not experience a vastness, an infinity like Deirdre's. For the universe of the Earthmother was most definitely contained and limited, surrounded by the Trackless Sea and marked only by the outcrops of rock, earth, and life known as the Moonshaes.

In this domain, the High Queen had witnessed the awakening of Grond Peaksmasher, had observed the trials and dangers endured by her husband and his companions. And then, most terrifying of all, her spiritual journey had allowed her to look directly into her daughter Deirdre's heart.

It was the latter vision that had jolted her awake and filled her with a sense of the most dire alarm. Though her return to awareness struck her at sunset, she had immediately taken to the air, chagrined that her musings had apparently lasted a full day. But then several hours had passed, and the moon had not risen, had not even glimmered in the east. And when it finally made its appearance, halfway to midnight, it had already shrunk well below the circle of its fullness. The meaning was apparent to Robyn: Her trance had lasted not just for a full night, but for three or four *days!*

Thus the desire that drove the wings of the white hawk had become a keen desperation. What had already happened? What was left to do? These were the questions that raged through her mind as she soared from Myrloch Vale, arrowed through the sky over Winterglen, and finally crossed the Strait of Oman. Here, even at her lofty elevation, the summit of the Icepeak loomed above her, and she was forced to veer around the mountain.

For, at the very least, her meditations had shown her where she had to go.

Finally the north valley of the Icepeak came into view, and as she saw the colossus there, she felt no overwhelming sense of surprise. The vision had been too clear, too undeniable. Instead, she felt a growing sense of outrage and violation, a sense that grew from beyond herself, as if the whole island had been corrupted.

The mountain that was Grond Peaksmasher, she knew, was a tool of the gods who had so long strived to overwhelm the Earthmother, to drive that goddess from the magical domain of her islands. It had been the mission of Robyn's life to stave off those incursions, and it was a task wherein she had already failed once. She remained well aware that it had been only her elder daughter's faith and tenacity that had previously broken the spell holding the Earthmother in thrall.

Now, however, it was up to Robyn to make sure that her goddess's freedom remained unchecked. This looming god was a great threat to that vibrant vitality, and it was one Robyn could not let pass unchallenged.

As she soared lower, the figures on the ground became visible. She saw the deep pit and recognized Tristan and Alicia. She saw other humans and many dwarves trapped there as well. Desperately Robyn wished that she could spare the time to go to them, could at least share with her family the sense of overwhelming love that drove her now into her most desperate attack.

Outside the pit, Robyn saw her daughter Deirdre and the patriarch of Helm. When she recognized the latter, a squawk of anger burst from her hawk's beak, for even the self-disciplined druid was unable to entirely contain her outrage.

Then she dove, feeling the power of the goddess surge through her. She was more than the great druid now, more even than the druid queen. As her spirit expanded, nourished by her days of meditation and trance, and she faced the looming bulk of the New Gods' power, she became something awe-inspiring, immortal in her own right.

In the force of that swooping dive, Robyn Kendrick, High Queen of the Isles, became the avatar of the Earthmother.

* * * * *

"Damn the curse that blinds her!" Tristan swore, shaking his fist at the disappearing firbolgs. Beside him, Ranthal paced and barked.

The brutes had just lowered them into the pit with the rest of his companions, and now he railed at the backs of the giants, arms clasped around swords, shields, and axes, who walked away with the weapons of the humans and dwarves. The firbolgs quickly disappeared from sight, since the prisoners in the pit could see only a short distance beyond the rim of the enclosure.

Just then the shriek of the white hawk pierced the breezy air in the valley, and the king peered anxiously into the sky. "Robyn! It's a trap!" he cried, his voice lost in the wind that suddenly arose.

"What are you guys doing in here?" asked Newt, appearing between Tristan and Alicia as they stood beside the gray barrier of the granite wall.

"We have to get out!" Tristan barked, returning to his inspection of the sheer surface. It was only twelve feet high or so, but the sides had been thoroughly smoothed and provided no handholds. It made a very effective prison.

"Well, don't be mad at *me!*" the faerie dragon huffed, quickly disappearing again.

Keane approached, his gait maddeningly nonchalant to the king. Yet Tristan sensed something conspiratorial in the man's walk, so the king turned back to the cliff, as if continuing his inspection. Keane came to a stop beside him.

"There may be a way—at least for one of us to get out of here," the young wizard said, his tone low and elaborately conversational. "I have a spell of levitation. It can lift me to the top, where I just might be able to do some good."

Tristan looked at him thoughtfully. "Just you?" he asked.

"Well, just a single person," the mage amended. "Though I thought that I could do the most—"

"Please!" the king said, his voice desperate. "That's my wife and my daughter up there! Use the spell on *me!*"

"But . . . Your Majesty," Keane objected. "You have no

weapons!" He bit back another remark, concerning the king's missing hand. He saw the desperation in Tristan's eyes but tried to dissuade him rationally. "At least I could use my spells to some effect!" he concluded lamely.

"Think about the fact that they put you in here without restraint," Tristan urged, his eyes turning crafty. "They know of your powers! Perhaps they're watching you right now, waiting for you to make some move for freedom! They won't expect the same from me!"

"But . . . the danger—!"

"Keane!" Tristan's voice was level and tense. "I won't, I *can't* order you to do this. The goddess knows you've earned the right to rule yourself. But *please*, man . . . it's Robyn!"

"Very well, Sire," Keane said miserably. He looked around the fringe of the pit—at least, at as much as they could see of it from inside the hole. None of the firbolgs were in sight, and Deirdre and the cleric, so far as they knew, had gone over to the base of Grond Peaksmasher.

"*Gravatius . . . deni,*" muttered Keane, touching a hand to the king's arm. Immediately Tristan started to rise from the ground. "Be careful, Sire!" the wizard whispered after him.

The High King kept his hand close to the wall, looking over his shoulder. As he rose higher, he saw several firbolgs across the pit, but fortunately their eyes were inevitably drawn to the scene above them. When he looked up to follow their gaze, he understood why. The queen, his wife, flew in the body of the white hawk, circling and diving at the mountain that was Grond Peaksmasher. The struggle would have seemed ludicrous to the king, if not for the fact that he understood the stakes.

The Peaksmasher reached outward with craggy fingers of granite at the bird, which seemed to swirl effortlessly away from the blunt, sweeping hand. Robyn screeched again, and the sound was a jarring note that rocked the giant backward. Grond threw his hands over his ears with a thunderclap of noise and bellowed his outrage against the affront of the Earthmother's cry.

The bird came to rest upon a high outcrop of rock, a spire that approached the very crown of the Icepeak, beyond the reach even of the colossal giant. The Peaksmasher reached down and grasped a huge shoulder of rock, breaking it free from the mountainside in a showering landslide of rubble. Hoisting the solid chunk, the size of a large house, he hurled it at the spire where Robyn perched. Moments before impact, however, the great druid once again sprang into the air.

Still rising gently, Tristan soon reached the top of the pit wall, checking to see that the firbolgs remained raptly engaged in the battle above. His feet on the ground again, the king sprinted for the cover of some nearby trees, tumbling over a low hummock and seeking the shelter of a streambed. He lay there for a moment, his mind whirling with tension—not for himself so much as fear for his wife and daughters.

Where was his weapon? The question jerked him up to spy over the bank of the shallow stream. He looked around, cursing as he saw the gleaming pile of armaments that the firbolgs had piled on the ground—*across* the pit from him.

Desperately, knowing that speed was as important as stealth, Tristan started down the rocky creek bed. The waterway twisted through a thick stand of trees, offering a modicum of concealment from the firbolgs. The king decided that he would try to circle the pit and somehow get to his weapon before the giant-kin reacted.

The king failed to see, as he slipped along, that one of the giants had already observed him. Carrying a stout club, the firbolg moved into the woods not far away and started stalking carefully along the king's tracks.

Instead of checking behind himself, Tristan looked above, watching a piece of massive rock soar through the air, hurled by the colossus toward the flying druid. The chunk of mountain missed the hawk to shatter against the ridge, sending shards arcing through the air, showering into the valley below, and obscuring the shape of the gleaming white bird. Then Robyn screamed again and dove, plunging like an arrow toward the broad, mountainous surface at the base of the Peaksmasher's back.

* * * * *

Hatred and rage burned in Baatlrap, flaring like a black flame in his evil, tortured mind. The shock of his wound expanded until it climaxed in a monstrous outrage, like a great wrong done not only to him, but also to the entire race of trollhood. Now vengeance awaited!

The paths of the Rockbound Ways guided him, and he knew that he followed close upon the heels of those he hated, those who had rendered upon him the intolerable insult of his missing hand.

Accompanying him were the survivors of the battle in Winterglen. These, too, were hateful and driven trolls. None of them bore the wounds of the Trollcleaver, but all had suffered hurt and indignity during the fight, even to the point of being slain, before regeneration gave them the mobility to limp from the field and heal completely.

Pressing along the darkened passage, Baatlrap had no difficulty following the trail left by the human and dwarven party. Even if the dust on the floor hadn't been disturbed, the troll's keen nostrils would have been able to follow the hours-old scent of warm-blooded creatures in the dank air of the cavern, so long had it been since these corridors had seen the footsteps of such surface dwellers.

The trolls' fabled endurance and impressive speed didn't require them to rest as often as their quarry. Thus the one-handed humanoid and his companions were only a scant hour or so behind the king's party when they finally reached the long ascending stairway and the shimmering waterfall that screened the sunlit world beyond.

Here, sensing the nearness of his quarry, Baatlrap wouldn't allow his trolls to rest. Quickly the lanky creatures fell into file and continued the march to Icepeak Glacier.

They loped up the trail in the narrow valley, winding their way easily around switchbacks that had slowed the humans and dwarves to a trudging crawl. Finally, as they neared the end of the valley, Baatlrap discerned through the trees the huge bulk of Grond Peaksmasher, and the awesome reality of the living mountain almost halted him in his tracks.

"So the old hag was right!" he hissed, impressed in spite of himself. Yet the firbolgs weren't the ones who had drawn him this far, and the hatred for the man with the deadly sword hadn't begun to flag. He would continue on the trail of vengeance, though it seemed only reasonable to stay out of sight of the colossus.

The trolls dropped into a narrow gully, skulking along a shallow streambed in an effort to creep up the valley without exposing themselves to view. And then it seemed that the gods truly smiled upon Baatlrap, for as the monstrous troll came around a bend in the stream, he saw, not twenty feet away from him, the hateful man who had wounded him.

A snarl escaped from the troll's lips, and the man looked up, his eyes wide and frantic. Good—he knows his fate! The troll gloated silently. Then he noticed another fact, a thing that caused his craven heart to bubble with cruel glee.

Now the man was unarmed, and Baatlrap could see no sign of that cleaving, deadly sword!

* * * * *

Thurgol followed the riverbed, observing the figure of the human who had somehow floated from the great pit. He watched the man sneak between the shallow banks, looking outward at the pit and the strange woman who had come so easily to master the independent firbolgs.

The chieftain still wasn't exactly sure how that had happened. In the instant that the Silverhaft Axe had been taken from his hands, it was as if his own will had been taken at the same time. After the theft of that mighty artifact, he'd had no power to resist any command of the black-haired human woman. Indeed Grond Peaksmasher, immortal lord of giantkind, apparently willed it so.

The woman had told him to watch the humans, to see that they didn't escape, and so he had set to the task resolutely. He'd been smart, it seemed, to post himself back in the woods, where he could observe any break for freedom without being seen himself.

So now the one-handed man, the human who had seemed to be their leader, had somehow scaled the wall and tried to escape. Thurgol would simply have to see that this attempt failed. Unconsciously he tightened his grip on his club, picking up the pace of his own stealthy pursuit.

Then he froze in his tracks, astounded, as he saw a large green shape springing up the streambed toward the escaped human and Thurgol. It was Baatlrap, leading a company of his savage humanoids! The giant-kin chieftain thought he must be going mad, but the troll was certainly real, for just then the human saw him, too.

The one-handed man immediately reversed course at the sight of the troll, spinning so quickly that he saw Thurgol before the giant could even try to hide. The human leaped from the streambed, breaking through the underbrush and sprinting toward the clearing where Deirdre and the cleric stood.

The troll sprang after him, but a sudden explosion of flames crackled through the woods, blocking Baatlrap's path. The monster twisted out of the way as a small, brightly colored little dragon popped into sight, shouting shrill insults at the troll and pleading with the king to run faster.

Bulling through a stand of pines, Thurgol charged forward to cut the man off. Firbolg, human, and troll all broke into the clear at once, and the man stumbled to a stop, too shrewd to get run down by the fleet-footed trolls.

Thurgol felt a flash of pity for the human. It seemed that his valiant effort deserved something better than this. The firbolg watched as Baatlrap raised his sword and stepped closer to the unarmed human. The duel looked increasingly incongruous, the troll every bit of ten feet tall, with that evil-looking weapon reaching like a tree limb over his head. The human crouched, ready to dodge to either side, but without a weapon or shield, his situation was desperate in the extreme.

Other trolls emerged from the trees, following Baatlrap to gather in a semicircle around the giant troll and his victim. The appearance of the green-skinned humanoids inflamed Thurgol. Just when he thought he was rid of his noxious comrades, they had arrived to dog his presence again. He shook his head and growled in frustration.

"Wait!" Thurgol barked. "Put down your sword!" he commanded Baatlrap.

"What?" objected the troll, pausing long enough to glare at Thurgol. "Shut up!"

"No. Put down the sword and fight him fair—only you fight him," commanded the firbolg, hefting his club for emphasis and advancing slowly on the troll. Perhaps Baatlrap remembered the fight on Codscove's dock. Whatever it was, the troll's brows lowered in an expression of sullen fear.

Baatlrap snarled again while the man's eyes flicked from one humanoid to the other. Finally, with a scowl of irritation, Baatlrap threw down his sword. Without another word, he sprang at the one-handed man.

* * * * *

Robyn's body changed in the instant before she collided into the stones at the base of Grond Peaksmasher's mountainous torso. Her shape shifted, as it had so many times before, but this time it did not assume the form of an animal. Instead, her wings tucked backward, her head outstretched, and she became an arrowhead of stone, driving toward bedrock. The transformation was instantaneous and complete, fusing the power of the goddess and the will of the druid queen.

The Earthmother reached out, grasping Robyn's physical shell and melding her into the raw, elemental power of the ground, joining them in a linking of power and will. The queen met the face of slate and merged, sinking through layers of rock to become one with the earth. Her soul remained intact, centered below the bulk of the Peaksmasher, but the physical reach of her body expanded to encompass the entire narrow valley, its sheer ridges, and even the massif of the high peak.

Like a fundamental force of the earth, Robyn surged through dirt and stone and deeper layers of sand and shale. She seized the bedrock of the highlands with wrenching might, using every bit of her power—power expanded by the fresh presence of the vengeful goddess.

The strength of the Earthmother, transmuted through mountain and hill and vale, twisted the surface of the world with violent, wracking force. Grond Peaksmasher bellowed like a continuous, booming thunderclap as the quaking earth took hold of him and tore at his vitals.

"O Mighty One!" The demigod reeled as the words, the message, came to him, so it seemed, from within himself.

"Hear me, Lord of Giants—hear me, *please!*"

Robyn focused her will on the message, and as the earth convulsed from the pressure of the conflict, she waited, wondering if Grond Peaksmasher would understand.

* * * * *

Tristan ducked his left shoulder in the briefest of feints and then dove to the right, rolling away from the crushing pounce of the grotesque troll. It was as he rose to his feet that the earthquake struck, slamming him heavily back to the ground.

Great fissures ripped along the ground, splitting into deep crevasses. Steam burst upward, and here and there rocks flew into the air, hurled with explosive force by the power of the contractions within the earth.

The huge troll bounced upward with the first shock of the temblor. A fissure snaked past Tristan, and he felt a stab of hope as he saw the one-handed monster, flailing madly, slip over the rim and vanish. The other trolls had been knocked to the ground, and now they scuttled around in panic, seeking some shelter from the onslaught.

Lurching to his feet, the king felt the ground still rocking underfoot, but he lunged away from the momentarily helpless trolls. Breaking into the clear, he raced toward the edge of the pit, hoping to get around the hole and reach his weapon. Another wave of force rolled across the valley floor. Large pieces of rock tumbled free from the high peaks, smashing downward to shatter on the lower slopes. Craggy shards shot through the air with death-dealing force, leaving dusty trails hanging in their wakes.

Where was Robyn? Desperately the king looked around, fighting a growing sense of panic when he couldn't see her. Had she vanished? Did she live?

Then, looking across the regular outlines of the deep pit, Tristan saw the opposite rock wall crack and tumble away, great boulders plummeting straight down to shatter among the prisoners. Falling again as the ground bucked, the panicked king bounced to his feet and stumbled toward the enclosure. In his heart, he feared to look, feared what he would find beneath the rockslide. The most horrifying picture of all was an image of Alicia, trapped beneath the crushing weight of stone.

He saw figures move, scrambling up the loose, treacherously shifting stone. In a moment of hope, Tristan realized that the edge of the pit had collapsed enough for the prisoners to escape. Reaching the opposite edge, he recognized Brigit's blond hair, Brandon's trailing braids. Then, with a palpable sigh of relief, he saw Alicia, with Keane's lanky form right behind her. Ranthal, bounding like a panther, sprang after them.

As soon as he reached the rim of the makeshift prison, the wizard blasted a lightning bolt full into the chest of a firbolg who stood guard over the cache of weapons taken from the companions upon their capture.

Tristan risked a glance behind him, seeing the one-handed troll crawling forth from the crevasse. The monster picked up its jagged blade, which lay at the rim of the gap, and started toward the High King. A bright blue shape appeared in the air next to the troll, fluttering away from the monster's vicious swing. Newt disappeared as another tremor swept the valley, slamming the king to the ground and knocking him senseless for a moment.

When he recovered, he saw Hanrald kneeling beside him. There were tears in the earl's eyes, tears that he shook away as soon as he saw Tristan blink and try to sit up.

"Thank the goddess, Sire! I thought—" He couldn't finish the sentence. "Here—I brought your sword!" he said instead, offering the hilt of Trollcleaver to Tristan as the king climbed back to his feet, keeping his stance wide in case the tremors returned.

"Thanks yourself," Tristan replied, feeling the good weight of his sword in the palm of his hand. He turned back to the troll, ready to use the weapon, ready to finish the task he had started with it once before.

* * * * *

Robyn, a force of nature, struggled to master the fundamental might of the earth. Pain wracked her nerves as the unnatural environment pressed against her, striving to extinguish the spark of her vitality. Yet only here, within the mountain itself, could she reach the demigod with her all-important message. Desperately, forcefully, she projected her thoughts into the awakening, immortal mind of Grond Peaksmasher.

"You are *part* of this world, Mighty One—a living piece of the isles! Don't make yourselves a tool of those who would slay that magic!"

She urged and pleaded, not knowing if he heard. The idea was simple—for so long he had rested in the body of the Earthmother. Did he *want* to destroy her? Or would he, instead, resent the intrusion of external and disruptive forces?

A dim, nebulous response reached her—not words, as such, but a vague, groaning question. It was a query that gave her hope, for it showed that Grond's will was subject to doubt.

"The Silverhaft Axe is merely a tool from the past. It is *not* a key to bind you against your will! You are being used—used to serve the invaders, those who would wrack the world of your body!"

The response grew more definite, becoming a sense of anger, of dark and implacable resentment that began to swell into a rising force. She struggled to continue, striving against the overwhelming weight of the mountain.

"Your enemies are not these humans and dwarves, nor those who wield the axe. Strive instead against those who seek to steal your will! You must assert that power before it is too late!"

The strain of her expansive form tore at Robyn's soul, and the rock smothered her. Desperately, like a foundering swimmer seeking a breath of air, she turned her soul upward, seeking to break free from the bedrock of the world. It was too late; she sensed that she would perish here, unheralded, failing once again to work the will of the Earthmother. Strata of rock split and twisted around her as once again the convulsions shook the land.

But now, finally, she could see light, feel air against her face. As the earthquake ripped a crack through the world, the druid queen reached upward and scrambled out, standing on the edge and seemingly impervious to the pitching rock beneath her feet.

Overhead, the monolith of the Peaksmasher settled its great arms to the ground. The massive head slumped, the eyes closing, as if the demigod suffered a loss of power and will. For a second, silence hung over the valley, broken only by the receding rumbles of the quake's echoes.

A screech of inhuman rage spun Robyn around, and she

saw the body of her younger daughter, her face distorted by rage and the massive axe raised high in her hands, charging toward her. But it was only the form of the princess, Robyn told herself. Deirdre's soul was already gone.

Or so the queen argued, savagely determined to make herself believe. It was the only way she could prepare herself for the terrible thing she had to do. She's *already* dead!

Coldly impassive, the druid queen raised her hands and prepared to meet Deirdre in an embrace of doom.

* * * * *

Hanrald and Brigit raced toward the trolls in Tristan's wake, charging on either flank of the monarch. Ranthal, too, lunged, snarling, toward the enemy. The darting shape of Newt, his scales a bright crimson for battle, flashed through the air. Flushed with hope, the warriors attacked valiantly, determined to capitalize on their good fortune. Leading the attack, the High King sprinted toward the massive troll with the evil, jagged-bladed sword.

More trolls emerged from the woods to try to block the king's path. Tristan cut down the first one and kept going, while the earl and the elfwoman raised their blades against another pair. Dimly he saw the great firbolg, surrounded by his giant-kin companions, standing mutely at the side of the battle. They watched, but they did not attack. He didn't have time to wonder why.

Hanrald chopped down a troll, but then the blow of a second sent him reeling. Twisting, he saw a golden-haired figure fly past him, driving a shining steel blade deep into the troll's belly. The monster bellowed and tumbled away.

But a third troll had avoided discovery for a second too long. It leaped from the shadows behind a rock, dodging around Brigit's sharp parrying blow. With a sweeping dive, the creature ripped a clawed hand across the sister's knight's face. Brigit made no sound as her head twisted around. Instead, the Llewyrr knight fell soundlessly to the earth, lying in a growing pool of blood.

"No!" Hanrald screamed, hacking his sword through the body of the hateful beast, dropping the troll in two pieces. The grotesque remains writhed upon the ground, each scrambling away from the fight, but the man's horrified eyes had already turned back to the pathetic, motionless figure on the ground.

Groaning unconsciously, he knelt beside Brigit, gently reaching out to touch her cheek. Her eyelids were shut, and no sign of breath disturbed the golden strands of hair that had fallen over her mouth and nose.

But she was not dead—not quite yet, in any event. Her eyes, large and almond-shaped, fluttered open, and she looked up at him in a mute expression of her love. And when he clasped her small hand in his, he felt the slight returning pressure of her grip.

Then, as his heart broke, she died.

* * * * *

Tristan confronted the one-handed troll as the monster raised his toothed sword. When the beast leaped at him, the king slashed deeply into one of his legs, knocking him to the ground. Grim and implacable, as the monster wriggled at his feet, screaming, the High King drove the tip of Trollcleaver through the troll's foul heart.

A circle of the monsters had collected around him, standing well back from his gory blade, silently staring at the dead body of their leader. Tristan wasn't certain whether they intended to attack or flee, but the question quickly became immaterial as Grond Peaksmasher extended a stony arm and brought the massive, rock-studded club of his fist to earth, crushing the monsters in a single, smashing blow.

Too surprised to wonder about the colossus's apparent change of sides, the king turned back to his companions. Then, closer, he saw Deirdre and Robyn facing each other. Racing to them, he stumbled in between the two.

"No!" shouted Robyn. "This is *my* fight!"

"There won't *be* a fight!" he shouted back. "This is Deirdre —*your daughter!*"

"She is *not* our daughter! She has become the sword of the New Gods!" Robyn screamed back.

Deirdre lunged, swinging the axe into an arc that would have cut through Tristan and into Robyn had it landed. But stone fingers dropped from above with surprising quickness, plucking the diamond blade from Deirdre's fingers. Grond raised the axe, the artifact looking insignificant and tiny in his hands. Then, with a flick of his fingers, he crushed it to dust.

The dark-haired princess shrieked in rage, her face distorted beyond humanity. Like a deranged banshee, she raised her hands, spitting the initial commands to a destructive spell.

Before the incantation was complete, the tip of a steel blade erupted from Deirdre's chest in a fountain of blood. The princess looked down, gaping without comprehension, before slumping face forward to the ground.

Her sister, High Princess Alicia, stood behind her, blood still trickling down her blade while she stared at Deirdre's body in uncomprehending shock.

* * * * *

Exalted Inquisitor Parell Hyath stood upon the brink of pitching chaos, his hands held over his stomach in a posture of reflection and contemplation. This goddess, this Earthmother, was a deity of power beyond his calculations. Clearly it was time to summon his chariot, to return to societies more fertile to the dogma of Helm.

But before he could cast that spell, another man stepped from behind a tree. Hyath recognized Keane.

"It was you," said the wizard, his voice level. "I know that now. Once before I saw a spell cast in that pose, hands clasped over a fat belly. It was *you!*"

"What are you talking about?" demanded the priest.

"It's the earthquake that made me remember," Keane explained, slowly approaching the cleric. Hyath took a step backward, frightened by some vague menace in the magic-user's demeanor. "I saw you during another one, another earthquake, but not so great as this."

"Explain yourself!" shouted Parell Hyath.

"In Baldur's Gate," the wizard continued, his voice still low and calm. "You cast the spell that consumed Bakar Dalsoritan. You killed him!"

The inquisitor's face went pale. "You're mad!" he shrieked, his voice cracking with terror, a terror that revealed beyond doubt to Keane that his memory was correct.

The cleric suddenly pulled a hand from beneath his cloak, raising three fingers toward the magic-user in a desperate attempt to cast a spell, *any* spell that might divert the Ffolkman's righteous wrath. But the wizard was ready, and his own finger pointed, his own voice barked a word before the cleric could strike.

Destructive magic whirled forth, commanded and controlled by the wizard's grim enchantment. The force ripped into the cleric's body, working in the space of a deadly instant, tearing flesh and bone and blood into insignificant fragments, scattering those pieces toward the four winds. When the violent spell expired, there was nothing left to show where the cleric had stood.

This was the power—and the grim, ultimate finality—of the disintegration spell.

* * * * *

"You had no choice," Tristan said, numb with shock as he held his daughter in his arms.

"What happened to her?" demanded Alicia, her voice almost a wail. "Why did she do it?"

"It wasn't Deirdre," Robyn said softly, her own voice numb with grief and shock. "It was all the enemies of the goddess . . . all those jealous deities who wouldn't let her survive in peace. They were the ones who killed Deirdre, and the only thing we could do was try to stop the monster she'd become."

"But why?" Alicia persisted, shaking her head in disbelief.

"That's not a question we can answer—but at least it's over now," Robyn said.

Slowly the others came limping back. Hanrald, his face blanched with his own grief, bore a slight form in his arms. Ranthal dragged a twisted leg, while even Newt settled, unspeaking, onto Tristan's shoulder. The earl brushed Brigit's golden hair, now streaked with blood, back from her face, and when he laid the sister knight gently on the ground, it almost looked as though she slept. Even the gruff Finellen couldn't hold back her tears at the sight of her old rival's lifeless body.

Brandon, too, came up to the king. The northman's battle-axe was stained with green trollish blood. "Where's Alicia?" he asked Tristan, and the king looked around in surprise.

"I don't know—she was just here."

"There she is," Brandon said, his voice falling. Following the northman's gaze, Tristan saw his daughter run into Keane's arms as the wizard slowly approached them. The lanky magic-user held the sobbing princess silently, allowing her grief to fall against him, soothing the pain that she felt.

The Prince of Gnarhelm turned away, his face tinged with the sadness of his own loss, when Brandon's eyes fell on someone else. "Tavish!" he cried. "I thought you were lost with the *Princess of Moonshae!*"

"No," chuckled the bard ruefully, rubbing a bruised lump on her head where the priest's spiritual hammer had struck. "And your ship's not lost, either. That big giant had the sense to pull it up onto the shore."

"He's a shrewd one, that firbolg," Brand agreed as several of Finellen's dwarves approached with the surviving giant-kin under guard. "I wonder what made him do it."

"You know, they didn't fight at the end," Tristan remarked

thoughtfully. "They could have turned the tables by joining the trolls, but they just stood there and watched."

"The firbolgs?" Finellen asked grimly. "What should we do with 'em?" The tone of her voice indicated that she favored a quick and permanent disposal of the captives.

"This one saved my life," Tristan said, picking out Thurgol among the dejected giants. "He made the troll put down his sword when I was unarmed. Otherwise I'd have been dead before the earthquake."

"They deserve a pardon," Robyn noted.

"I don't want them back in the vale!" Finellen protested.

The king looked around at the wilderness of rocks and trees that surrounded them. No firbolgs lived on Oman's Isle, so far as he knew, but perhaps that could change. There were far fewer humans here than on Gwynneth.

"Can you make a home here?" Tristan asked Thurgol. "Can your people live in these highlands and stay away from the settlements of humans?"

The giant-kin blinked in surprise, obviously having expected a more brutal suggestion. "Yes—we stay," he agreed with a jerk of his head. The king saw an old hag of a giantess nodding at the chieftain. The new community would get off to a solid start, he suspected.

"I have learned a truth about my own home," Robyn said quietly. "For too long I have ignored the depth of my calling, the commitment that is rightly the cost of our triumph. I wanted it both ways—the strength of spirit within, while I surrounded myself with the trappings of royalty. But it was wrong.

"I cannot live in the castle, nor in the shelter of the town. My calling is real and true. I am a druid again, and such shall be my destiny until I die. There is only one place I can live."

"Where . . . ?" Tristan began, but of course he knew the answer. He surprised himself by greeting the knowledge with a sense of pastoral calm, almost of relief.

"I must go to Myrloch Vale, return to the grove of the Great Druid."

For a time, no one spoke. Hanrald looked at the queen in wonder, Tristan and Finellen in shrewd appraisal. The king nodded once, with regal dignity, and then again as the idea settled in.

"Will you have room for another there?" Tristan asked. "One who will be a hard worker, although he has only one hand?"

Robyn smiled gently, touching the king's arm. "You'd come to live in the wilderness with me? What about the kingdom? How will you rule?"

"We've ruled together for twenty years—a good, long reign," Tristan replied. "But you don't think I could do it apart from you, do you?"

"But what . . . how . . . ?" The queen's eyes shone as she looked at her husband. He smiled and took her in his arms without at first replying.

Alicia and Keane came up arm in arm. The princess's eyes were red, but at least her grief-stricken expression had given way to a look of, if not joy, a mixed sense of happiness.

"Our daughter will make a splendid queen," Tristan continued. "She has proven many times over that she's ready to rule. And now, perhaps, she may even be ready to announce her king!"

As if signaling approval, a high, keening voice rolled through the highland, and all the companions grew silent as they listened for several moments to the cry of a proud, lone wolf.

FANTASY ADVENTURE

The Icewind Dale Trilogy

By R. A. Salvatore
New York Times best-selling author

Follow the adventures of an unlikely quartet of heroes – the dark elf Drizzt Do'Urden, the halfling Regis, the barbarian Wulfgar, and the dwarf Bruenor – as they combat assassins, wizards, golems, and more in a struggle to preserve their homes and heritage. The Icewind Dale Trilogy is a fascinating tale filled with mystery, intrigue, and danger you won't want to miss!

The Crystal Shard
Book One
ISBN 0-88038-535-9
Sug. Retail $4.95

Streams of Silver
Book Two
ISBN 0-88038-672-X
Sug. Retail $4.95

The Halfling's Gem
Book Three
ISBN 0-88038-901-X
Sug. Retail $4.95

Look for Drizzt's return in
Starless Night
Book One in R. A. Salvatore's new fantasy trilogy in hardcover goes on sale in October 1993!